5h

W9-BGI-649

THE
LOVELY
AND THE LOST

ALSO BY PAGE MORGAN

THE DISPOSSESSED SERIES

The Beautiful and the Cursed

The Lovely and the Lost

The Wondrous and the Wicked

THE
LOVELY
AND THE LOST

PAGE MORGAN

EMBER

This is a work of fiction. Names, characters, places, and incidents either are the product of the author's imagination or are used fictitiously. Any resemblance to actual persons, living or dead, events, or locales is entirely coincidental.

Text copyright © 2014 by Angie Frazier
Front cover photograph copyright © 2014 by Marcus Ranum, manipulation by Ericka O'Rourke; back cover photograph copyright © 2014 by Victor Torres/Shutterstock, manipulation by Ericka O'Rourke

All rights reserved. Published in the United States by Ember, an imprint of Random House Children's Books, a division of Random House LLC, a Penguin Random House Company, New York. Originally published in hardcover in the United States by Delacorte Press, an imprint of Random House Children's Books, New York, in 2014.

Ember and the E colophon are registered trademarks of Random House LLC.

Visit us on the Web! randomhouseteens.com

Educators and librarians, for a variety of teaching tools, visit us at
RHTeachersLibrarians.com

The Library of Congress has cataloged the hardcover edition of this work as follows:
Morgan, Page.
The lovely and the lost / by Page Morgan. — First edition.
pages cm.
Summary: "Ingrid and Gabby Waverly continue to battle dark forces in turn of the century Paris while being protected by gargoyles"—Provided by publisher.
ISBN 978-0-385-74313-6 (hc) — ISBN 978-0-307-98082-3 (ebook) [1. Supernatural—Fiction. 2. Gargoyles—Fiction. 3. Sisters—Fiction. 4. Paris (France)—History—1870–1940—Fiction.] I. Title.
PZ7.M82623Lov 2014
[Fic]—dc23
2013020052

ISBN 978-0-385-74314-3 (tr. pbk.)

Printed in the United States of America
10 9 8 7 6 5 4 3 2 1
First Ember Edition 2015

Random House Children's Books supports the First Amendment and celebrates the right to read.

For my parents, Michael and Nancy Robie

Because you believed in me

The quiet ached.

After all the crying and screaming, the pleas for Léon to *stop!,* silence crushed the dining room. Now Léon trembled on the rug beside the table, his arms wrapped tightly around his knees.

He wanted to shut his eyes, but terror froze them open. He wanted to clap his palms over his ears so he wouldn't have to listen to the weak, muffled cries coming from all around him—but his fingertips were still *leaking.*

Léon's father was at the head of the table. Every inch of the man, from his thinning crown to his polished brogans, even the spindle-back chair upon which he sat, had been bound in a cocoon of thick white silk. The untouched plate of coq au vin still steamed in front of his father's mummified figure. The scent of mushrooms and wine, a sauce his mother had spent the afternoon stirring at the stove as she hummed little songs, now turned Léon's stomach.

Unblinking, Léon turned his head. The lacey trim of the

tablecloth hung low, but not low enough to block the sight of his mother's cocoon as it wriggled on the floor. And moaned.

Léon jumped to his feet and crashed back into his chair. A third, smaller silken cocoon, the one imprisoning his younger brother, had already gone still. The venom had worked its way through his sticklike limbs the quickest. Léon's wriggling mother would stop moving next. But his father, whose meaty frame was fully upright in his chair, might remain conscious another few minutes. Five at the most.

Léon hadn't wanted to hurt them. But he'd lost his temper when his father had started to shout the way he always did whenever Léon had done something wrong in their pâtisserie downstairs. He had thought he'd become immune to his father's blustering, but lately, things had started to change. With every flare of Léon's temper, Léon *himself* had started to change: the swelling pressure at each of his fingertips and the piercing pain in the roots of his eyeteeth were always the first signals.

Tonight, they had come on too quickly.

With his father's insults pounding in his ears, the white drops had pushed through Léon's skin and beaded at each of his fingertips. Within seconds, marble-sized globules had dripped free like white icing, distending toward the floor as long ribbons of silken web.

Léon's eyeteeth had erupted from his gums next. They had pushed past his lips into plain view, transforming into thin, hooked fangs and shocking his father into silence.

And then the screams had shattered the air.

Léon had wanted to assure them that this body wasn't his. That the sticky tangle of webbing was as repulsive to him as it was to them. But they had all kept wailing, and Léon had lost himself. It was the only way to describe it. It hadn't been *Léon* sinking his fangs into his father's neck, or his brother's forearm, or his mother's shoulder. It hadn't been *Léon* who had then used the endless strands of silken thread oozing from his fingers to swathe each of them in tightly wound pods.

But this was Léon now, eyes blurred by tears, body shivering. There was no way to help them. The antivenin Monsieur Constantine had promised was still at least a week away from being complete. There was nothing Léon could do. Nowhere he could go. Constantine had said Léon would be able to get better, that he'd be able to control himself. All he'd wanted to do was hide what he'd become from his family—and now they were dying. Because of *him*.

Léon gasped for air and stumbled away from the table, toward the dining room door. He whimpered as he passed the white cocoons, trying to ignore the way they twitched.

CHAPTER ONE

Ingrid's body had gone numb in the snow. She lay on her back, staring up at steel skies, and wondered how long this was going to take. The grounds surrounding Monsieur Constantine's home, set in the airy outskirts of the city, just beyond the Bois de Boulogne, were quiet, just as he had promised. Ingrid needed privacy, and here, she could have as much as she wished.

If any of her old London friends were to see her now, splayed out in the snow, they would likely think she'd gone mad. A smile tugged the corner of her lips. Perhaps she had. If that was the case, then mad she would remain, because chilled to the bone was the only way Ingrid could feel anything at all.

The clouds rumbled like a hungry belly, promising not snow but a cold February rain. It would likely wash away the hard, thin blanket of snow that had fallen the night before. Ingrid closed her eyes and ordered the first spark to light. She cried out at the sharp twinge in her shoulder, which was followed by a burst of heat. Pain crackled down one arm, coming alive with an electric rush. With her gloves already cast aside, a serrated line of lightning sputtered from her fingertips. It hit the trunk of a poplar less than a body's length away. Simultaneously, a quick, bright flash of lightning stabbed down from the brooding clouds and struck the poplar. From each striking point, thin trails of smoke eddied toward the sky.

Ingrid's eyes flew open and she belted out a laugh. She'd done it! After nearly two months of visits to Constantine's chateau, spending hours upon hours practicing control over this new side of her—a side that her London friends would most definitely believe insane—she had finally done it!

Ingrid pushed herself up, her violet woolen cape and fur-lined hood damp from the ground. The motion set her slushy blood back into circulation, and more tingles pricked at her shoulders. They flooded her arms, pooled at her elbows, and fanned out toward her fingertips. The sudden rush of feeling gave her arms the sensation of being large and unwieldy compared to the rest of her body. But it had happened. For the first time, the electric pulses hadn't come of their own volition. They hadn't been ruled by her temper or by fear or any other emotion. She had commanded them.

Ingrid had finally grasped a sliver of power over her demon half.

She still sometimes thought it was preposterous that she had anything other than human blood coursing through her veins, and that demons were real creatures with unspeakable appetites. Some mornings, Ingrid would wake and, for the first few seconds of consciousness, forget that she belonged to two worlds—one of ordinary humans, with their duties and titles, families and responsibilities, the other filled with demon hunters wielding blessed silver weapons, steel-scaled gargoyles protecting territories and humans, untouchable angels that enslaved those gargoyles, and of course, people like Ingrid herself: Dusters, humans gifted at birth with demon blood.

The damp cold closed in as her mind hitched on the memory of one dark-scaled gargoyle in particular. Reluctantly, she let the memory go. Learning that demons were real had thrown Ingrid's life into a spin. But it had been the reality of living, breathing gargoyles that had surprised her the most. They were far more complex than demons. Shape-shifting slaves to the angels, gargoyles were charged with protecting the humans living within their designated territories. Most humans didn't know gargoyles were anything more than stone statues or waterspouts, like the ones scattered about Notre Dame. Sometimes Ingrid wished she could still count herself among the ignorant.

She was in too deep to turn back now, though.

Behind her, the brittle layer of icy crust broke underfoot. "I didn't realize making snow angels would be part of your education."

She really ought to have been used to his American accent by now. His words were fast and efficient, though softened by his rich, satiny tenor. It warmed her blood a few more degrees.

Ingrid picked up her gloves and got to her feet, the leather of her bright ocher boots stiff from the cold. She quickly flipped back the hood of her cape and shook the snow free before turning to greet Vander Burke. His pale brown eyes were especially radiant in this moody light. She'd first met Vander two months before, inside his cramped Saint-Germain-des-Prés bookshop. Her younger sister, Gabby, had deemed him a handsome bore, much too intellectual and staid.

Gabby had been partially correct. Vander *was* handsome. He stood a full head taller than Ingrid, with athletically broad shoulders and classic Roman features weakened only by the wire-rimmed spectacles he wore. He *was* intellectual and staid, aiming—surprisingly enough—to become a reverend. He'd even quit the apartment above his bookshop to live and study at the American Church. But a bore he most certainly was not.

How could any handsome bookseller-cum-demon-hunter who aspired to the clergy be boring?

"You're not usually this early," she said, but then stopped to think. Just how long had she been supine in the snow? Vander met her at Clos du Vie after each of her lessons to drive her home, but he usually waited for her in Monsieur Constantine's foyer. She peered at him. "Are you checking up on me?"

Ingrid wasn't the only Duster who came to Clos du Vie to explore the powers of demon blood. There were others, Constantine had told her, but he was always careful to schedule their visits so none of them overlapped.

Vander nudged his spectacles higher on his nose and smiled. "I'm checking up on Constantine."

Ingrid sighed. Vander had made it clear that he didn't trust Constantine. Not that Ingrid blamed him for his skepticism. Monsieur Constantine had fooled them all, beginning with her twin brother, Grayson. Masquerading as an estate agent, he had helped Grayson select a property for their new residence and their mother's future art gallery here in Paris. He'd led Grayson to L'Abbaye Saint-Dismas, which consisted of an old, crumbling stone church, a cold stone rectory, and a dilapidated carriage house, all of which had been adorned with a number of *les grotesques*—gargoyles.

Then, when Ingrid, Gabby, and their mother, Lady Charlotte Brickton, had arrived, it had been Constantine who had informed them that Grayson had gone missing. Constantine had been at Lady Brickton's beck and call, playing the helpfully ignorant family acquaintance, when in reality, he had known just about everything.

He'd known about Ingrid and Grayson's demon dust; that Ingrid and Gabby had started working with the Alliance, a well-established underground society of demon hunters, to find their missing brother; and that Ingrid's demon blood had given her a supernatural ability, one that she had no control over. He'd even known about gargoyles; that L'Abbaye Saint-Dismas, with its sacred ground and the stone gargoyles covering the place like creeping ivy, would doubly protect whoever lived there.

Constantine had bided his time, observing Ingrid from a distance, and then, when she'd needed it most, he had offered his assistance. She was glad he had, even if Vander wasn't.

"Monsieur Constantine is a gentleman, Vander. He's helping me." She hesitated to tell him about the electricity she'd just conjured. It had only happened once. She didn't want to brag prematurely.

"Perfect gentlemen allow their guests to lounge in snowdrifts?" he returned, but she caught the mischievous gleam behind those spectacles of his.

"It helps, believe it or not," she answered, avoiding his gaze as she shook snow from one of her ocher gloves. "When I can't feel anything at all . . . it's like having a blank slate before me. I don't understand it, but Constantine suggested it might help me focus. And it did."

She dropped a glove, her fingers too stiff to hold it. Vander stooped to snatch it up.

He held it out to her. "It might also help you catch your death."

Ingrid tried to take the glove, but Vander must have seen her blanched skin and purplish-blue fingernails. He slipped the glove onto her hand himself and then lifted her palms to his lips. She felt his hot breath through the soft kid, and the warmth brought out an embarrassing moan of relief.

She gathered her wits and pulled her hands away from the press of his lips. "I won't catch my death."

It was the truth, and it was also a reminder of how different Ingrid was from other Dusters. Axia, the guardian angel who had been cast into the Underneath for her sin of gifting babies with strains of demon blood, had given Ingrid and her twin something more: she had hidden her own blood within their veins.

Axia had needed to safeguard her blood from the toxic Underneath, where its power would wither. She had chosen Ingrid and Grayson to harbor her angel blood, and for all of their lives, the two had been blessed with good health and fast-healing bruises and cuts. Recently, Ingrid had discovered something more. She didn't know why or how, but on two occasions, she had been able to force gargoyles into submission. And once, she had actually *glowed*. All this because of the angel blood.

So no, a little time in the snow wasn't going to give her pneumonia. The only thing Ingrid had to fear was Axia herself. The angel wanted her blood back, and she'd already proven she had the power to get it.

"All right, so you're healthy as an ox," Vander said, taking her by the elbow. "But what about Constantine?"

"I think he's rather healthy himself, for a man of his age," she said, knowing full well that she was being cheeky. She liked making Vander smile.

"Minx," he muttered. "You know what I mean. Have you figured out his mystery? Why does he have my demon gift when I can't trace a speck of dust around him?"

That was yet another reason Ingrid felt so at ease with Vander Burke. He was a Duster as well; his gift was the ability to see the colorful dust particles demons left in their wakes. Constantine had once told her that his students' demon gifts ranged all over the map. There was an endless variety of demon breeds, it seemed, and Vander hadn't yet discovered what demon he shared blood with. Whatever it was, his was a useful gift for a demon hunter.

"I don't know why Constantine can see dust," she said, knowing her comment would only cause Vander's brow to pull together into a frown.

Constantine shared Vander's ability, but he himself wasn't a Duster, so Vander's question remained: why could Constantine see dust?

"I'm sorry," Vander began as they slowly retraced their footprints in the snow back to the chateau. "I know this is important to you, but, Ingrid . . . I'm not alone in this. The rest of the Alliance here in Paris, your sister, even Grayson . . . we're all suspicious of Constantine's motives."

"Well, I'm not," she replied.

Constantine, a man of about fifty years, had devoted his life to the study of demons and their influences on the human world. When he had discovered the existence of Dusters, however, he'd also discovered a new purpose. A whole new field of study.

"What could he possibly receive in return for showing me how to control myself? He doesn't ask for compensation. He doesn't ask for anything at all," she said as the chateau's slanted glass-and-iron orangery roof came into view.

"Doesn't that make you suspicious?" Vander asked. "It was enough for Grayson to turn down Constantine's offer."

Ingrid tugged her elbow free. "Grayson didn't refuse the offer because he was suspicious. He refused because he's afraid of what he is."

Ingrid and Grayson might have both been given Axia's angel blood for safekeeping, but the twins' similarities ended there. Instead of gifting him with lectrux blood, as she had Ingrid, Axia had given Grayson the blood of a hellhound. Hellhounds were her dearest demon pets, massive dogs that hunted human prey at her command. And Grayson had, at least for a short while, become one of them.

From what Grayson had reported, Axia's hellhounds could shift between human and bestial form in the Underneath, but not on the earth's surface. That seemed to be something only Grayson had been able to do. He hadn't shifted for weeks, but he hadn't gone back to his normal human self, either.

Ingrid knew her twin well—or at least, she'd known him well once. Grayson had cut himself off from her lately, choosing to stay holed up in the rectory, their small home behind the abbey.

He'd refused to acknowledge anything regarding this new world they'd been thrust into. She wanted him to come with her to Clos du Vie, but he wouldn't budge.

"And you're not afraid?" Vander asked. She felt him close to her shoulder, saw his breath in the frigid air.

Ingrid stopped walking and noticed how cold her toes were. Wickedly, she imagined Vander drawing her stocking feet to his lips instead of her gloved hands, his hot breath turning her into a raging furnace. But it was no use. She couldn't escape his question.

"Of course I'm afraid," she whispered. "Just not of Monsieur Constantine."

Axia was stronger now that she had reclaimed the angelic blood Grayson had always harbored. She wouldn't kill the Dusters, or as she called them, her seedlings. She had given them demon halves for a reason. Ingrid didn't know what it was, or what Axia's plans for them might be. She only knew that Axia wanted to use her Dusters in some way against the Angelic Order. Against the human race, too, she suspected.

Vander came to stand in front of her, his arms folded tightly across his chest. He locked her in the steady gaze he wore when he shifted from intellectual bookseller to deadly serious demon hunter.

"I promised you once, and I'll promise you again now: I won't let anything harm you, demon, human, or angel."

She knew he meant it. She also knew she had other protection, which she didn't want to think about just then. Not with Vander standing so close, looking so earnest. Instead, she thought of her sister, Gabby, and how she had gone the opposite direction from Grayson, wanting to soak up everything there was to know about the Alliance and Underneath demons—specifically, how to destroy them in hand-to-hand combat.

Vander held out his hand. He didn't wear gloves like a refined gentleman would, and his fingertips were ink stained. He would have never been permitted into Ingrid's social circle back in London. But as she took his hand, her chest filled with warmth and gratitude. Yes, Vander Burke had romantic feelings for her. She didn't know how to define her feelings for him just yet, but first and foremost, he was her friend.

They walked in silence the rest of the way to the orangery. Inside, balmy air wrapped their chilled bodies. The glass roof and walls drew in the sunlight, trapped it, and created a tropical zone. A maze of bamboo; glossy green palms; bright red, orange, and pink flowers; lemon and lime trees; coconut and mango, too. Constantine's orangery should have felt like a miniature paradise. Unfortunately for Ingrid, every time she stepped inside it, she remembered *him*.

Luc.

His wavy dark hair, and the way he pushed it out of his eyes, which happened to be the brightest shade of green Ingrid had ever seen. His lashes, coal-black and thick. His expression of constant irritation. His creamy velvet skin as it checkered over into glimmering jet scales.

Vander could make a thousand promises to keep Ingrid safe, but it was Luc who was her true protector. It was Luc who could sense her every emotion as clearly as if it were his own, whether it was fear, excitement, or joy. It was Luc who knew where Ingrid was at any given moment, and who could be there within seconds should she require his help.

Luc was her gargoyle. And Ingrid was in love with him.

"Lady Ingrid?" Monsieur Constantine's voice came from a clearing amid towering bamboo.

She walked through the cut path of green stalks, blindingly bright compared to the gray winter day outdoors.

"Oh—Mr. Burke." Constantine frowned as he rose from his wicker chair.

Vander had apparently let himself onto Constantine's grounds without announcing himself first. *How rude of him,* Ingrid thought with a grin. Vander saw it and flashed her a smile in return.

When she glanced back at her teacher, she saw that he was still frowning. The frown was directed not at them, however, but at the newspaper clutched in his hand. He sat back down in his chair.

"Monsieur Constantine?" Ingrid said, edging closer to the table. He didn't often smile and rarely allowed a laugh, but he didn't usually glower. Constantine's expressions were always as gray as the clothing he wore—all different hues of gray, from gainsboro to silver to platinum. The color suited him perfectly.

"It is this morning's paper," Constantine stated, his fingers crushing the edges.

"Is it very bad?" she asked.

Her teacher set the paper down and smoothed the wrinkled pages. "I am afraid so. A family was found dead in their home."

Ingrid blinked, unsure how to respond.

"Their bodies were intricately wrapped in a mysterious silken thread. 'Sticky,' the reporter wrote. A *sticky* silken thread."

Ingrid glanced questioningly at Vander. He raised his chin.

"As in *cocooned*?" he asked.

A meaningful look passed between the two men. Ingrid had taken off her gloves and unbuttoned her cape. She draped them over the back of a wicker chair and sat down.

"The police found the work of a demon?" she asked.

"No," Constantine answered. "They found the work of a Duster."

Ingrid stared at him, her mind at a gallop.

"A Duster?" Vander echoed.

Constantine leaned back, the wings of his wicker peacock chair enfolding him. "My student, Léon Brochu. He has the blood of an arachnae demon. It appears the victims were his parents and younger brother."

A swirl of nausea cramped Ingrid's stomach. A Duster had murdered his own family. "But why?"

"The boy only came to me twice," Constantine answered. "He hadn't been handling his gift well, and from what I observed, it bubbled to the surface much like yours does—with emotion."

If Léon had slain his entire family, it could have been because of any raging emotion: fear, embarrassment, anger. She closed her eyes, trying not to see the memories of the fire she had once started—a lifetime ago, it seemed—in London. It had been a mixture of emotions that evening, humiliation especially, that had sent hot sparks from her fingertips. The nearby drapes had caught fire, and by the time the flames had consumed the ballroom, with people fleeing for their lives, Ingrid's closest friend, Anna, had been badly burned.

Ingrid knew what it was to lose control. But this Duster had killed his family. She ached for him. For them all.

"And Léon?" Vander asked. "What happened to him?"

Ingrid opened her eyes and found Constantine's gaze on her. As if he knew where her mind had taken her.

"The police are searching the city," he answered. "But I doubt they are looking in the right place."

Vander braced himself against the table, glaring at Constantine. "Tell me he isn't here. Duster or not, he's wanted for murder."

Constantine sat forward, his mustache twitching with defiance. "I would give refuge to any Duster in need of it, monsieur, but Léon Brochu is not at Clos du Vie."

Ingrid stood up and rested her hand on Vander's shoulder. She was certain he would give refuge to any Duster who needed it, too, all ethics aside.

"But you do know where he is?" she asked.

Constantine gave a curt nod. "I would like to ask for your help," he said, his gaze still on Ingrid. "Léon feels very alone, my lady. I've always respected the Alliance's request to keep their existence from common knowledge, so Léon knows nothing of them, or of the Dispossessed, as you do. Most Dusters are unaware of these things. They only know that they are different. Most do not know there are others out there like them. I believe Léon might respond better to another Duster. Especially one of the gentler sex."

Vander snorted, unimpressed. But Ingrid stepped forward. She didn't consider herself gentle, but she understood what Constantine meant. "I want to help."

She was lucky, all things considered. She had found out about the Alliance, about demons and gargoyles, all before Vander told her she had demon dust. She had known right away that she fit in somewhere. Léon and the rest of the Dusters out there didn't have that.

Vander rolled his shoulders. "Fine. If Ingrid's going with you, so will I. But if this boy poses any sort of threat—"

"He is a good boy," Constantine interrupted.

"A good boy who murdered his family," Vander retorted.

Ingrid took Vander's hand, lacing her fingers tightly with his. It surprised him into silence. *As intended,* she thought with a slight grin.

"We'll help," she said again.

Her teacher pushed back his chair and stood, his gray eyes flickering with unusual vigor. "Excellent. Tell me, then—is either of you familiar with the Paris sewers?"

CHAPTER TWO

Gabby gripped the handle of the sword and felt the balancing weight of the silver blade. The bridge was empty, closed to traffic, both pedestrian and wheeled. Tattered canvas sheets draped over long-forgotten bricks and granite blocks fluttered and snapped in the winds coming down the Seine. The river was the color of Connemara marble, and above, cement-gray skies threatened more icy rain.

She followed the scuttling movements of the rattilus demon as it rushed toward her from behind a pyramid of bricks. She hopped onto the bridge's footpath, then up onto the metal railings of some scaffolding, the tip of her sword aimed at the ratti.

The name was deceiving. The creature advancing on Gabby was no river rat. It was the size of a greyhound, and just as long and bony. The ratti's tail, saw-toothed and twice the length of its body, was its killing feature. Gabby had narrowly missed being struck by it twice in the last five minutes.

This was not going well at all.

"Come on, you nasty Underneath rodent," she muttered as she grabbed a vertical bar and braced her foot on the next crossing of rails up the scaffolding. Poised as she was, Gabby would have the advantage. She'd hack off that vicious tail and send the demon back to the Underneath in a burst of green sparks.

Foresight. Gabby truly did think it was her strength when it came to hunting demons.

She pulled herself up—and felt her foot slip out of the notched crutch of the two crossing rails. The back of her knee landed hard on the notch, and she lost her grip on the cold metal bar. Gabby flopped backward, dangling upside down from the scaffolding. Her hat, pinned as it was, stayed in place, but her skirts rushed down around her face, exposing her knickers and completely blocking her view of the rattilus demon.

She'd have to work on that foresight.

Gabby slashed her sword through the air blindly, knowing the demon's razor tail could be coming for her from any direction. In that moment, she felt fear. It jolted her pulse out of the calm rhythm she'd taught herself to maintain these last many weeks, hoping to hide her feelings. Because Gabby knew that she wasn't the only one who could feel her pulse. She could never truly hide or mask what she felt. Just like her sister, brother, and mother, Gabby was never entirely alone.

She took a deep breath and, still upside down, chased the fear away. She did not need Luc to rush to the bridge, all black wings and sharp talons, to save her. He didn't like to coalesce during daylight, but Gabby knew that he would. If her fear set off his trigger to shift, he would come. But Gabby could save herself.

She straightened her hitched-up leg and released her hold on the scaffolding. She fell, smashing her shoulder on the pavement. *Luc will definitely have felt that.* Skirts back in place, Gabby finally saw the ratti again—less than a foot away, with its tail cutting through the air toward her head.

Gabby ducked and the saw-toothed tail bit into the metal

scaffolding. She rolled to the side and lifted her sword—and then a firestorm of green sparks exploded right in front of her face.

Two silver throwing stars with sharp, gearlike edges, polished to a radiant shine, clattered to the pavement in front of Gabby as the demon's death sparks vanished.

Gabby groaned. "How am I supposed to learn how to kill demons if you're always leaping in and doing it for me?"

Light footsteps came up behind Gabby, and then a petite figure dressed in crisp breeches and a stylish Zouave jacket knelt down in front of her. Chelle picked up the two blessed silver stars and rolled her eyes at Gabby.

"How are you supposed to learn if you are dead?"

Gabby got to her feet, her backside cold from the frozen pavement. The bridge had been the perfect place for Chelle and Gabby to stand about idly for the last half hour or so, looking like a pair of stupidly innocent humans and luring any demon worth its salt. The bridge repairs had been postponed long ago, the city workers engrossed in constructing scores of palatial exhibition halls and pavilions along the riverfront and the Champs de Mars for the Exposition Universelle. The world's fair would open in April, as would Gabby's mother's gallery.

Gabby only hoped that by April, she'd be able to kill a demon without Chelle's help.

She sheathed her sword in the leather straps she'd sewn into the lining of her cape as Chelle tucked her twin stars back into the folds of the red scarf wrapped around her waist.

"I should not be doing this," Chelle muttered.

"But you are," Gabby said. "And you have to admit that you need me."

Chelle gawked at Gabby, her round eyes made wider. "What I need is a demon hunter, not an apprenticing nuisance."

The weight of Gabby's sword was a comfort, even if Chelle's words were not. She kept the blessed blade close to her whenever she could manage it, and not just because a few weeks before,

Chelle, one of the last two Alliance members remaining to safeguard Paris, had reluctantly agreed to train Gabby in the art of demon slaying.

The sword reminded her of Nolan.

It had been his gift to her for her sixteenth birthday, and Nolan Quinn, another Alliance member in Paris, had promised to teach her how to use it when he returned from Euro-Alliance headquarters in Rome. But he'd been gone for more than six weeks, and Gabby had been champing at the bit to train. She'd needed something to obsess over, and she certainly hadn't wanted it to be the set of ugly scars that marred the right side of her face.

Her encounter with a hellhound in December had left a three-pronged track of deep claw marks down her right cheek. Sitting around the rectory while she waited for the doctor's judgment that the wounds had fully healed had been torture. The moment the bandages had come off, Gabby had gone to Hôtel Bastian, Alliance headquarters in Paris.

"Give me one more week," Gabby said as Chelle rewrapped a thin woolen scarf around her neck and tugged down the short brim of her cap against the gusting wind. She avoided Gabby's pleading stare. "I almost had this one."

And if Nolan knew, he'd be furious. Chelle didn't have permission to train Gabby, even though the Paris Alliance was hurting for fighters. It had been thinned out months before when higher-ranking members had gone to Rome for some big summit. Gabby didn't know much about it, but she did know that with Nolan gone and two treasonous members, Tomas and Marie, in Rome for their trials, Vander Burke and Chelle were the only two Alliance left in Paris.

They needed all the demon hunters they could get.

Secretly, Gabby imagined with pleasure how stunned Nolan would be when he returned and saw how well she fought. Impressing Nolan wasn't her main desire, but it was one of them.

Before he left, he'd assured her that the scars the hellhound's claws had carved wouldn't matter. He'd made Gabby that promise and she'd accepted it with a slow, heated kiss. But she still felt the need to make up for the puffy pink marks. If she couldn't be beautiful anymore, she had to be skilled—and demon hunting was a skill she knew Nolan admired.

"As if I could rid myself of you anyway," Chelle said, starting for the bridge's Left Bank exit. Gabby wasn't one of Chelle's favorite people. Nolan had a lot to do with that. Chelle harbored old feelings for him.

"Thank you," Gabby said, following Chelle's brisk footsteps. The words wouldn't make Chelle like her, but she *was* thankful.

Gabby nearly trod on Chelle's heels a moment later when Chelle ground to a halt and held up an arm, her short, well-manicured nails poking through the open tips of her gloves.

"What—" Gabby sealed her lips when she saw a man emerge from behind a stack of steel beams. He brushed aside the frayed, flapping canvas cover.

"This bridge is closed." The words traveled to their ears clearly on the wind. His voice was calm and measured, but firm. Gabby had no doubt that this man, whoever he was, had every right to order them gone.

"This bridge is also marked," Chelle replied, twisting around to look past Gabby's shoulder. Gabby pivoted to follow her gaze to a rampart topped by a canvas-wrapped statue. She had noticed it earlier but paid it no attention—the whole bridge seemed to be wrapped in canvas. But now, on second glance, Gabby saw a bit of the statue poking out. A pair of sharp stone claws curled into a ball of granite atop the rampart. The stone around the claws had been carved to look like shaggy fur. Lion's paws. What lay beneath the canvas seemed so obvious now, especially given the hump where the figure's back must be: wings. It was a gargoyle, and it had a twin directly across the center of the bridge.

Gabby turned back to the approaching man with new clarity. The presence of those two statues meant this bridge had a gargoyle protector. The number of statues didn't determine the number of Dispossessed assigned to a territory—there were scores of gargoyles upon the abbey, yet Luc was the sole Dispossessed there. Gabby didn't know how many gargoyles protected this bridge, but this man, his black hair streaked with ribbons of silver at the temple, was most certainly one of them. And Gabby was trespassing on his territory.

He wore an old-fashioned jacket and waistcoat, and his pinstriped trousers had been tailored at least a quarter century ago. He came to a stop directly in front of Chelle. So close that Chelle, squeezed as she was between the man's chest and Gabby's front, was forced to slip off to the side. The man stared at Gabby, his eyes two pools of ink.

"You're one of Luc's humans," he said.

"Who are you?" she whispered. She hadn't met another Dispossessed before.

"Yann," the man answered. She wondered how old he was. How many centuries he'd lived through, what he'd seen. He wasn't human, that much Gabby knew.

"And you, Alliance," Yann said, sparing Chelle a pointed glare. "Are you luring demons to my bridge?"

Chelle huffed. "It took you long enough to get here."

She had known? She had taken Gabby to a protected place on purpose? Chelle caught Gabby's incredulous stare. "What? It's called tactics, Gabby. Added protection is never a bad thing. Even if it is from one of *them*."

Chelle turned her back to Yann, who then resumed inspecting Gabby. "Where is Luc? If I felt humans in danger on my bridge, he should have felt your fear as well."

Gabby lifted her chin. "He didn't feel my fear because I wasn't afraid."

Except for that one blip, of course, and Luc had learned to ignore the blips. At least, Gabby hoped he had. He was intuitive but also reserved. If he didn't have to go chasing after one of his humans, he wouldn't. He'd wait for the real emergency instead.

Yann's smile surprised her. "You may be interesting, human, but you're also troublesome." He inclined his head, his smile drawing into something wicked. "I don't like trouble. This bridge. Is. Closed."

Gabby refused to inch back. She wouldn't be bullied by anyone, not even a gargoyle.

"Don't worry, gargoyle. We won't be coming here again. From the looks of your bridge, you'll be in hibernation soon," Chelle said, adjusting her cap and strutting past Yann. "The best gargoyle is a sleeping gargoyle, after all."

He lowered his dark lashes, closing his eyes for a long moment. What Chelle had said was correct. Not about sleeping gargoyles being the best gargoyles—Gabby didn't scorn the Dispossessed the way Chelle did. But with this bridge being shut down for as long as it had been, the Dispossessed guarding it should have slipped into the stony sleep the gargoyles called hibernation. Without humans to protect, there was nothing to keep a gargoyle awake. From what Gabby had learned so far, though, it sometimes took months for a gargoyle to go into hibernation. Perhaps Yann was already beginning his sleep. Maybe that was why it had taken him so long to sense a human in danger on his bridge.

Chelle half turned to see if Gabby had followed her, but Yann had opened his eyes and was spearing her with them again, a new edge to his stare.

"You should return to the abbey. Demons are out in droves lately," he said. "Luc has a hard enough time as it is keeping tabs on you."

"I don't require anyone to keep tabs," Gabby replied. That was the reason she'd started training her fear reflex in the first place. Besides, if she was going to be fighting demons, Luc couldn't be coming to her rescue every time.

"Regardless," Yann said, suddenly smug. "You and your family seem to need more than one pair of watchful eyes. Luc will soon be joined by another Dispossessed, isn't that so?"

Gabby let out her breath. Yann was right. Luc had told them that another Dispossessed would be coming to live at the abbey, but so far, the Angelic Order had not sent anyone.

Gabby lowered her chin and started to walk around Yann, who stood like a pillar in the middle of the bridge. He followed her with his dark, inquisitive eyes. She saw them hitch on her crescent of scars. They throbbed, as if each scar knew it was being inspected. Yann's throat made a mean little gurgle as she rushed past him.

This was what Gabby had feared. Not the unlimited supply of demons she might come face to face with when she became a member of the Alliance. She could fight those demons; she could send them back to the Underneath, where they belonged. She couldn't do the same with the marks on her skin. They would always be right there: the first things people noticed about her. If a creature like Yann—a gargoyle, for heaven's sake!—looked at her with such disgust, how would others see her?

How would *Nolan* see her? He'd left before the bandages had come off. Would he change his mind about her when he returned to Paris and saw the scars for the first time?

Gabby brought down the black tulle of her veil, which she'd rolled atop the brim of her hat while battling the rattilus. Covered, she felt better. She felt more like the old Gabby, the Gabby who'd been pretty and confident.

She wanted that Gabby back more than anything.

CHAPTER THREE

Hope was a futile thing.

Luc had known better than to harbor any, even after two months had passed and he remained the only Dispossessed at l'Abbaye Saint-Dismas.

Irindi had promised the arrival of another gargoyle, and the angel of heavenly law had finally kept her word. That morning, just as the servants were finishing up their breakfast in the rectory kitchen, Luc had felt the telltale chime at the base of his skull. He'd set his fork down, taken one last sip of his coffee, and raised his eyes as the new groom entered the kitchen with the butler.

Gustav had gone around with introductions. Dimitrie was his name, with some long surname Luc couldn't care less about. The Dispossessed had no use for last names.

The boy's eyes rested only a half beat longer on Luc than the other servants. A boy indeed. Dimitrie matched Luc's height, but he was gangly and smooth-cheeked. No older than fourteen,

Luc had suspected at the time, but now, as he followed the boy into the stables, he gave him the benefit of perhaps another year. Dimitrie had just enough breadth around the shoulders for fifteen.

Luc closed the stable doors behind him to shut out the kicking wind. Dimitrie had entered a stall and was speaking in soft tones to the snuffling mare.

"She doesn't like you," came Dimitrie's voice from within.

Luc approached the stall entrance and crossed his arms. Fourteen. The boy's voice was still a warbling pitch.

"The mare. She doesn't like you. See how nervous you make her?" Dimitrie went on. He ran his slender fingers down the horse's meaty shoulder, then along its back. He finally looked at Luc.

"Irindi sent you?" Luc asked. A little warning would have been nice.

Dimitrie didn't so much as blink. "You required help."

From an infant? Luc wanted to reply. He stayed quiet. Dimitrie could have been trapped within his fourteen-year-old body for one year or one hundred. Maybe more. There was no way to tell without asking, and it wasn't a question one Dispossessed asked another so soon after meeting. Luc himself had been seventeen for 327 years. This was the first time he'd met another gargoyle whose human age was younger than his.

His age didn't matter, though. Neither did it matter how awkward and spindly the boy looked. He was no innocent— Dimitrie had committed the same crime every other gargoyle had: the cold-blooded murder of a man of the cloth. Priest. Reverend. Bishop. It didn't matter their title or rank. If a man killed an ordained soul, he was barred from heaven upon his death and cast into the ranks of the Dispossessed.

Luc was a murderer. They all were, even this waif of a boy.

"I understand. This has been your territory," Dimitrie said.

Luc had been guarding this place on his own ever since his first day as a gargoyle. When the abbey had been a functioning church, Luc had protected all its parishioners while they were on sacred ground. The priests usually lived alone, except for a few servants here and there. Even when the abbey fell out of use before Luc's last hibernation and an old Sorbonne professor and his blind wife had taken up residence in the rectory, Luc hadn't had much trouble seeing to their safety.

He had shaken free of a thirty-year hibernation just over four months before, and almost immediately he'd been challenged with humans who were pure disasters: in league with the Alliance, completely aware of the Underneath, two of them with demon dust and one with an appetite for demon hunting. . . . Luc *did* need help. And he should have been relieved to have it.

"I mean no disrespect, but it's also my territory now," Dimitrie said, giving the horse's snout a gentle rub. "And they are my humans as well."

Luc launched himself into the stall, his boots scattering fresh hay. Dimitrie jumped back and the horse whinnied and stomped. Luc curbed his temper, fast. It wouldn't be wise to show this boy just how little he wanted to share his humans. Especially one human in particular.

Ingrid.

Once Dimitrie met Ingrid Waverly and breathed in her scent for the first time, he would be able to call it up at any moment. He would be able to feel the echo of Ingrid's heartbeat, the flutter of her pulse. He would be able to know exactly where she was at all times, whether she was afraid or happy or sad or anxious. He'd feel her every emotion. Dimitrie would be connected to Ingrid just as Luc was. Luc stifled a growl of irritation.

"Where do you come from?" he asked to change the subject.

There were hundreds of Dispossessed in the city, thousands in Europe, perhaps hundreds of thousands the world over. The

Dispossessed guarded any territory where *les grotesques* stood, whether it was a public park, a cemetery, or a private home. Dimitrie didn't look familiar, but Luc's circle of acquaintances was rather slim.

"Not far. Bourges," Dimitrie answered, his eyes still on the horse's quivering flesh. Luc supposed he did make the animals a bit jumpy, but he was Lady Brickton's driver. The horses had no choice but to work with him.

"The other servants tell me the family is unnatural," Dimitrie said. "Especially the twin brother and sister."

Luc arched a brow. He'd thought Irindi would explain things to Dimitrie. But perhaps she simply tossed the boy into his new territory and washed her hands clean of it.

"You should keep yourself separate from the other servants," Luc advised. "Give them no reason to gossip about you."

After the debacle in December, Lady Brickton had raised the servants' pay significantly to secure their silence and to keep them on staff. The servants knew almost everything now. They had witnessed not only Grayson in hellhound form, but two gargoyles as well, one of which had shifted from true form to human form directly in front of them. They had also seen Ingrid, whose angelic blood had lit her up like an incandescent bulb and given her the power to subdue the attacking gargoyles—all on the front lawn of the churchyard.

Only the butler, the cook, and two lady's maids had chosen to remain. Nora, Gabby's maid, had been killed by a hellhound. Luc supposed that was reason enough for the others to have flown the coop.

"Besides," Luc added, a knot at the base of his throat coiling tight. "It isn't wise to become friendly with the humans."

Luc had learned his lesson.

Dimitrie's bony shoulder rose in a shrug. "I don't mind humans so much."

The confession silenced Luc. Admitting something like that

to another gargoyle was a serious risk. There were plenty of gargoyles who *did* mind humans. Despised them, even. Especially Alliance humans. They were supposed to be allies to the Dispossessed, and yet there were rumors going around now that Alliance leaders wished to enslave gargoyles even further. Make them bend to Alliance edicts. Suffer Alliance punishments.

Luc would love to see the fools try. Gargoyles were already slaves enough. Irindi and the rest of the Angelic Order ruled over them. They watched and listened. They knew everything. *You have an affinity for the child christened Ingrid Charlemagne Waverly.* The memory of Irindi's hollow, monotone voice as she had accused Luc of such a disastrous and unorthodox breach of conduct still flooded him with shame. Yes, he did have an affinity for Ingrid. Worse yet, he'd kissed her, and he'd wanted more—much more—than a kiss.

He still imagined sometimes, when feeling particularly weak, what that *more* might be like.

But it was a waste of Luc's time to continue with such pointless imaginings. He was a gargoyle, and the angels or God or whoever had created gargoyles in the first place had covered all the bases. No Dispossessed could take a human lover. Anything more than a kiss triggered an involuntary shift, and a painful one, too: bones snapping, muscles and tendons stretching to unnatural lengths.

Not to mention that the Dispossessed considered such relationships treasonous, punishable by death. Just last December, René, a member of the Wolves caste, had been ripped apart and discarded into the Seine for his indiscretion.

How could Luc protect Ingrid if the same was done to him? Protecting her had to come above all else. He supposed Dimitrie would at least be able to help him in that respect. Still, for the boy to admit he liked humans was a dangerous—even foolish— move. Luc wondered what kind of gargoyle Irindi had sent him.

He was still inspecting Dimitrie when the stable doors heaved open. Heeled boots hit the raised floorboards, and with one deep breath, Luc caught the heady perfume of hibiscus and water lily. Almost identical to Lady Brickton's scent, just slightly milder.

"What were you doing on that bridge?" Luc asked before Gabby had come into view.

"I was certain you already knew, so I thought I'd come make nice," she replied as she swung around the corner of the horse stall.

Gabby's smoky eyes landed on Dimitrie. She bit her bottom lip and Luc felt her heart throb with alarm.

"It's fine," he said, nodding his chin toward Dimitrie. "Meet my new roommate."

The black veil of her hat had been cut at an angle to shroud the scarred half of her face, exposing just one of her stormy eyes. It was wide and unblinking as it traveled from Luc to Dimitrie.

"This is . . . I mean, have you finally . . ." Gabby trailed off.

Luc sighed. "Just ask if he's a gargoyle already."

Gabby scowled at him. "Well, now I don't have to, do I?"

He held back the smile fighting to leap to his lips. Ingrid's younger sister reminded him so much of his own, Suzette. Impetuous and witty, with a sharp tongue and plenty of spirit. Luc looked away from Gabby as the memory of his sister slid like a dull knife between his ribs.

Dimitrie stepped away from the horse and, bending at the waist, dipped into a low, proper bow. He even nicked off his tweed cap and crushed it against his chest.

"My lady," he said, face still aimed at the floor.

Luc knitted his brow, taken aback once again. "Straighten up," he barked, and Dimitrie snapped up to his full height. "You're her gargoyle, not her servant."

"Actually, he is my servant," Gabby said. "As are *you*. I don't see you returning the wages my mother pays you, now, do I?"

Gabby waited for Luc's reaction, her lips in a pointy pout.

Lady Brickton knew gargoyles existed. She knew they were at times men and at other times beasts. But she did not yet know that Luc was one of them.

"My name is Dimitrie," the boy said when Luc stayed silent.

"Lady Gabriella Waverly," she returned.

"You didn't answer me," Luc interjected. "What were you doing on that bridge?"

Earlier, her scent had surfaced and Luc had been able to trace a mix of emotions: fear, fast drowned out by disappointment. He'd nearly been able to feel Gabby stomping her foot in frustration. And then she'd been fine, all fear vanquished, and the trembling of Luc's bones, preparing to shift, had stilled.

"I met a friend of yours," Gabby said, avoiding his question.

"Yann isn't my friend," Luc replied, already knowing where she'd been and which gargoyle had probably been there.

She frowned. "Good. I don't like him."

"I advise you not to like any gargoyles," he said.

Gabby began to push the black netting away from her face but remembered Dimitrie hadn't yet seen her scars. She quickly tugged the veil back into place.

"Not even you?" Gabby asked, turning playful.

Luc hitched up the corner of his mouth. "Especially not me." He saw a flash of her white teeth. "You shouldn't cross into other gargoyles' territories."

She sighed and wheeled around on her heel, heading for the stable doors. "Their territories are everywhere. What am I to do, play hopscotch around Paris to avoid running into any of them?"

Sarcasm. Suzette had had plenty of that as well. Gabby was dark like Suzette, too, with her caramel hair and smoky eyes. Perhaps all these resemblances to his sister explained why Gabby rankled Luc so much. She, more than anyone else, even Ingrid, reminded him of what he'd done in his previous life. The sin he'd committed defending Suzette's honor.

"Can you just stay at the rectory for now? Until your sister returns, at least?" Luc asked, disgusted by the queasy churn in his stomach.

That morning, Ingrid had gone to Monsieur Constantine's home as she did twice a week, on Mondays and Fridays. Constantine sent his driver to pick her up, and she usually returned home with Vander Burke, the Alliance Seer. Luc wasn't with her these mornings; she didn't need him. But that didn't stop him from eavesdropping on her every now and again. The bubbling of her pulse when she was in the Seer's company bothered Luc.

Out of habit, he called up her scent: a springtime morning of sweet-smelling grass; rich, dark soil; and of course, that additional bitter tang that Luc now knew was the scent of her demon blood. She was on her way back to the rectory. He felt her location as clearly as he knew his own.

"There she is now," Gabby said as the clatter of wheels came from the churchyard drive. The wheels crunched through the snow and the frozen gravel beneath.

"Not yet," Luc said, and walked with Gabby toward the stable doors. Dimitrie stayed in the horse's stall, acting more like a servant than master of the territory.

Luc and Gabby peered out into the churchyard and saw not Vander Burke's gleaming new carriage—his old one having suffered irreparable damage in a crash—but a rough and chipped hansom cab.

Gabby frowned. "I wonder who it is," she whispered. Luc saw her fingers swish through the black veil once again. She worried about those scars, but they weren't as hideous as she imagined them to be. At least, Luc didn't think so. Then again, he *was* a monster.

The hansom drew to a stop, the brake lever was thrown, and the carriage door opened. Luc and Gabby waited as the set of steps crashed down. A pair of polished oxblood boots appeared on the first step, and then the visitor himself filled the frame of the door.

Gabby gasped. Then let out a high, tinny moan.

"Who is it?" Luc asked as the man, tall and broad-shouldered and wearing what looked like an expensive greatcoat, stepped onto the snowy drive just in front of the rectory's front door.

"Oh no," Gabby whispered. "It's Papa."

CHAPTER FOUR

Vander's wagonette came up rue Lagrange. The abbey's twin bell towers stood like stone exclamation points at the far end of the street.

"I think you're overreacting," Ingrid said, not for the first time since leaving Clos du Vie.

Vander sat beside her at the reins, straining for control over his temper. He'd lost it when Monsieur Constantine had asked them to enter the Paris sewers to search for the missing Duster, Léon. He had grabbed hold of Ingrid's arm and all but dragged her from the orangery. Since leaving the chateau, Vander hadn't said more than three words: *In* when they had reached his carriage, and *Hold on* as he'd slapped the reins and torn down Clos du Vie's long, winding drive.

He'd breathed loudly, inhaling and exhaling with little growls when Ingrid had asked why he'd reacted so badly. Finally, as the abbey and rectory loomed on the horizon, he spoke.

"Do you have any idea how dangerous the sewers are, Ingrid?" he asked. "Constantine does. He knows how many demons, and how many fissures between our world and the Underneath, are down there. And he still played on your sympathy to force you to risk yourself for a boy who murdered his entire family."

The sewers did seem like the perfect place for demons to lurk. Vander's assessment of the dangers didn't surprise her. But something else did.

"He's a Duster," Ingrid said. "Like us, Vander, but alone. We have each other. He has no one."

Like them, Léon would have somewhere on his skin the two strawberry ovals that could easily pass as birthmarks. Ingrid and Grayson had always thought the matching marks on their calves were just that. But then she'd seen the same marks on Vander's neck, and Axia herself had explained to Ingrid what they really were: the brand of a Duster.

Vander took another long breath. This time, he chased it with a glance at Ingrid. He'd calmed, and she knew it was because of what she'd said. *We have each other.*

"I know," he said. "But if we're going to go into the sewers to look for him, we're going to do it smart. We'll need more Alliance. More silver. Maybe even a pair of wings."

Luc. *He means Luc.* Ingrid smiled as Vander steered the horses through the break in the hedgerow along the cross street of rue Dante. The hedges stayed thick and green during the winter months and blocked the view of the old stone rectory from the street.

If Vander was jealous of Luc, he didn't usually show it. Luc was Ingrid's protector, and because of that, Vander accepted him. In fact, Vander had accepted much about Ingrid that she'd never thought he would. He knew about the fire that had harmed her friend, Anna. He knew she'd made a fool of herself over Jonathan Walker. It had taken a heavy dose of humility to part with the secrets, but Vander had rewarded her for it. He hadn't judged her. Hadn't done anything more than stroke her cheek and say "Jonathan Walker sounds like an idiot."

The only time a flicker of jealousy flared underneath those wire spectacles of his was when he came upon Luc and Ingrid together. It didn't happen often. Luc had made her a vow that whatever he'd led her to believe was happening between them was over—and impossible anyway. He'd been true to his word. But now and then, Vander would come to the rectory and see Luc either handing Ingrid down from the landau or working with her in the abbey, cleaning it out to make way for the gallery. It always made Ingrid uneasy. Which of them was she supposed to look at? Speak to?

She quickly scanned the carriage house and stables, then the abbey's doors. No sign of Luc, even though she knew he'd already sensed her return. Vander held out his hand once he'd braked and descended.

"I'll send word to Constantine," he said as they walked to the front door. "Maybe Chelle will help. Gabby, perhaps?"

Her sister was training for the Alliance, yes, but Ingrid still shook her head. "I don't want her in any danger."

Vander cocked his head. "But you don't mind putting yourself in deep?"

Ingrid looked away and opened the front door. Of course she wanted to protect Gabby: she was only sixteen, and she was dangerously eager to prove herself.

The moment Ingrid stepped into the small foyer, a familiar voice boomed from the sitting room. She went still, one of her gloves peeled halfway off. Vander had come in as well, and he passed her now, craning his neck to see inside the room. The peacock-blue drapes had been only partly closed.

"How could you?" the voice boomed again. It struck Ingrid and rattled her to her bones. She must have given a gasp, because Vander whipped his head toward her.

He was mouthing *Who?* when she raced past him and threw open the drapes, one glove on, one off.

The sitting room fell quiet as all heads swiveled to look at her. Her mother, Lady Charlotte Brickton, sat pale-faced on the sofa closest to the hearth. Gabby stood at the half-shuttered windows, her eyes red rimmed. And between them, standing in the center of the sitting room, his dark navy pinstriped suit perfectly pressed and starched, was Lord Philip Northcross Waverly III, Earl of Brickton.

Otherwise known as *Father.*

"Papa?" Ingrid said, stepping into the room. The surprised grin hadn't yet formed fully on her lips when Lord Brickton stabbed a rigid finger at her.

"You!" he bellowed. Ingrid noticed his crimson cheeks, the pronounced vein down the center of his forehead. "You wrote that she had been injured, not that half of her face had been torn off!"

Ingrid froze, holding the ridiculous half-formed grin. Her father was shouting at her. She hadn't seen him in nearly three months. Now here he was, a surprise arrival, and he was *shouting* at her. Ingrid felt as if she'd just tripped over something and gone sprawling face-first.

"I—" she started, quickly meeting Gabby's wide eyes. She'd been crying.

"Where is your brother?" her father demanded.

Her mother was on the edge of the sofa cushion, her lips pursed as if in indecision: intercede, or let her husband have it out?

Their father was supposed to have been on his way to Paris when the hellhound attack had happened, when Ingrid and Grayson had been taken into the Underneath. But a few days later a telegram had arrived, announcing that an issue had arisen in the House of Lords. Their father would need to stay in London indefinitely. Ingrid's letter to him had been brief, and yes, she'd played down the gravity of Gabby's wounds, but only because she hadn't wanted to worry him. And perhaps, if she was honest, Ingrid hadn't been ready to have her father come to Paris just yet. He would be an outsider to the world she, Gabby, and Grayson had become a part of. How could they explain any of it to him?

"I believe your son was to meet with an architect this morning," Vander said, entering the sitting room from behind Ingrid. "For abbey repairs."

Lord Brickton's scowl deepened. "And you are?"

"Vander Burke, my lord," he answered, and Ingrid was impressed at just how unruffled he sounded. This was not an ideal first meeting. "I'm a friend of your—"

"Mr. Burke, this is a family affair. If you don't mind."

Ingrid held her breath. She had never witnessed her father being so rude before. Lady Brickton flushed violently, and Gabby's eyes grew wide with disbelief. Vander, however, bowed deeply.

"Of course," he said. He straightened and took Ingrid's hand. He pressed his lips to the leather. "I'll call on you soon."

He had made a point to take her gloved hand, not the bared one. Pressing his lips to her skin in front of her father would have been scandalously wrong.

Vander was already trying to gain her father's favor, she realized. Though at the moment, she couldn't understand why. Her father was being an absolute beast.

"You're protecting him," he said as soon as the front door had closed behind Vander.

Ingrid turned back to her father. "Protecting whom?"

Brickton swiped an arm out. "Your brother! Don't lie to me, Ingrid. You didn't relate the severity of your sister's injuries because it was *he* who caused them!"

They all stared at him, momentarily shocked silent. Gabby recovered first.

"Grayson caused nothing!"

"He did this to you—don't lie to protect him. He doesn't deserve it," their father quickly retorted.

Gabby and Ingrid shook their heads, their eyes meeting quickly. What was their father saying?

"He would never," Ingrid said. What would make their father even suggest something so awful?

"Philip, it was that crazed man," their mother said, finding her voice at last. "Ingrid wrote you. She told you about Nora and the other girls he kidnapped and killed. Gabriella was lucky. She got away—"

Lord Brickton hacked at the convenient excuse they had fed all the news reporters and police in the days following Gabby's injury and Nora's murder.

"Lucky? You call this *lucky*?" He stabbed his finger again, this time in the direction of Gabby's inflamed cheeks. The flush made her pink scars ever brighter.

"My point is, it wasn't our son who harmed her," Lady Brickton said.

Ingrid's father turned on his heel and stormed toward the windows overlooking the churchyard. Gabby, standing near them, darted away, toward Ingrid. They shared a horrified glance.

"He's a fiend. You think you know him, but you don't. None of you does," their father said, staring out at the snowy lawns.

What on earth was happening? Their father had shown up unexpectedly, exploded into a rage, and was now calling his own son a *fiend*? Ingrid took hold of Gabby's hand and pulled her close. She felt her little sister tremble. A spark shuttled from Ingrid's right shoulder, like a shooting star arcing toward her fingertips. Anger. She was getting angry, and that always set the sparks off. She breathed deeply and remembered the cold. She closed her eyes and imagined shoving her arms into a bank of snow.

"It wasn't Grayson." Ingrid's whisper cracked loud against the silence. She opened her eyes. Her father was still staring out the window, his face pinched.

It hadn't been Grayson, though it very well could have been. When he'd been in hellhound form, he'd tried to kill Gabby. He'd sunk his fangs into Ingrid's skin, injecting her with enough demon poison to take her through a fissure and into the Underneath. He'd certainly had the claws to do the kind of damage that had been done to Gabby's face.

But to tell their father this, to confide in him the truths those at l'Abbaye Saint-Dismas now knew, would ruin everything. If he knew the truth, he'd whisk them all back to London. It was a fate none of them wanted. Mother, with her gallery on the horizon and artists barraging her with requests to exhibit; Gabby, with her Alliance dreams and Nolan's promised return; Grayson, who was nothing at all like the young man who'd left London in the fall. And as for Ingrid, returning to London could be a disastrous move. Axia could get to Ingrid anywhere. Paris, London, the darkest corners of Africa—it didn't matter. There were fissures all over the world. When the Alliance leaders, a group known as the Directorate, had strongly urged Ingrid and Grayson to go to Rome for better protection, she had flat out declined. At least here in Paris, Ingrid had Luc. She had Vander and the Alliance members she knew and trusted. Leaving them simply wasn't an option.

"Philip—" their mother started to say, but the front door opened and then slammed, silencing her. Ingrid turned to the blue drapes. Grayson never had quite grasped how to gracefully shut a door.

The drapes swished aside and her twin stepped into the sitting room. His dark blue eyes settled on their father immediately. His blond hair was a tousled mess, his jaw tight, nostrils flaring. Grayson still held one panel of the drapes in his clenched fist.

"I half expected you to have disappeared again," their father said to him.

He still believed Grayson had driven their mother into a panic last December when he'd gone out carousing, sending no word at all. Grayson had actually been a prisoner in the demon realm, but of course their father couldn't know that.

"Grayson has taken charge of the abbey's repairs," Lady Brickton offered, slipping into her role as ambassadress between warring father and son. She would have a new role now: protector of her children's secrets.

Lord Brickton gave a sarcastic snort, the kind he reserved for anything he found ridiculous or a waste of time. Ingrid flicked her gaze back to Grayson. She couldn't be sure that it actually had happened, but for the briefest moment, she thought she saw a ripple of color roll over the whites of his eyes, turning them pale rose. In a flash, it was gone, and Grayson quickly averted his gaze, staring at the floor.

"The architects will be here Monday," he said to their mother, ignoring their father's presence completely. "The restorers can't begin on the final stained-glass panel until next week, and they think the rose window will need more time than they predicted."

The report floated out into the dead silence. Finally, their mother cleared her throat and thanked him. Grayson didn't spare them another moment. He turned on his heel and disappeared through the drapes, into the foyer, and back out the front door. Slamming it yet again.

Ingrid let out the breath she'd been holding.

"One more incident," their father said, his attention resting on Gabby and her scars. "*One more incident* and I will put an end to this. We will all go home—where we belong, might I add."

He rushed from the sitting room, barking to the butler to send for his valet. Ingrid, Gabby, and even their mother, who was still seated, seemed to sway, exhausted, in his wake. One incident? Ingrid's heart plummeted. In a house filled with demon gifts and a gargoyle, incidents were bound to happen.

Grayson slipped along boulevard Saint-Germain's slushy pavements. His only objective was to get as far away from the rectory as possible. He felt his feet go out from underneath him, but he shot out a hand and grasped a lamppost before he went down on his arse like a fool in front of everyone on the whole damned street.

He swore beneath his breath and raked a hand through his hair once he'd righted himself. Why come to Paris now? Couldn't the mighty Earl of Brickton have stayed in London for the rest of the winter? As if the old man even cared about the bloody gallery. In all the years Grayson's mother had dreamed aloud about her future endeavor, Father had answered with long sighs and vague promises such as "I'll think about it, my dear."

No, the only reason Lord Brickton was here now was because of Grayson's disappearance back in December. He'd been gone a little less than two weeks, and he remembered his time in the Underneath well. He remembered his prison, that hot, dry hive flickering with blue light. Grayson still woke from nightmares about the hooded woman, Axia, and the fanged man—a hellhound, Grayson had realized, though in human form, something hellhounds couldn't maintain while on the earth's surface. *I require more flexibility in my pets,* Axia had said. She needed her pets to look human on the outside, even when they were monsters at heart.

Monsters like Grayson.

He had besmirched the Brickton name plenty back in London, long before Mama had called on the police to search for him, hired the fake private detective Nolan Quinn, and sent urgent telegrams to Waverly House pleading for assistance from Scotland Yard.

Of course, Grayson's father had refused to help, and without a good explanation. Had he been honest, Lady Brickton would have needed smelling salts to revive her. Grayson would have loved to have seen *that* telegram:

> *No to Scotland Yard -(Stop)- Our son killed a girl*
> *-(Stop)- The police are already nosing about -(Stop)- Be*
> *glad you are rid of him -(Stop)-*

Being flippant was the only way to endure the harsh truth of it. Lord Brickton had shipped Grayson off to Paris for one reason: to shield him from the London police should they connect Grayson to the prostitute found dead on the rocky mudflats of the Thames last September.

Because Grayson had indeed been the one who'd killed her.

And now here he was, drawing more attention to himself in Paris. Attention his father had wanted to avoid entirely. No wonder he'd shown up. No wonder he'd looked ready to throttle Grayson back in that sitting room.

Then again, he was pretty sure his father wouldn't have made it halfway across the room alive. And that was why Grayson had fled the rectory for the frigid February air. For the slippery streets and the nameless faces crowding the pavements along the main boulevard in their arrondissement. He'd needed to calm his racing heart, his building fire. Grayson had felt it come close to the surface, and he knew Ingrid had seen it, too.

No, Grayson hadn't shifted from human to hellhound in months. But it was getting harder and harder to resist. He thought again about the man with fangs. He came to Grayson in nightmares sometimes. The man would taunt him, saying that in the end, he wouldn't be able to fight what he was.

Grayson's feet stopped carving a path through the slush and he stood still, hands in his pockets. Axia had said she'd wanted more flexibility in her hounds. If they couldn't hold human form on earth, how valuable would someone like Grayson—someone who could shift—be to her?

The scent of coffee and bread came at him, pulling him away from the panic that question always inspired. He knew exactly where his aimless wandering had taken him. Or maybe it hadn't been aimless after all. He always seemed to end up here.

Café Julius wasn't busy. Through the windows, where the café's name had been etched in red and gold across the glass, Grayson saw maybe a half-dozen patrons. He pushed open the door, the small brass bell ringing in his arrival. From the corner of his eye, he saw her turn, look up from what she was doing at the counter.

Grayson went to a small round table near the window and pulled out a chair. Why did he keep doing this to himself? He shrugged off his jacket, his temperature from encountering his father in the rectory still cranking. Maybe he kept coming here because he knew he deserved to be punished. What he'd done . . . Grayson had wanted to forget it. He'd wanted to pretend that it had never happened. Being in the Underneath and hearing Axia speak about it with such nonchalance—as if she had been *proud* of him—had made him ill.

The truth was, he didn't remember killing the girl. He didn't remember anything beyond seeing her in that greasy tavern. She'd hooked him with her eyes, an unspoken offer lingering there. And then an intoxicating, all-consuming need had overcome him.

That was where Grayson's memory started to haze.

A desire for her had driven him out of his chair. He'd followed her though the tavern's back door, into a dank, dark alley. He remembered the confusing hunger pangs clenching his stomach, closing off his throat. He didn't want the girl the way he'd wanted other girls.

He had simply been . . . hungry.

"If you've come to ask me to stop training your sister, you're wasting your breath," Chelle said. She stood beside the table with a shining silver coffeepot in one hand and a cup and saucer on a tray in the other. His usual request.

Grayson smiled, but not just because she'd anticipated his order. He could never hold back a smile when Chelle spoke. She sounded like a gruff military general. He sat back in his seat and put an ankle on one knee before glancing up at her. He furrowed his brow. No doubt she'd pour the contents of that silver pot in his lap if he said the wrong thing.

"I've come for the coffee, actually."

Chelle narrowed her round eyes at him in suspicion. She wore what she always did when working her shifts at Café Julius: male waiters' attire, complete with a white blouse, black vest, and tie. She'd put on breeches today, though sometimes she wore a long black skirt. He liked her in breeches. And the bright red scarf tied around her waist accentuated her petite hips.

Grayson had imagined spreading his palms around those hips. She was beautiful. She was Alliance. And she didn't like Grayson at all.

"So, may I?" he asked.

Chelle stared at him. "May you what?"

He looked pointedly at the silver coffeepot. "Have a coffee?"

She saw the pot in her hand and seemed to startle, as if just remembering she was holding it. With an ungraceful motion, she set the cup and saucer on the table and splashed in some steaming black coffee. She spilled, drops splattering on the white linen tablecloth. Chelle flushed.

Grayson smiled, liking the color on her cheeks. But then another scent cut through the bitter aroma of roasted beans. Sharp and decadent. At once sweet and tart.

A memory sparked. Grayson, rising from his engorged haze in that London alley. Warm blood smeared over his hands, his shirt. He'd licked his lips and tasted it in his mouth. So sweet. So delicious. And then he'd seen her on the stones beneath him. So much blood. Her blood.

Grayson bolted up from his chair and Chelle jumped back, the flush still on her cheeks. *Blood.* That's what he smelled. The rush of Chelle's blood to her cheeks.

"Did I spill on you?" she asked, looking at his lap. "It wasn't intentional. I only purposely spill hot liquids into the laps of old men who wink at me."

Grayson brushed at his trousers, going along with it. "What about young men who wink at you?" he asked, attempting to laugh off what had just happened. What had been happening for some time, actually.

He could smell blood as it sluiced through a person's veins. He could hear the heart pumping it. And every time, it made his throat hot and tight.

"Forget their laps," Chelle replied. "I aim for their hands."

She didn't smile. Grayson wondered whether she might be serious. He sat down, searching for something else to say to her. After all, she was the reason he always found himself here.

"I didn't realize you were so devoted to my sister's training." He held his coffee closer to his nose, wanted to smell that instead of another whiff of Chelle's coppery blood. It made every muscle in his body tight, as if he were holding himself together by will somehow.

"I am practical, not devoted. We need the help." She held his gaze and vaulted a brow with obvious expectancy.

Grayson pushed his coffee away. "No. I've already told Ingrid and Gabby and Vander—and *you,* if I recall. I'm no demon hunter."

They all wanted him to be one, though. They wanted him to join. Pick up a silver sword or dagger and prowl the streets at night. Protect the city and its people.

"You know about us, Grayson. You know about the Underneath and the Dispossessed," she said.

He stared into the coffee he no longer wanted. Yes, he knew about them. But they didn't know about *him*. They didn't know how hard it was becoming to fight the urge to shift, and he certainly didn't wish to tell them.

Chelle exhaled loudly. "Don't you feel as though you should do something?"

"Like what?" he asked, more curtly than he liked. It made his pulse jump, which was never a good thing. Not anymore. He got to his feet and Chelle stared up at him.

"*Something,*" she answered. "Anything other than hide. You've already proven you do that well enough."

She drew back as soon as she'd said it. Her lips parted and her expression betrayed a look of regret. But it was gone just as fast.

"Is it because of your dust?" she asked. "Vander has it, too, and it hasn't stopped him from doing good things for the Alliance."

"Don't compare me to Vander Burke," Grayson muttered, reaching into his pocket for a few coins. "He doesn't turn into an enormous rabid dog."

"It only happened once, Grayson, and you were under Axia's influence." Chelle lowered her voice. "If you would just try—"

"You want the wrong things." Grayson tossed the coins onto the table. "You shouldn't be asking me to join you. You should be asking me to stay away."

Grayson started for the door. Why did he keep doing this to himself? Going to Café Julius, seeing Chelle. It never made him feel better. The Alliance was interested in him and his sister because of their dust, and had gone so far as to request that they go to Rome for observation and interviews, even protection from Axia, if need be. Neither he nor Ingrid had accepted, though. He couldn't imagine anything worse than being drilled with questions about his demon half or letting the secret he clutched come out into the open.

If anyone knew what he'd done in London, knew the urges he fought every single day, they would realize he shouldn't be hunting anything.

They would realize *they* should be hunting *him*.

CHAPTER FIVE

Everything was going to be different now that Papa had arrived. Ingrid trudged through the snow behind the rectory and tried to convince herself that she wasn't already hiding from him.

Wasn't that what they would all be doing from here on out? Hiding from the truth? Hiding from what they were? What they had become? So much had changed since London. What frightened Ingrid the most sometimes was that she didn't want to go back. Everything she'd been born and bred to be as Lady Ingrid Waverly—a prim and mild society rose whose only ambition was to marry high and well—had disintegrated over the last few months. But her father didn't know this, and he most certainly couldn't find out. With one word, he could command them all to pack up and leave Paris. What would Ingrid do . . . refuse? The thought made her sick to her stomach.

She loved her father, but he had a weight to him. Had he always been so overbearing? Or maybe it was their newfound freedom here in Paris that had made his sudden presence feel like a wet sheet of canvas tossed over all their heads.

Ingrid felt guilty for it, but she wished he had stayed away.

She slowed down as she neared the abbey's cemetery. Her feet were cold, her boots still damp from that morning. Ingrid looked around, the back lawns new for her. She'd seen a corner of the cemetery from the rectory, but she hadn't yet been out this way. The icy, drizzly snowfalls had kept her from exploring.

The bars along the iron fence enclosing the cemetery had gone to rust. The gate hung from one hinge and was frozen open by a drift of snow. Her feet were the first to break the perfectly smooth blanket of white as she entered through the gate. The headstones slanted like gray, crooked teeth, and the engravings were all in French, of course—a language Ingrid had, sadly, never grasped. She knew enough to get by, but nothing more.

She wound her way among the rows of headstones, wondering how she might explain to her father the twice-weekly visits to Constantine's chateau. What if she said she was receiving French lessons? Ingrid sighed. But then her father would expect her French to improve.

She didn't need to know the language to know the headstones here were old. The most recent death she saw dated from a century ago. There were more graves through a second gate on the other side of the cemetery, though these were marked with simple wooden crosses or nubs of stone. A pulpy wooden sign hanging on the entrance gate bore one word: PROFANE.

She knew the English meaning for this word. Did it mean the same in French? With a forceful shove, the gate swung in, plowing through the snow. This second plot was smaller and wasn't fenced in; trees and shrubbery made up the perimeter instead. Ingrid stepped inside, wondering how much farther the abbey grounds went. Maybe she'd avoid her father a bit longer and walk the whole property.

But as soon as she entered the plot, her legs seized. Her knees trembled. A swirl of nausea slammed into her. The whole cemetery seemed to set off on a wobbly spin, blurring around her shoulders. Ingrid squeezed her eyes shut, trying to clear her vision, but with the blackness came a racing cold.

She opened her eyes and found herself flat on the ground, her cheek buried in the snow. The world around her still shook, unhinged. Her mind was slow to respond, but her hands moved fast. They plunged into the snow and she pushed herself up, her head spinning.

After a few long blinks, the cemetery plot steadied. The snow and the stones, the trees and sky all came back into focus. And when everything had stilled, Ingrid saw that she wasn't alone.

Standing amid the trees that bordered the other side of the cemetery was a girl in a bright white cape. If not for her pink cheeks and the dark brown curls framing her face, she might have blended into the landscape perfectly. Ingrid, still on the ground, peered at the girl, completely confounded.

"Anna?" she whispered.

It didn't make any sense. Anna Bettinger was supposed to be in London preparing for her wedding later that month. Ingrid tried to stand, battling the nauseating fog. Her skirts tangled beneath her in the snow.

Had Anna traveled with Papa to Paris? Was she surprising Ingrid with a visit?

Giving up on trying to stand—her legs were so *tired*—Ingrid looked back at her friend. She'd expected to see Anna coming through the snow, shaking her head at Ingrid's ridiculous position, a hand pulled free from her mink muff and extended toward her. But instead, Anna stood motionless. The only change at all was a sly little lift at the corner of her lips. It was a smug grin, and it was just as cold as the snow Ingrid knelt in.

It wasn't one of Anna's smiles at all.

"Ingrid?"

She startled at his voice. Luc came through the second

cemetery gate behind her, halting a split second when he saw her crumpled in the snow. And then he was surging forward, his mouth twisted into a scowl.

"What are you doing out here?" He jerked her out of the snow. Her knees wobbled, but she refused to slump against him. She forced them to lock and stood on her own.

"I—" She turned back toward Anna, but there was no one there among the trees. Anna and her white cape and smirking expression were gone.

"I . . . I was just walking. I must have hit a headstone buried in the snow and tripped." It was an awful excuse. Luc kept his firm grip on her elbow.

"Do you know where you are?" he asked.

"The headstones give it away, Luc," she answered, shaking off his hand. He wasn't wearing a jacket, and she realized he must have had to race away from whatever he'd been doing when he'd felt her . . . her what? Fear? Confusion? Whatever it had been, he'd believed she was in trouble.

He hooked his chin toward the pulpy wooden sign strung with wire over the center arch of the gate. "*Profane*. This is unconsecrated burial ground."

Oh. It wasn't blessed, then. But so what? Ingrid couldn't stay on holy ground forever.

"Why is it set apart?" she asked as Luc led her back through the gates into the first, consecrated burial ground.

"Because that's where they buried the people who weren't good enough for this supremely blessed soil," he answered with unabashed sarcasm, spreading his arms wide. "Nonconformists. Suicides. The generally unworthy."

Luc shut the gate behind them. "Whatever the reason, the spirits buried in profane lots lie restless. Certain demons feed on those restless souls. And demons beget demons." Luc speared her with his pale, lime-colored eyes. "You should remember that."

Ingrid remembered a lot of things, including the fact that to

Luc, she was just a human. Just a duty. He'd come to her aid just then because he *had* to, not because he wanted to.

"Did I hear you speaking to someone out there?" he asked, scanning the profane plot once more.

He hadn't seen Anna. Ingrid drew in a breath and shuddered. "No."

Again, he stared at her just a beat too long. He knew she was lying. She wondered if he could feel her emotions, her senses, that well. Did everything about her echo within him?

They went through the consecrated plot in silence, and Ingrid started wishing for dry clothes and a steaming cup of tea to wrap her fingers around. She'd been in the snow far too long for one day.

At the gate, though, another person stood waiting for them. It was a boy, thin and gangly, about a year younger than Gabby, Ingrid presumed. He met Ingrid's eyes and smiled at her. She slowed, suddenly wary. Luc stiffened, no doubt feeling her hesitation.

"Lady Waverly," Luc said, his formal use of her name out of character. "This is Dimitrie, the new livery boy."

The boy immediately dropped into a deep bow, his chin drawn in so that the crown of his head was pointed at Ingrid's feet. "My lady," Dimitrie said, his voice muffled.

Gustav, their butler, should have hired a new groom in December, right after Bertrand, their first driver had died and Luc had ascended from his position as groom. But Lady Brickton had been distracted with the disappearance of her son, and then, once Grayson had returned, she'd told Gustav to hold off on hiring new staff. The fewer people to encounter Ingrid's and Grayson's abnormal abilities, the better.

"Stand up," Luc ordered, and the boy did. But he was smiling, his bright eyes as blue as a spray of forget-me-nots.

"Your scent is delectable," the boy said.

Ingrid frowned. "Excuse me?"

"Your scent, my lady," he replied.

"My *what?*" she asked, her cheeks quickly heating.

Luc stepped between Ingrid and Dimitrie, glaring at the new groom with the kind of ferocity he might show a hellhound.

"Irindi sent him," Luc explained. Ingrid felt herself inch back a step. She inspected Dimitrie again. *He* was a gargoyle? But he was so young.

"Oh," she replied, unable to think of anything else to say at first. But then, "I have a scent?"

Dimitrie, unfazed, nodded eagerly. "Of course. We keep our humans' individual scents in a kind of olfactory memory," he said with a nervous laugh. "It's how we trace you. How we call you up inside ourselves."

Ingrid immediately looked at Luc. He hadn't told her any of this, and yet, here Dimitrie was spilling forth information less than a minute into their first meeting. Why had Luc held back? She'd already known that he could trace her, but she hadn't known how. Her scent was the key.

Luc ground his jaw, clearly annoyed. She recalled Luc's words the last time she'd been in his loft, in December. *You're just a human. You're not supposed to know.*

Dimitrie caught Luc's harsh stare and seemed to shrink back.

"Go inside," Luc said. Ingrid startled when she saw that he was looking at her, not the new gargoyle. "And stay out of that cemetery."

Ingrid bristled. How dare he? Luc couldn't order her to stay on hallowed ground forever. She marched past him, keeping her gaze locked on his. "I will go where I please."

She turned away and stormed through the snowy back lawns, her ire stoked high enough to keep her raging hot from head to toe. Luc might be her gargoyle, but he wasn't her master. Ingrid wouldn't be returning to that profane cemetery plot anytime soon, but not because he'd ordered it. Something had happened to her there. It was as if she'd been attacked somehow, and then that vision of Anna . . . a trick. Something had played a trick on her.

It had been a quiet two months, and Axia seemed to have forgotten about Ingrid. There hadn't been a single attempt to reclaim Ingrid's angel blood. Axia had said that if she ever got it back, it would give her enough power to challenge the Angelic Order. She would be an untouchable fusion of demon, human, and angel. But how she planned to wield her power was still a matter of speculation among the Alliance and gargoyles.

Ingrid had known the quiet wouldn't last forever. Axia had already reclaimed the angel blood Grayson had harbored all his life, and if angel blood turned toxic in the Underneath, Axia had to be desperate for the rest of her blood. She needed Ingrid.

Perhaps she'd just made her first strike.

CHAPTER SIX

Gabby crushed the small note in her fist. The carriage wheels rolled along boulevard Saint-Germain, lurching up and sideways over frost heaves, jostling Ingrid, Grayson, and Gabby.

The note had arrived via messenger less than an hour before, just after luncheon. The envelope had been blood red, the single square of cardstock inside matching crimson. Red was the color of the Alliance, and it never failed to stir her, filling her head with a whooshing roar.

"Luc just passed Café Julius," Grayson said, leaning forward and following the café with his eyes as they trotted past. He groaned. "*Where* are we going, Gabby?"

"I apologize for the ruse," she replied. "Having you with us was the only way we could leave the house without Mama or Papa objecting."

Grayson would have never agreed to a call on Alliance headquarters, but he would also have never turned down a chance to glimpse Chelle at the café. Gabby had done what she'd needed to do, and no accusatory glare from her brother would make her feel sorry for it. The note had made her too elated to feel guilty about anything.

Nolan had returned!

He was back from Rome and he wanted to see her. *Immediately.*

Fortunately, Gabby had been alone in the music room when the note arrived, tapping distractedly on the ivories of an old, out-of-tune piano. She hardly ever went to the music room—it was musty and the light was dim, and really, her musical skills were as poor as Ingrid's French. However, in the forty-eight hours since her father had arrived, Gabby had been trying to find places to hide from him. No. Not just him, but the way he looked at her. He couldn't meet her eyes, not without first frowning at her left cheek and the track of scars there.

She had reread Nolan's slanted script and noticed, with a slight dip in excitement, that he'd requested that Ingrid and Grayson come, too. So it wouldn't be a private reunion, then. It didn't matter. Nolan was back, and she was more than ready to set eyes on him again.

"We're going to Hôtel Bastian, aren't we?" Grayson asked.

Ingrid bit back her grin, though not very successfully. "Don't be angry with Gabby."

"She used me to escape from under Father's nose," Grayson retorted.

"It was my idea, really," Ingrid said.

At Grayson's bug-eyed reaction, Gabby leaped in. "It's not just Papa. Even Mama wouldn't have let us go."

Their mother knew about gargoyles; she knew that her twins possessed strange abilities, and that their friends Nolan and Vander were part of a group of people who stood against demons. But if she knew that her youngest daughter was training to hunt those demons, Gabby was sure that would be the line in the sand for Lady Charlotte Brickton.

"Nolan's returned from Rome," Gabby said, unable to mask her thrill. Her brother gave a nearly imperceptible shake of his head.

"Bring out the marching band," he muttered. Gabby ignored him. Ingrid did as well. At least the two of them were of the same mind. Plus, Gabby suspected her sister wouldn't be too upset should Vander Burke be waiting for them there.

By the time they'd arrived, Grayson still hadn't said anything. He didn't move when Luc, whose expression was equally gloomy, opened the carriage door for them.

"At least walk us up?" Ingrid asked, calling on his chivalry. It worked. Grayson sighed and hopped out of the carriage behind them.

Luc shut the door and, as he usually did when dropping Gabby off at Hôtel Bastian, glanced up at the sloped black mansard roof that topped the five-story town house. As if expecting something or someone to be perched there, looking down at them. All Gabby could see was a decorative black iron fence scrolling along the roof.

"I'll be here," Luc said, as always. He no longer kept his eyes on Ingrid when he said those words, but Gabby still felt that the reassurance was meant for her sister alone.

They went inside and climbed the first three stories, the last twist in the stairs leading them to a heavy oak door with a grid of iron in the center. Gabby touched the slanted veil of her hat to make sure the moss-colored tulle covered her well. She couldn't hide the hooked ends of the scars near her lips, but at least the veil obscured the worst of them. Perhaps Nolan wouldn't see the scars straight away.

The square of wood behind the iron grid slid to the side and the top half of an unfamiliar face peered out at them.

"Name?" the stranger asked.

After a pause—*who was this?*—Gabby recovered the quickest. "Waverly," she answered.

The peephole slammed. The chains on the door rattled. And then they were being ushered in by a tall, broad-shouldered young man. He wore a brown leather vest adorned with glimmering silver daggers, three strapped into individual sheaths on each side panel, and on the back, two swords in crossed scabbards.

"This way," he said, and Gabby was reminded of the person who had first shown them into the Alliance headquarters.

Tomas's face and neck had been badly scarred—worse than Gabby's, by far. Tomas had turned out to be a traitor, and he'd been taken to Rome for his trial. Could this young man be his replacement? He led them down the short hallway and into the wide-open, loftlike apartment. He had a stealthy gait, the set of his chin and shoulders disciplined. He was a hunter, she knew.

Then Gabby saw the rest of the apartment. It was packed to the corners with people, mostly men. There must have been close to two dozen of them, ranging from Gabby's age to men older than her father. Some were simply talking; others were hovering over tables, with maps and papers spread out before them; and another handful were passing around a particularly beautiful sword, each one admiring it with raised brows. They were all Alliance. The red sash worked one way or another into their clothing made that perfectly clear.

Gabby felt Ingrid go still at her side. Grayson had his arms crossed, his glower deeper than before. Gabby had definitely not expected so many people. Chelle had been living here alone the last few months, everyone else having been in Rome. It was such a change from before, when their voices had echoed off the exposed beams and plaster ceilings.

Gabby saw him through the shoulders of a crowd that had been standing in the open kitchen, huddled together in serious conversation. He met her gaze, and it was as if she had snared him with a fishhook and immediately commenced reeling him in. Nolan broke away from the others and came toward her, deftly avoiding a practice jab with the much-admired sword. He didn't flinch, his focus steady. The rest of the apartment slipped away, and Gabby could only see him. His morning-glory eyes, his glossy black hair, the waves grown out and even more unruly. He came toward her with an easy swagger, sure-footed and mischievous rather than predatory.

The veil and what lay underneath it didn't matter to him. She saw it in the coy grin lifting the corner of his mouth. Oh, how she'd missed him. How she'd missed just looking at him.

But before Nolan could reach them, someone from deeper within the apartment bellowed, "Ah! Here they are."

The entire apartment went silent, and the invisible line on which Gabby had strung Nolan was severed. He stopped moving. His playful smile crashed.

A man made his way toward them through the crowd. Gabby didn't need an introduction. She saw Nolan in every facet of him—his overwhelming height, his dark features and fathomless blue eyes. Nolan's father, Carrick Quinn.

Apparently, the elder Quinn knew no introduction was necessary. He didn't spare them one.

"Where is your gargoyle?" he asked.

For some reason, Gabby and Grayson automatically looked to Ingrid. Silly, since they both knew the answer.

"Outside," Ingrid told him.

"Good. See that it stays there," Carrick Quinn quickly replied. Out of the corner of her eye, Gabby saw Ingrid's chin lift. *It.* Luc wasn't an *it.*

"I won't waste your time, or mine," he went on, all business. "Recently, there has been a breakdown in proper Alliance command in this city." There was no missing the pointed look he sent his son. Nolan ignored it, his eyes remaining on Gabby.

"I've come back from Rome with plenty of Alliance ready

to set things to rights. With what we've learned about the fallen angel Axia and this much-too-vague Harvest of hers, we cannot allow for even the slightest dip in our standards," he said. His Scottish burr was just as soft and unpronounced as Nolan's.

"You and you," Carrick said, stabbing a finger toward Ingrid and then Grayson. "The Alliance is still interested in the two of you, even though you both declined an urgent request for your presence in Rome. You"—he stabbed his finger toward Gabby—"I have to ask that you leave."

Gabby stilled and felt a stupid expression slacken her jaw. "I—I beg your pardon?"

Chelle's petite figure emerged from between two taller Alliance men, followed by Vander.

"The Alliance insists that you forget everything you've learned about us these last months," Nolan's father answered without an ounce of remorse. "My son made a mistake bringing you into our circle, informing you of our practices."

Nolan stood rigid, the only change in his expression the downward slant of his brows. *Open your mouth!* Gabby wanted to shout. *Say something!* Even Chelle's and Vander's lips were sealed, though their eyes were bright and clearly troubled.

"This is an underground society, one that has been built upon a solid foundation of Alliance families around the world. Your sister and brother possess certain abilities that—*if* controllable— could aid our hunters, just as Mr. Burke has done. Otherwise, we do not make it a regular practice to take in first-generations. Not without good reason, at least."

So Gabby had nothing to offer. No demon gifts, no special abilities. Nothing but her own will and a glimmer of fighting skill.

Without a parting word, or an apology, Carrick Quinn nodded once to show he was finished and folded back into the stunned crowd. Gabby's whole body shook with embarrassment and fury. Forget the last few months? Forget the Alliance and everything she'd learned? Was the man absolutely insane? There was no way she could forget. It was like asking someone to forget what a crack of thunder sounded like, or the sum of two plus two. It was just there, and there was no getting rid of it.

She didn't *want* to be rid of it. The Alliance was supposed to be her chance. This was what she'd been working for, training for. And as pathetic as it sounded, even to her, this was where she'd thought she'd be accepted.

Nolan came forward as the others went back to their conversations. No doubt they were already forgetting her. Gabby blinked, her eyes stinging. No. She would not cry, not here in front of everyone.

Nolan stopped a foot away from her. Before, she had pictured throwing her arms around him, feeling him catch her and return the embrace. Maybe even stealing a kiss. That fantasy reunion shriveled.

"I'll come to you," Nolan whispered so low that no one else could hear.

He wasn't going to fight for her.

Gabby backed up without a word. Her heels trod on something solid and she felt a pair of hands grip her waist. Spinning around, she found herself looking up into the face of the young man who had opened the door for them.

"Will ye be all right?" he asked. The question startled her. She didn't know him, and yet he sounded genuinely concerned.

Gabby had no answer. She shook her head and bit her lower lip to fend off a new threat of tears. She rushed past him, away from her sister and brother. If the Alliance didn't want her, well, then she wanted no part of it.

Ingrid started after Gabby as she barreled down the entrance hall. Nolan's father had been horrible, and Ingrid's eyes burned with anger.

Grayson caught her elbow. "I'll go." He looked around the apartment as if it were infested with vermin. "I don't want anything to do with this place anyway."

Chelle stepped into his path. "We can help you. That's all we've been trying to do."

Grayson huffed a laugh, but Ingrid knew her twin was miserable, not amused.

"Unless you can help me get rid of my demon dust, there isn't a damned thing you can do." He followed in Gabby's wake.

Ingrid spun on her heel in time with the slam of the front door. She saw Carrick Quinn across the apartment, his back to her.

"How could you be so awful to her?" She hadn't shouted, but her voice carried.

Nolan's father held still. Vander clasped Ingrid's hand, implying a warning in the way he pulled her closer. She unthreaded her fingers and pushed herself forward.

"You can't discard my sister so heartlessly. She isn't worthless."

Ingrid forced her lips sealed before she could go on about how hard Gabby had been training. A slip like that would have landed Chelle in scalding water.

Vander didn't try to take Ingrid's hand again, but he did lean close to her ear, his breath hot against her skin.

"This isn't wise. You don't want to cross—"

"So you're the lightning girl," Carrick Quinn interrupted, finally turning to look at her.

She didn't know why, but having this man whittle who she was down to those two words stabbed like an insult.

"My *name* is Lady Ingrid Waverly," she replied, attempting to keep her voice even.

Carrick waved his hand in the air before him. "Your name isn't important. Neither is mine, or my son's, or that man's over there." He loosely wagged a finger, indicating pretty much everyone. "What matters is what you can do. Whether your talent be wielding blessed silver, tracking demons, keeping peaceful negotiations between us and the Dispossessed, healing wounded fighters, or, in your case, handling a supernatural power."

He'd come closer as he'd been speaking, masterfully captivating the eyes and ears of every person in the apartment.

"So, lightning girl," Carrick repeated, lingering on the epithet just to goad her. "Show me what you can do."

Ingrid's natural reaction was to laugh. Show him? What, just conjure up a little lightning right then, right there? She looked around and realized it was no joke.

"You want a demonstration?" she asked, her gaze flicking to Nolan, then Vander. The two of them stood like sentries on either side of her, their chins slightly raised, their jaws set, but they were watching Carrick, not her.

"We wanted a demonstration in Rome, but considering you declined our invitation . . . ," Carrick said, opening his arms as a gesture for her to begin.

Ingrid rubbed the tips of her fingers together, feeling the smooth friction of her kid gloves. She'd done it. Just the other morning, she'd made the sparks fly down from her shoulders. The electric charge had overrun her arms, filling them up the way water gushing from a tap would fill a bottle. When the water reached the mouth of the bottle, it would geyser, the same way her electricity would geyser from her fingers.

The tips of Ingrid's ears began to burn. Everyone stared at her, even Nolan and Vander, waiting for her to fulfill Carrick's request.

"It's not always so easy," she said softly.

"Why not? It's a part of who you are, isn't it?" he asked with all the sympathy of an asp being prodded with a stick.

Ingrid opened her mouth to argue with him, but he was right.

It was a part of her. It also belonged to her. Not to him. Not to the Alliance or anyone else. She exhaled, her decision final.

"I won't give you a show," she said, her eyes tearing up from holding his scorching stare for so long. "I have nothing to prove to you."

Vander's fingers brushed the back of her arm, as if poised to clutch her and draw her away in a flash. The stunned, and then furious, expression contorting Carrick's face made her think Vander wasn't overreacting in the least.

But a few measured breaths later, the flush upon his cheeks lightened. If possible, his stare softened. "Very well, Lady Ingrid. We shall all wait until you deem us worthy of your light."

Carrick swept into a low, mocking bow before snapping his fingers at a few other Alliance and brushing past her.

"That's not what I meant," Ingrid said to Vander as he hooked her elbow and led her toward the rear of the apartment, along the corridor of curtained makeshift rooms.

Nolan followed them. "We know what you meant, and my father does as well."

"He's a manipulative old rooster," Chelle said, catching up with them. "He's hoping to make you feel guilty."

"The only one who should feel guilty is him," Ingrid said, exasperated. "The way he threw Gabby out . . . he humiliated her."

She was probably sitting in Luc's carriage at that very moment, sobbing. Or, more likely, plotting her revenge.

Released from Carrick's hold, Ingrid wanted to return to the carriage.

"He's getting worse," Nolan muttered to Chelle and Vander.

Chelle reached out and touched his arm. "There is nothing you can do."

Nolan covered her hand with his, gave it a squeeze, and then walked away. Chelle angrily murmured something in French before rearranging her cap, pushing back her shoulders, and rejoining the others. Ingrid and Vander stood alone in the corridor.

Vander held a finger to his lips and parted a curtain, indicating that he wanted Ingrid to go inside. She should have been more reluctant—these were obviously bedrooms. But her feet moved quickly and Vander shut the curtain behind them. He sighed.

"I'm sorry," he said. "I would have warned you if I had known Carrick would be like that. Nolan's right. He's gotten worse."

She still didn't know what that meant. "Worse how? Is he ill?" He didn't look sick at all. He was older, in his late forties, perhaps early fifties. He was still robust and vibrant, though.

"In a way," Vander answered. He came away from the curtains, toward her. "Nolan's father is one of the best hunters the Alliance has. He's fought almost every kind of demon we know about, and he's trained hundreds of us. But that also means he's been exposed to a lot of mercurite over the years." Vander passed Ingrid and pulled aside another wall of curtains. Behind it was a door. He opened it and Ingrid saw steps leading both up and down.

"Come. I have something to show you," Vander said.

Curious, Ingrid climbed the twisting set of steps up to the fourth floor, coming out into a long, empty corridor. Electric lamps lit the way, though sparely. There were four doors, two on each side of the hallway, the walls covered in deep maroon silk. More bedrooms, was her initial guess. But why hide bedrooms away like this?

She kept in Vander's shadow as he walked along the rust-red carpet. "What has the mercurite done to Mr. Quinn?" Ingrid asked.

Vander twisted the handle to one door and held it steady. "Have you heard about the mad hatters? The toxic amounts of mercury hatmakers are exposed to?"

"The mercurite has made him insane?" she whispered.

"Not quite. But he's changed. The mercury has started to break down his tissues and organs. Some days he can't even get out of bed. It's also changed his behavior."

Vander opened the door then, and every thought about Carrick Quinn and poisonous mercury was set free.

All she could see were books. The room was filled with them. Ingrid glided over the threshold, her jaw unattractively slack. Vander laughed.

"I remember the first time I saw this room, too." He shut the door behind them. It was completely silent inside. Ingrid could almost hear the dust motes floating through the air.

"It's beautiful."

Vander scratched his head. "No, not really. It's a mess."

Yes, the shelves along all four walls sagged from the weight of so many books, and where some were placed upright with spines facing out, there were just as many tipped onto their sides, spines facing in. On most shelves, books and scrolls had been stuffed in to rest on top of other books, and there were at least a half-dozen towers of homeless books piled up on the floor.

"It's a beautiful mess," she said, compromising.

Vander straightened one leaning tower with his knee. "I thought you'd like it. But the collection is limited. This is an Alliance library. You won't find Chaucer or Shakespeare, but if you want to know anything regarding the Alliance, demons, the Dispossessed, or the Angelic Order, this is where you'll find the answer."

There was a book about the Dispossessed? Ingrid's pulse fluttered in her neck. *Luc will have felt that.*

"Why did you bring me here?" she asked, running her hand along the top book of one towering pile.

Vander came up behind her without disturbing the floorboards. Not a single creak. It reminded her how much of a hunter he really was.

"I don't want you to fight demons," he said. "I don't want you in the sewers looking for crazy Dusters, or in any situation that puts you at risk. But I do want you here." He touched her then, sliding his hands up her arms. "You belong here."

Did she? The words fell through her, unable to find a foothold anywhere. Did she truly belong there, with the Alliance? She didn't want to fight, not like Gabby did. Ingrid couldn't even imagine holding a sword and stabbing at a demon. It was all so violent and dangerous. But if she didn't belong here, where did she belong?

"I was supposed to go through this room . . . organize, categorize, read and research, and then be that one person any Alliance could turn to for answers," Vander said, his hands still on her.

A mellow spring of electricity went down through her arms, the way it usually did when Vander touched her for longer than a few seconds. She had started to wonder whether it was because they both had demon dust.

"It made sense. I ran a bookshop—who better to be the Alliance academic?"

"But you don't want to anymore?" she asked, trying to focus. The mellow current had started to fizzle, leaving behind a lovely kind of weightlessness. When the last prickle dissolved, Ingrid slumped back against him. Her arms felt like they were made of silken ribbons instead of flesh and bone.

Vander didn't react. He only held her tighter. "It's more a matter of time. My studies at the church are taking more of it than I thought they would."

"So you think I can do this?" she replied, seeing the stacks of books with new, overwhelming wonder.

"Be an Alliance academic? Absolutely." He turned her to face him. She needed the help. The silky feeling had spread to her legs.

"Do you feel that?" she asked.

A coy little grin worked at Vander's lips. "I most certainly do."

She swatted him on the arm, though she was sure the slap

landed like a goose feather. He feigned injury but then put on his sly smile again.

"I mean it. I feel an electricity whenever we touch," he said, stepping closer, leaving an inch, maybe two, between them. Ingrid already felt hot, and when Vander reached up to run his thumb across her lower lip, she thought she might combust.

"Do you feel anything now?" he asked. Before she could answer, Vander had his lips against hers.

Ingrid held her breath, her eyes still open.

She shouldn't be kissing him.

Should she?

Her lips moved on instinct. Her eyes slowly fluttered shut. Vander's arms wound around her and tucked her body against his. Ingrid's hands, trapped between her chest and his, gathered up fistfuls of his soft tweed jacket. Their kiss broke off and Vander tilted his head to press his lips to the curve of her jaw. He tasted her skin, nuzzling the slope of her neck, his breath hot. Vander held her tightly, his arms solid, his fervor rising. He felt so good and strong, and she began to yearn for his lips to climb back up to hers. *If* she should even be kissing him. A small voice called for her to stop and breathe. Step away. Vander's mouth came back upon hers, silencing the voice altogether.

The knob on the door to the library creaked, the hinges squealed, and Chelle stood, openmouthed, in the doorway.

"Oh. Ah." She averted her eyes as Vander pulled away and adjusted his spectacles. Ingrid stumbled back against a tower of books. They toppled into a heap.

Chelle recovered first. "Your gargoyle is darkening our doorstep. He's taking your brother and sister home but refuses to leave without you. Are you, ah, finished here?"

If Luc's sixth sense had felt the stirring of Ingrid's blood, or the sudden stream of static that had strangely dissolved a minute later, then he very well might have entered the building to interrupt her.

Or, Ingrid reasoned as she said an awkward good-bye to Vander and followed Chelle, he had simply grown tired of waiting for her. Why did she keep doing this to herself? Hope always felt so good and buoyant—until truth sank it. Luc could lust, not love. And Ingrid wanted love.

Vander could love her. Perhaps he already did. She certainly hadn't disliked kissing him, even though that small voice had implored her to stop. Still, kisses were one thing. Ingrid had to start thinking seriously about whether she could love Vander in return.

CHAPTER SEVEN

The thing Luc disliked most about being the Waverlys' driver was the amount of time he spent sitting on his ass, waiting. It wasn't the cold, which tonight was more of a bone-chilling dampness. Or the horses, even though they smelled. No, it was just his backside, aching now that he'd been sitting on it for nearly two hours while Ingrid and her family ate a leisurely dinner in a restaurant near the Champs de Mars.

The drizzly snowfall had amounted to a half an inch of dirty slush along the pavement. It gathered on the short brim of Luc's driver's hat and dripped steadily into his lap. Had it only been Lord and Lady Brickton dining out, Luc would have been more annoyed than he already was. But Ingrid was with them, along with Gabby and Grayson, and so Luc sat vigilantly in the driver's box, doing something the other drivers lined up and down the curb couldn't do: eavesdropping on his employers.

It had become a disgraceful habit, but Luc couldn't stop himself. There was something about this family that intrigued him.

However, Lord Brickton was not a welcome addition. For Luc, he was one more human to protect, and for Ingrid and the others, he was a source of nervous tension. Ingrid, Gabby, Grayson, and even Lady Brickton had all responded to his arrival with the same tightness in the chest, the same unease. It bothered Luc, the way this one man could have such an instant and dreary effect on them all.

He had tried to figure out Lord Brickton a bit more by surfacing his scent a few times. The oil and leather filling his nostrils and falling into the back of his throat hadn't told him much. So far all he'd learned was that Ingrid's father was angry. Bitterly angry and unhappy.

It was Ingrid whom Luc eavesdropped on now. It was so easy, her scent always just *there* whenever he thought of her. And he thought about her a lot. Too much.

Ingrid was content. For the first time, he didn't feel anxiety closing like fists inside his chest. He thought about checking in on Grayson, who had been in a constant state of discomfort for weeks now. He decided to stay with Ingrid a little longer. He could taste her sunshine. A watery morning light on his tongue. It was a pleasant contrast to the hard, cold bench, the drizzle, and the slushy streets around him.

The chime at the base of his neck broke her scent's spell. He focused ahead of the landau and saw a person walking toward him on the sidewalk. He wore a black wool coat and hat and held a black silk umbrella against the snow.

"Gaston?" Luc called when the gargoyle's face came into the yellowy light of a lamppost.

Monsieur Constantine's personal valet and heavenly appointed bodyguard raised the scalloped trim of the umbrella an inch and looked up at the driver's bench.

"Luc," he returned with a dip of his head. Oddly enough, Gaston reminded Luc of a piece of wood: Solid, quiet, boring.

Lacking in any personality whatsoever. He was a perfect servant. Most likely a perfect gargoyle, too.

"Is your human here?" Luc asked, glancing toward the restaurant windows, fringed with russet silk drapes and filled with a low amber light.

"No. I've come to warn you," Gaston answered. Luc sat forward, curiosity piqued. "Monsieur Constantine had a visitor this afternoon, a man by the name of Robert Dupuis. I felt my human's pulse spike when the man was shown into the orangery, and so I stayed close. Hidden, but close."

There were plenty of places to hide within Constantine's miniature jungle. Luc and Ingrid had hidden under a domed canopy of furry pink moss once. He had nearly kissed her there.

"Dupuis spoke of your human girl, the one who makes lightning," Gaston said. Luc was listening fully now. "He told Monsieur Constantine that his interests in the girl will not cease, and that she should be turned over to them sooner rather than later."

"Who is 'them'?" Luc asked.

"I do not know," Gaston answered. "I just know I do not like this man Dupuis. Neither does my human. Whatever his interests are in your human girl, they are not good."

Luc let the warning settle. Gaston had just done him a favor, which of course only made him suspicious. "Why seek me out to tell me this?"

Gaston kept his expression as wooden as ever. "We are both Dogs, are we not?" They were. In fact, Luc and Gaston, with their dark coloring and green eyes, looked nearly identical when in true form. Ingrid had even mistaken Gaston once for Luc. But Luc hadn't thought Gaston had such deep loyalty to other members of his caste.

"We are," Luc replied. He gave a nod, a silent thank-you, and Gaston turned to walk back down the sidewalk the way he had come.

He didn't have more than a second to contemplate who Robert Dupuis might be before another chime throbbed at the base of his skull.

"More people sniffing around your humans, brother?"

Marco approached from behind the carriage and stood streetside, next to Luc. Yann came up beside the bench seat on the sidewalk, closing Luc in properly. Marco and Yann had brought together the Wolves and the Chimeras into a steady Alliance. Theirs were the strongest castes, with the largest numbers and influence among the Paris Dispossessed. The Dogs ranked with the Snakes just below that, while the Monkeys and Goats and a few other castes languished in the background, generally unnoticed and unheard.

"What do you want, Marco?" Luc asked, already wary.

Marco was the butler for a family that stayed but three or four months of the year at his territory, a fine old place in Montparnasse known as Hôtel Dugray. His humans were not yet in the city for the season, so he was free to roam around, unencumbered by duty.

How nice for him.

"An update," Marco replied. "Is yours still the only cursed soul at the abbey? I'm beginning to think our dear Irindi has forgotten all about you."

Marco and Yann had been checking in regularly to see if Irindi would follow through with her promise. They tended to visit the carriage house at night, when Ingrid and the others were asleep. Probably for the best, considering Marco and Yann had tried to kill Grayson. Ingrid hadn't forgiven them just yet.

"She didn't forget," Luc answered. Yann and Marco took a moment to adjust to his response. Usually Luc just told them to go to hell.

"Anyone we know?" Marco asked, clearly excited.

"No."

"How does he seem?" Marco pressed.

"He seems very Dispossessed," Luc said with a sigh. "He's a gargoyle. He's on my territory. What more do you need to know?"

"Touched a nerve, have we?" Marco said with a snort of laughter. "Bring him to common grounds. Lennier will need to meet him."

Marco nodded to Yann before disappearing behind the carriage.

"And keep your human girl off my bridge," Yann said before following Marco. "If she'd been killed on it, I would have suffered an angel's burn. I happen to like my scales the way they are, even if they become crusted with stone."

Luc watched him as he walked away. So Yann was slipping into hibernation, then. His bridge had been closed for quite a while. Marco, too, had gone nearly seven months without anyone to protect. If his humans didn't arrive soon, he might descend into hibernation as well. The idea was enough to make Luc grin.

He straightened his spine as the doors to the restaurant opened and the Waverlys emerged. Other carriages packed the curb outside the restaurant, so Ingrid and the others weaved through and began to cross the street to their own carriage. Luc hopped down from the driver's seat, and his boots landed in an ankle-deep puddle of slush. Magnificent.

He saw Ingrid first, her hat's burgundy veil drawn down to her chin. He could see through it, though, and she was clearly biting back a laugh. Her lips struggled to remain level as Luc remained rooted in that cold puddle. Those lips, he knew, were like silk. Soft as the petals of a rose. Her pale hair a sheet of satin. He remembered running his fingers through the strands. Pulling her closer against him.

Ingrid's wavering grin flattened out, her eyes turning dark and serious. As if she knew what he was thinking of. Was he so transparent?

He cast his eyes down to his soaked boots, but a shrill cry of alarm brought his attention back up. Each one of his humans, crossing to the carriage in a staggered line, had come to a reeling stop, eyes wide as they looked down the boulevard. Luc heard the clapping of shod hooves on the pavement. A horse and rider barreled down the center of the street, cutting a manic path between carriages and bicycles—and heading straight for his humans.

"Ingrid!" Gabby screamed from where she stood, close to their landau, and Ingrid's only thought was that at least her sister was safely out of harm's way.

Mama's scream came from behind her, along with her father's absurd warning to *look out!* But Ingrid's feet refused to move. In her peripheral vision, she saw Luc running toward her, but even if he'd traded skin for scales, he wouldn't have reached her before the horse cut her down.

Something solid slammed into her from behind, pitching her forward and onto the wet pavement just as the horse's muscular legs streaked by.

"Goddamn it!" her brother—and rescuer—shouted. Grayson rolled onto his back and leaped up, chasing after the horse and rider while hurling profanities.

Having reached her, Luc lifted Ingrid from the boulevard, his hands squeezing her shoulders, his voice shaking. "Are you hurt?"

She didn't answer. The rider had stopped farther down the road and turned back, as if to view the destruction he'd left in his wake. His blond hair was radiant in the bath of a streetlamp. He wore no hat to cast shadows over his face, so Ingrid could see him well. She knew that face.

She'd fallen in love with it once.

"Jonathan," she whispered, tugging her shoulders free from Luc's grip. "Jonathan?"

He looked back at her, belting out wild laughter. With Grayson closing in on the horse, Jonathan's laughter cut off. He merely grinned. It was the same cold smile Anna had given her before, in the profane cemetery plot.

He drew up the reins and whirled around, charging off before Grayson could reach him.

Gabby and Mama converged on her then, pushing Luc out of the way.

"Are you bleeding?" her mother asked as her father bellowed for them to get out of the street before someone else ran them over.

"Oh, your dress!" Gabby exclaimed, plucking at Ingrid's top skirt, wet and torn from the slide along the pavement.

"I'm—" Ingrid began, but couldn't finish. She wasn't fine. She wasn't fine at all.

"My God, that madman looked like Jonathan, didn't he?" Gabby said as she helped Ingrid straighten her hat.

"Don't be absurd, Gabriella," their mother said, breathless. "It couldn't have been Mr. Walker."

Mama was right. It was absurd. Even though the rider had looked identical to Jonathan, it couldn't have been him. What would he be doing in Paris, let alone trying to run Ingrid down in the street?

"Into the carriage!" their father ordered, herding them all out of the center of the road and toward the curb. There were people enough staring at them from the pavement, some having pulled carriages to complete halts in order to look on.

"We shouldn't be made to cross a filthy, dangerous street, boy!" he railed at Luc.

Luc ignored him, though, his attention solely on Ingrid. He peered at her the same way he had before, right after Ingrid had thought she'd seen Anna in the cemetery. She didn't know what was happening, but she was willing to bet her dowry that Luc did.

CHAPTER EIGHT

"What a fright that must have been for you, my lady," Cherie said as she unbuttoned the first of a dozen satin-covered buttons along the back of Ingrid's dress.

Ingrid stood within the flickering light from the fireplace in her room, the flames too small to provide any real warmth. She stared into them. Nearly getting trampled in the street had been upsetting, yes. But even more worrisome was the fact that the incident hadn't produced a single lick of electricity. If she'd been getting anywhere at all with her training, she should have been able to use it for protection. A few staggered jolts of lightning would have dropped that rider straight out of his saddle. The fact that the rider couldn't have possibly been Jonathan made her all the more quiet and confused as Cherie worked at the buttons.

"Are you cold, my lady? I'll warm a pan for your bed," the maid said timidly. Cherie had been her lady's maid for four years, but now that she knew Ingrid could fire off electricity, she acted as if Ingrid would lose her mind at any moment and do just that.

"Yes, thank you," Ingrid said distractedly. There was a knock on her door and Cherie abandoned her unbuttoning to answer it.

"Lord Fairfax." Cherie bobbed into a curtsy before Grayson, who stood on the other side of the door.

"Grayson?" Ingrid clutched the shoulders of her loose dress to hold it up.

Her brother hadn't sought her out in weeks. In fact, she'd felt completely separated from him lately. Their connection, the one she'd always counted on while growing up, had withered away to practically nothing.

"I wondered if you would walk with me a bit around the churchyard," he said.

Without a moment's hesitation, Ingrid asked Cherie to close the door and redo the buttons on her dress. If Grayson offered to spend time with her, then she would gladly accept.

Maybe he had changed his mind about visiting Constantine.

As soon as they were outside the rectory's front door, Grayson held out his elbow for Ingrid to grasp. She took it, feeling as if they were back in London, stepping out to take a stroll through Hyde Park like they used to every Sunday. *Attached at the hip, I see* or *Two eggs in a basket, as always* had been a couple of the comments they'd grown used to receiving each week.

But after an entire turn around the rectory with little more than a few words passed between them, Ingrid began to feel desperate. How could she not know what was happening inside her brother's head? She'd always been so intuitive with him before, and he with her. How was it possible that her own twin now felt like a distant relative?

Well, she was finished with it. Finished treading so carefully around him. Besides, it was still misting flecks of ice and it had to be close to midnight.

"Why did you ask me out here if you weren't going to speak to me?"

"If you'd rather go back inside . . . ," he replied testily. Ingrid sighed.

"No. I'd rather talk with you for once. Grayson—" Ingrid stopped to gather the right words. Something soothing. Something heartfelt. But nothing came to her.

"What happened between you and Papa? I need to know." She hooked his arm and brought him to a halt. "He called you a fiend. He thought you were the one who'd harmed Gabby. Why would he think that?"

Grayson hunched deeper inside his fine woolen coat.

"I can't tell you." He swallowed hard. "You have no idea how badly I want to go back to the way things were, but . . . I'm different. I've changed."

"We've all changed."

"Not like I have." He jerked his arm free.

They were behind the rectory, near the ell where the servants were housed. No doubt their voices were carrying, providing bits of juicy gossip to be passed around the next morning.

"Would you stop?" she said, exasperated. "Grayson, I'm not afraid of you. None of us is. You haven't shifted in weeks. You're controlling it, so please—stop setting yourself apart like this. You're a Duster, just like I am. Just like Vander is. There are more of us, and if you'd just try—"

"You wouldn't say that if you knew what I've done," he said, pulling even farther away.

The icy mist had built up on her skin. It beaded and rolled like teardrops down her cheeks.

"We've all done things, Grayson. I set a ballroom on fire. I could have killed someone."

"I *did* kill someone!"

Ingrid stared at his black outline, unable to blink. No. He couldn't have.

"How? When? My God, Grayson—" Ingrid stepped forward and reached for him. He sidestepped her.

"It was in London. It's why Father sent me here instead of to university like he'd planned. He knows what I did, and he's right. I am a fiend."

She heard the sob trapped in his chest, strangling each word.

"Were you—I mean, did your hellhound blood have anything to do with it?"

She wanted to know everything. Who it had been, what had happened and why. Perhaps it was self-defense. Or an accident. Or—

"Stop. I know what you're doing. You're going to tell me it wasn't my fault. That it was the demon blood. Well, the demon blood *is* me. *I* am *it*. You can work all you please at taming your demon half, but you're nothing like me. Your demon half doesn't transform you into a bloodthirsty animal."

Ingrid forced herself into his line of vision. "I don't know what Axia did to you in the Underneath to make you become that hellhound, but she can't touch you here. Your demon half might not transform you again."

"I don't want to find out," Grayson murmured, unable to look her in the eye. "I just know I don't want to live this way."

He pivoted on his heel and jogged toward the stables. She started after him, but her blasted heeled boots slipped on the snowy lawn, her right leg sliding out into an ungainly split. She cursed as she righted herself and saw Grayson dash around the stables and into the thicket of trees bordering the abbey property.

I don't want to live this way.

What did he mean by that? Ingrid's pulse fluttered. He'd taken a life. Ingrid stood still and wrapped her chilled arms around her chest beneath her cloak. No wonder he'd been so distant. He'd cut himself off from her and Gabby and everyone else because he loathed himself. The fire Ingrid had started in Anna's ballroom didn't seem so terrible all of a sudden.

Grayson's guilt had to be eating away at him. He wouldn't do anything rash. Would he? The old Grayson, the one she knew, never would. But *this* Grayson? Honestly, Ingrid wasn't sure.

She began to follow him again. His footprints were firmly marked in the snow. The moon was nearly full, though hidden behind a misty cloud cover.

Luc came out from behind an angelic statue just ahead of her. "If he needs me, I'll go to him."

"But he said—"

"I know what he said," Luc cut in.

"You were spying on us?"

"I prefer to call it 'observing,'" Luc replied coolly. Then, finished with preamble, he said, "I want to talk to you."

He walked away. Just as Grayson's invitation to take a stroll with him had been irresistible, so was Luc's. But Luc's was a command rather than an invitation, and Ingrid built up to a simmer while she followed him around the abbey, to the far, western transept.

"Where exactly are we going?" she asked as Luc opened the door for her. She was blind as soon as he shut it behind them. The gem-colored stained-glass windows on either side of the long nave and the massive rose window behind the pulpit weren't letting in a single drop of moonlight.

"Luc?" Ingrid's voice echoed off the vaulted ceilings. For all the cleaning Mama's hired workers had been doing inside the abbey, it still smelled like an old hatbox.

A warm, dry hand snaked under hers and grasped it. Luc led her through the blackness, his speed notched just enough to convey irritation.

"I apologize if my eyesight isn't on par with yours," she muttered.

He didn't reply, only led her through the rest of the cold abbey, toward the narthex and the new arched front doors, the first things Mama had replaced. Once there, their direction shifted to the right. Ingrid's vision was beginning to adjust, and she could make out the black stamp of a doorway ahead.

"Stairs" was all Luc supplied before her feet stumbled upon the first step. He steadied her with his arm. It felt like falling against a solid block of granite.

"I've got it," she assured him, and after another moment, he apparently decided to believe her.

They climbed what Ingrid now realized was one of the bell towers. The stone steps spiraled up and up, with narrow arrow slits in the wall every other turn. Even in the dark, the constant rotation made her dizzy.

Ingrid had an idea what Luc wanted to talk about, and it put her on edge.

"Why here?" she asked, a little breathless from the steep climb. They must have taken at least a hundred, if not two hundred, steps.

"Privacy." Luc was a whole rotation ahead of her. He didn't sound breathless, either.

Ingrid trudged up the last few steps and emerged onto a thin walkway that ran the square perimeter of the belfry. The top of the bell tower was open on all four sides. The night sky was surprisingly bright. An enormous bell, twice her height and three times her width, hung in the center of the belfry. Ingrid could smell its rust from where she stood, her hand on the open, waist-high ledge. Directly below the bell was a series of steel wheels that, with rope and pulley, she guessed, had once been used to mechanically ring the bell.

She searched for Luc and found him tucked into the corner of the belfry.

"That wasn't a man tonight," he said. "It was a demon."

"I thought so," she whispered.

"The profane cemetery plot," Luc said. "You didn't trip on a headstone, did you?"

Ingrid started to wish she had.

"I don't know what happened. Some sort of dizzy spell hit me and I . . . I saw someone."

"Who?"

He was angry. She should have told him, she supposed, but until seeing Jonathan on that horse, she had hoped it had been a unique episode.

"My friend Anna Bettinger."

Luc's pale emerald eyes were too bright to be completely human. She shouldn't have been able to see them squinting as he frowned, not from this distance and not in such murky light.

"She looked so real. Solid. As solid as the trees around her. But then . . . she was gone."

"And tonight?" Luc asked. "You called the rider Jonathan. Who is he?"

Ingrid looked out over rue Dante, toward the Seine.

"Anna's betrothed," she answered, rubbing her fingers over the casement ledge in an attempt to distract herself. She didn't care. Not anymore. Jonathan was in the past. Ingrid took a long breath, realizing that the old excuse she'd used time and again was no longer an excuse.

"But he's in London with Anna, not here." Ingrid turned back to face Luc. "Grayson came the closest to him, but he said he was too angry, that he only saw red. So who was it really? Am I delirious?"

Luc left the corner of the belfry and came toward her, his palm running along the open ledge. The moonlight, free from the clouds for the moment, lit his face. It was drawn into a fierce scowl. "No. You did see Anna and Jonathan."

"I did?" Ingrid asked, more confused than before.

Luc stopped and braced both palms against the ledge. He hunched his shoulders and hung his head, muttering a string of oaths.

"Luc, what is it?"

He pushed himself up. "A mimic demon. They latch on to

humans and within a few seconds dig through memories, soaking up everything. Your dizzy spell? That was the mimic searching through your memory."

She remembered feeling the nausea slam into her, then blacking out. A demon had been inside her mind? She ran her fingers through her hair and massaged the back of her head.

"Why?" she asked.

"To find out how to play with you," Luc answered darkly. "It saw Anna and Jonathan in your memories and knew who they were. What they meant to you. And then it used your memories, down to the last detail, to look like them."

Ingrid dropped her hand. "But how is any of that playing with me? It nearly trampled me in the street! It could have killed any one of us."

Luc shook his head. "A mimic won't harm anyone other than its target. And it won't kill you outright. It takes its time teasing and confusing you first. Scaring the hell out of you. Once it's finished playing, *that's* when it kills you."

Ingrid turned back toward the open sky. "Perhaps it's just me, but that doesn't sound very fun at all."

She thought she heard Luc laugh, but when she looked over, she saw he was just as serious as before.

"How do I get rid of it?" she asked.

If this thing had targeted and attached itself to her, did that mean it could pop up anytime, anyplace?

"I don't know." Regret pulled Luc's voice. "They're rare, though. I know about them, but I've never dealt with one myself."

"Do you think it could have something to do with Axia?"

She whispered the fallen angel's name, as if Axia might be able to hear Ingrid speak in her dry, hellish hive in the Underneath.

"It could. I suppose—" Luc paused. "I suppose we could ask the Alliance what they think."

And by Alliance, he meant Vander. She thought it might

actually be the first time Luc had alluded to Vander since he'd made his pledge to stay away from her. To act only as her gargoyle.

"I could ask Constantine, too," she said, but this only seemed to sharpen Luc's stare.

"I had a visit from Gaston tonight," he said. She recalled Constantine's gargoyle. "I think you should stay away from Clos du Vie for now."

Ingrid wanted to throw up her hands. First Vander, and now Luc?

"Why? What did Gaston say?"

Luc took a few steps closer as he told her about the man named Robert Dupuis and his unsavory interest in her.

"And then Constantine sent him away?" Ingrid asked.

"Yes, but he could come back."

"And if he did, he'd try to what, kidnap me? Wrap me up in one of Constantine's Persian rugs and smuggle me into his carriage?" Ingrid couldn't help but laugh at her own wit.

Luc, however, didn't laugh.

"No. Gaston wouldn't allow it. But—"

"Let me ask Constantine who this Dupuis is. If he refuses to tell me, then perhaps I won't go back. But for right now . . ." She shook her head, not sure she could explain it. "I have to go. I have to do something about *this*." She rubbed her hands and then clasped them together in front of her skirts. Her life had been in peril tonight, and she'd failed to protect herself. Conjuring the lightning on her own the other morning at Clos du Vie must have been a fluke.

The cords in Luc's neck stood out as he tensed. He cocked his head and seemed to be listening to something in the distance.

"Dimitrie?" she asked.

"Your lady's maid. She's anxious. You should go back."

The adjacent bell tower blocked the view of the rectory, and yet Luc was connected to the people inside it. Connected to

86

Cherie. Because of her scent, Ingrid thought, remembering what Dimitrie had told her.

"Why didn't you tell me?" she asked. "About our scents?"

Luc hesitated. He didn't seem to like that she knew about this ability of his. But it was fascinating the way he could tap into someone's consciousness using something as natural as his sense of smell.

When Luc continued his silence, Ingrid added, "He said my scent was delectable. What does that mean? What exactly do I smell like, food?"

Luc smiled. "No, not food. It's sweet grass, the kind that flowers in the summer, and if you tug up a strand and chew on it, it tastes sweet, almost like vanilla. And then, underneath that, your scent is like rich, black soil. Earth that will grow anything seeded there."

Ingrid knew she had been the one to ask, but she hadn't expected Luc's reply to be so intimate or detailed. It was almost as if he could taste her, rather than just scent her. He turned away from her after a moment.

"I'm not used to sharing my secrets with humans," he grumbled.

"Dimitrie was probably only trying to be friendly," she said.

Luc leaned both elbows on the ledge and peered down. "A waste of time."

Ingrid jerked back, stung, especially after the tender way he'd described her scent. "If he's anything like you, he'll learn it's much easier to be heartless."

She stumbled toward the stairwell and took the first step down. Luc seized her arm before her foot could land and pulled her back up onto the walkway. His hand lingered, his fingers tight around her elbow.

"I don't trust him," he whispered.

She recalled how young Dimitrie appeared. "He's just a boy."

Luc, his hand still clasped around her arm, shook his head. "He's a gargoyle."

Trust between the two Dispossessed seemed like it should be a given, considering they both held guardianship over the same humans.

"But he's our gargoyle, isn't he?" Ingrid asked. "He's compelled to protect us just like you are."

Luc let go of her only to take her shoulders this time. His strength didn't surprise her, but the way he pressed her shoulders together did. There was passion in it. Urgency in the downward slant of his brow, his pale lime eyes lit as if from within.

"*I* am your gargoyle," he whispered, his breath sweet and warm against her lips.

This was what Ingrid had been wanting. This was what she'd been missing. Luc, showing her that he actually cared. Not the cold, aloof, emotionless Luc. *This* one.

"Your heart is racing," he said, taking a long, discouraging step away. He dropped his hands and Ingrid listed to the side, against the belfry wall. She felt cold, her temperature dropping along with her heart and stomach.

"If I can feel it, so can Dimitrie," Luc explained. "Go. I'll watch you from here."

She didn't want to leave, but she knew she couldn't stay. Luc wouldn't be able to see her to the rectory, of course. Not in the normal sense. But he could watch her just the same.

Ingrid took the tower steps down, rotating slowly, her legs suddenly tired and weak. She went easily through the abbey, her vision having adapted, then across the courtyard to the rectory. She felt Luc's eyes on her the whole time, even after she'd closed the front door and started up to her room. He could watch her whenever he pleased, she supposed. He could stay with her all night, if he wished.

Perhaps he did.

Perhaps he kept her scent with him at all times, and that was the reason why he hadn't wanted her to know about it. It was ridiculous how much the notion stirred her.

I *am your gargoyle.*

Yes, he was. But that wasn't all he was. By the way Luc had held her, saying those words like a vow, he'd let slip that he still considered himself something much more.

CHAPTER NINE

Grayson wasn't sure where he was, but he knew there was blood nearby. A lot of blood. Freshly spilled.

He'd crossed the Ile de la Cité to the Right Bank and had started wandering through a few middle-class neighborhoods and squares. He wore his suit and tie from that evening's dinner, his coat draped over his arm. The heat was unbearable, like blue-hot coals being stoked inside his stomach and chest. He'd cooled down a little since leaving Ingrid on the rectory lawns, but the flecks of ice were still a relief against his sweltering skin.

Why the devil had he told her?

He'd only wanted her company while walking a circuit around the churchyard. He hadn't wanted to talk. Hadn't planned on confessing the one secret that could destroy the way everyone, including his twin, saw him. He had only wanted her there beside him while he'd cooled down. She had always been able to steady him, and he'd needed that desperately. Father hadn't said a decent word to him all day, and then that reckless rider after dinner had sent Grayson plunging over the edge.

The uncontrollable trembling had set in after that. His muscles had coiled painfully and his bones had ached as if some great weight from within them were pushing out, trying to break free. He'd had the sensation of trying to hold himself in. Hold himself together. He'd thought a bit of cold air and his twin's presence would help.

But he'd gone and told her the truth. His darkest sin. And then he'd needed to run.

Now the smell of blood stopped him short.

He slowly ducked into the opening of a mews. The slim alley stretched behind one side of a residential square. High walls enclosed each home's backyard, so no one could see Grayson creeping along the bricked road, which was slanted toward the center to allow horse waste to run freely toward the sewers.

He followed his nose, allowing it to root out the source of the smell. He pushed aside the niggling thought that he was sniffing like a hound when he came to the arched entrance of one family's stable. The doors stood ajar. The coppery bite of blood landed hard on the back of Grayson's tongue. The origin of the scent he'd been tracking was inside.

He listened for a moment before pushing a door open and slipping in. A small carriage was parked inside, the single horse pointed toward the far wall, as if it had been led in. The animal was still hitched, and a pair of beveled-glass lamps sputtered on both sides of the driver's bench. The horse tossed its head nervously and stomped the cobbled floor. With good reason—two slumped figures sat upon the bench.

The driver, a man, had fallen against the seat back, his arms limp at his sides. His head lolled toward his spine at an unnatural resting point. The passenger, a woman, had fallen forward against the curved dashboard, her profile craned toward the quivery light of one carriage lamp. Her eyes were wide, her lips parted. And on the ground beside her was yet another figure. A young man, Grayson noted as he edged closer.

The smell of their blood thickened Grayson's throat, though thankfully not with thirst. Splattered as it was over the slumped bodies, carriage, and cobbled floors, the blood didn't affect him the way it did trapped within a person's veins. He breathed out, relaxing a bit.

But there was still the matter of the three bodies.

Something moved in the corner of the stable, near a pile of stacked hay and bags of feed. A quick, darting motion. By the time Grayson focused, it was gone, replaced by a scratching sound, like nails on stone. It came from the driver's side of the carriage. A dog? Grayson slowly went around the back of the carriage and a foul odor hit on top of all the blood. Sour milk and fetid meat.

A creature scuttled out from behind a crate and under the chassis. The horse whinnied and stomped, lashing its tail back and forth. Grayson leaped back.

That was no dog.

The thing had darted by on three sets of pitchfork-type legs, its nails clicking on the cobbles. A wicked spike tipped its long, curled tail, which resembled a scorpion's.

Grayson had seen something like it in the Underneath.

The demon shot straight toward Grayson's feet. He staggered backward into a long workbench. Tools rattled on the surface and Grayson swept his hand over them, searching for a heavy, blunt object to swing at the miniature beast. He closed his fingers around something just as the spiked tail whipped forward over the demon's ratlike skull and snapping teeth. The spike struck the stone an inch from Grayson's foot. He smashed a long wrench into the demon's tail, but the demon only recoiled, uninjured, and immediately dove forward again.

Grayson braced himself against the worktable and tucked up

his legs. The stable doors flew open and a gleam of silver spun low through the air, inches above the cobbles. The silver embedded itself in the demon's ridged back and the creature flashed into a cloud of death sparks.

Grayson lowered his feet when he saw Chelle and Vander standing in the doorway. The two Alliance members looked at Grayson, then the bodies, and then back at Grayson.

"What are you doing here?" Grayson, Chelle, and Vander all asked in unison.

Chelle sighed and closed the doors behind them. "We were out patrolling when Vander caught the scorpling's dust trail. What were you doing?"

Grayson set the wrench back on the worktable. He took deep breaths, willing his heart to calm. He didn't need Luc showing up right now. If Luc could sense that Grayson was no longer in danger, perhaps the gargoyle would turn right back around for the abbey.

He crouched to pick up Chelle's silver star. "I, ah . . . I was taking a walk."

Chelle propped a hand on her slim hip. "And *this* is where you ended up?" She took a suspicious glance at the dead bodies.

Grayson set his jaw. He didn't want to admit the truth, but there was no excuse he could give that would make sense.

"I smelled them," he said softly, gesturing toward the carriage with the razor-edged star. "I tracked them."

Chelle stood still, her frown frozen in place. Vander crossed behind her, heading toward the bodies.

"Their blood, you mean?" he asked.

Grayson nodded, his throat cinched tight.

"Well, there's a lot of it," Vander said casually. He crouched by the boy's body, careful to keep his boot soles out of the surrounding pool of blood.

Chelle watched Grayson as he left the workbench and extended his hand. He half expected her to take the weapon back and immediately fling it at him. She only tucked it inside her red sash and appraised him in silence.

"The slashes at his wrists are deep," Vander said evenly, as though he worked with dead bodies all day instead of books. "They look self-inflicted."

"And these two?" Chelle asked, nodding toward the adults in the bench seat.

"I doubt either of them would have had the fortitude to cut their own throats," Vander answered. Chelle made a sickened sound when she saw the gaping dark smiles across their necks.

"The boy's parents?" Grayson asked. Vander shrugged.

"All I know for certain is that he was a Duster."

Grayson stood back, staring at the boy's body with new interest, unable to trace the demon dust that Vander could so plainly see.

"You're sure it's his own dust? What about that thing? The scorpling?" he asked.

Vander stood and pushed up his spectacles again. "The boy's dust is a different shade from the scorpling's." He circled the boy's still frame and ran his hand soothingly along the horse's trembling haunch.

"What is it?" Chelle asked, apparently seeing some conflict in Vander that Grayson didn't.

"Constantine. He has a student who killed his entire family a few nights ago. And now . . ." Vander crossed his arms, circling back around the pool of blood. "It looks like another Duster might have done the same thing."

"But the scorpling," Grayson said, picturing the spiked tail. Could it have made clean sweeps across two throats and then the boy's wrists?

"It's nothing but a bottom feeder," Chelle replied. "That thing was here for the dead flesh. It didn't kill them."

Grayson didn't know this boy at all, but the fact that he was a Duster—or had been one, he supposed—made him a little less of a stranger. It made the boy something much closer to Grayson himself.

"We can't stay here," Chelle announced.

"What, we're just leaving them?" Grayson asked.

Chelle pulled her cap lower. "Before the police are summoned? Yes. Definitely."

She was right, of course. None of them had any right to be there, and no clear reason, either. Grayson didn't need to attract any attention from the police, French or English.

"Did you drop anything?" Chelle asked.

Grayson saw his coat lying on the floor near the workbench. He scooped it up and then helped them scatter a few armfuls of hay around the stable floor where their shoes had made slushy footprints.

"Thanks," Grayson said as Vander checked up and down the mews to be sure they wouldn't be seen leaving the stable.

"For what? Making sure you weren't implicated in a triple murder?" Chelle asked, eyeing his coat.

They slipped outside, dragging their feet in a messy line so no specific prints would be left behind.

"No," Grayson answered. "For saving my life. Gabby said you were pretty good with those stars."

Chelle snorted. And even though it *was* a snort, she somehow managed to make it lovely. "They're called *hira-shuriken*. And I'm better than 'pretty good.'"

"She also said you were extremely insecure," he replied.

Chelle scowled at him from under the short brim of her cap as they turned out of the mews, away from the dead Duster.

Had he lost control? Had the boy's anger overrun his senses? Grayson could understand, if so. It made him shiver with nausea. Perhaps this boy just hadn't been able to get away fast enough to simmer down. As they walked toward the Seine, Grayson wondered how many more Dusters were out there, perched on the edge of a killing spree.

CHAPTER TEN

Gabby doubted her plan the moment the demon emerged. It slipped from under the stone bench, looking, at first, like a shorter version of the bench it had been hiding beneath, one of many benches within the closed and gated park along rue de Babylone.

The demon had four stumpy legs and a long, flat back. It remained in its benchlike form for another moment. Plenty of time for Gabby to consider whether she should have stayed at the rectory instead of sneaking out, fully armed with two blessed daggers and the short sword Nolan had given her. She gripped the handle of the sword, her leather gloves sticking to the cold silver.

Damn that Carrick Quinn! He'd made her so furious, wounded her so deeply, that all she'd been able to do the last two days was formulate her revenge plan. If the Alliance wasn't going to take on any regular first-generation members, then she'd be something spectacular. She'd prove that she could fight. She'd hunt demons on her own until Carrick Quinn got wind of it and finally accepted that he'd been wrong.

The benchlike demon started to change. The flat seat grew longer as new vertebrae appeared like leaves being inserted into a grand dining room table. Two more sets of stumpy legs fell down from where they'd been tucked up beneath the seat, and those, too, began to lengthen.

Gabby skittered back as one end of the bench curled up, peeling back like a banana skin. One set of stumpy legs, another pair, and then a third, drew off the ground, until only a single pair of legs supported the thin, flat demon. The rest of it stood erect, and to Gabby's utter horror, it also had a head. Like the two hidden pairs of legs, the demon's head had been tucked in. It unfolded now, the higher end of the bench becoming a neck.

It probably had eyes and a nose, but really, all Gabby saw was its mouth: a round hole with two sets of spiked teeth rotating and gnashing together like cogs. Upon seeing its dangly legs—no, arms, she now saw, each tipped by a thick, tusklike horn—Gabby realized what this demon was: an appendius.

For the first time, she felt her resolve slip. Like before, on the abandoned bridge, she unintentionally gave in to fear. But unlike before, she failed to push it back out. She knew what the appendius could do. Tomas, the traitorous Alliance member, had been attacked by one. The appendius's horns had left gruesome scars on his face and neck—worse than Gabby's by far. *The appendius would have skinned me alive. It would have devoured me piece by piece, taking time to digest between meals.* The memory of what Tomas had told her about the appendius sent her skittering back another few steps. Her pulse hammered in her throat.

Then the demon took its first swing.

The horned tip of one arm slashed toward her. Gabby barely leaped out of its reach, ducking behind a tall, deep green cast-iron Wallace fountain. The appendius slammed its horned tip into one of the four sculpted caryatids, their raised arms holding up the fountain's domed top. Gabby scrambled farther back, behind a box hedge, her fear completely unleashed. Luc would already be in his scales and on his way, she was certain.

The ground shook beneath her feet as the appendius plodded along, following her as she weaved deeper into the park. *Fool!* What did she know about fighting demons? A few lessons from Chelle and one from Tomas, and that was it.

She threw herself behind a massive tree trunk and gasped for air, forcing herself to breathe evenly. Tomas had taught her that the appendius's weak spots were in the center of each arm, where there was nothing but soft cartilage.

With both hands gripping her sword's handle, she jumped out from behind the tree and took an upward swipe at the appendius's oncoming arm. The blade cut through with barely any resistance. Her victory was short-lived, however—the other arm pierced her shoulder with its tip. She went down on the packed dirt and rolled against the knotty base of the tree. Her ears started to ring with panic.

But she still heard the wings.

A shriek rent the air, and clutching at her wounded shoulder, Gabby watched as a pair of sapphire wings unfurled in front of her, shielding the appendius from view. The blue-tinted scales of the strange gargoyle glimmered in the moonlight. What gargoyle was this? She'd chosen this spot purposefully. It wasn't marked. There couldn't be a Dispossessed guarding it.

The gargoyle, though smaller than Luc, brutally sheared off the rest of the demon's arms with two powerful strokes of its talons. The appendius reeled back, no longer balanced, and fell. Instead of destroying it, the gargoyle turned to Gabby, plucked her from the ground, and spiraled into the air.

The wind rushed up her nostrils and drove down her throat, stealing away her breath. She closed her eyes to shut out both the pain of her throbbing shoulder and the sight of the ground that she knew was far, far below. The flap of wings filled her ears, the gargoyle's stony arms and legs enclosing her like a cage.

If this wasn't Luc, and if the park wasn't protected, then this had to be the new boy. Dimitrie. *His scales are beautiful,* Gabby thought as her head grew heavy.

The rhythm of the gargoyle's beating wings changed, and Gabby forced one eye open. They were descending toward the top of a building, its flat roof covered with raised garden beds filled with snow-dusted crushed gravel. And there was a man.

She closed her eyes again as Dimitrie landed.

"Stop where ye are, gargoyle." The brusque voice rang familiar to Gabby. She was still cradled in a pair of arms. She startled when she saw that they were no longer covered with shimmering blue scales.

"Who do ye have?" The voice had grown closer and had softened. Gabby forced open her eyes again. It was the man from Nolan's apartment. The one who'd opened the door for her and asked her if she'd be all right. The gargoyle had brought her to Hôtel Bastian.

"Give her to me," the man said, but Dimitrie, in his human form, clutched Gabby closer.

"Fine," the man said with a sigh. "But stay wi' me. Ye're not supposed to be inside, gargoyle."

Gabby let her eyes rest as she was taken through the roof door and jostled down a stairwell, then down a long corridor. Her shoulder felt worse than before, the pain starting to spread. Her neck and shoulder blades ached, and the throbbing had even extended to her hand.

Demon poison, she realized as her back hit a cold table. Dimitrie's arms slid from underneath her.

"Gabriella, open yer eyes." The man's voice was so close that she complied with a start. He was directly above her, palms planted on the table on either side of her head. He smiled down at her, his ice-blue eyes crinkling at the corners.

"Nolan's coming, lass," he whispered. His Scottish burr nudged some awareness deep inside her. The eyes. Not Nolan's, but somehow the same.

"Who are you?" she asked. Her body shook with fatigue and what felt like a creeping fever.

"Rory, *laoch*," he answered, again with that familiar grin.

Rory *what*?

The door sailed open and plowed into a wall. "What happened?"

Where Rory's voice had nudged, Nolan's kicked. He thundered into the room, a wrathful storm darkening his eyes as they inspected her shoulder.

"*You.*" Nolan thrust a finger toward Dimitrie, who stood at the foot of the table without a stitch of clothing on. Thankfully, everything from the waist down was hidden from Gabby's view.

"What was it?" Nolan demanded.

"An appendius." Dimitrie's voice cracked on the last syllable.

"Well, what have you been waiting for? You're the new Dispossessed at the abbey, aren't you? Get on with it. Slice open your hand or your arm—your jugular, for all I care. Just give your blood!"

"I wouldn't have brought her to you if I could heal her myself," Dimitrie said through clenched teeth. He turned, showing his pale back. Gabby tried to sit up when she saw the paper-thin horizontal lines, but she couldn't do more than lift her head.

Angel's burns. Ingrid had told her about them. Dimitrie's burns started at the nape of his neck and descended to the small of his back. Most were white and healed, but some at his lower back were pink and new. He'd failed his human charges so many times Gabby couldn't begin to count the scars before she fell back against the table.

He would be punished for her injury tonight, too. So would Luc. Gabby felt sick with guilt, on top of everything else.

"You know what these do to a gargoyle's blood," Dimitrie said, his head drooping low in shame.

Nolan raked his hand through his hair. "Your blood's useless. Why didn't you take her back to Luc at the abbey?"

Gabby didn't understand what was happening, but she did know that she'd never heard Nolan so furious.

"She was in a park one street away from here," Dimitrie answered. "And if Luc wasn't at the abbey when I arrived with her . . ."

Dimitrie had only been thinking about healing her, and fast. Even Gabby could see that.

"For Christ's sake! Where is Luc?" Nolan hissed. He unbuttoned his cuffs and rolled up his sleeves. "Rory, guard the door. My da can't know she's here. Or him," he said with a nod toward the naked boy.

Rory nodded and slipped out of the crisp, sterile room. It was a medical room, she noticed with detached wonder. Hôtel Bastian had a medical wing? There were two walls of glassed-in cabinets holding bottles and linens and strange-looking contraptions. Gabby lay on one of many metal tables—gurneys, she realized. A moment later, after Nolan rummaged around in one of those glass cabinets, he came back to her side.

"Gabby," Nolan whispered. He brushed her hair from her sweaty forehead. "Lass, you've demon poison in you. I can't wait any longer for Luc to find you. It's got to be mercurite, or the poison will spread too far and deep."

And that would be that, Gabby concluded.

She nodded, and without further ado, Nolan ripped the bloody and battered sleeve of her dress, tearing it straight off at the shoulder seam. Gabby remembered applying mercurite to one of Nolan's wounds, and the way the viscous silvery liquid had beaded up and seeped down through the curving line of stitches. The liquid silver and mercury worked together to surround the poison and then destroy it. She also remembered the grimace on Nolan's face.

The first splash touched her shoulder and shocked the breath out of her.

"It won't last long," Nolan said, as soothingly as a mother tending her sick child.

The bone-crunching cold gave way to an itch, then heat. And with every passing breath the heat intensified, until it clawed deep into tissue and then bone. Gabby's whole arm, and a path across her back, felt as if it had been consumed by flames. She whimpered but swallowed a scream. Nolan was trying to hide her presence.

He pressed his mouth against her forehead and mumbled words she couldn't comprehend. Gabby heard only the rush of blood through her ears, the pealing scream she held blocked in her throat.

And then it was over. The burn collapsed inside her and she dragged in a gulp of air. Every tensed muscle sagged toward the table.

"It's over," Nolan confirmed. "God, Gabby, I'm sorry. I know what it's like, especially the first time. But—" He paused, and even though her eyes were closed, she could see him screwing up his face in frustration. "How the *hell* did this happen?"

She rolled her head away from him. Lying wounded before Nolan hadn't been part of her plan tonight. She'd failed. And now he knew.

"You picked a fight with it," he guessed, and when Gabby didn't deny it, he slammed a fist onto the metal table. "What were you thinking? You could have been killed!"

"I can fight," she said, testing her shoulder. She wanted to get up and away as fast as she could.

Nolan brought his palm to her opposite shoulder and held her down. "How the devil can you fight, Gabby?"

She couldn't tell him about Chelle's lessons. She couldn't send Chelle to the guillotine like that.

"I can prove to your father that I belong here," Gabby said instead.

"If he found out about this it would only prove how much of a liability you are," he growled, but then reached his fingers into her hair, combing the tangled strands. "I don't agree with my da. He's wrong about you, Gabby, but there's no telling him. He won't be swayed. You don't know him."

He stopped, dipped his chin, and picked up the bottle of mercurite he'd set beside Gabby's hip. The black glass had no label. "Hell, I don't even know him anymore."

He corked the bottle roughly as Rory returned to the room.

"We're clear. Uncle is still out on patrol," Rory relayed.

Nolan thanked him, then turned back to her. "Gabby, this is my cousin."

Cousin. Those eyes made sense now. Gabby met them again and Rory nodded a hello.

"We've met," he said.

Nolan's cousin was a half head taller than him, and at least twenty pounds heavier, though Gabby was sure it was all muscle. Again she noticed his brown leather vest, strapped with a half-dozen gleaming silver daggers. Clearly his weapon of choice.

"She needs a second dose of mercurite," Rory said, his eyes on her bared shoulder.

"I'll wait for gargoyle blood," Nolan replied. He seemed to just then remember the gargoyle standing at the foot of the table. "Luc's, by the look of it."

Dimitrie lifted his head. "He's here."

Rory calmly strode back out into the hall, and Gabby knew it was to meet Luc on the roof.

"I don't need Luc's blood," Gabby said, feeling more embarrassed and angry by the moment. And guilty, too. She'd screwed up, and Luc and Dimitrie would suffer for it. It wasn't fair. Her actions were her own. She should suffer the consequences for them, no one else.

Nolan came to her side and cupped her cheek. In all the madness, she hadn't once thought about the scars along her face. He tenderly swept his thumb over them. "I won't use any more mercurite than I need to, lass. After a while . . ." He sighed and pulled his hand back. "After a while, it changes you."

It had changed his father. Gabby pieced together a few of the comments he and the others had made about Carrick Quinn. The mercurite had changed him, and not for the better.

She couldn't help but wonder: how long until it changed Nolan?

Luc's talons had barely touched down on Hôtel Bastian's flat roof when a flood of hot white light split the night sky. It poured over him, searing his scales, but it was a warm caress compared to what Luc knew was coming. An angel's burn.

Gabby had gotten herself hurt, and Luc hadn't been there to protect her. He hadn't even known she had sneaked out of the rectory. He'd been so focused on Ingrid, on getting her up to that tower, and on hiding from Dimitrie. Which infuriated him. He shouldn't have to hide from anyone while on his own territory.

"You have erred," Irindi said.

The gravel beneath Luc's talons shook when she spoke. He couldn't look at her, not directly. Her presence forced him into a neat bow, his forehead a spare inch from the crushed gravel and snow, his wings spread out behind him. From the corner of his eye he could see the pearly contours of her lithe shape, though she had no solid features. She was nothing but a quivering mass of radiance. Irindi was what an angel of the Order was supposed to look like. Nothing like Axia and her grotesque form, stripped of her angelic glow and power.

The roof door opened, and to Luc's deep humiliation, a human emerged. Here he was, stuck in his scales, bowing like a fool to something this Alliance human couldn't see. To the human, the only change at all was an unexpected whipping wind. No light, no heat, no radiant shine, and certainly no chiming, monotone voice telling Luc that he had failed.

Irindi got on with it. The angel's burn seared into Luc's scales along his back. It ripped through the steel-like armor, and though he wanted to groan in pain, he swallowed the urge. He wouldn't look any more of a fool in front of this Alliance member than he already did. At least the human stood back in silence, as if completely aware of what was happening to Luc.

And then Irindi's glow was gone. All that was left was the sizzling echo of her punishment. Luc surged to his feet. Remaining in true form, he stalked toward the roof door and the Alliance member standing patiently on its threshold.

The man stood aside and allowed Luc to take the stairs first. Luc didn't need to be shown the way. He had caught Gabby's heady scent like a fist in the kidney earlier, and he'd been following it ever since. Her location had changed, though, and his destination had gone from a park along rue de Babylone to the town house along rue de Sèvres.

As soon as he crashed through the door and saw Gabby lying on the table, her eyes wide and cheeks burning, Luc felt the release of his true form. As if a finger had come off a trigger, everything inside him loosened and his muscles and bones shrank and slid back into their human places. His scales turned to skin.

Gabby jerked her chin up and fixed her eyes firmly on the ceiling.

"Ugh, why must you all be so naked?" she groaned, and Luc knew for certain that she was all right.

Dimitrie stepped away from Gabby's table. He, too, was in human form. He looked even younger and scrawnier without clothing.

How had Dimitrie gotten to her first? Luc had only felt her fear in the moments before an echoing pain slammed into his shoulder, signaling her wound—and setting his punishment in stone.

"It was an appendius," Nolan informed him, moving away from the table to give Luc space to work.

Without a word, the Alliance member from the roof plucked one of the knives strapped to his vest and held it out to Luc. He took it, drew the blade across his hand, and built a well of blood in his closed fist. He crossed the room, his eyes on Dimitrie—why hadn't he given Gabby his own blood yet? Luc opened his hand and pressed his palm against the deep tear along her shoulder.

She squeaked in pain.

"It's better than—" Luc stopped as his hand started to itch. Within a second, it felt like he'd pressed his hand against the glowing end of a cattle brand. He ripped his hand away and clutched it at the wrist.

Gabby lifted her head, concerned. "Luc?"

The skin covering his hand had turned a mottled gray, sickly and ancient compared to the skin that joined it at the wrist.

"Bloody hell," Nolan ground out. "I'm sorry, Luc—I administered mercurite."

Luc tucked his hand close to his body, his fingers stiffened open.

"You could have warned me," Luc growled.

"What is it? What happened to him?" Gabby resisted Nolan's attempts to keep her down on the table. She pushed herself up into a sitting position, though not without a grimace of pain.

"It's nothing," Luc said, just as Dimitrie said, "The mercurite."

The glare with which Luc speared Dimitrie shut him up fast.

Nolan took over rubbing Luc's blood into Gabby's shoulder and explained to her anyway. "They can't touch mercurite. The mercury and silver poisons them—a lot faster than it does us."

Luc tried to bend his fingers, but they were too stiff. Like stone, he thought. Mercurite did more than just poison Dispossessed. It rendered them useless. As far as Luc knew, it was the only thing the human world had that could harm a gargoyle. Unfortunately, the Alliance also knew it, and they always kept a full stock. For healing, yes, but it was also a nice insurance policy.

"You shouldn't have needed mercurite," Luc said, again eyeing Dimitrie, who had shrunk even farther into the corner of the medical room. He shuffled around until he faced the corner like a schoolboy caught in some punishable act.

Luc forgot his stinging hand and his throbbing back. He had never seen so many angel's burns on one gargoyle before. Line after line after line, so many that there wasn't even one inch of smooth, bare skin.

Dimitrie was a shadow gargoyle. A failure. Incompetent and as useless as Luc's stiff hand. Every angel's burn weakened a gargoyle's blood a little, but after being lashed by scores of them . . . Dimitrie's blood was no longer able to heal at all.

"Why would Irindi send you?" Luc asked. *This* was her idea of help?

Dimitrie didn't stay in his human form long enough to answer. He coalesced fast, the silvery-blue scales along his back turning every angel's burn into a crusty ridge. Dimitrie fled the room, wings pleated behind him as he went.

"I'll do the stitches and you can take her home," Nolan said to Luc, ignoring the exchange. "You can't be here when the patrols return."

Luc knew gargoyles weren't allowed inside Alliance headquarters, just as Alliance weren't welcome at the Dispossessed's common grounds, a territory held by the gargoyle elder Lennier.

He suddenly dreaded taking Dimitrie there. To be saddled with another Dispossessed was humiliating enough. When Marco and the others found out Dimitrie was a shadow gargoyle, there would be no end to the jesting.

It didn't make any sense. Why would the Order send someone like Dimitrie? A gargoyle with no power to heal? Luc hadn't trusted the boy in the first place, and now he questioned the Angelic Order's decision even more. There was a reason behind it. What it was, however, Luc couldn't begin to fathom.

CHAPTER ELEVEN

"**I**f this were a real date, I believe it would be our last."

Ingrid shivered as the wind buffeted her cloak, every other gust carrying a frigid spray of water from the Seine.

Vander stood close beside her on the quay passing underneath pont de l'Alma. It had been overcast all morning, and now, standing beneath one of the numerous bridges that spanned the Seine, Ingrid thought it looked more like evening than early afternoon.

"If I must remind you," Vander said, bouncing on his heels to keep warm, "this date was your idea."

It had actually been Constantine's. They were waiting for him now. Vander had picked Ingrid up at the rectory under the pretense of taking her for a carriage ride around the city. A bold, courting move, Ingrid thought, and one that had earned him a rigid interrogation from her father first.

Of course, it wasn't a *real* date. It had all been a farce so they could meet Constantine as planned and search for Léon, the missing Duster. Still. Ingrid had felt strangely giddy when her father had ordered Vander into his study and the door had shut solidly behind them.

"For our next date, I was thinking we could tour one of the city's slums," Vander said lightly. "Considering dirty, smelly places of filth are your cup of tea and all."

She lightly stomped on his foot and then promptly ducked out of his reach as Nolan Quinn came scuffing down the stone quay steps. He had his hands in his pockets and dark circles under his eyes.

"You're going to owe me one, Burke. I don't generally like to spend my afternoons in the Parisian sewers." Nolan joined them beneath the bridge. "What's this all about?"

Constantine had sent Ingrid and Vander notes earlier that morning as well. Ingrid's note had specified a meeting place and a time when Vander would be coming to fetch her. When he had arrived, Vander had told her he'd sent for Nolan, too. The more blessed silver they had in the sewers, the better.

"It's about the missing Duster," Ingrid answered Nolan.

"The one who killed his family?" he asked.

Vander exhaled long and hard. Ingrid knew he still objected to combing the sewers for Léon, but he'd agreed to help her find the boy anyway. If Léon was caught by the police, he would be tossed into prison, where he would no doubt cause more chaos. If they could find him before the police did, perhaps Constantine could truly help him.

Last night, Grayson had returned from his midnight walk unscathed, but what if he hadn't? What if his life turned down the same path as Léon's? He'd already killed someone. Ingrid still couldn't comprehend it. How and why—and who—were the questions she desperately needed answered.

"The boy mentioned the sewers once." Constantine had come up behind them, but Ingrid was the only one who'd jumped at his refined, unmistakably aristocratic voice.

"Léon said that if his family ever discovered what he had become, he would take refuge in the sewers like Jean Valjean. This entrance is relatively close to his home."

Hearing that Léon had read *Les Misérables,* a book Ingrid had recently read, too, only made him all the more human to her.

"It has been a handful of days," Constantine said, with an accusatory glance at Vander. "Perhaps by now he will have calmed a bit. He might even be willing to come to Clos du Vie." He tapped his cane on a brass manhole cover at their feet. *"Messieurs?"*

Ingrid watched distractedly as Nolan and Vander crouched and started to discuss the best way to pry the cover free. She looked past the underbelly of the bridge, where pigeons trilled and cooed from their roosts. The Zouave statue molded to the base of one of the bridge's arches seemed to stare at them with rapt distaste.

It was daylight. What if something happened down in the sewers? What if Luc felt even a nominal resonance of fear from her? He'd have to shift. He'd have to fly through skies that would reveal him to anyone who happened to look skyward.

He would know where she was. Luc had watched from the stables as she'd left with Vander. Not for the first time, Ingrid wondered if afternoon was the best time for this.

"Maybe we should come back at night," she suggested.

Using Nolan's sword as a lever, Vander and Nolan heaved the round brass cover and slid it to the side. It scraped along the paved walkway.

Vander stood and brushed his hands on the sides of his trousers. A few seconds of eye contact was all he needed to read Ingrid's mind.

"You won't need him."

The words weren't an attempt to reassure her. They had been sewn together with a black look that flashed behind his spectacles. It was gone fast, before Vander could return his focus to the open manhole. But she'd still seen it. Her thoughts for Luc had upset him.

"It's not about me needing him," she said as Nolan shinnied through the manhole. Constantine followed without difficulty, as if he descended into the sewer every day. "His instinct won't care that two Alliance members are beside me with their blessed weapons. He'll be forced to come to me. And in daylight—"

"He might be seen. So what?" Vander interrupted. "Why should that bother you, Ingrid? It's Luc's problem. Let him worry about it."

Her eyes watered as if he had struck her. Vander saw it and looked away, lips pursed.

Ingrid gathered her skirts and concentrated on lowering herself to the edge of the manhole, then finding the metal ladder with her feet. So she'd been wrong about Vander. He was jealous of Luc after all. How well he'd covered that up, she thought as she climbed down the two dozen or so rungs and stepped onto another stretch of pavement.

It was warm and dark, with only two electric jets visible along the railed-in walkway. The humid air wasn't as overwhelming as it had been in Constantine's orangery, and it wasn't nearly as fragrant. There was a smell, though. A dank, sulfuric odor that reminded her that human wastewater flowed nearby.

Above, Vander slid the cover back into place before climbing down. The cover sealed with a *gong,* and the dense air immediately felt harder to breathe.

"Well, this is cozy." Nolan's voice rolled off the arched tunnel walls and briefly ate up the steady hum of fast-moving water. It ran in a gushing strip just beside the raised walkway where they stood.

Thick, sweaty pipes snaked overhead, but they were lost to the murky darkness outside the limited sphere of light.

"It is the picture of solitude, is it not?" Constantine said, and with a flourish of his cane began walking.

Ingrid started after him, the water rushing at such a fast clip it threw wind up over the railing. Vander grabbed for her arm and roughly jerked her back, his crossbow already aimed into the darkness.

"Stop."

Nolan swung his broadsword into an offensive position. "How many are there?"

Demons. Vander could see their dust.

"At least four," he answered. "We should leave."

"No." Ingrid wrested herself from Vander's death grip. "One of those streams of dust could be Léon's."

She squared her shoulders and continued on Constantine's heels. The old man had already started walking again.

"He could be dangerous," Vander said for what felt to Ingrid like the millionth time.

"And he could be scared and confused, just like I was when I started lighting things on fire," she returned.

She peered over her shoulder and saw Vander and Nolan following closely, their weapons at the ready. "Don't you remember what it was like? Knowing something was wrong but not having any idea what or why?"

"I know helping him is the right thing to do, Ingrid, but this isn't one of your lessons at Clos du Vie. This is real. You're in no way prepared to fight demons, so it's left to me to make sure you're safe."

Vander was probably aiming for chivalry, but his words smacked of patronization instead.

"Protecting me is Luc's problem, isn't it? Let him worry about it," Ingrid said, throwing Vander's earlier words right back at him. She didn't care if they stung. This was exactly why she'd wanted to take lessons with Constantine. She didn't want her safekeeping to *fall* to anyone. Her safety should be her burden alone.

If only she could direct her power the way she needed to.

Nolan passed Ingrid, taking the lead in front of Constantine.

Vander brought up the rear, and he was quiet there, no doubt stewing over her retort. Their first argument. Ingrid kept her eyes on the steel railing that she speculated kept the sewer workers from taking a misstep and falling into the rushing, debris-laden water.

After a few minutes of silent procession, the railings began to look, well . . . *odd*. Whitish strings wrapped them, forming wide nets between each section of post. The nets jiggled here and there, and when Ingrid stopped to bend closer to one, she saw why. They weren't nets. They were spiderwebs. Spiderwebs the size of pillow shams, and they had trapped all manner of things. In the web closest to Ingrid, a cockroach struggled pointlessly. Its hairy legs had become tangled in the sticky gossamer, along with a number of flies and centipedes, and in one far corner—Ingrid peered closer, before gasping and standing back up. It was a rat's tail, chewed off from the rest of its body.

"Constantine," Nolan called from farther ahead. The tip of his sword sliced through a web that stretched the width of the walkway. The broken strands fell away, but not with a ghostly flutter. The threads dropped to the cement with a wet slap.

"Either the evolution of spiders has worked at miraculous speeds here in the sewers, or this was spun by the Duster we're looking for."

Nolan was right. It had to be Léon. Ingrid stepped away from the webbed railing. Her heel nudged something. It looked like a dirty, oversized mothball in the dim underground light. She quickly corrected herself: it was a cocoon. She didn't want to know what was inside.

"He's close," Vander said, his crossbow raised.

The next voice that rang out didn't belong to any of them.

"How do you know this?"

Léon was above them, perched on one of the thick pipes, his chest and legs folded tightly together so that he could fit in the small space. His shoulders hunched forward until they were on his knees, and his short blond hair hung in limp, ragged clumps around his face.

"How do you know this?" he repeated, his English heavily accented.

"Because I can see your dust," Vander answered, nonplussed. Ingrid admired him for that; her heart raced like one of Pamplona's stampeding bulls.

"I have it too," Vander went on, his crossbow still aimed true.

"Léon," Constantine said, walking back toward the pipes that he had just passed beneath. "We only wish to help you. Won't you come down?"

Léon's sweaty face pruned up into a grimace. "You. You said I would get better. You said I would be able to control it." He rocked forward, letting his hands come out and brace against a parallel pipe. He hung over Constantine, seething. "Well, I could not! And now they are dead! You can't help me."

He sounded as angry as Grayson had the night before. Ingrid knew not to pull Vander's crossbow from its target, but she placed a hand on his arm to stay him.

"It takes patience, Léon," she said. The boy's eyelids, which had been sealed in agony, sprang open. "I hurt my friend. I didn't kill her, but I could have. I could have killed a number of people. We all make mistakes—"

"I murdered my family," Léon spit. *"Mon père, ma m-mère."* His chin quivered as he spoke. "And Charles. *Mon petit frère . . ."*

They let him sob. His shoulders shuddered and his nose ran and Ingrid had to look away. Was this how Grayson felt? Did he hate himself the way Léon did? Something about Léon's sobbing must have put Vander at ease. He lowered his crossbow and hitched it back inside his overcoat.

"My name is Ingrid Waverly," she said once Léon had composed himself a bit. "I have the blood of a lectrux demon. My brother, Grayson, has hellhound blood. We know how frightened you are. How confused. Please, let us help you."

Léon watched her from his perch, his pale lashes blinking rapidly, as if he was considering her offer. She held her breath.

"Non," he finally said, shaking his head for emphasis. "You want to help me live with this curse, but there is another who will free me of it. I am going to him."

Constantine's feet scraped the cement as he lurched forward. "You cannot."

"What man are you talking about?" Nolan asked, his broadsword still poised.

"Dupuis," Léon answered.

Ingrid knew the name. Dupuis was the man Luc had told her about the evening before. The one who had called on Constantine and asked about her.

Constantine jabbed his cane at Léon as if it were a saber. "Monsieur Dupuis is lying to you, Léon."

"You lied to me!" Léon shouted, and with a grating shriek let go of the pipes. A pair of long, hooked fangs had erupted from his top gums by the time he hit the walkway. They were thin and black and reached to the underside of his chin. Léon went for Constantine's shoulder with them.

The old man had spry reflexes. He bashed his cane into one side of Léon's face. It stunned the boy long enough for Nolan to shove Constantine aside and connect the flat of his broadsword with Léon's shoulder. He didn't want to hurt Léon, or he would have angled his sword quite differently.

Vander pounced on the Duster from behind. He pinned Léon's arms and kept him from taking another leap for Constantine. But the boy's hands were still free, and Ingrid watched with wonderment as each fingertip secreted what looked like a white bead. The beads grew larger and rounder and then dripped from his fingers.

Léon flicked his wrists and ten ribbons of thick white silk

spewed toward Nolan. The webbing lassoed him, twisting and weaving until Nolan's arms were bound to his sides.

"Stop, Léon!" Ingrid shouted.

Then something began to happen to her own fingertips. They prickled and stung, the shudders of electricity dancing wildly from her shoulder to her hands. She hadn't called on it, and yet here it was, as unwelcome as ever. She closed her eyes and tried to use the imagery Constantine had taught her: Plunging her arms into snow. Or into icy water. But a moment later the current was still live and kicking inside her.

Her fingertips throbbed and swelled with need. If the electricity came out here, now, it might travel anywhere. Strike anyone. Unless she could direct it. Give it someplace to go.

Her ears rang with panic, cutting through the roar of the sewage river. Ingrid's eyes sprang open. The water! She threw herself toward the webby railing and leaned over the edge, her hands reaching for the aqueduct. A warm shudder rippled through her as forks of lightning flowed from her, driving into the brown water. The river of sewage turned into an electrical tide, illuminating the tunnel in bursts of skittering white light. It crackled and hissed, and Ingrid's eardrums itched. And then it was over. She sagged against the railing, feeling drained yet again. Tears of frustration rimmed her eyes.

Ingrid rested her head against the railing before remembering the sticky webs encasing it. She pulled back and swiped at her forehead as Constantine hustled to her side.

"My lady, are you hurt?"

She shook her head, avoiding his eyes. "I just . . . I couldn't stop it."

Constantine patted her shoulder. "Electricity begets electricity, I am afraid. Once you begin generating it, the current must be very difficult to quell. Come."

He left her side.

All sounds of the struggle between Léon and Vander had

fallen silent. Vander still held the boy's arms pinned, but Léon now stared blankly at his raised fingers. The tacky liquid had stopped seeping from them.

"How—? It . . . it stopped," Léon whispered. Vander freed him.

"You can control it," Ingrid said, jealousy hot in her chest.

Léon curled his fingers into his palms, tucked his fists to his stomach, and ran. He dodged Vander and disappeared like a shadow into the sewer tunnel. After a few seconds, Ingrid couldn't even hear the slap of his feet against the cement.

"Burke," Nolan said, still wrapped tight in Léon's webbing. "If you have a moment? I feel like an idiot over here."

Vander sheared the threads binding Nolan, the webbing falling again with a heavy, wet smack. Vander then reached up and massaged his upper lip.

"Are you hurt?" Ingrid asked.

"Léon might have thrown his head back," Vander answered. "It's nothing."

"Who is Dupuis?" Nolan asked as he peeled leftover threads of silk from the buttons of his coat.

Ingrid turned toward Constantine. "He visited you recently."

Her teacher didn't react to her knowing this detail. He simply gestured in the direction of the entrance with a flick of his cane and began retracing their steps. Ingrid fell in behind him.

"I hadn't taken Gaston for such a gossip," Constantine said, laughter lifting each word. "Indeed, Monsieur Dupuis and I are acquainted, though it does not rank among my fondest acquaintances—he is a member of the Daicrypta."

Ingrid kept walking, waiting for more of an explanation, but Vander and Nolan both stopped.

"The *Daicrypta*?" Vander asked.

"Why would any of them visit you?" Nolan tagged on.

"Wait—" Ingrid held up her hand. "What is the Daicrypta?"

The skittering of claws sounded above them, along the cast-iron pipes.

"Keep walking," Vander advised, and then explained, "They're demonologists."

Like Constantine. "So they study demons?"

And how could this Dupuis man offer to free Léon of his curse?

"They do more than that," Nolan answered. "They're occult. The Alliance's goal is to push back the demon realm, but the Daicrypta would rather keep the demons right here, in *our* realm, so they can learn from them. Manipulate them. And they couldn't care less if people get injured in the process."

Ahead, an electric jet reflected light off the rungs leading up to the manhole cover.

"What I'd like to know is how Constantine came to be acquainted with one of their disciples," Vander added.

Constantine had finally reached the foot of the ladder leading out. "I know many of them, monsieur. I was once a disciple myself."

Vander and Nolan advanced on the old man so quickly that Ingrid jumped back, and Constantine held up his cane to ward them off.

"I said *once*," he repeated. "I could no longer condone a number of their practices and decided to take my leave."

"Which practices were those?" Nolan asked, his broadsword still level with Constantine's throat. "Observing humans possessed by demons and allowing their torture instead of performing a simple exorcism? Or perhaps it was the practice of buying asylum patients and using them as flesh rewards for the demons they were attempting to tame and train?"

Ingrid stared hard at her teacher, her stomach in a knot.

"Yes, those practices," Constantine admitted, his nostrils flaring. "Those and many more. You may judge me as you see fit for becoming a disciple in the first place, but there is no one—*no one*—who regrets it more than I."

He took a rattling breath to calm his own fervor before continuing. "It has been over a decade since I parted ways with the Daicrypta; however, no inoperative disciple can ever go very far. They will always be watching me. Robert Dupuis was a colleague, and you might have guessed that he has an interest in Dusters—particularly in Lady Ingrid."

She took another step back. "What does he want with me?"

Ingrid wondered whether the Dispossessed knew about the Daicrypta, and whether Luc would be as upset as Vander and Nolan seemed to be.

"Shall we discuss this aboveground?" Constantine asked.

Ingrid made for the rungs right behind Nolan, eager for the cold, fresh air. Down here, the air was too thick and rank to take a full breath without gagging.

At the top Nolan put muscle into shoving the manhole cover up and aside. The bleak afternoon light kissed the crown of Ingrid's head, and when she climbed out, the gritty walkway and splattered pigeon droppings were a welcome sight. Even the curious glances from the occupants of a passing river barge didn't affect her.

Once Vander and Constantine were out and the cover had been slid back into place, the conversation picked right back up and blew Ingrid's good spirits to smithereens.

"Dupuis wants the same thing as Axia," Constantine said. "Lady Ingrid's blood. The angelic quotient of it, at least."

Vander took a protective stance in front of her, as if Constantine were going to do the attacking right then and there.

"I am sure they would not intend for her to die," her teacher went on. "But their blood-draining and -separating experiments have failed more often than they have succeeded."

Ingrid's knees went a bit weak. Brilliant. So now she had to worry about not only a crazed fallen angel coveting her blood but a secret occult society as well?

"Dead girl or no dead girl, they'd have angel blood. I don't even want to think about what they could cook up with that," Nolan said. "Why has Dupuis come to you? Has he made some kind of offer?"

"None that I am tempted to accept," Constantine replied, cutting his eyes toward Ingrid. "They cannot simply take you and perform their experiments. When you accepted me as your teacher, I laid claim to you. Even though I am an ex-disciple, they must honor my claim."

His *claim*? Ingrid's ears began to burn in spite of the buffeting wind.

"I am not a plot of land or some lost puppy you found in an alley. You have no claim over me, monsieur. No one does."

Constantine put up his hands in surrender. "Forgive the phrasing. Let me say it this way: it is much like Luc's claim over you and the humans within his territory. You are under my protection, that is all, and I give you my word that I will not betray your trust—or the trust of any of my students. You are, however, free to give yourself to the Daicrypta."

"If Léon's curse stems from his demon blood and they've promised to rid him of it . . ." Ingrid took Vander's hand as she worked it out. "That's what they're going to do, isn't it—drain his blood?"

The deepening frown on her teacher's lips was answer enough.

"Speaking of blood," Nolan said, pulling out a pocket watch and checking the hour, "I have an appointment to keep."

"We're discussing how an evil society is plotting to drain Ingrid's blood, and you have an *appointment*?" Vander asked.

Nolan tucked the watch into his vest and shrugged. "It's a pressing appointment. Besides, you heard the man: the evil society can't touch her. I'll see you at Hôtel Bastian tonight?"

Vander grumbled his assent, and with the tip of an invisible hat, Nolan headed toward the quay steps. He turned back as he took the stone steps two at a time. "And don't go after spider boy!"

Vander squeezed Ingrid's fingers. "I think he's talking to you."

Constantine eyed their joined hands and raised his brow. Ingrid and Vander unlaced their fingers, but as they parted, she felt something cold and sticky pull at the skin on the back of her hand. Looking down, she saw strings of white gossamer waving in the wind. Spider silk. It ran from Vander's fingers to Ingrid's hand like an undulating bridge.

"Is that—" Ingrid stopped and tried to shake the webbing free. Vander did the same, wrenching his hand back. The silk stretched, firmly affixed to the tips of his fingers.

Ingrid stared at him. "Is that coming from *you*?"

CHAPTER TWELVE

An E-flat wheezed from one of the abbey's wooden organ pipes, belching yet another off-pitch note into the fan-vaulted ceilings. Gabby gritted her teeth as her linen cloth came off the ivory keys coated in gritty black dust. It had taken her the last half hour or more to clean the pipe organ's dual keyboards, her fingers bringing up ages of dust and playing the keys with all the finesse of a toddler.

"You can cross *butchering pipe organ music* off your things-to-do-before-I-die list," Grayson mocked from where he crouched, brushing the newly painted choir stalls with varnish. Their mother had reimagined the choir stalls as a spot to smoke, drink champagne, and mingle between viewing exhibits.

"How was I supposed to know the thing was still able to play?" she shot back.

That morning at the breakfast table, she and Grayson had promised their mother they would help with the abbey, and Lady Brickton had put them to task. It wouldn't normally have taken

Gabby an hour to clean fifty-six keys, even if they were the size of a giant's knuckles. But the soreness in her shoulder slowed her down significantly. The stitches were small and neat—Nolan had seen to them himself—but they still pulled and stung.

Gabby supposed that was what one got when one tussled with an appendius demon.

"How did you get that wound?" Grayson asked.

Gabby crumpled the dusting linen and went still. She'd told Ingrid about the appendius before her sister had gone out that morning with Vander, but not Grayson.

"You're left-handed, and yet you're using your right to clean," Grayson explained, popping up from between stalls. He wiped his sweaty forehead with the back of his arm. "And I can smell your blood better than usual."

For whatever reason, this didn't surprise Gabby as it probably should have. Her brother had been acting strange for weeks, and knowing he had hellhound blood in him . . . well, heightened senses didn't seem all that out of the ordinary.

"Because of your demon gift," she said.

Grayson mashed the bristles of the varnishing brush against the ledge of the choir stall. "I wish people would stop calling it a gift. It's a curse, not a gift." He made a messy stroke of the brush. "And why, of all demons, did it have to be a bleeding hellhound? Why not a lectrux, like Ingrid? Or whatever it is Vander has the blood of?"

He jammed the brush back into the tin bucket and a wave of clear, tacky varnish slopped over the edge. Grayson swore.

Gabby wished she knew what to say, but she was caught with an open mouth and no words at all. Her brother didn't usually speak so much to her, and definitely not about important things like this.

The sound of shoe soles on the tile floor made them both peer toward the narthex. Their father strode into the abbey foyer, the loose cowl of his black woolen great coat fluttering like a raven's wings. He appraised the interior of the church with a wrinkled brow. He was not impressed. He would have been had he seen the wreck the place had been in early December. Then again, Gabby thought, had he seen it in early December, they would have all been home in London before Christmas.

"Papa?" Gabby's voice carried far, echoing off the ceiling. She thought the ceiling might be the abbey's most beautiful feature. Each fanned-out section had been painted into a mosaic of color: sapphire, viridian, iris, onyx, and ruby. She had often gazed at the patterns it made until her neck ached.

"Gabriella, you're to come with me," her father replied.

Blast. What had she done now? Gabby put down the dusting cloth, her mind racing. Had he found out about her sneaking out the night before? No. If that had been the case, that telling vein of his would have been standing out in the center of his forehead.

She took a quick glance toward the choir stalls. Grayson had sunk out of sight. The coward!

She brushed a few tufts of black dust from the front of her skirt, picked up her coat and gloves and followed her father outside to the rectory drive, where Luc waited with the landau. Luc avoided eye contact. He was probably still angry with her for sneaking out and getting injured. Gabby did feel awful about the angel's burn. She'd said she was sorry the night before while he'd been flying her home—which was, Gabby had to note, the most exhilarating thing she had ever done in her life. But Luc had been in his scales and unable to respond. By the look of his stony face, he hadn't accepted her apology yet.

Once in the carriage and rattling down rue Dante toward the Seine, Gabby could no longer stand the suspense.

"Where are we going?"

Her father tugged on the shade's string and blocked out the milky sunlight.

"We're paying a visit to Dr. Frederic Hauss," he answered.

"I'm sorry . . . who?"

"Dr. Hauss is a renowned surgeon, Gabriella."

The carriage jerked over a particularly deep rut. It shook her and set her injured shoulder blazing.

She didn't understand. "A surgeon?"

Lord Brickton held out his hand and gestured toward her face. "You cannot possibly wish to endure such marks for the rest of your life. Dr. Hauss might be able to help you overcome this deformity."

The carriage bucked again, providing nice cover for the look of pure shock spreading over her face. Was that how he saw her scars? As a deformity? Her father continued to ramble about Hauss's celebrated rhinoplasties in Germany and in Great Britain and how fortunate Gabby should consider herself now that he was practicing here in Paris.

Her chest felt like it was caving in.

"I'm not deformed," Gabby said, too hurt to put much fire behind the declaration. Her father ignored her.

"If anyone can fix you, my dear girl, Hauss is the one."

Their landau slowed to a stop and her father sent the shade up. They'd pulled alongside the arcaded entrance of a fortresslike limestone building. Hôtel-Dieu. He'd taken her to the hospital.

Since the morning after the hellhound had shredded half of her face, Gabby had dreamed of being able to erase the damage. How miraculous and lucky she would be if she woke up one day to find the pink, waxy-looking scars gone and her supple, unblemished skin back.

But hearing that someone might be able to do it, hearing her father wish for it as well, hurt more deeply than Gabby could have imagined.

Luc opened the landau's door and this time looked straight into Gabby's eyes. He could feel what she did: the sensation of being turned inside out. Luc's wrathful glare speared Lord Brickton, but Gabby's father wasn't paying his driver the slightest bit of attention.

"I'm not going in," Gabby announced. She sat farther back on the bench.

"You needn't be embarrassed," her father replied. He rested his hand on her knee, and for the briefest of moments, she saw true compassion in him. He wasn't trying to be cruel. He was just blinded by what *he* wanted. What he thought was best for an earl's daughter.

"I'm not—" She was going to say embarrassed, but then he'd want to know what the problem was. She didn't know how to explain it. "I'm not ready."

Her father was clearly disappointed but agreed to let her wait inside the hospital while he and Dr. Hauss consulted alone this first time. As they entered the building and found their way into a vaulted corridor, her father admitted that perhaps he'd sprung this visit on her too suddenly. He gave her a moment to reconsider joining them—during which she stood resolute and silent—before entering Dr. Hauss's office without her.

Left alone in the corridor, Gabby paced a small swath of floor. Her father's rich baritone carried from behind the closed doors, but she didn't want to listen to him talk about her. She moved away down the hall until her father's voice faded.

A string of tall, arched windows running down the corridor overlooked a narrow inner courtyard and, across from that, the exterior of another wing of the hospital. The windows on that side were also arched, and she saw more people walking back and forth.

A head of thick black curls caught her attention. Gabby stopped. Practically pressed her nose to the glass as she watched Nolan Quinn march through the arcaded entrance into the courtyard portico and enter the opposite wing. She held her breath. What was he doing here?

Gabby lifted her skirts and ran as fast as her heeled boots could take her to the exit and outdoors onto the portico. She ignored the startled glances of two nurses in long white skirts and starched hats and dashed through the same door Nolan had entered. Just in time. He was slipping through a pair of swinging doors farther down the hallway.

Gabby considered her father for all of two seconds before she headed straight for those doors. The wonderful thing about a hospital, she realized, was that anyone who passed her had problems of their own to tend to. No one paid her any mind as she got to the doors and went through. They opened onto a descending set of stairs that twisted to the left. Nolan's footfalls were still audible.

Gabby opened her mouth to call out to him but stopped. Instinct told her that neither she nor Nolan belonged down here. She took the steps quickly and quietly, making it to the bottom in time to see Nolan darting through yet another pair of doors ahead to the left.

The air was markedly colder on this level, and Gabby had the creeping suspicion it wasn't just because they were underground. The sign above the door Nolan had passed through confirmed it.

MORGUE.

What was Nolan doing in there?

She pushed the door open an inch and the chill of the vast room hit her in the nose. White-sheeted bodies topped rows of steel tables. Pale feet stuck out everywhere, an identification tag hanging from each body's big toe. Nolan was the only person inside. Well, the only living person.

He was walking through the maze of tables, flipping up toe tags. Gabby shoved the door open wide.

"What on earth are you doing?"

Nolan nearly ripped the tag off one corpse's toe. "Gabby! Christ in heaven, don't sneak up on a man like that."

"Says the person who is clearly in a place he shouldn't be," she retorted, closing the door behind her.

He recovered with a roll of his shoulders. "I happen to be on

Alliance business. Benoit is diverting the mortician, so I have a time limit."

The Alliance's trusted doctor friend, Benoit, had been the one who'd cleaned and stitched Gabby's scars.

Nolan flipped another toe tag and read the name. "And how is it you just happen to be at the hospital?" Nolan let go of the tag and stood up straight, his eyes suddenly bright with concern. "Is it your shoulder? What's wrong?"

"No, it's fine," Gabby said. "I mean, it hurts, but I'm fine."

She cringed at the idea of telling him the true reason her father had dragged her here. The two times she and Nolan had seen each other since his return from Rome, neither of them had mentioned the state of her cheek. Broaching the subject was too uncomfortable. And what if he thought surgery was a good idea?

Gabby cleared her throat. "It's my father. He's feeling a touch of rheumatism about the knees."

Nolan spared her feeble answer a moment of deliberation before lifting another toe tag.

"Are you looking for a specific corpse, or will any serve?" she asked, and to her horror, he tossed back the sheet on one body, exposing a pale thigh and buttock.

"Here he is," he answered, and then, to Gabby's further horror, Nolan reached inside his coat and removed a needle and syringe. Without a second's hesitation, he stuck the dead flesh with the tip.

"You can't do that!"

Nolan proceeded to draw up the plunger, sucking the corpse's blood into a clear glass barrel. Gabby's stomach rolled. The body belonged to a man—the clinging drape of the white sheet failed to conceal *that* much—and the exposed skin showed a mottled kind of bruising on the flesh pressed flat against the metal table.

"Stop it, Nolan!" she said again.

"When Carrick Quinn gives an order, it's wise to obey," he

replied as the barrel reached capacity. He extracted the needle and capped it.

"What could he possibly want with a dead man's blood?" Gabby asked with a quick check of the door. Could they be arrested for this?

Nolan tucked the filled syringe back into his coat pocket. "He's a Duster, and he murdered his parents before killing himself last night." He replaced the sheet but then turned down the edge covering the man's head. Gabby shrank back. It wasn't the first time she'd seen a dead body, but the experience hadn't gotten any more pleasant.

"What's his name?" she asked. He was younger than she expected, perhaps right around Grayson and Ingrid's age. His bloodless skin looked like rice paper, his brown hair a shock of color in contrast.

"Gilbert DeChamps," Nolan answered, before draping the boy's head once again. "You weren't the only one who sneaked off abbey grounds last night. Grayson found the boy and his parents."

Well. Her brother had kept that juicy bit of information to himself all morning.

A pungent odor filled her nostrils: ammonia, and something else. It was sickly sweet, and Gabby somehow knew it was coming from the cold, decaying flesh all around them.

Nolan must have seen her color drain. He took her by the arm and steered her toward the door.

"I'm fine," she said, and meant it once they'd left the morgue.

"Right as rain," he said in that sarcastic tone of his. Only this time, Gabby didn't smile.

She stepped out of his hold. "So you think I'm a fool, then?"

Nolan frowned. "For turning green around a bunch of stiffs?"

"No," Gabby answered, thoroughly vexed. "For not obeying your father's order to forget the Alliance. You said the wise obey Carrick Quinn. But I can't. So that must mean I'm a fool."

Nolan guided her toward the stairs, his palm at the small of her back. "Lass, I think my da's the fool, not you." He wrapped his hand around her waist and brought her to a halt, spinning her to face him. The cold focus he'd shown in the morgue while drawing the corpse's blood had gone. "If I could, I'd start training you right now. I'd bring you all the way in, get your oaths ceremony lined up in Rome—everything."

There would be an oaths ceremony? In Rome?

"Gabby, I don't know how to change his mind. The mercurite's made him something he isn't. Or at least, something he never was." He kept his hands away from her shoulders, remembering her wound, and settled for sweeping his fingers along her chin. He lowered them until he'd circled half of her slim neck in his palm. There was something entirely possessive about the way he touched her. Possessive and protective. Gabby liked it. "I want you with me."

She didn't care that they stood down the hall from a morgue. She would kiss him anywhere. Even had they still been standing beside the dead bodies, she would have kissed him. Well, all right. Maybe not *right* next to the dead bodies.

But it wasn't to be. Nolan's lips were still a few inches from hers when the morgue doors swung open and crashed against the corridor walls. Gabby shot back, and Nolan released her as they turned to see who'd caught them.

No one else had been in the morgue, Gabby reasoned in the split second before the interloper stumbled into the corridor. That he was naked was Gabby's first thought. The second was that he was also very much dead.

"Bloody hell," Nolan hissed.

Gilbert DeChamps shuffled out of the morgue, his waxy white arms hanging at his sides. There were long, gaping black slashes across his wrists.

"What did you do to him?" Gabby asked, suddenly and unreasonably angry. Nolan had stuck him with a needle and now he was up and stumbling around!

"I didn't do anything," Nolan answered. The boy swung his head toward them. His jaw hung loose, his eyes heavily lidded.

"It's a carcass demon, Gabby. Get back." Nolan unsheathed his broadsword from inside his ankle-length coat.

The dead boy surged forward a few graceless steps. Gabby tried not to look at his exposed bits and instead kept her eyes trained on his slack face, his unseeing blue eyes.

"What's a carcass demon?" Gabby asked, reaching for her own sword.

"A demon that feeds on the dead flesh of anything recently touched by another demon," Nolan answered, backing Gabby farther away from the shambling boy. "They usually feed quietly, but when disturbed, they can reanimate the dead bodies they're in."

Gabby held her sword the way Chelle had taught her—with one hand, her elbow tight to her side.

"What the— Gabriella, what are you doing? Put that away! Didn't you learn your lesson last night?"

"Let me take him," Gabby said. "He doesn't look all that silver-footed."

"Absolutely not! Carcass demons can be extremely deceiving. If you're not careful—"

Gilbert DeChamps lunged forward, arms outstretched. No longer stumbling awkwardly, his bare feet pounded the green-and-white-tiled floor of the corridor as he came at them.

Nolan swung his broadsword in a clean upward stroke, on a straight path for the dead boy's neck. But at the last moment, Gilbert's body took an impossible detour.

He planted one pale white foot, toe tag still affixed, on the wall to his right and propelled himself up. His other foot slapped against the next wall tile and he pushed off into an arcing leap over Nolan's head. The broadsword connected with the wall just as the carcass demon landed in front of Gabby with stealthy precision.

"Swing, Gabby!" Nolan barked. He needn't have. Gabby knew what to do. She lunged forward and sliced into the corpse's torso with the tip of her blade. The blessed silver melted away the flesh in a spit of green sparks, but the cut hadn't been lethal.

She swung again, the short sword feather-light compared to Nolan's cumbersome broadsword. But Gilbert's reanimated corpse had once again cartwheeled into the air over her head, landing adroitly at the base of the stairs. Heaven only knew what would happen if a naked dead body escaped into the upper floor of the hospital, or worse, out into the street.

Gabby reached for her blessed dagger, strapped at the lip of her boot, and without thinking, hurled it at Gilbert. The dagger struck home between his ribs, and the flare of green sparks proved it had been a killing blow.

Gilbert dropped to the floor, legs and arms bent at awkward angles, like a marionette with slackened strings.

The corridor was probably silent, but Gabby's heart rampaged; her blood cascaded through her ears. Nolan grabbed her arm and swung her around to face him, his expression a cross between fury and admiration.

"Who taught you to do that?"

She was saved from having to answer when Luc appeared at the base of the steps. He was in his human form, but barely. His cheekbones had shifted into sharply cut ridges beneath his skin, which was itself on the verge of becoming closely knit scales.

"I'm not hurt, Luc," she said, desperate to turn off whatever alarm was ringing inside him. "Really, I'm all right."

Luc took an indifferent glance at the dead body lying in a twisted heap. He didn't say anything, and Gabby wondered if it was because his voice would have been gargled.

"A carcass demon," Nolan explained, his chest heaving. "The boy was a Duster."

"And you took a sample of his blood," Gabby said. "You never answered me—why does your father want it?"

Nolan raked his fingers through his hair. "The Alliance isn't all about demon hunting. There's a scientific element, and no, I can't discuss it." He sent a pointed look at Gabby. "Let's just say this Duster's blood is meant for research."

Voices traveled from down the hall, far past the morgue doors, which were still wide open. Nolan ushered Gabby toward Luc and the steps, stopping to retrieve Gabby's dagger from Gilbert's torso. They eased around his grotesquely used body and took the stairs two at a time.

"Two Dusters within the last week have murdered their families," Nolan said once they'd reached the main hallway. He bent to one knee and pretended to tie his bootlaces while slipping the dagger back into Gabby's boot.

She turned away from a passing doctor, who slowed and sent them a suspicious look. Her scars were all too noticeable, as would be the stain of color on her cheeks from having Nolan's hands roving about her ankles.

"One of them is running around the Paris sewers, and the other is at the bottom of those stairs," Nolan continued.

"Ingrid was in the sewers this morning," Luc said, his voice hoarse.

Nolan nodded. "She was worried you'd have to come after her."

"She wasn't frightened," Luc replied. "Just nervous for a moment."

Gabby frowned. Her sister and Nolan had gone into the sewers to search for a Duster, Grayson had discovered dead bodies, and Gabby had just taken down a carcass demon. They were all keeping rather busy.

"She's too trusting," Nolan said. "First with Constantine, who turns out to be ex-Daicrypta—"

Luc snapped to attention. "He's Daicrypta?"

"*Ex,*" Nolan stressed. Gabby watched the exchange with growing confusion. What was the Daicrypta? "He says an active Daicrypta, Robert Dupuis, wants Ingrid's angel blood."

"Who is Robert Dupuis?" Gabby nearly screeched.

Luc cocked his head and breathed in sharply. "Your father is leaving the meeting."

Without another word, he moved like the wind down the corridor, out onto the portico, and to the arcaded entrance.

Nolan walked Gabby toward the exit onto the portico, his hand once more on the small of her back. Her skin responded with a pleasant throb. Glancing through the arched windows and across the courtyard, she saw her father in the opposite wing, passing by one of the windows there.

Nolan brought his hand around the side of her cloak and patted the spot where her sword was sheathed inside. "Where did you learn how to use this?"

Her father pushed open the door to the portico. He looked toward the arcaded entrance and then swept his eyes over the rest of the courtyard, searching for her. The muscles in her legs tensed, prepared to break into an unladylike trot. And yet the gentle touch of Nolan's hand was powerful enough to hold her back.

"I can see him turning purple from here," she said. "I really must go."

Nolan pressed his lips together and dropped his hand. Gabby rushed forward to meet her father. She could feel Nolan's eyes on her as she stormed outside and met her father's irritated glare.

"I became restless," she explained lamely. He merely grunted before taking the stone steps down toward the entrance and their waiting landau.

After they had climbed in and Luc had nudged the horses forward, her father told her all about the illustrious Dr. Hauss and the procedures they had discussed. Gabby blocked out her father's voice easily. Her hands were still trembling from the fight with the carcass demon—and from being so close to cornered by Nolan's question.

The next time she saw him, she would need a ready answer. Preferably one that didn't incriminate Chelle. At least Gabby had shown him what she could do. Perhaps he would take the account back to his father.

It wasn't meant for him, but the smile Gabby directed toward her father as he finished speaking wasn't entirely false.

CHAPTER THIRTEEN

Humans called gargoyle common grounds Hôtel du Maurier. Luc was sure they called it a number of other things as well, like *a disgraceful eyesore* and *a rubbish heap*. They weren't wrong. Lennier's territory had been abandoned decades before, and what had once been an elegant four-story estate on the outer rim of the Luxembourg Gardens had slowly deteriorated into a ramshackle limestone shell.

Overrun by ivy, rust, and shattered glass, it was the perfect meeting spot for the Dispossessed. Humans tended to turn away from the unsightly, and Hôtel du Maurier was unsightly indeed.

Luc and Dimitrie finished dressing in the courtyard. It was empty and quiet, and, except for the low dance of firelight in two windows on the second story, dark. The light wouldn't be visible from the street. Lennier evaded hibernation only because of the vagrants and inebriates who often sheltered within his walls. Those kinds of humans weren't a threat to him. Sober, curious passersby who could have sworn the place had been deserted for years were.

"You're going to tell them, aren't you?" Dimitrie asked as they made their way into the shadowed town house. The ballroom's double doors had been left wide open and were now banked in by snow.

"Tell them what?" Luc's breath steamed in front of him as he strode through the old ballroom. He heard the squeak of mice coming from under the lid of the rotting piano. The prisms of the chandelier chinked together as a squirrel hopped along its column to a hole in the ceiling plaster.

"About the burns," Dimitrie answered. "You're going to tell them I'm a shadow gargoyle."

Luc led the boy down a hallway, his keen vision turning the utter blackness into grays and whites. He avoided an old credenza, several white-sheeted chairs, and a dead skin-and-bones cat before taking the carpeted steps up to the next level.

"That's your own burden to bear, no one else's," Luc returned.

Being a shadow gargoyle wasn't a crime. It was just pathetic.

It had been a few days since Marco and Yann had told Luc to bring Dimitrie to common grounds. A few days since Gabby's incidents with the appendius and then, less than twenty-four hours later, the reanimated corpse. The girl was starting to become more troublesome than her sister.

With a mimic demon on Ingrid's tail and the cultish Daicrypta wanting her blood, Luc had hesitated to take himself, or Dimitrie, very far from the rectory. But the last few days had been quiet, and Lennier was waiting.

Luc knocked on the door to the elder gargoyle's rooms. He expected Lennier's raspy voice to command them to enter, but instead the door opened and another man appeared before them.

Luc had seen him before at common ground gatherings. He was middle-aged, with a dartlike chin and nose, a wan complexion, and twiggy black hair. He regarded Luc the way Luc had regarded the dead cat downstairs: with narrowed eyes and flared nostrils.

"You are the guardian at l'Abbaye Saint-Dismas," the man stated.

"Allow him in, Vincent," came Lennier's familiar voice. Vincent pulled the door wider and Luc stepped inside.

Marco stood at a window, his arms crossed, a smile spreading slowly across his face.

"This must be your new companion," Marco quipped. "How's the honeymoon going?"

Again with that slow, lordly smile. Perfectly shaped for Luc's fist.

Dimitrie entered Lennier's suite with hesitation. The decay eating away at the rest of the house stopped at the door to Lennier's rooms. Instead of being covered with water stains and creeping ivy, the walls in these rooms were papered with a floral print. The bare wood floor had a high gloss, and the furniture, though aged, was well taken care of. A working tall case clock stood against one wall, and there was a leaping fire in the hearth. Lennier sat close to it in a Louis XIV chair. He held his hand up to Luc, a signal to wait. He then turned to Marco.

"I am sorry to hear of this," Lennier said, resuming a conversation Luc's arrival had interrupted.

Marco bowed to Lennier. "I only hope my hibernation won't last long."

Luc moved forward into the apartment. "Your hibernation?"

Marco pushed off from the window frame and went to the fire beside Lennier. "My humans won't be returning to Hôtel Dugray this season."

Which would leave Marco too long without humans to protect. He was probably already feeling the sleep coming on. A weight in the chest, Luc remembered. Like a stone settling there, growing heavier with every passing day. The stone eventually made it impossible to move or breathe—or even care.

"A shame," Luc said, trying to keep the pleasure from his tone. Marco heard it anyway.

"You'll miss me, brother, I know you will," he said. "And I have to admit, I'll miss watching you scramble around trying to protect those pesky humans of yours. Such entertainment."

"The one with angel blood is particularly troubling," Vincent piped up. He had remained near the door.

Luc kept his back to him. "I don't know why she should trouble you at all."

"She is unnatural," Vincent said.

Luc lifted his chin. He would not react. He would maintain a show of disinterest. Marco, however, knew a show when he saw one.

"Careful, Vincent," he said. "Luc turns a bit rabid whenever someone speaks ill of his favorite human."

Lennier, used to Marco's snide remarks, continued to warm his bony hands by the fire. Vincent, though, snapped up the dangling bait.

"You have a favorite human?" He balked. Luc wondered what he'd been in his first life. An overworked professor or an eccentric scientist, perhaps.

"At least I have humans enough to keep me awake," Luc said, simultaneously avoiding Vincent's question and taunting Marco.

Funny. Not too long ago, Luc had been wishing for hibernation. Now the idea of it was unnerving. Going into hibernation would mean Ingrid had gone away. The next time he woke, who knew where she would be? She would have aged. Married, perhaps. Had children, grandchildren. She might have even died.

And Luc would still be *this*. He would still be the same. Never changing. Eternally damned.

"Having a favorite human is just as unnatural as the one you favor," Vincent retorted, a sneer spreading his thin-lipped mouth. "Not to mention her unfortunate ties to the Alliance."

Letting it stand that he had a favorite human could be dangerous, but Luc kept silent, his stare blistering. He would not grovel at this gargoyle's feet.

"The Alliance here have given us aid in the past," Lennier said. He sat forward and propped his hands on the armrest. He probably wanted to rise, but his human movements were often torpid. At least his transformed figure, cut of albino scales and powerful wings, was something to be feared. "We shall continue to show them the same courtesy. Peace between us is paramount."

"And what about the abominations?" Vincent asked. "The ones with demon blood and dust? Surely you agree they should be considered our enemies."

Though Lennier said nothing, Vincent received a response.

"But they're still human."

Luc turned toward Dimitrie, having nearly forgotten that he was there. The boy started to wither under the other surprised looks he received. "Isn't it our duty to protect the human part of them?"

Luc was starting to understand why Dimitrie had so many angel's burns. He was a diplomat. Diplomacy between nations was difficult enough; between different species it was almost impossible.

"A point well made," Lennier intoned. "Your name?"

The boy ducked his head. "Dimitrie."

Lennier's wrinkled lids shuttered his eyes. "I wish to speak with Dimitrie alone."

Marco and Luc exchanged dubious glances, but when Lennier wished something done, it was done. Without a word, Luc, Marco, and Vincent, the last sniffing at his dismissal, exited into the corridor.

"The boy worries Lennier," Marco said as soon as the door had closed.

"Anyone with a weakness for humans worries me," Vincent put in.

Luc had had enough. He dove into Vincent's space, close

enough to smell the musty age of his cloak. "And gargoyles who mistake duty for weakness worry me. You're not a residential Dispossessed, that much I know, or you wouldn't have made that mistake. Where is your territory?"

Luc's boldness garnered a snort of amusement from Marco and a torrid glare from Vincent.

"Notre Dame," he answered with a curl of his lip.

Of course. Those Notre Dame gargoyles were all the same. They strutted around as if guarding the most recognizable piece of architecture in Paris had made their wings turn to gold. Vincent was no doubt waiting to see the awe on Luc's face.

He'd be waiting for quite a while.

"You'd best leave us lowly residential gargoyles to our shenanigans, then, wouldn't you say, Vincent?" Marco asked, but the humor in his voice didn't reach his eyes. They demanded Vincent's departure.

The older gargoyle drew up his cloak and heeded Marco's words.

"I don't think he likes you," Marco said once he'd fallen from view.

"Does anyone?" Luc returned, realizing the answer was most likely no. That was fine by him. Dimitrie the diplomat couldn't say as much, and look where it had gotten him.

"I think I know of one person," Marco said. "Though from what I've been hearing, she might like the Seer more than she does you. Or I should say, the future Reverend Seer."

Luc had been preparing to brush off Marco's jab until that last sentence. "Reverend?"

"The Alliance's little pet aspires to the clergy, or didn't you know? I have allies who tell me the Seer is studying under a reverend at the American Church."

Luc hadn't known. He and Vander Burke weren't exactly chatty.

"It doesn't matter," Luc said, and it didn't. The Seer could do as he wished. Though for some inexplicable reason, the fact that Vander would become an ordained man sat heavy in Luc's stomach.

He ignored it, throwing the attention from himself back to Marco. "Have a nice nap."

"It won't be for a while yet," Marco said, attempting to sound indifferent. It wasn't working. Luc could tell Marco didn't want to slip into the cold, dreamless sleep of hibernation. "Go back to your humans, Dog." He started down the hallway, shoulders pressed down and chest thrust out. "And don't trust the boy."

Luc stopped grinning. "What?"

Marco kept walking toward the cherub-topped newel posts that marked the stairwell.

"Dimitrie. I know a liar when I see one." Marco took the stairs.

Helpful as ever, Luc thought. He'd already known not to trust Dimitrie. But there was something satisfying in knowing Marco shared the sentiment. He was older, and though it pained Luc to admit it, he had unrivaled senses. Marco was a predator—sharp, skilled, and dangerous. So had he caught on to Dimitrie's secret of being a shadow gargoyle? Or had he sensed something more?

Grayson needed to get out.

His muscles shook beneath his skin, burning as if he'd just finished an hour of vigorous calisthenics. Sweat rolled from his unbuttoned collar down his chest and back. He was in his room, pacing before the window, and he felt caged. Trapped, the same way Axia had trapped him in that damned hive. Only now it was his father who'd done the trapping.

Ingrid, Gabby, and Mama had all gone out to some artist's salon, and though Grayson and Lord Brickton had also been extended invitations, the old duffer had refused on both of their behalves. *Too many bohemians,* his father had mumbled, and then, with a piercing look at Grayson, he'd added, *and temptations.*

Grayson had considered arguing. He'd gotten dressed and nearly left with his sisters and mother. The salon would be crowded, though, and hot, and Grayson knew how easy it was for people to work themselves up over art. His mother certainly did. It made the pulse race. The blood run swift and fragrant.

Perhaps being alone in his room was for the best.

He crouched and ran his hands through his hair. It was damp from sweat. His bones. God, they hurt more than ever before.

A scattering of dirt struck his window. Grayson stood up and a second rain of dirt and snow pelted the glass. He went to it and shoved the window open.

His room overlooked the rear of the rectory, and standing directly below his window on the back lawn was Chelle. He couldn't see her face, but the moon lit her slender figure and distinct cap.

"What the devil are you doing?" he called.

"Shhh!"

Grayson waited for her to say something more, but instead she crossed her arms and hugged herself against the cold.

"If you've come to serenade me, I believe your next move is to sing," he said, knowing it would only vex her. He couldn't help himself. He liked seeing her vexed. And talking helped him forget the state of his body.

"I am not serenading you," Chelle hissed. She then groaned and threw up her hands. "Never mind!"

She started to stomp away.

"Wait," Grayson called lightly. He couldn't shout. The servants' ell was too close, and his father's study was only two rooms down near the corner of the rectory.

Chelle kept walking.

"Girls," Grayson muttered, and swung his foot over the ledge of the open window. The second floor wasn't terribly far from the ground. If he hung from the ledge and dropped, he probably wouldn't even sprain an ankle. Besides, it wasn't as if attractive girls threw pebbles at his window every day.

He dropped and landed with surprising agility. The action eased the ache of his muscles slightly, and the cold air in his lungs helped bring down his temperature. Chelle must have heard his feet breaking the snow. She turned back, shook her head in aggravation, and then signaled for him to follow.

It felt good to move, even if he had no clue why Chelle had come to him. It didn't really matter, he supposed. She was here, wasn't she?

Chelle didn't speak until they'd left the abbey grounds. It was past ten, well after dark, and the streets were starting to empty.

"I'm patrolling the Latin Quarter tonight," she said.

"Alone?" He searched behind them and up ahead, but he didn't see Vander's tall frame anywhere.

"I don't get a partner every night, and I don't need one, either," she answered, prickly as a hedgehog.

"And you were wooing me at my window because . . . ?" he said.

"Certainly not because I felt I needed a partner!" Chelle sped up. "I *thought* you might be useful."

She mumbled something in French, too fast and breathy for Grayson to understand. He got the gist of it, though: she regretted having fetched him.

"Useful how?" Other than engaging the architects and laborers who were refurbishing the abbey, Grayson hadn't felt useful here in Paris at all.

"Your nose," Chelle answered, and then, without a beat of hesitation, "Can you scent more than just blood?"

Grayson stopped in his tracks. So that was what she meant by useful. "You want me to sniff out demons so you can kill them."

She faced him. Her jacket was too thin, he noted. She had to be freezing.

"Would that be a bad thing?"

"I thought I'd made it clear that I don't want anything to do with the Alliance," he answered.

Chelle lifted her chin and crossed her arms, trying to look down her nose at him. Their difference in height made it a challenge.

"*Bonsoir,* then," she said, and left him standing there.

She looked like a petulant child storming off in a fit of temper. A child with blessed silver hidden in the folds of her clothing and a highly skilled and lethal aim. He didn't have to worry about her. Chelle would be fine on her own.

Still, he found himself catching up and swinging in front of her, blocking her way. "That doesn't mean I want you roaming the streets at night alone."

Chelle stared hard at him before doing the oddest thing: she laughed.

"You are a gentleman, aren't you?" she said, as if it were the silliest thing he could possibly be.

It almost made him relieved to deny it. "Trust me—I am no gentleman."

Gentlemen didn't turn into monsters and kill prostitutes in back alleys like demonic versions of Jack the Ripper. Again he regretted having told Ingrid what he'd done. She only knew half of his evil deed, but that was enough to have built an awkward wall between them the past few days.

He wouldn't make that same mistake with Chelle. Or anyone else.

Chelle walked beside him, her pace slowed. They'd passed rue Lagrange and had come to the wide boulevard Saint-Germain. For one of the main thoroughfares in Paris, the traffic was slim. A buggy puttered by, along with a horse or two, and a covered carriage coming from the other direction.

"What exactly do you do on patrol?" Grayson asked to fill the silence. It wasn't an awkward silence, but he certainly didn't want Chelle to grow bored with his presence.

"We look for demons," she said.

"I'm not *that* slow," Grayson replied. "What I mean is, if demons come in every shape, even in human form, how do you know what's a demon and what isn't?"

She kept her hand at the red sash tied around her slim waist, where she hid her throwing stars. Her *hira-shuriken*, he corrected himself.

"Every demon has a trademark," Chelle explained, her eyes never straying from the street or sidewalk. "Some are more intelligent than others, and are better able to acclimate to the human realm. But most demons are base creatures, unable to think beyond *want* and *attain*. They don't work hard enough to cover up the trademarks that Alliance are trained to spot."

Chelle crossed in front of him and hitched her foot on the bottom rail of a length of iron fence. She pulled herself up to peer over the spikes, into a private garden.

"Appendius demons can shorten or lengthen their bodies and legs, allowing them to crawl low to the ground, through grass and beneath shrubbery, until they rear up and attack unsuspecting humans."

Chelle let go of the fence and landed beside Grayson.

"But their horns leave specific impressions on the ground, making it easy for Alliance to track them."

Grayson listened intently. Chelle had an alluring voice. It was steady and confident, and completely devoid of the acerbic sweetness that plagued so many debutantes back in London.

"Corvites are like demon messenger birds. They carry information to and from the Underneath. They look like ravens or crows, but their calls set them apart. A corvite's call breaks off in a growl."

They turned onto a winding side street off Saint-Germain.

The lack of streetlamps and the resulting shadows slowed him, but Chelle kept her confident pace. She must have come this way alone plenty of times before. Grayson didn't like that thought at all.

"Demons with enough power to glamour themselves into human form are working so hard to maintain that glamour that they usually fail to mask their behavior. They froth at the mouth or hobble around. . . . I can't explain it. They just look uncomfortable in their skin," she said, and then shrugged. "We know what to look for, and when we see it, we close in."

"And have you ever made a mistake?" he asked. "Have you ever attacked what you thought was a demon but was really just a hobbling, frothing-at-the-mouth human?"

"There is no room for mistakes. If any Alliance harmed an innocent human, we would turn ourselves over to the Directorate for punishment."

The noble thing to do, Grayson thought. Unlike him, who'd ripped apart a girl, apparently with his teeth, and had been running ever since. He hadn't even known her name. If Chelle knew what he'd done . . . He let out a joyless laugh.

"What is so funny?" Chelle asked.

Grayson's next step faltered. His hands, tucked deep into his trouser pockets, balled into fists as an odor wafted under his nose. It was smoky and sweet, and he shivered uncontrollably.

"Grayson?" Chelle stopped. "What is it?"

Walking had relieved the soreness of his muscles and bones, but now they seized again, the pain immediate and fierce. The scent grew stronger, and with an awareness rushing up his spine, Grayson understood what it was.

"Hellhound," he rasped. His muscles had coiled so tightly he could barely breathe.

Chelle's hand flew to her sash. She pulled out a throwing star and crouched into a defensive position. Her nose wrinkled as if she'd just smelled the inside of a latrine.

A shadow moved up ahead. Two red eyes flickered and flared, as if someone had just run a lit match over wicks. The hellhound slinked toward them, its greasy, shaggy fur taking shape out of the darkness.

"Stay back," Chelle said. Grayson didn't know if the order was for him or the hellhound. He couldn't have moved even if he'd wanted to. Every bone in his body, from his tibias to his skull, stretched and pulled until he was certain they would all splinter into dust, leaving him a writhing mass of burning skin and muscle. He doubled over and ground his teeth.

"Grayson!" Chelle's cry of alarm brought his head up.

The hellhound was in front of him. Their eyes did more than just meet. The circles of fire latched on to Grayson's eyes and dug in; they made him focus. They seemed to pull everything that was inside of him forward, away from his quivering body.

For a moment the pain was gone. And with one shattering quake, Grayson was gone, too.

CHAPTER FOURTEEN

Ingrid sipped her punch in the corner of an apartment on rue Bonaparte. The place was stifling. At least two dozen people milled about in shuffling half steps throughout a scant three-room apartment. The walls were covered from ceiling to baseboard with oil paintings, some canvases still fresh. It was all enough to make Ingrid's temples throb. She lifted her cup to her lips again and accidentally elbowed an older gentleman who had sidled up beside her. He grinned forgivingly before saying, "It speaks of my youth." He nodded toward the canvas that hung in front of them both.

Ingrid hadn't yet looked up at the oil painting, and when she did, she wished she hadn't. It showed a woman at the beach. She was taking tentative steps into frothy seawater. And she was nude. How on earth could *this* remind him of his youth? Ingrid smiled dumbly and fluttered her lashes. Appearing dimwitted was but a small sacrifice to avoid the man's attempt to discuss the artist's oeuvre, which seemed to focus on the nude female body.

Ingrid knew it was art. She knew better than to blush and appear scandalized. But if she had to look at one more dimpled buttock or fleshy thigh, she thought she might chuck her punch at the nearest canvas.

The man moved away a moment later, and Gabby slid into his place.

"Dreadful," she whispered.

"How many interpretations of a woman's rump must we be subjected to?" Ingrid whispered back.

Meeting artists had to be one of the most tedious elements of preparing for her mother's gallery debut. This was the third such salon this month, and while Gabby and Mama seemed to enjoy them, Ingrid wished to be anywhere else. None of it felt real anymore. Whenever she was out, she couldn't stop herself from glancing around and noting that, most likely, no one else present had demon blood in them. They didn't know about Luc's kind or the Alliance or the Angelic Order. She held these secrets with a kind of reverence, and the weight of them felt more real and significant than any salon or social gathering could possibly be.

"We certainly have an endless bounty of bare rumps here to admire," Gabby murmured into her punch before taking a sip. Her thick, dark plum veil hung diagonally across her face, as did the veils on all of her hats, exposing just one of her smoky quartz eyes, fringed by dark lashes.

Ingrid had heard all about what happened during the visit to the surgeon, including Gabby's foray into the morgue, Nolan's drawing the blood of a dead Duster, and Gabby's successful slaying of a corpse demon. Gabby had only wanted to discuss those things; Ingrid's mind, however, had stuck to how thoughtless their father had been.

Gabby's scars weren't small, but they weren't grotesque, either. The hellhound's claws had carved three deep curving lines into her cheek, but Benoit's stitches had been neat.

Gabby had feigned indifference about the visit to the surgeon, but Ingrid had seen her sister hurt and humiliated before. She always blinked rapidly and shrugged too much. And that was when Ingrid had noticed something was wrong with Gabby's shoulder.

"Is your wound better?" Ingrid asked.

Gabby lowered her glass. "Practically healed. I know the Alliance looks down on it, but Luc's blood works miracles." She eyed Ingrid cautiously. "Speaking of Alliance . . . have you heard anything more about Vander's leaky fingers?"

Ingrid still couldn't shake off the feeling of the viscous webbing: the itchy, sticky pull of the silk as it clung to her skin. Or how it had looked streaming from Vander's fingertips. Constantine had demanded that Vander come to Clos du Vie for Ingrid's next lesson. He required time to scour his books for a reason why Vander would have taken on Léon's arachnae ability, if only to a minimal degree.

"I'll see him tomorrow," Ingrid answered. "Let's get some air."

She pulled her sister toward a pair of open doors that led to a narrow terrace. There was barely enough room for the two of them to stand side by side, but they could at least revel in the cold night air. Unfortunately, they couldn't quite escape the crowd.

A man approached their balcony hideaway. He was middle-aged, with faint lines branching out around his eyes when he smiled at them. And he apparently knew they weren't French.

"Good evening," he said with a small bow.

"And to you," Ingrid returned politely. He wore a crisp black suit with delicate stripes of gray.

"Are you an admirer of the artist?" Gabby asked with false enthusiasm.

"I am not." He fastened his attention on Ingrid, his eyes so intense they practically shoved her. "You are Lady Ingrid Waverly of l'Abbaye Saint-Dismas."

Ingrid blinked. She fought the urge to back up a step—not that she could go very far. "And you are?"

The man dipped into a bow so deep his forehead nearly reached his kneecaps.

"I am Robert Dupuis, Daicrypta doyen and primary research facilitator."

This time Ingrid did step back. She dragged Gabby by the elbow, too, until they were fully outdoors on the two-foot-wide terrace. Dupuis laughed.

"I see André has told you about me, mademoiselle."

"André?" Ingrid repeated.

"Monsieur Constantine," Dupuis answered with a second roll of laughter. "Of course he would not have shared his given name with you. Far too informal for him, I suppose."

Gabby's eyes narrowed to wrathful slits. "You're the one who wants to drain my sister's blood?"

"Not all of it, my dear," he said, keeping his previous humor.

"You aren't getting one drop!" Gabby shouted.

Ingrid clamped her fingers around Gabby's arm. Now was not the time for her fire. If Luc felt her swirling temper and Ingrid's alarm, he'd abandon the carriage and horses below and be on the terrace railing within seconds.

"Monsieur Dupuis, why have you followed me here?" This was no chance meeting.

"I do not come on an errand of malice," he answered. "I am concerned for your safety and for the safety of those you hold dear. I trust you have heard of the two families murdered this week?"

"I know they were killed by Dusters, yes," Ingrid said. Her initial alarm was quickly dissolving. This man couldn't harm her, and not just because Luc was so close. Dupuis couldn't touch her unless Constantine handed her over or she gave herself to the Daicrypta.

"Those who are infected with demon blood are at great risk," he said.

"As are those put under your knife," she returned.

The humor left his expression. "André Constantine has been gone from the Daicrypta many years, Lady Ingrid. Our research has vastly improved, as have our technologies. You need not fear me."

She didn't fear him. Their being alone on the terrace without the shadow of Luc's wings was proof of it.

"The doyens and disciples of the Daicrypta know of the fallen angel, Axia, and her desires for your blood. *Her* blood, I might say," he said. "If you allow it, I can remove that temptation for her."

"By taking my blood," Ingrid clarified. She felt Gabby tense at her side.

Dupuis shook his head. "By cleansing it."

This gave Ingrid pause. He sounded so sure of himself and this procedure of his. What if he was right? It wasn't as if the angel blood were doing anything inside her anyway. It kept her unusually healthy, yes, and she had been able to command a handful of Dispossessed, including Luc, a couple of times. But she didn't need Axia's blood.

"And my demon blood," she said. "You would take that as well?"

She didn't need lectrux blood any more than she needed angel blood. What might it feel like to be normal?

Dupuis bowed. "If you wish."

Ingrid clasped her hands behind her back, fingers woven tightly together. Constantine knew only the Daicrypta's past failures. What if there had been recent successes?

"Has a Duster named Léon come to you yet?" Ingrid asked. Dupuis lifted his chin sharply.

"No."

She didn't know what it was about that brief answer that rang so false, but she didn't trust him.

"My sister won't be coming to you, or to your bloodletting

carnival, either," Gabby said. "All of her blood will be staying right where it belongs, thank you very much."

Dupuis waited, expecting something more from Ingrid. She stayed quiet, letting Gabby's response be hers.

He shrugged. "You will come to me in the end."

He fell into another deep bow and then folded back into the crowd. Ingrid stayed on the terrace. She leaned over the curved iron railing, peering three stories below to the street, and saw the black tops of carriages, an aerial view of waiting horses, but no Luc. She'd expected him to be on the curb, eyes turned up toward their terrace.

"Ingrid?" Gabby touched her arm. "Please tell me you aren't considering that man's offer."

Ingrid lifted her eyes and met her sister's exacting glare.

"Never," Ingrid answered. "I promise."

The lie slipped out like oil. It left a greasy feel in Ingrid's stomach, too.

Grayson knew he was in trouble when the hellhound's growls came through as words. No. That wasn't the right way to explain it. The growls coming from the demon hound still sounded like rocks being ground between two stone wheels, but Grayson could understand what they meant.

He had shifted. Fully and completely, there was no mistaking it. No denying the truth. Grayson looked down at what had once been his hands and saw in their place a pair of bulky, sharp-clawed paws planted in the slushy pavement of the back alley. His arms had lengthened until the cuffs of his coat had been brought up tight around his elbow joints. Exposed was the thick pale yellow fur that had enveloped his body. He felt more fur rubbing uncomfortably beneath the clothing he wore, like an unwanted skin. But he was still human. He still thought like one.

Mistress will be pleased.

The notion chimed through Grayson's head, and he knew it had come from the other hellhound stalking a slow circle around him. *Mistress.* Axia.

"She is not my mistress," Grayson tried to say. It came out an abrasive snarl.

Behind him, a startled cry squeaked from Chelle's throat. He turned sharply to peer at her. She had both *hira-shuriken* in her hands, ready for flight.

"Grayson?" Chelle's voice quavered. He smelled it then, stronger and more potent than it had been before. Her blood. It sluiced through her, fast, hot, and fragrant.

The other hellhound groaned. It knew Chelle was frightened, and that made it joyous. Grayson felt its ravening thirst mirrored within him—and then, in an instant, he remembered.

The fog that had cloaked his memory was gone, and he recalled everything that had happened in that back alley in London: The girl's gargling screams, drowned by her own blood as Grayson's fangs ripped into her jugular. Her fingernails digging into his face and shoulders but slipping through thick, greasy fur without purchase. And here he found himself in another dark alley with another girl.

Join me. Mistress desires it.

Grayson knew that the hellhound had been commanded to rip into Chelle—and that Axia wanted Grayson to take part.

He swallowed the spate of saliva that had pooled in his mouth, and closed his eyes. His body felt right. Utterly right. The new state of his muscles and bones was pure relief. He'd been fighting them, denying them the change for too long. But the other hellhound's lusts, throbbing through Grayson like a tremor, weren't right. They were base and cruel, and he didn't give a damn what Axia desired.

"Stop," Grayson said, stunned once again to hear his voice roll out as such an inhuman growl.

The hellhound turned its flaming eyes toward him. It wanted

to know why. Behind him, Chelle's boots scuffed nervously along the pavement. Grayson looked and saw that the fear had gone out of her eyes. She was ready to fight. The hellhound must have sensed it, too, because it abandoned its focus on Grayson and darted forward, straight for Chelle.

On all fours, Grayson surged to intercept it. He moved faster than he'd thought possible, skidding to a stumbling halt in front of the hound. It weighed at least three stone more than he did and had the powerful flanks of a Belgian horse. *It* was the demon, not Grayson, but he didn't stop to think about what the hellhound could do to him. He lowered his head, keeping his eyes firmly on the hound.

He didn't need to say anything. If he could sense this hound's wants, then it should be able to sense his. He would not allow it to attack Chelle. He moved toward the hound, his shoulders pressed into a flat, taut plane. If this beast came at him, so be it. He'd go down fighting, and Chelle might have enough time to run away.

Grayson felt the slap of wind just seconds before a gargoyle landed on the pavement beside him. Luc screeched at the opposing hellhound, one of his great black wings coming down protectively in front of Grayson's transformed figure. Grayson knew Luc was only doing his duty, but it still pricked his pride. He could do this himself.

Grayson sidestepped the tip of Luc's wing and advanced another few paces, receiving a warning screech from Luc in the process. The other hellhound's growl faltered, then broke into a thin whine. The beast dropped low to the pavement, even lower than Grayson stood, and shambled backward. It had curled its great tail and tucked it between its legs. Was it submitting to him? Or to Luc? Grayson took another assertive lunge to be sure. With a final whine of dismay, the hound pivoted and disappeared into the shadowed turn behind a building.

And then Grayson was empty, the hellhound's intrusive

presence inside him lost. He let his shoulders sag, his rugged form suddenly too heavy to bear. How had he done it? That hellhound could have ripped him to shreds. And yet it had fled the moment Grayson had opposed it.

He collapsed to the pavement, hearing Chelle timidly call his name. He could still smell her blood, but its ripe fragrance was fading. He shivered as the sensation of a hundred fingers plucking at his skin, pinching and pulling and twisting, overtook him. He was going back to normal, and it felt like trying to stuff a foot into a shoe two sizes too small. He wasn't going to fit back into his human form. How could he, when there had been such relief within this one?

"Grayson?" Chelle said again.

He lay still on the pavement, the wet snow melting through his clothes and chilling his skin.

The fur. It had disappeared. He had skin again, and as he ran his tongue over his teeth, he felt blunt canines instead of wicked fangs.

The two buildings lining the alley loomed over him, a strip of night sky between. Luc's wings and long, dragonlike tail cut into view, sailing up, over the edge of the building, and out of sight. Luc had come—but Grayson hadn't needed him.

Chelle's pale face hovered into view, as did her razor-edged *hira-shuriken*.

"I won't hurt you," Grayson said, and though it was hoarse, it was his own voice.

She held still, eyelashes fluttering in consideration. She then sheathed her weapons and reached one of her gloved hands toward Grayson.

"How many times has this happened?" she asked once he'd stumbled to his feet. He was still shaking, and it made him feel like a palsy old drunkard.

"It hasn't. Although . . . I think I've wanted to."

His stomach churned. God, he wouldn't be sick here, in front of Chelle. She'd just watched him become a monster, and now he stood in front of her with his clothes split at the seams in places; she didn't need to see him vomit, too.

"When have you wanted to?" she asked.

Grayson closed his arms around himself, trying to still his shaking. "Whenever I'm angry." He forced himself to meet her gaze. "Whenever I smell blood. Which is . . . well, it's pretty much all the time."

Chelle dropped her gaze and played nervously with the brim of her cap.

"I don't want to hurt anyone," Grayson said, wishing she'd look up at him again. She had to believe what he said. "I won't hurt you, Chelle."

She gave him what he wanted and met his stare. He wanted to promise her, wanted to ask her whether she trusted him enough to believe him. But there was no need. The way she looked at him, chin hiked, eyes softer than Grayson had yet seen, was her answer.

"I know, Grayson," she said, taking him by the arm and leading him back toward the alley entrance. "I know."

CHAPTER FIFTEEN

It was cold inside the landau, the sun not having risen high enough in the morning sky to warm it. In London, it would have been fodder for the scandal sheets for Ingrid to be out just after dawn without a chaperone. But here in Paris, the rules of the game had all changed. The only person who would have made a scene was her father.

He thought her still asleep in bed at the rectory; Mama had made sure of that. Her mother had shocked her less than an hour before when she'd entered her room and woken her with a shake. It was Monday. The day Ingrid normally visited Clos du Vie. "You must go now," her mother had whispered. "Before your father wakes."

Ingrid had been in a fog while dressing herself in the dark, her maid not yet up to assist. Her mother's help was as foreign as it was thrilling. Lady Brickton had never interfered with Ingrid's visits to Constantine. She knew what Ingrid was supposed to be learning, and though she never requested details, every now and again, Lady Brickton would pleasantly inquire how her lessons were progressing. But until that morning when she'd hustled Ingrid out of the house, she had never acknowledged her daughter's *need* for them.

Luc had been waiting with the landau on the curb, just beyond the hedgerow. And now here they were, parked outside a shopping arcade, killing time while the sun rose. It was far too early to call on Clos du Vie yet.

"I didn't think my mother understood," she said to Luc, who sat awkwardly on the bench seat across from her. She'd made him come in, out of the drifting snow and bone-cold weather.

"He'll be furious when you return," he replied. He was right. There would be the devil to pay, but perhaps Mama might have some excuse planned. Ingrid hoped so. She wouldn't worry about that just yet.

After a minute or two of silence, Ingrid started to wonder if she should have heeded Luc's protestations about staying out on the driver's bench. Each time she dared lift her eyes, he would shift his gaze to the floor, or the seat cushion, or the window. Ingrid was aware of him, of his every breath, the slide of his foot over the carriage floor, the way he tugged at his collar as if it were choking him.

"Vander Burke is going to be a reverend?" he said, breaking the silence.

The mention of Vander's name suddenly made the carriage feel crowded.

"He wants to become ordained, yes," she answered. "Why do you ask?"

Luc sat up taller. "It just seems like an odd choice for someone who's always been so willing to work with the Dispossessed."

"Why should his becoming a reverend change that?" Ingrid asked. As far as she knew, Vander had no intention of quitting the Alliance. In fact, he'd said an Alliance reverend could be useful. The old reverend at the American Church had been blessing their silver weaponry for decades. When he died, Vander could take over the task.

Luc held her gaze. "You don't know, do you?"

Ingrid frowned. At her confusion, Luc added, "Why we're gargoyles? What we did to be cast into the Dispossessed?"

It was her turn to shift uncomfortably on the bench.

"I had wondered, but . . ." But she hadn't had the courage to ask. Not just Luc. She knew she could have asked Vander or Constantine. Even Gabby would have known.

Whatever it was, it had to be awful—an unforgivable sin. She had considered what it might have been time and again but hadn't made any move to learn it explicitly. Knowing Luc's sin might change the way she saw him. The way she thought of him.

She was being a coward.

Luc looked away from her, confessing to the window instead. "We're all murderers, Ingrid."

She forgot the cold seeping in at the tips of her suede boots.

"Priests. Reverends. Any man of the cloth. We all took a holy life in cold blood, and in doing so gave up our eternal souls, along with any chance of entering heaven."

He turned from the window to see how his confession had landed. Ingrid hoped she didn't look as shocked as she felt.

"Why did you do it?" she whispered.

He didn't hesitate to answer. "Vengeance."

"For what?"

Now he hesitated. His eyes clouded over and went distant. He was somewhere else, remembering, and she could read his expression well enough to know he didn't want to be there. Luc didn't want to talk about what he'd done, and she was willing to bet that he hadn't done so for a very long time. Perhaps never.

"Did a priest do something to you?" she asked, then bumbled, "Or perhaps a reverend, or—"

"To my sister," he said, voice low and dangerous. "Suzette."

He said her name with unexpected gentleness. He'd loved her.

"What happened?" Ingrid asked.

The distance in Luc's eyes closed, and he was back with her in the carriage. He stared at Ingrid, unflinching. He was going to tell her, and he wasn't going to look away until he'd finished confessing.

"He was the priest at our church. I liked him. My family trusted him. And Suzette . . . he seduced her. Got her with child. When my father turned her out, the bastard wouldn't take her in. He denied everything. Said the babe inside her wasn't his."

Ingrid listened, rapt. She wanted to move to the bench beside Luc but held still. Any movement and he might startle like a bird and fly away from her.

"I didn't get to her in time. She drowned herself in the Seine." His voice had gone thick.

"So I killed him." The spell broke and he averted his eyes. "I was in a fury. I wasn't careful."

She wanted him to look up at her again, but he wouldn't.

"They hanged me at Montfaucon in front of a crowd, every last one of them believing I'd murdered an innocent priest."

Luc huffed a laugh, but Ingrid felt sick. She could see it all. Luc, standing at a gallows with his hands bound behind his back, a noose around his neck. A jeering crowd the last thing he saw before a suffocating black hood was thrown over his head. And then the fall. The snap of his neck.

"I didn't repent then, and I still don't," he said.

Ingrid no longer just felt sick. She worried she might actually *be* sick. "I'm sorry, I need some air," she said, her hand clasped lightly at her throat. "I'm fine. You needn't come with me." She scrambled forward and shoved open the carriage door. The steps were already lowered and she took them, fast.

She headed straight for the arcade entrance, a pair of glass doors under a fanned-out awning of iron and glass. To her relief, the doors were open, and she hurried inside.

He had died.

Of course, she'd known Luc had died and that he'd been young, but . . . she hadn't been prepared to learn *how*. That he had been executed.

The arcade's main doors swung closed behind her. She slowed, the tap of her heels echoing along the long, empty corridor. The shopping arcade was an indoor plaza, with storefronts on either side of a wide corridor, topped by a glass roof. The stores weren't open yet, and Ingrid hoped she wouldn't come upon any vagrants taking shelter. Though she supposed that was what she was doing, in a way.

Ingrid started for the stone fountain up ahead. Here, in the warmth of the greenhouse-like building, water burbled from the fountain. There were benches nearby. She needed to sit and get the wretched image of Luc swinging from a gallows out of her mind.

She walked along the marble-floored corridor, passing over a short stretch of glass and iron that was in fact the roof of an underground arcade directly below. Little stretches of glass-and-iron bridges allowed the sunlight down to the subterranean arcade where Ingrid and Gabby had once shopped for hats and gloves.

She had nearly reached the benches when something moved near the tip of the fountain's spout. The fountain was a basic tiered design with three bowls, the smallest at the top and the widest at the bottom. Water overflowed at each bowl's rim, creating a cascade into the basin. Ingrid stopped walking and stared at the falling water. There was something moving through it, dropping from one bowl to the next. It looked like a white braided rope, thicker even than rope used to moor ships. But it wasn't rope.

It slinked from the widest bowl into the main basin and then up over the lip of the fountain edge. Ingrid froze.

Axia's serpent.

The snake's diamond-shaped eyes fixed on Ingrid, its pale scales glistening and wet. Ingrid had nearly forgotten about the serpent and the way it had darted out from Axia's robes to attack Ingrid when she'd been in the Underneath.

Axia couldn't leave the demon realm, but her serpent clearly could. And it had come to fetch Ingrid.

The front doorbell rang its grating trill throughout the rectory, and Gabby slouched with relief. The breakfast table had become a war zone. The opposing armies were her parents, and Gabby had somehow become the innocent citizen caught in the cross fire.

"I don't see the scandal in French lessons," her mother said to Gabby, though her words were directed at her father. Lord Brickton sat at the opposite end of the table, the skin around his club collar mottled purple.

"Sending her off at the crack of dawn, without a chaperone and to a man's home, isn't scandalous?" he roared at Gabby, refusing to meet his wife's eyes.

Gabby stared into her tea, which was far too milky, but her arm had jumped when her father had shouted earlier and she'd spilled in more than she preferred. Grayson had been smart enough not to come down to the dining room. The weasel had probably sneaked out altogether.

Their butler, Gustav, entered the dining room, his hands clasped behind his back. "My lord, my lady. Monsieur Quinn to see you."

Gabby startled again, and this time a splash of tea crested the lip of her cup and sloshed onto her saucer. She sat with her back to the foyer entrance and heard Nolan's footsteps as he entered. What on earth was he doing here? It was far too early to call, and Gabby hadn't even pinned on one of her veiled hats yet. She resisted turning to face him.

"Detective Quinn, what a surprise," Lady Brickton said, addressing him as she had in December when Nolan had pretended to be a detective searching for Grayson.

Her mother knew the truth now, of course, and her greeting had sounded cool.

"I apologize for arriving at such an early hour, my lady," Nolan said. His voice set off an unexpected craving inside Gabby. As much as he vexed her, Nolan also had a way of making Gabby want more of him.

"I haven't had the pleasure," her father said from his chair. He peered at Nolan, who had moved almost directly behind Gabby. She was disturbingly aware of him, and it brought a most unwanted flush to her cheeks.

Her mother introduced Nolan, and when she explained that he was the detective who had helped her search for Grayson, humiliation hung on her every word. Her husband had thought her a fool for making such a fuss of their son's disappearance, and it was clear that having to thus play the fool wounded Lady Brickton's pride to no end.

"And Lord Fairfax is well?" Nolan inquired, using Grayson's title with astounding propriety. No doubt he wanted to roll his eyes.

"As well as he'll ever be," Gabby's father answered, making little attempt to mask the disdain he felt for his own son. If he felt this way about Grayson now, Gabby didn't want to imagine how it would be should he learn about his son's demon half.

"I apologize if my wife had you mucking about Paris trying to find the boy."

Her brother straightened her back and leveled her chin. It

was only a matter of time before she burst. Gabby didn't wish to be there when it happened.

"No apology is necessary. She did nothing wrong. Any decent parent would have taken the same course of action," Nolan replied.

The room fell silent and Gabby's jaw went slack. Even the footman in the corner of the dining room raised his eyebrows at Nolan's cutting insult. No one spoke to her father that way. Before she knew what she was doing, Gabby shifted slightly in her seat and peered up at him in awe. He and Lord Brickton had become locked in an arctic glare.

"I wanted to deliver an invitation to you personally, rather than through a messenger," Nolan went on, as if he'd said nothing at all. "My father and I would like to request the pleasure of your family's company at our home, Hôtel Bastian, tomorrow evening for dinner."

Had Gabby been eating, she would have choked. Nolan must have gone utterly mad. He wanted her *father* at Alliance headquarters? Gabby's mother seemed to be having the same concerns. Her lips twitched as she started, then stopped, and then started once more to respond.

"Oh, why . . . of course, that would be marvelous. Indeed, we shall come."

Lord Brickton said nothing but continued to stew in his chair.

"Excellent," Nolan said, at long last meeting Gabby's eyes. "I know it's early, but would you care for a stroll around the churchyard, Miss Waverly?"

His smooth manners unsettled her—she much preferred the improper Nolan Quinn who called her *lass* and winked devilishly at her. Gabby folded her napkin and set it on the table, avoiding her father's eyes, which were no doubt simmering with displeasure. She stood up, half wishing her father would bluster and refuse to allow her to leave. Once she was alone with Nolan, she'd have to explain how she'd destroyed the carcass demon. But then, staying with her parents at the breakfast table wasn't a much better prospect.

Gabby and Nolan left without hearing a word of objection. They stopped in the foyer to gather her cloak and gloves, but all of her hats were up in her room. She felt exposed as they walked outside onto the thin layer of crusty snow covering the drive. Nolan kept an arm's length between them. He was silent, and when Gabby ventured a peek, she saw that his eyes were fastened on the abbey, his lips drawn into a taut line.

He was angry.

They were nearly to the transept doors when Nolan finally said, "It was Chelle, wasn't it?"

It wasn't worth the effort it would take to feign ignorance. Gabby nodded. "You don't know what it was like, sitting around the rectory waiting, doing nothing. I'd catch a glimpse of myself in a mirror, see my face, and remember that hound . . . how powerless I was." Gabby stopped at the doors while Nolan reached for the handles. "Don't be angry with Chelle. I practically begged her to start training me."

"I'm not upset with her." Nolan gestured for Gabby to enter.

They weren't alone in the eastern transept. A pair of workers were crouched along the aisle, scrubbing the white marble frescoes that had gone brown and yellow with age and neglect. They spared Nolan and Gabby a single glance before setting back to the delicate work of cleansing the carved robes of the portrayed saints.

"But you're angry with me," she whispered as they walked toward the pulpit.

Nolan didn't reply. He took her by the arm and led her toward the ambulatory. Pink marble columns lined this rounded end of the abbey, creating a walkway past numerous small alcove chapels dedicated to individual saints. Nolan continued to lead Gabby deeper into the sanctuary, behind the freshly varnished choir stalls. The columns rushed past them, and Gabby's slippers hit the tiles with echoing slaps. Finally, he jerked her to a stop underneath the great rose window, took her by the shoulders, and dragged her behind a column.

And then he kissed her.

It wasn't a soft kiss, either. He backed Gabby up against the column and pinned her there, his lips hard against hers. She opened her mouth and he stole inside with a husky groan of satisfaction. Gabby tried to free her arms, longing to wind them around his neck, run her fingers through his black curls. But he held them firmly at her side.

"You're not angry?" she gasped when he pulled away for a breath of air.

"Furious." He kissed her again. Nolan released her arms and curled his own around her hips, pulling her away from the column and against him.

"You don't seem furious," she whispered, eyes closed, a smile tugging at her throbbing lips.

He held her so closely that the rumble of laughter in his chest passed to hers. "All right. I'm jealous. I wanted to be the one to train you."

Gabby opened her eyes. The unexpected kiss had plunged her into a swirly kind of fog.

"But you can't," she said, an edge of sadness intruding. "Because your father won't allow me to join the Alliance." She closed her eyes. "And now I'm to dine with him so he can whisper enticing persuasions to Ingrid and Grayson so that *they'll* join and wield their demon gifts for the greater good."

Nolan leaned his forehead against hers and sighed. "My da's decision is final, so no, lass, you can't join the Alliance. Not yet." He rubbed his nose against the tip of hers. "But that doesn't mean you can't keep learning how to fight. If it's done between us, in private, there's no reason anyone else has to know."

Gabby liked how that sounded. She brought her mouth to

his, kissing him first this time. She felt Nolan's lips stretch into a smile. He captured her bottom lip with a soft nip of his teeth.

"Do you have anything you wish to confess?" he murmured.

Gabby drew back, confused by his question. She followed his gaze to an old, worn confessional tucked back in the closest alcove chapel. The two connected wooden booths, one for the priest and the other for the sinner, still had their solid doors attached.

Nolan snaked his arm around Gabby's waist and stepped up onto the raised floor of the alcove chapel.

"You're wicked," she whispered. "May I remind you that we are in a house of the Lord?"

Nolan continued toward the confessional, pulling her with him. "And how hospitable of him. Look, he's provided us a room of our very own."

He reached for the small knob on the confessional door and twisted. It swung open with a groan of its rusted hinges.

Gabby peered into the dark booth. There was a small wooden seat inside, and a carved iron grate set in the wall. She thought of all the sins whispered through that latticed ironwork. She rose onto her toes and kissed Nolan, loving the feel of him. How he gathered her against him in that stubborn, unyielding way of his. What she felt for him wasn't a sin.

"If you'll remain a gentleman?" she asked.

Nolan swiveled on his heels and twirled her into the shadowy booth. He stepped inside the small space with her, their bodies forced even closer together. "Define *gentleman*," he said, his breath already hot against her neck.

She giggled, feeling somewhat relieved when he left the confessional door open partway.

If she could, she'd stay tucked away like this all day. Just her and Nolan, kissing. But she'd soon be missed. If not by her mother, who kept busy most days with her gallery plans, then definitely by her father, who seemed far more idle than he ever had in London.

"I can't," she said. Nolan froze. Pulled back.

"You know me, Gabby. Of course I promise to be a gentleman," he said, brow furrowed in earnest.

She laughed. "Not that. My training. It's too difficult. My father watches me constantly, and if I keep sneaking out at night, I'm bound to get caught."

Nolan loosened his arms from her waist. He probably hadn't considered Gabby's constraints. He'd never had them himself, she gathered. His father had raised him within the Alliance, after all. She bet he'd never even had a curfew.

"Then I'll come to you," he answered.

"But how?"

"You won't have to sneak out at night. I'll sneak in," he said. "We can practice in your room at the rectory."

"Don't be absurd—you can't come to my room in the middle of the night!"

He formed a slow, arrogant smile and began to reel her back in, closer to him. "You don't want me there?"

The confessional booth was growing warmer by the second. "I—" She sealed her lips. She shouldn't say yes, but of course she wanted him there. *To train,* she scolded herself.

"My room is on the upper floor. How will you get in?"

"I'll fly him up."

Nolan and Gabby tore out of their embrace and turned toward the booth's open door. Dimitrie stepped into the alcove chapel and stood just outside the confessional. How long had he been watching them? Gabby flushed.

"My lady," Dimitrie greeted her. "I can bring him to your window."

As she and Nolan spilled out of the confessional, Gabby tried to imagine Dimitrie's scrawny frame lifting Nolan's muscled one.

Of course, Dimitrie's body in true form was a different thing altogether.

"Why would you do that?" she asked. Luc would never have offered to help.

Dimitrie shrugged. "Any human willing to fight demons is an asset to the Dispossessed."

Gabby wanted to smile and say thank you, but she couldn't stop remembering his pale back and the scars running the length of it like the ridges of a metal washboard. Nolan had called Dimitrie useless, but he wasn't. He'd saved her from that appendius and had swallowed his pride by taking her to Hôtel Bastian for mercurite.

"All right," Nolan said. "I'll come to the carriage house tomorrow night, after midnight."

"Thank you," Gabby said quickly. Dimitrie bowed. He was so much more gracious than Luc. It was a bit disarming.

Nolan called after Dimitrie as he stepped down out of the alcove chapel. "One more thing. Can you trace Grayson for me? I'd like to speak to him."

Dimitrie stilled. His fingers tensed into fists. He kept his back to Nolan, his head bowed forward. When he answered, it was through gritted teeth.

"I prefer not to use my abilities to please the whims of humans."

He strode away without a look back at Nolan or Gabby. She immediately took back every kind thought she'd just had for the gargoyle.

"He's a bit touchy," Nolan muttered.

"He could have easily told you," Gabby said.

Dimitrie's refusal to trace Grayson didn't make any sense, especially since he'd practically begged to fly Nolan up to Gabby's window, as if facilitating some preternatural rendition of *Romeo and Juliet.*

"Never mind." Nolan took Gabby's wrist in hand and persuaded her back to his side. She liked it there, and promptly forgot Dimitrie.

"If I'm going to be coming to your room, I suppose we won't need this relic," Nolan said, kicking the confessional door closed with his foot.

Gabby jabbed a finger into his chest. "We'll be training, not kissing."

He nodded and sputtered promises of good behavior. Gabby didn't believe him for a second.

"Why did you want to see Grayson?" she asked.

Nolan ran his thumb across the tender underside of Gabby's wrist. "He hasn't told you?"

"He doesn't talk much lately," Gabby said with a weary laugh. The sound caught in her throat as Nolan's thumb coursed over her wrist again. "What happened?"

"He shifted into a hellhound last night," Nolan answered with stark brevity. Gabby pulled her wrist away and stared, disbelieving.

"Chelle saw the whole thing. She said it wasn't like before," he went on. "He was a real hellhound. Smaller than most, but—he didn't look human at all."

"But it doesn't make sense. Why would he shift fully? He hasn't been in the Underneath, like last time."

Nolan and Vander had determined that Axia must have done something to him there. Given him some sort of poison to make him shift. That was why his body had come out of the Underneath riddled with bite marks.

"I don't know," Nolan said. "But, Gabby, for now, it might be best if you kept your distance."

She huffed, waving off his concern. "He's my brother. He isn't going to harm me."

"No doubt you'd put him in a hospital bed should he attempt to," Nolan said as he cupped her cheek, her puffy scars against his palm.

Gabby flinched.

"Just be careful around him," Nolan pressed. "And tell Ingrid as well."

He kissed the tip of her nose before stealing back down the ambulatory, toward the transept. Kissing in a church. In a confessional booth! Gabby should have felt sinful. Instead, the only thing clenching in her stomach was dread. How was she supposed to tell Ingrid that Grayson had fully shifted? That their brother had become even less human than before?

CHAPTER SIXTEEN

Ingrid backed away from the fountain. The arcade entrance wasn't far, perhaps fifty yards. She could make it if the serpent kept its sluggish pace.

Luc. She stole a glance over her shoulder. He wasn't there, coming for her in full battle regalia. And the glass doors seemed farther away than she remembered.

Ingrid's soles scuffed over the marble, a rush of desperation making her clumsy. Luc would come. Any moment he would swoop overhead, his wings like black pennants. There were no other humans here to witness him. But a second passed, and then another, and a fast look showed Axia's pale serpent now gliding over the marble tiles, its shining scales leaving a track of fountain water in its wake.

Where was Luc?

Ingrid hated that she needed him so desperately. The first moment of fear and here she was, wishing for him to fly to her rescue. She'd started going to Constantine so she could learn to defend herself. She had the power. She'd defeated this serpent before, too, sending spikes of lightning through its boneless coils.

All she had to do was face it. Let Axia's pet come at her. Her body would react, her lectrux blood would boil and surge all on its own, and she could *make* the lightning.

Ingrid slid to an abrupt stop on the glass-and-iron floor she'd just crossed a few minutes before. It was a gamble. She tried to imagine the sparks lighting at her shoulders, tried to feel the numbing current coming down her arms. She *needed* to feel it.

"Don't fail me," she whispered, and then spun on her heel to face the serpent.

But the demon was gone.

She let out a shallow breath and searched the corridor, eyes wild. A creature of that length and mass shouldn't have been able to hide very well.

Ingrid let her shoulders drop, the urge to run overwhelming. It wasn't gone. The thing was still here. She could feel it.

She took a step toward the entrance, but a strange squelching, like a sweaty palm dragging along a pane of glass, stopped her again. The sound resonated in her gums and made her cringe. It was coming from beneath her.

She lowered her gaze slowly, but she wasn't prepared for what she saw.

Axia's serpent was on the underside of the glass-and-iron floor, directly beneath her feet, stuck to the glass like a leech. How it had gotten into the underground arcade and maneuvered its way onto the stretch of ceiling wasn't something Ingrid had to worry about for very long. Because at that moment the tip of the serpent's tail reared back and smashed against the glass. Ingrid threw out her arms for balance as the floor shook—and then cracked.

She sucked in a breath as the fissure in the glass carved a path between her feet, branching out in fits and bursts like the overflow of a flooded river.

The serpent rubbed at the glass as it peeled free, curling down toward the strip of white marble floor that ran between the underground shops at least three stories below. Ingrid held still, her muscles seizing. If she shifted her weight, the weakened glass would shatter. Her lightning wouldn't save her then. She needed Luc.

Where *was* he?

As the serpent hit the floor below, it coiled its body into a stack of thick corkscrew rounds. The pale scales flashed to gray, then black. And then the coils were gone. The *serpent* was gone.

Axia stood in the corridor below, her cloaked and hooded figure just as Ingrid remembered it. The fallen angel's head tilted up until Ingrid was staring into the black cavern of her hood.

But it couldn't be Axia. She couldn't walk the earth, not without first taking back her blood from Ingrid. If this wasn't Axia . . .

It uses your memories, down to the last detail. Luc's words. First Anna, then Jonathan.

It was the mimic demon, using her memories of Axia. Her fear. Leading her like a lamb to slaughter.

The floor bowed under her feet and Ingrid yelped. A black mass filled the corridor below, racing in like dark smoke. Luc collided with the mimic, shearing through the black robes with his talons. A killing blow. Ingrid expected a burst of green sparks— every demon she'd seen destroyed had disappeared in such a manner. But this one simply vanished. No sparks. Nothing.

Luc was alone in the underground arcade corridor when the floor finally gave. Ingrid fell in a rain of glass shards, a scream locked in her throat. She squeezed her eyes shut against the grating chime of breaking glass, the whistle of air as it rushed past her ears. Her skirts billowed and flapped around her, and she prepared for the sickening crack of bone against marble.

She should have known better.

Luc caught her midair, his arms slamming into her back with such force it drove the breath from her lungs. It was an awkward catch, but once he had her in his arms, curled in tight against the hard, square plates of his chest, he folded in his wings and dropped to the floor.

Ingrid's eyes were still squeezed shut, her hands balled into fists. Slowly, she opened both, but she couldn't take a breath. She hadn't been this close to Luc in ages. He was so warm, as if his dark reptilian scales had been exposed to glaring sun.

She turned her face up and saw his pale lime eyes flash with concern. They were the only part of Luc—the *human* Luc—that was left. The rest of him was monstrous, the featherless black wings looming over each of his hulking shoulders, the clipped ears of a dog set high on his bald skull, and small, tightly knit jet scales covering his face. They shimmered, even in the poor light of the underground arcade.

How could someone so handsome turn into something so hideous?

Ingrid uncurled the fingers of one hand and reached timidly toward the squared plane of his chin. Luc's scales felt like slate. Ingrid let her fingertip travel lightly up the curve of his jaw and then in, toward his mouth. Luc's gargoyle lips weren't full and lush like his human ones. They were thin and black, and he kept his mouth in a tight seam, his eyes cautiously following the motions of her hand.

"Thank you," she whispered.

Luc jerked his head to the side, dislodging her exploring fingers. He set her down roughly. She shouldn't have touched him. Her legs weren't steady, and her shoes crunched broken glass underfoot. They needed to leave, and fast. The entrance stairwell to the underground shops descended directly from the sidewalk along the street. At the base were Luc's shoes and clothes. He would need to shift and dress.

"I'll wait in the carriage," Ingrid said, and started to walk away.

She felt a tug of resistance. Glancing down, she saw Luc's talons tangled in the velvet folds of her cloak. Each talon was sharp enough to cut through the velvet with one swipe. But he was holding her back gently, and she didn't know why. She watched in awe as his talons receded, changing from obsidian hooks to fleshy pink fingers.

He was Luc again. The human Luc she was used to seeing, at least. He stood behind her, stark naked. She kept her eyes fastened on his hand, still balled in the velvet of her cloak. Still holding her as if he didn't want her to leave.

"We should hurry," she finally said.

He waited another moment before letting her go. Ingrid ran for the stairs with the nagging feeling that Luc had wanted her to say something else. Exactly what, she didn't know. Somehow, she still felt as if she had failed.

Morning sun bled through the skeleton-limbed trees surrounding Clos du Vie. Ingrid had thought of Dimitrie on the long ride to the Bois du Boulogne and wondered why he hadn't arrived at the shopping arcade. Perhaps it was because Luc had already been with her. It made sense, but Dimitrie's absence bothered her nonetheless. Not that she'd needed him. Or wanted him. Luc was protector enough.

It was still too early to call on Constantine, but his butler showed them into the orangery without a fuss. He didn't even react when Luc refused to leave Ingrid's side. Ingrid wouldn't have dared ask Luc to stay with the carriage, and not just because she feared the mimic might pop up again. The fierce determination in his expression brooked no argument, not from her, and definitely not from Constantine's butler.

For once, Ingrid appreciated the suffocating heat of the orangery. She hadn't been able to shake the shivers wracking her body since leaving the arcade. The gathered heat in the glassed-in jungle immediately seeped into her skin and relaxed the tremors.

And then she saw Vander.

He was standing by the garden table in his mustard-colored waistcoat and creamy white shirtsleeves, his coat and bowler hat slung over the curved back of a chair. When he saw her coming through the stand of bamboo, Ingrid forgot herself. She forgot Luc and Constantine, who was seated at the table surrounded by a dozen texts. She ran toward Vander and crashed into his chest. His arms went around her back and he folded her to himself.

"I thought Constantine was supposed to send his carriage for you. What happened?" he asked, his mouth pressed against the side of her head. His breath ruffled her hair. It had come loose from its bun in the arcade and she hadn't thought to fix it.

Ingrid hadn't yet told him about the mimic demon, and she didn't know how to start. She pulled away as a shudder of electricity raked down her arms. Why now? Why now and not when she'd needed it?

When Ingrid didn't answer, Vander turned toward Luc. "Tell me."

And so Luc told them. He was brief, and his voice didn't shake the way Ingrid's would have. He knew what to say, when Ingrid was certain she would have mumbled incoherently. A demon wanted to kill her. And it had come very close to succeeding.

"This is quite grave, I am afraid," Constantine said once Luc had concluded. He sat back in his chair. If possible, he appeared even grayer than he had moments before.

"I tried to kill it," Luc ground out, unmistakably frustrated that he hadn't been successful. He didn't like to fail. Though at least she hadn't been injured. Not even a scratch from all that falling glass. Luc wouldn't suffer another angel's burn on Ingrid's account, not if she could help it.

"Next time, I *will* kill it," Vander said.

Luc glared at him, but Constantine interrupted before he could make a retort.

"Mimic demons are almost impossible to destroy. Unlike other demons, mimics can appear and disappear at will. They can vanish before any harm is done to them, whether it's by a gargoyle's talons or blessed silver."

That explained the absence of the death sparks Ingrid had been hoping to see.

"You said *almost impossible*," she remarked, self-consciously running her fingers through her tousled locks. She probably looked as if she'd just rolled out of bed.

Constantine sat forward, crossing his arms on the green wrought-iron table. "The only way I know of to destroy a mimic is to simultaneously kill the human or animal that the mimic has taken the appearance of. Luc says the mimic took on the form of your friend from London? If she had been at your side and you had plunged a dagger through her heart while the mimic still wore her appearance, the deed would have been done. It requires a sacrifice, my dear."

Ingrid's uncontrollable tremors made another attack. "That's impossible," she whispered.

Constantine fanned out his hands. "As I said."

"There has to be another way." Vander loosened his jacquard tie and the first few buttons of his shirt, nearly exposing the strawberry-colored marks he, Ingrid, Grayson, and every other Duster shared.

"Capturing a mimic requires advanced technologies that are unavailable to me," Constantine replied. "However, if you were to go to the Daicrypta with such a request—"

"No!" Ingrid, Vander, and Luc all shouted in unison.

Ingrid sighed. Asking the Daicrypta for anything was out of the question. There had to be another method for stopping a mimic.

"There's a library room at Hôtel Bastian full of books. They haven't been touched in years," Ingrid said, looking at Vander. He'd invited her to be their academic. And then he'd kissed her.

Ingrid turned back to Constantine, avoiding both Vander's and Luc's eyes.

"I could try to find something there," she said distractedly.

But then she saw the stacks of books on the table. Constantine had a library three times the size of the one at Hôtel Bastian, and he'd been studying demons for decades. Ingrid fiddled with her hair again, tucking a lock behind her ear.

"We can search together," Vander said with a step in her direction.

"How pleasant." Luc moved between Ingrid and Vander. "What are you doing here, Seer?"

She saw again the books at Constantine's elbows. Ingrid had forgotten. Vander had come to hear what Constantine had learned about the webbing that had spewed from his fingertips.

"I thought I'd come early. Get it over with," he said to her with a timid glance toward Constantine's books. He was nervous.

Constantine got right to it.

"Léon's ability to produce silk protein is a main characteristic of the arachnae demon, just as electric pulses are of the lectrux, and perhaps just as the ability to shift is of the hellhound. When you were pinning Léon's arms, he lost that ability, and you, Mr. Burke, adopted it. Only to a slight degree, but you still adopted it."

Luc slowly rotated toward Vander, a strange light dawning in his eyes. Ingrid held her breath. He didn't know about Vander's dust. No one within the Dispossessed did.

"Why would that have happened?" Luc asked.

Constantine opened a book, oblivious to the tension brewing between Vander and Luc.

"After much research, I believe I've discovered the source of Mr. Burke's demon blood and his demon gift."

Luc and Vander stared at one another. If either of them was breathing, Ingrid couldn't see evidence of it. They were both so still, they looked like wax replicas.

"You're one of them," Luc whispered.

"There are many of us," Vander replied.

Constantine sighed. "My apologies, Mr. Burke. I wasn't aware Luc was in the dark about your demon blood."

"It doesn't matter." Vander broke off from Luc's daggered glare. "My blood doesn't come from an arachnae, I know that much. My dust is multicolored, not pale yellow like Léon's. I also already know what my gift is: I see dust."

Constantine opened to a marked page within the thick text. "That is a gift, most certainly. But I do not believe it is your *demon* gift. Just as it is not mine, for I do not possess demon blood, and yet I, too, see demon dust. You understand?"

Vander rounded the table, headed toward Constantine. "No. I don't."

Ingrid quickly looked at Luc. He was already watching her, and he was livid. She hadn't told him the truth about Vander, but it hadn't been her secret to share.

"The ability to see dust has nothing to do with your having demon blood. May I inquire as to when you received your calling from Our Lord?" Constantine asked.

Vander drew back. "Why?"

"Was it about the same time you started being able to view the dust around certain animals or people? Perhaps in random clouds or airstreams?"

Vander considered this in silence while Ingrid wondered what exactly a calling from the Lord was. Had Vander woken up one day with the unexplainable desire to serve God? Or had his family expected it of him for some reason? He spoke sparingly of his plans for the church. He spoke sparingly of his family, too, who she assumed still lived in America. All she had to go on was what he'd given her—and with a start, she realized that it wasn't much at all.

"It was about the same time," Vander said, sounding guarded.

Constantine nodded excitedly. "Excellent!" He stood from

the chair and balanced the open book with both hands. "Just as I presumed from the beginning, Mr. Burke. Your ability to see dust is not terribly uncommon. A number of the devout develop the same sort of sight when they receive their calling from the Lord. A *true* calling, mind you. One that cannot easily be explained or reasoned out. I suspect your family was rather surprised when you announced your intentions for the clergy?"

Ingrid watched Vander closely. His expression softened with wonder, and Ingrid was certain Constantine's guess had been dead-on.

"We share the ability to see dust because we have both been called, Mr. Burke. I have followed my calling by studying Christianity's darkest mysteries, while your calling has led you along a very different path."

"What's your point?" Vander asked.

Constantine set down the book he'd been holding, spun it toward Vander, and gave it a short push.

"You have the blood of a mersian demon," he said.

Vander touched the edge of the open book with his fingers. "I haven't heard of a mersian demon before."

"Neither have I," Luc said as he approached the table. "And I've been around a little bit longer than you have, Seer."

Ingrid stayed quiet. The only demons she knew of were the ones she'd come into direct contact with. Unfortunately, she knew there were many, *many* more.

"That is because they don't hunt humans," Constantine answered. Ingrid, Vander, and Luc gave him their full attention. "They hunt other Underneath demons and feed on their dust. By feeding on a demon's dust, a mersian will leach its prey of power and will in turn soak it up, making the power its own."

Constantine again pushed the book in Vander's direction. "When a mersian comes close enough to another demon, it absorbs that demon's field of dust. Like any demon, the mersian will eventually exhaust whatever it has consumed, and will therefore need to feed again. However, until it exhausts the dust it has fed on, the mersian will take on the abilities of its prey."

They all took a silent moment to make sense of what Constantine had just said. So when Vander had pinned Léon's arms, he'd come into contact with arachnae dust. He'd absorbed the dust, and then that dust had . . . what? Given him Léon's powers?

Vander removed his spectacles and rubbed his eyes. "I can't have mersian blood. I've fought demons before, and I've never taken on their abilities after."

"Yet haven't you always had your sword or some other weapon to keep your body at a distance from those demons?" Constantine countered, his expression confident. He already knew what Vander's answer would be.

"You held Léon's arms at his side for at least a minute, perhaps longer. Enough time to absorb his dust," Ingrid's teacher went on, taking up his cane from where it rested against the table.

"But wouldn't Vander have noticed something like this before now?" Ingrid asked. He was nearly nineteen, and she and Grayson, at seventeen, had started noticing their abilities months ago.

"That depends on how many opportunities he's had to touch another Duster—or a demon, or gargoyle, I suppose, since all those things have dust fields," Constantine answered.

The temperature in the orangery intensified, and the flora seemed to creep in closer. Ingrid didn't know how many Dusters Vander had touched, but she did know that he had touched her. Held her. Kissed her. Each time, she'd noticed a thorny stirring in her arms. The last time, in the Alliance library, it had surged and then drained away. And the next day she hadn't been able to conjure up her electricity, even when the Jonathan mimic had been bearing down on her in the middle of a street.

Vander was watching her as she remembered these things. Unfortunately, so was Luc.

"I've touched Ingrid," Vander said.

She had wondered before if the connection Luc had with her

was deep enough to have pierced her, giving her the same connection to him that he had to her. At that moment, she was sure it had. Rage blistered underneath her skin, and Ingrid knew it wasn't her own.

"You have?" Constantine blinked owlishly behind his spectacles, looking from Vander to Ingrid, and then back again. "Oh. Well, ah . . . did you, ah, notice anything?"

"Yes, Seer. Did you notice anything?" Luc asked with unmasked menace.

"I did," Ingrid said, drawing Luc's ire. "I think Monsieur Constantine is right. I couldn't produce a single spark the following day."

It hadn't even come to her unwanted, as it usually did.

Vander reached for the book Constantine had pushed toward him. He slammed it closed, making her jump.

"So that was your lectrux power I felt?" he asked.

"You actually felt it?" she asked, almost giddy. Someone else had felt it!

Vander put his spectacles back on and looked at his hands. "I didn't know it was that. I mean, I thought it was—"

"Enough," Luc growled. "Whatever happened is over. You won't touch Ingrid again."

Ingrid's smile collapsed. "Luc, stop."

He approached fast, stopping a hairsbreadth away from her. "If he touches you, he takes away your ability to protect yourself."

I can't protect myself anyway! she wanted to blurt, but was too ashamed. Besides, though she abhorred being told what to do and what not to do, she knew Luc was right.

Vander did as well. "I won't risk that, Ingrid, not with a mimic demon stalking you."

What was she going to do, argue? Beg Vander to reconsider? Stomp her foot and shout that it wasn't fair? Because it wasn't. First Luc couldn't kiss or touch her without shifting into gargoyle form, and now Vander couldn't touch her, either, not without rendering her a weak, ordinary human.

Luc turned away from the table and moved toward the bamboo, keeping his back to them. The blistering sensation beneath Ingrid's skin ebbed.

"Would a demonstration be too much to ask, Mr. Burke?" Constantine said after a moment, reminding them that he was still present. "We're all in agreement that Lady Ingrid's dust must not be disturbed, but perhaps . . . Luc?"

Luc paused at the entrance to the bamboo path.

"You are neither demon nor Duster, but you do have dust," Constantine went on. "If Mr. Burke could—"

"You don't honestly believe he could weaken me?" Luc asked. He looked over his shoulder and fixed Vander in his sights. "You share the blood of a pestilent demon. Mine comes from the Angelic Order."

"And yet you're still a slave," Vander rejoined.

Luc had no retort for that. He was a slave, Ingrid knew. Luc knew it as well, and for the first time, Ingrid saw something new flash over his expression: shame. It was there and gone again, and then Luc had recovered, pulling on his cloak of arrogance once more.

He spread his arms wide. "Try it," he said, sauntering up to Vander.

"Just for a few moments, Mr. Burke," Constantine interjected, and with a gentle hand on Ingrid's arm drew her away from Luc and Vander.

Vander hesitated. Ingrid understood why. She still doubted her own power every time, and usually with good reason. But if Vander's touch had been weakening her . . . maybe that was the problem.

With a steadying breath, Vander reached toward Luc. He didn't make contact but hovered an inch or two above Luc's outstretched arms, then ran his spread fingers down their length and along his ribs and torso.

Luc gave a skeptical roll of his eyes when Vander sank into a crouch and swept his hands down Luc's legs, past his knees, and then up again, never once making contact.

"His dust is moving," Constantine whispered to Ingrid. She wished she could see it too.

Vander let his hands fall back to his sides. "I don't think it's working."

"Give it another moment," Constantine urged.

Luc groaned, arms still wide. "I'm getting bored."

"This isn't exactly a carnival ride for—" Vander's jaw hinged shut. He lifted his head and tensed his back. "What is that smell?"

Luc's arms dropped. "What did you say?"

Vander sniffed the air, his eyes searching for the source of the smell that was distracting him. He moved toward Ingrid, breathing in deeply.

"That smell," Vander repeated. "Can't you smell it? It's . . . grass. It's like I'm in a field and it's just been hayed." A huge grin crossed his face and he laughed. "This is amazing." He looked to Luc. "What is this?"

Ingrid stared in wonderment at Vander's infectious smile. Constantine looked especially pleased. The only one who didn't was Luc.

"It's Ingrid," he answered darkly. "It's her scent."

Vander turned back to her, his honey-wheat eyes bright. "It worked."

He could scent her the same way Luc always did. Could he feel her heartbeat, too? It was unsettling to think so. It was odd enough knowing Luc could.

She met Luc's glare. "Can you still . . . ?"

He kept his lips pressed into a grim line and avoided her eyes. He didn't answer her, and he didn't have to.

He couldn't scent her. Vander had taken it from him.

"Exceptional! I hardly see a reduction in Luc's dust at all," Constantine remarked, unmindful of the panic creeping over Luc's expression. "I wonder, if Mr. Burke were to absorb more of Luc's dust—"

"I'm done. My dust stays where it is," Luc said, severing Constantine's theory at the knees.

For Ingrid, the question of what might happen continued to snowball. If Vander had adopted Luc's ability to scent her so quickly, what else could he adopt if given more time? Scales? *Wings?* What if he could take Luc's ability to coalesce?

Vander, a gargoyle? And Luc . . .

A human.

CHAPTER SEVENTEEN

Dinner at Hôtel Bastian was a complete and utter farce.

As Gabby sat at the long oval table inside Hôtel Bastian's modest dining room, she wished for that awful painter from a few nights before to come paint their portrait. She would command him to title it *A Meditation in Absurdity,* and who knew, she just might allow him to paint on a few bare, dimpled backsides.

The courses had all been served and cleared away, and even though each dish had been delicious, Gabby hadn't been able to enjoy any of them. She'd sipped her wine and prodded food around on her plates, waiting for something terrible to happen. It was inevitable. Her father and Carrick Quinn had been chitchatting merrily for close to two hours, feeding lies to one another and in turn consuming them with relish.

Apparently, Carrick owned a textile mill, and Nolan was in line to take control of it. Chelle, seated across from Gabby, was playing Nolan's lovely sister, and Gabby wasn't sure which was worse: Chelle's atrocious Scottish accent or the calico-print dress she had clearly not even bothered to press. As for Lord Brickton, he was happily embracing his wife's new gallery venture. Grayson, seated at Gabby's left, had been proudly presented as heir to the Brickton earldom and had received an unsettling number of grins from their father. Ingrid, would you believe it, had quite a few beaux waiting for her in London, and Gabby . . . well, poor Gabby; Lord Brickton was sure Carrick had heard all about her shocking accident.

It was all so embarrassing. The fact that her father seemed to be the only one in the dark was especially mortifying. She almost felt sorry for him.

Nolan, seated to the right of his "sister," had caught Gabby peeking at him a few times, and she had caught him peeking once or twice as well. There was nothing flirtatious about their glances, though. They were both nervous.

He sat rigid in his seat, his steel-blue eyes watching his father spin lie after lie. Just like Gabby, he was waiting for something to happen.

She jumped when Carrick pushed back his chair.

"If the ladies will allow us to take our leave, I have a bottle of single malt waiting for us, gentlemen."

They all stood, Nolan and Grayson seeming to do so with added weight. They had to go off to some smoky room and endure more of their fathers' absurd conversation. Gabby only hoped the Scotch whiskey went down smooth and fast.

Upon exiting the dining room, Carrick led the men off to the right, and Chelle led the ladies to the left. They had seen the parlor when they'd first arrived. It was just off the foyer, and like the rest of the rooms, it had a starched look about it. The furniture was all too new and underused. Proper, but not loved. It was a stage, Gabby knew, and right now they, all of them, were acting.

Chelle closed the foyer door behind her.

"Miss Quinn," Gabby's mother called. Chelle plastered on a dainty smile—it looked rather painful—and turned to face Lady Brickton.

"Yes, Lady Brickton?"

Gabby's mother chose a sofa and lowered herself, patting out the folds of her skirts. "Would you be so kind as to tell me your real name?"

She said it as primly as if she were asking Chelle to ring for tea.

"Thank goodness. I thought I'd go mad if we had to keep playing make-believe," Gabby said, dropping to the cushion beside her mother.

Chelle let go of the posture suited to a lady and slouched. She tugged at the waist of her dress. "I can't believe I volunteered for this." She eyed Lady Brickton bashfully. "My name is Chelle, but it isn't followed by Quinn."

"That isn't surprising, dear. You don't look a thing like them," Gabby's mother said. "And your accent is deplorable."

Gabby snorted. It really was.

Ingrid moved toward the fireplace, her terra-cotta dress glowing like coals in the firelight. "Chelle, why on earth did Mr. Quinn invite us here?"

Chelle fell back into her soldierly gait as she crossed the room, headed toward a door that servants might use. "He wants to align your families."

"What?" Ingrid asked.

"How, exactly?" Gabby demanded.

To the queue of questions, Lady Brickton added, "Why?"

Chelle opened the narrow servants' door and gave a small whistle before turning back to the three Waverly women.

"The old-fashioned way: by marriage. The marriage of Ingrid and Nolan, more specifically. And you, Lady Ingrid, have your magical blood to thank for it."

Gabby shot up from the sofa. "*Ingrid* and Nolan?"

"I am not going to marry him!" Ingrid exclaimed just as Nolan's cousin Rory appeared in the servants' door.

He wore his standard outfit: trousers, shirtsleeves, and a waistcoat armored with daggers. Lady Brickton gasped at the sight of him.

"It wouldna be a death sentence for ye, Lady Ingrid," Rory said. "But I'm afraid 'twould be for Nolan once Vander Burke got hold of him." He finished with a smile that could have easily knocked a weaker girl down flat.

It wasn't even directed at Gabby, and she still felt the shock wave of it.

"Come, Lady Ingrid. We havna much time."

Ingrid looked at Gabby and their mother apologetically, hands clasped before her. "I sent a note ahead of us," she explained. "I need to do something, and I didn't know when I'd have another chance to come to Hôtel Bastian."

Their mother puckered her brow, an expression her children had long ago learned to translate as "Not in a million years."

"I helped you leave the rectory yesterday morning, but if you think I'm going to allow you to go off with this young man, you are sorely mistaken," she told her elder daughter.

A show of solidarity was the only thing Gabby thought might work. She left the sofa and stood beside Ingrid.

"I'll go along, Mama. She'll be fine." Their mother didn't appear swayed in the least.

"Lady Brickton, I'm takin' yer daughter to a library on the premises," Rory said, his charm somehow softening the fact that he wore daggers upon his waistcoat. "No harm will come to her, ye have my word."

Why Lady Brickton was convinced by Rory's vow and not Gabby's didn't matter. Sneaking about Hôtel Bastian promised to be ample compensation for Gabby's wounded pride.

"Quickly," Lady Brickton finally said. "I don't know when your father will tire of this charade."

Clearly, she already had.

Ingrid and Gabby followed Rory through the door and up a set of stairs. Chelle stayed in the parlor with their mother and shut the door behind them. The narrow stairwell went black..

Thick carpet muffled their footsteps, but their breathing seemed unnaturally loud.

"One more flight," Rory announced. Gabby followed his voice and Ingrid's swooshing skirts while feeling for the steps with the tips of her slippers.

"Lady Ingrid, pay no mind to my uncle's plans," Rory said once they neared the next landing. "He isna himself lately."

Because of the mercurite, Gabby knew. He must have used a lot of it over the years. All Alliance fighters did. But how much was too much? She couldn't help thinking of Nolan. Did all Alliance fighters eventually . . . change?

Rory opened the door to a dimly lit hallway. Ingrid seemed to recognize it. She led them toward a door to the right.

"I trust Nolan wouldn't wish to marry me anyway," Ingrid said with an all-too-obvious glimpse in Gabby's direction. Rory didn't miss it. He smiled widely.

"Aye, ye may have trouble wi' the *laoch* who fancies my cousin. I hear she's fierce."

Ingrid laughed, while Gabby blushed. *Laoch?* He'd used that word before, but at the time she'd thought he'd been telling her his last name.

"What does that word mean?" she asked.

Rory opened the door for Ingrid and about a decade's worth of musty, closed-up air escaped. Gabby gagged. It smelled like one of those stinky old bookshops Ingrid and Grayson went all cuckoo for. Ingrid stepped into the room and maneuvered between towering piles of books.

"It's Scots for *warrior*. Isna that what ye are, lass?" No smile now. He wasn't jesting with her. "Lady Ingrid, ye have fifteen minutes, no more."

It wasn't a lot of time to sift.

"What are you looking for, anyway?" Gabby asked her sister.

Ingrid craned her neck and read the spines along one shelf. "It's difficult to explain."

"That makes it a bit hard to help," Gabby replied.

Ingrid kept her focus on the shelves. Gabby and Rory stood watching her.

"Well, this is uneventful," Gabby muttered.

"I could show ye round," Rory suggested.

He cocked his head and slipped back into the corridor. Gabby followed.

"Stay out of trouble," Ingrid called, as if her snooping around were proper behavior. Of course, if Carrick came upon her, he would probably take her interest in the library as a promising sign of upcoming nuptials.

Gabby shook off the shudder of nausea the image of her sister and Nolan's wedding gave her and concentrated on following Rory. He moved with purposeful strides, his shoulders squared. On his back he wore two short swords in crossed sheaths. The handle on each, she imagined, would be easy for him to reach and pull free.

Gabby wanted to see him in battle. If fighting skill ran in the family, he would be just as impressive as Nolan.

At the end of the corridor, Rory took hold of the banister on a spiral staircase and climbed. His feet scuffed along the metal lightly, making hardly a sound. It was strange how something as basic as walking and climbing stairs could display so much about a person, but in watching Rory, Gabby saw that he was observant and careful. Precise.

And that was when Gabby ran into him, treading on his heels. He'd stopped, and she'd been too focused on the way his body moved to notice.

"Careful, *laoch*. Ye don't want to fall in this room." He shoved open a pair of sliding pocket doors.

They rolled aside, and a moment later, a series of lightbulbs fixed to the ceiling buzzed to life. The light wavered at first. When it finally held steady, Gabby saw that the room was large, perhaps the size of the rectory's sitting room. There were no windows, but none were needed. It was already bright enough, and not just from the electric bulbs.

Polished silver lined the walls. To her left, swords of every shape and size—rapiers, *katanas,* cutlasses, broadswords, and styles she couldn't name—hung from silver dowels drilled into the walls. Directly ahead, daggers, dirks, and knives, straight-handled and bowed, hung in rows, from longest to shortest. And to Gabby's left there were crossbows and darts, throwing stars, and even a few battle-axes.

She could barely breathe. It was all so beautiful.

Beside her, Rory crossed his arms. "I thought ye might fancy it."

Gabby went for the daggers first. She had her sword from Nolan, and as gorgeous, light, and natural to wield as it was, it was hard to transport in the inner folds of her cloak.

"Are they all blessed?" she asked.

Rory nodded. "We do them in batches. The reverend at that church of Vander's disna ask many questions."

Gabby couldn't imagine he would get many answers if he did.

"We all have our weapon of choice," Rory said from where he stood by the door, watching her. She didn't dare touch any of them. Her fingers would leave spots on the silver.

"What is yours?" she asked before remembering the daggered vest. She smiled back at him. "Never mind."

"Vander has his crossbow and Nolan his broadsword," Rory said.

"And Chelle her throwing stars," Gabby added.

"Aye, nothing rips the air better than Chelle's stars."

She liked the dagger she'd stolen from Vander's desk a while back. He knew about it now, and he'd been gracious enough to let her keep it.

"I don't know what my weapon of choice is," she said, moving toward the swords. It was funny. It wasn't long ago that she wanted baubles, dresses, and hats with the same sense of longing she now felt for these silver weapons.

What would her London friends think of her?

"Dinna worry, *laoch*. It'll find ye."

Gabby stopped at the corner where the sword and dagger walls met. A floor case started there. It reached to her hip and ran the length of the sword wall. Beneath the display glass, Gabby saw more silver things: some swords and daggers, but mostly crossbow darts. They were laid out neatly, and at first glance Gabby guessed there were perhaps fifty darts, maybe more. They weren't as shiny as the weaponry hanging upon the walls. Instead of high silver, they were like polished pewter.

"What are these?" Gabby asked, also noticing a thick padlock on the case cover. She lifted it and gave it a small tug. Locked fast.

"Those aren't blessed," Rory answered. He came up to the stand and peered through the glass. "They've been dipped in mercurite."

Gabby dropped the padlock, the memory of the burning mercurite still fresh in her mind. "I thought demons weren't affected by anything but blessed silver."

"These aren't for demons," he answered. "They're for killing gargoyles."

CHAPTER EIGHTEEN

For the first time ever, Ingrid hated books.

There were far too many of them, all unorganized and uncategorized. And her time was dwindling. So far, none of the random books she'd flipped through had mentioned anything about mimic demons. Constantine had needed days to search his own massive (and neatly organized) collection, and here she was scrambling like an idiot with fifteen bloody minutes!

"A fool's errand," she said under her breath, and then sneezed as dust traveled up her nose.

Maybe there was no other way of getting rid of a mimic. But Ingrid didn't think she could kill a living thing to destroy one.

She slammed the cover of the book she was skimming and then jumped out of her crouch as a loud crash echoed it. Ingrid faced the door, expecting someone to come charging in, but no one appeared. The crash had sounded like it came from the floor below. Perhaps even from the second level, where Mama still sat with Chelle in the parlor. She thought of her father and Grayson. What if the crash was a signal from Chelle?

Ingrid opened the door and peered into the hallway. It was so quiet she began to wonder if she had heard a crash after all. She decided it was best to err on the side of safety, so she started toward the servants' door Rory had led them through. She had barely made it halfway down the hall when indecipherable shouting shattered the silence.

Ingrid took a panicked glance behind her. The door to the library was too far away, but there was another, closer one off to the left. She went for the handle, twisted, and let herself in. A few lightbulbs overhead hummed with power, and thankfully, no one was inside.

The shouting continued, and Ingrid was frozen with indecision: Should she go into the hallway and risk running into someone? Or stay here and risk having her father discover her gone from the parlor?

She needed better options.

A chill ran through her, lifting the small hairs on her arms and neck. Whatever this room was, it was cold. At least ten degrees cooler than the hallway. The room was a laboratory of sorts, with long metal tables, microscopes, beakers, and machines that Ingrid couldn't begin to identify. Along one of the walls were two rows of wide, square, steel-fronted doors, each one nearly as tall as Ingrid, and with a combination lock. There had to be at least ten of these doors in each row.

She had to leave and make her way back down to the parlor. But those steel doors were too curious to ignore. Ingrid crossed the room, walking around a table strewn with tubes and piping. Each steel square had been engraved with a number, and in the center of each combination lock, there was a little temperature gauge. Inside one, an arrow trembled toward the negative-twenty-degree-Celsius mark.

Ingrid regretted putting her finger to the steel door the second her skin came into contact with it. It *was* freezing. She pulled her hand back, now even more curious. What could the Alliance be keeping inside such cold compartments?

She didn't have time to investigate any longer, though. She heard footsteps coming from the hallway, and as she went to the door, heard Rory's harsh whisper: "Lady Ingrid?"

She whipped the door open and came face to face with him and her sister. He frowned, looking over her shoulder into the odd laboratory. "I didna say ye could go in there."

"I'm sorry, it's just that I heard a crash and loud voices, and . . . didn't you hear them?"

Rory shook his head. "The fifth floor is insulated better than the others—it's where we train, and we tend to make a lot of noise." He looked again into the cold room. "Come."

Gabby remained unusually silent on their return to the parlor. She met Ingrid's questioning gaze with a small shake of her head. Something had happened. And she was the wretched sister who had let Gabby go off alone with this bulging, dagger-strapped stranger. Had Rory made some sort of pass at Gabby? They took the narrow servants' stairs to the parlor, where Rory stopped at the door and listened. The room sounded quiet enough. Rory whistled lightly and the door winged open.

"Hurry!" Chelle growled, and Ingrid and Gabby toppled inside. Chelle slammed the door in Rory's face just as the parlor's main door flew open.

Lord Brickton was the first to enter, followed by Grayson, then Carrick Quinn, and last, a bloody-nosed Nolan.

Gabby surged toward him, but their father blocked her path. "Gather your things. We are leaving."

The charade had most definitely ended.

"What has happened?" their mother asked, rising from the sofa, right where Ingrid and Gabby had left her.

Carrick worked his hand into a fist, curling, then uncurling each knuckle. "Nothing but a little bit of Scottish discipline. My apologies again, Lord Brickton."

Ingrid and Gabby stared with open mouths. Carrick had hit his own son? Nolan pressed the sleeve of his dinner coat to his bloody nose. Strands of black hair had fallen into his eyes from the tussle with his father.

"Well, you don't have my apologies," Nolan said to Lord Brickton before turning to Gabby. "You don't need surgery, lass, and you shouldn't listen to anyone who tells you different."

"It is none of your concern!" their father shouted.

"You have no idea how wrong you are, do you?" Nolan threw back.

Gabby's face flushed crimson. The veil of her hat obscured most of her scarring, but there was a small line near the corner of her mouth that stayed white. Ingrid felt her eyes water for her sister, who was no doubt festering with humiliation.

Their father practically ran Grayson down as he barreled through the door out into the foyer. Lady Brickton quickly followed her husband, failing to make the necessary compliments about dinner and their hospitality. Gabby fled the room next, unable to meet Nolan's gaze again. Grayson took Ingrid's arm as she approached the door, and pulled her to his side.

"I'm glad that's over," he mumbled as they all hurriedly wrapped themselves in cloaks and gloves. The footmen who had appeared at dinner had mysteriously disappeared.

"Are you?" Ingrid whispered back. "I thought you rather enjoyed ogling Nolan's dear sister all evening."

Ingrid felt a strong pinch just above her elbow and jumped away. "Stop it!"

"You stop it," Grayson jested.

He was smiling. For the first time in a very long time, her brother was smiling.

Perhaps dinner at Hôtel Bastian hadn't been a complete failure after all.

* * *

Gabby lay in the dark with three layers of blankets piled on top of her. She couldn't get warm. Her whole body shook, though she wasn't sure if it was with nervousness, rage, or mortification. All three could sum up how she was feeling.

The tall case clock at the top of the rectory stairs rang the hour: two in the morning. She was certain no one but her was awake to hear the chimes. Nolan was supposed to have come to her room two hours ago to train, but after the debacle at dinner that evening she wasn't surprised that he hadn't shown.

He, Papa, and Mr. Quinn had been discussing her face, how ugly and pitiful she was. Her father had refused to recount what exactly had occurred, but he'd said the boy was insolent. Nolan had been rude and arrogant, and Carrick had interfered when Nolan had rushed at Lord Brickton. And now Nolan had a broken nose and absolutely no invitation to call on the rectory ever again.

It was a disaster.

Gabby tossed in bed, rolling to her side and propping her head on her elbow. Nolan's bloody nose and her father's wounded pride weren't the only things keeping her awake. She kept seeing the mercurite-dipped darts in that horrible case in the weapons room. *They're for killing gargoyles,* Rory had said. The ease with which he had said it had stolen from her the next sensible question: *The Alliance kills gargoyles?* Instead, she'd stared at him, dumbstruck.

The waxing gibbous moon reflected off the panes of Gabby's single window. She had kept her curtains open, liking the silvery light. Hoping, just a bit, that Nolan would come. But she'd given up around one o'clock and had stripped herself out of her dinner dress and bodice and put on her nightgown. Maybe it was for the best that Nolan hadn't come. If killing gargoyles was a requirement for being an Alliance member, Gabby wasn't sure she wanted to be Alliance after all.

So of course, that was when she saw the shadow at her window.

Gabby sat upright in her bed, clutching the covers close to her. The shadowy blob split, becoming arms, a torso, and a head. *Nolan.* He struggled for balance on the narrow beam outside her window.

She didn't have time to dress. Gabby pushed the blankets back and flew to the window, pulling the panes inward. Nolan was alone on the ledge, chest heaving from the climb.

"Where is Dimitrie?" Gabby whispered, remembering the gargoyle's promise to fly Nolan up.

"It doesn't matter. Stone blocks make for easy scaling," Nolan answered softly, still clinging to the window frame. He raised a brow. "That doesn't mean my arms aren't tired."

Gabby leaped to the side and let him come in. Nolan's feet touched the floor and the wooden board creaked with his weight. They both cringed.

"If my father discovers you in here . . . ," Gabby said, closing the window.

"Haven't you heard? Pistols at dawn have fallen out of fashion," Nolan replied with his usual cocky grin. The moonlight showed purplish shadows under his eyes.

"If *your* father knew—"

"He'd break my nose again?" Nolan teased. When Gabby didn't laugh, he sighed. "I'm sorry I'm late. I had to wait until he was too tired to rail at me any longer."

She crossed her arms. The loose cotton against her skin made her wish she'd stayed dressed.

"In case you weren't aware," Gabby said, biting back a grin, "you've completely ruined any chance at winning my sister's hand in marriage."

Nolan stepped out of the moonlight and deeper into her blackened bedroom. "You know that wasn't going to happen, lass. My da's just grasping for ways to tie Ingrid and Grayson to the Alliance."

"Vander is Alliance," Gabby said, though guiltily. Ingrid would be furious if she knew Gabby was playing matchmaker.

"He's not from a root family, like mine. He's first-generation, and to a lot of Alliance, it makes a difference. To me, as long as Vander saves my life now and again, we're square."

Gabby wasn't in the spirit for his sarcasm. She went to her bedside lamp. "I need to ask you something."

The flare of light reached his face. She saw the bruises then. A crescent beneath each eye and one humped across the bridge of his already crooked nose. He was still startlingly handsome, though. Two black eyes only enhanced his devilish looks.

Nolan wrapped his hand around one of her bedposts and waited for her to speak.

"Have you ever killed a gargoyle?"

He lifted his chin. "Why would you ask me that?"

"I saw the mercurite-dipped weapons the Alliance keeps on hand. I know what they're used for."

Nolan pushed off the bedpost, his fists clenching. "Rory took you to the weapons room."

Gabby might have felt remorse for exposing someone else, but not Rory. He was more than capable of holding his own should Nolan confront him.

"Have you?" she pressed.

"No." There was just enough of a twinge in his voice to tell her there was more to that one-word answer.

"But?" she pressed.

He exhaled a long, husky sigh. "Gabby, there's more history between the Alliance and the Dispossessed than you know about yet. Things are stable now, but it wasn't always that way."

"You were enemies?" she asked.

"It was hundreds of years ago. The Alliance didn't know what the gargoyles were. They thought they were demons and hunted them as if they were." Nolan sat down on the edge of Gabby's bed. "For a long time, we didn't even know they shifted form. For decades—for whole generations—there were battles, all waged at night when the Alliance and the Dispossessed could move about without being seen. Then, during one of them, an Alliance healer was attacked. In a desperate attempt to defend himself, he broke a bottle of mercurite against the gargoyle's scales. He saw what it did. From then on we knew that what healed us harmed them."

Gabby sat down, careful to keep a decent distance from Nolan. She remembered the confessional booth and her pathetic lack of willpower.

"But then in the sixteenth century, a gargoyle and an Alliance member did something no one else had done before: they spoke. Once they did, once they knew the other's purpose, that's when the peace began. But it's still tenuous, and history tends to repeat itself. You know that, Gabby. That's why we keep mercurite weapons under lock and key. The closer we allow the Dispossessed to get, the more dangerous it is for us. We won't allow our numbers to be obliterated, as we almost were before."

She'd had no idea. She'd assumed, of course, that for quite a while the Alliance and the Dispossessed had been creeping toward friendlier terms, but she hadn't imagined they had ever hunted or killed one another.

"The summit in Rome," Gabby said, shifting toward Nolan. "The Alliance members in favor of forcing gargoyles to register and adhere to Alliance law want to use the threat of mercurite weapons, don't they?"

Nolan closed his eyes and rubbed them.

"In short, yes. I can't manage explaining the long answer right now." He leaned back, eyes closed, until he was fully reclined on the pink coverlet.

"Do you get to cast your vote?" she asked. "Are you for the regulations?"

She knew Chelle was. The girl had no reservations when it came to expressing her contempt for the Dispossessed. But Vander and Nolan hadn't let on as to where they stood.

He stared at her where he lay. "The Directorate weighs everyone's votes. And yes, I'm for the regulations."

It wasn't what Gabby wanted to hear.

"But why should they adhere to your rules when they aren't Alliance? They're of the Angelic Order, Nolan. They're not yours to command."

"Not all gargoyles are like Luc," Nolan whispered. "There are some who wouldn't bat an eye when it came to harming a human who didn't belong to them. They've committed crimes against humans in the past, Gabby. People I know—people *you* know—have been hurt by them. You know what they've done. They're all murderers. They weren't decent men in life, and an eternity of enforced service isn't about to change them."

She knew about their crimes. She also knew that they had already been judged and punished accordingly.

"It isn't right."

"It's a complicated matter. Even the Directorate had to postpone the summit talks. They couldn't reach a majority agreement." Nolan stretched his arms back, a forearm coming down over his eyes. "How did we get onto this subject? I'm not supposed to be telling you any of this. You could be a spy, for all I know." He peeked out from under his arm. "Lie down with me."

Her body tensed and sent her flying to her feet.

"Not like that," Nolan added with that maddening grin of his. "Didn't I promise to be a gentleman? Just . . . lie beside me for a little while."

Gabby glanced at his warrior-like figure, his long black coat fanned out under him like wings, glints of silver peeking out from hidden sheaths. His faded canvas trousers had been tucked into a pair of tall Hessian boots. The temptation to crawl beside him and let him hold her was almost irresistible.

But he was in favor of making gargoyles slaves to the Alliance. Disappointment was a sharp blade. Impossible to ignore.

"Not a chance. We'll fall asleep," she said, her voice shaking. "My maid will find you here come sunrise and I'll be ruined."

Nolan lugged himself up, his wicked smile even wider. "I've never ruined a lass before."

He was entirely too dangerous. Gabby moved away from the bed.

"I don't think this is going to work," she said, and the words seemed to snuff out Nolan's charm. He suddenly looked concerned. "The training. Here, in my room. The floors are too old and creaky. We'll be heard."

He relaxed. "Then it's the perfect place to train. Hunting demons is about stealth. You'll acquire it all the better if we manage to practice right under your parents' noses without being discovered."

She had backed up to the window while he'd been whispering. The wind leaked through the gaps and gusted against her nightgown. Nolan followed her. She could smell the wintry night air that clung to his coat.

He wanted to kiss her. His eyes gave it away as they kept skittering down to her lips. He took her chin with his thumb and forefinger and then cupped her scarred cheek. Nolan said nothing as he dragged his hand down to the curve of her jaw, along her neck, and to her exposed collarbone. His fingertips traveled along the lace top of her nightgown, his touch leaving a needful burn in its wake.

But they still hadn't spoken on the other important subject that had been keeping her awake.

"I don't want the surgery."

Nolan didn't flinch. She wondered what it would take to surprise him.

"You don't need it," he replied.

"But the scars," she started, determined to be honest. They were alone, in her bedroom, and she was in a nightdress and barefoot. If she couldn't be honest now, when could she? "They're ugly. Don't tell me they're not."

"I think you know me well enough to know I won't lie to you," he said, tucking a few strands of loose hair behind her ear. "Scars aren't pretty. I've got plenty of them myself. What they are is a story, and each one is a record. Each one's a victory. When I look at your scars I remember how close you came to being taken from me. And then I remember that you weren't. That makes it my victory, in a roundabout way." He leaned closer and rubbed the tip of his nose against hers. "And I think you also know me well enough to know how much I love my victories."

She did know him. At least, she'd thought she did. But she kept seeing the polished pewter darts and daggers. Nolan was a good man; she couldn't imagine he would use them to drive gargoyles into submission. But even good men could be wrong.

Gabby turned her cheek and reached for the latch. She swung the window open for him. "Be careful" was all she managed to say. Nothing clever or alluring. She wasn't feeling either of those things just then.

Nolan handled the snub with his usual pride and climbed onto the sill. He paused, as though he might say something more. But then he lowered himself, scraping lightly against the stones as he scaled the rectory before hopping to the ground and walking away.

CHAPTER NINETEEN

He probably should have gone back inside, straight into Gabby's room, and punched Nolan Quinn in the jaw. Crouching near the stables, Grayson had seen Nolan cross the churchyard, pick his way up the side of the rectory, and slip inside his little sister's room with all the stealth of a bandit.

Grayson had closed his eyes and breathed in the frosty night air instead. He didn't have the fortitude to play protective big brother, not tonight. One spike of his pulse and he'd shift. He didn't dislike Nolan Quinn enough to risk attacking him in hellhound form.

He'd waited another minute before stealing out from behind the stables and jogging off the sacred ground. Instantly, he'd breathed easier. Perhaps that was the problem. It made sense, actually. Holy ground might not be the best place for someone who was mostly demon.

The Saint Germain-des-Prés streets were sleepy and, aside from a few snoring vagrants, deserted. He didn't know if Chelle would be out on patrol, but aimless searching was better than pacing his room like some caged tiger. Even if he had been able to speak to her during the disastrous dinner at Hôtel Bastian, he wouldn't have known what to say. Sorry for turning into a hellhound? I promise I didn't want to eat you?

He ambled into a small residential square and started to lose hope. The moon reflected off the hard layer of snow, ice crystals winking everywhere. Four iron benches sat arm to arm in a diamond shape around a copse of trees. He wasn't ready to go back to the rectory yet. The place made his chest feel tight, like he was trying to breathe honey instead of air.

Grayson sat on one of the benches and looked up at the town houses that surrounded the square. The windows were all dark, everyone inside sleeping soundly and safely in their beds. None of them fearing a slip in their temper or the moment their skin sprouted fur.

He felt a tug on his ankle, and then, faster than he could look down, he was being jerked off the bench and onto the packed snow. Grayson tried to move his legs and jump to his feet, but they were bound. A strange kind of white rope had lassoed him from ankle to knee. He rolled onto his back and found a boy looming over him. The moon was so bright over his shoulders it blacked out the stranger's face.

"You are Ingrid Waverly's brother? The one with hellhound blood?" he asked before Grayson could speak. He had a French accent and his voice shook.

The boy held the ends of the ropes binding Grayson's legs. Ropes that kept *moving*. Strands joined, became one, and then split apart again. It wasn't rope at all, Grayson realized.

"You're Léon." He strained to loosen the spider silk wrapped around his shins. The silk dripping from each of the boy's fingers trembled in the slight wind. When Léon cocked his head, Grayson saw two hooked fangs protruding from his mouth.

"I followed you from the abbey," the boy admitted. "She said you are both like me. You have the dust also."

Like him? He'd murdered his whole family, hadn't he? Grayson was about to argue but stopped.

He *was* like Léon. More than he wanted to admit.

"Tell her to stay away from the Daicrypta," Léon said. He snapped his wrists to the side and detached the dripping spider silk from his fingers. "She tried to help me and I did not let her. Now I am helping her. I am helping all of you. Stay away from that place. Stay away from the man named Dupuis."

Léon backed away from Grayson, who sat on the ground trying fruitlessly to pry the tacky silk from his pant legs.

"Wait! What happened to you there?" Grayson called. "Wait!"

But Léon was running from the square, his feet kicking up snow in his haste. Grayson swore beneath his breath and yanked one of the strands of silk with all his might. It was like stretching a length of rubber. The silk stayed put, leaving a pitchy residue on his fingers.

"Damn," he hissed, just seconds before a gargoyle the color of jet landed on the snow beside him.

"I'm glad you can't say anything right now," Grayson said, knowing he looked like a complete fool. It was the second time in one week that Luc had been called to his rescue.

Luc snorted, his hot breath rolling from his snout in clouds of white steam.

"It's funny, is it? Well, don't bother shifting. I'm fine. It was a Duster. The one Ingrid tried to help," Grayson explained, shuffling his legs in an attempt to loosen the insanely strong webbing. What *was* this stuff?

"He came with a warning."

Luc's great black wings unfurled with a resulting crack. His rocklike arm, covered in thick, shimmering scales, reached for Grayson's legs. He sheared through the silk webbing with an easy slice of one talon. The binding fell away and Grayson leaped to his feet—just in time to see Chelle's slender form glide through the open gates to the square.

"He wants Ingrid to stay away from Dupuis and the Daicrypta," Grayson finished saying as Chelle hurried toward them.

"Grayson, is that you? What is going on?" she asked. A light popped on in one of the town house windows. Luc turned his beastly face toward it and dropped into a defensive crouch.

"Go, Luc. I'm fine," Grayson said. With another snort—this one agitated instead of amused—Luc pushed off the ground and sailed into the sky. His wings beat down a rush of cold air that knocked Chelle backward. Grayson steadied her.

"I was heading back to rue Sèvres when I saw someone running from this square," Chelle said, drawing Grayson into the shadows of the copse of trees. "What are you doing?"

"I was searching for you," Grayson said.

Chelle blew out a gust of air. It ruffled her short bangs. "You were being demon bait, you mean."

"It was Léon, a Duster. Not a demon. Besides, I'm pretty sure I could hold my own," Grayson replied, though he didn't feel as confident as he sounded. Hell, he hadn't even been able to untangle himself from Léon's web.

"Come on," Chelle said, and with a glance at the surrounding town houses—the lone light had been extinguished—she took his hand and moved for the gates.

Her fingers were small and delicate. Her hand fit nicely in his.

"Where is your other gargoyle?" Chelle asked at the same time Grayson opened his mouth and said, "About the other night . . ."

Grayson stopped. "What?"

"Your other gargoyle. Shouldn't he have come, too?" she asked, searching the skies.

It was embarrassing enough having one gargoyle fly in to save him from something as ridiculous as a spiderweb. Chelle had a good point, though.

"I'll ask him later. Listen, I want to apologize. The other night, when I . . . became . . . something else."

Chelle's boots ground to a stop, carving ruts in the snow. "You are sorry for protecting me from that hellhound?"

"Of course I'm not sorry for protecting you. That's not what I was trying to—"

"Wouldn't the hellhound have been happy to kill me?"

Grayson blinked, unsure when his apology had taken a turn. "It wanted to kill you more than it wanted its next breath. Your blood sang to it," he whispered. "It sang to me. I'm a hellhound, Chelle."

She considered this, her expression the serious mask she usually wore. But then her lips quivered and broke apart, and she was suddenly smiling.

She never smiled.

"There is no shortage of dangerous creatures in this world. Not all of them are demons," she said, her smile faltering a moment as her eyes drifted back up to the sky.

"Do you mean the Dispossessed?" Grayson asked.

She brought her gaze back to him, but it wasn't as soft as before. "It doesn't matter. What I mean to say is that you are no hellhound. I've faced them before. *Real* hellhounds. And none of them have ever worked so hard not to kill me."

Chelle kept smiling. Grayson was taken in by the novelty of it. There was a small gap between her top front teeth that he hadn't noticed before.

"I think you are more human than you give yourself credit for, Grayson Waverly," she whispered.

He didn't know where the courage came from—maybe it was from seeing that adorable gap between her teeth—but he reached up and cradled her cheek in his palm. His hand must have been freezing, because her skin was searing hot. Chelle's eyes fluttered shut and she parted her lips. If it was an invitation, Grayson wasn't brave enough to accept it. He wasn't sure of anything, not with Chelle.

Then it was over.

She tore her cheek out of his palm and batted his hand away. She stepped back and touched her face.

"Chelle—"

"My patrol is over," she said flatly.

"I'll walk you back," he offered, knowing it was absurd. She was the one with all the sharp, deadly objects.

"No!" Chelle shouted, but it was from fright, not anger.

She turned on her heel and sped away from him as fast as she could. Almost as quickly as Léon had fled. Grayson was repelling all sorts tonight: cryptic Dusters, beautiful Alliance, irritated Dispossessed.

Maybe it was time to go home.

Luc approached the bowed roof of the carriage house at top speed.

Where was Dimitrie? He hadn't heeded the last call to Grayson's side earlier that week, or the one tonight. He hadn't shown at the arcades, either, when the mimic had attacked Ingrid. Yes, the danger tonight had been trivial, but it had still curled around Luc's heart like a fist and demanded that he go to his human's aid. Was it the angel's burns? Did shadow gargoyles not feel the same awareness or need?

Luc pleated his wings as he glided through the open loft door. Inside, it was roughly the same temperature as the outdoors. He didn't care about the cold. His human skin was susceptible, but his scales weren't. He touched down on the rough floorboards and felt a chiming at the base of his skull.

"Dimitrie?" Luc called before he'd shifted completely. The sound had been a gravelly shriek, though any Dispossessed would understand the goyle language.

"Do I have a surprise for you, brother," came Marco's voice from the innards of the loft. His muscled form strode into the moonlight, fully dressed.

Luc's scales melted to flesh, his wings sinking back into his body and disappearing. He felt the prickling sensation over his scalp as hair grew out, fast as a wave of water.

Luc rolled the loft door shut. "Not tonight, Marco."

He was in a foul mood. For the last two days Luc had felt like a fool, a feeling he deplored above all else.

"Oh yes, tonight. And every night from this one to the end of eternity," Marco replied.

Luc grabbed his clothes from the cot where he'd been resting less than fifteen minutes prior and tugged on his trousers.

"You're being annoying," Luc said, not caring in the least if Marco thumped him for it. A set of knuckles to the jaw might actually make Luc feel better. He'd been such an ass telling Ingrid about Suzette. He had never told anyone, and he shouldn't have started with Ingrid. He'd confessed everything, poured out his sins at her feet, and she had nearly been sick. Her sudden nausea had been mirrored within him, climbing up his throat, clenching his stomach. He'd never be able to forget the revulsion she'd felt for him as she'd raced from the carriage into the arcades.

"Just wait," Marco said with a satisfied laugh. "I'm not saying anything more until—"

White light poured into the loft, drenching every corner with its molten heat. Luc collapsed beneath its crushing weight. Beside him, Marco fell into a relatively more graceful bow, his forehead nearly touching the floor. When Irindi finally spoke, Luc felt her voice reverberate up through his hands.

"It has been decided," Irindi began, her monotone voice

strumming Luc's eardrums. "A second Dispossessed has been chosen to aid you, Luc Rousseau."

He tried to lift his head, but it felt locked in place. It was a little late for the big announcement, wasn't it?

"Dimitrie has been here more than a week," Luc said.

"I am not aware of any *Dimitrie*," she said. "You will share your territory with Marco Angelis. Your human charges are now his as well. Receive him accordingly."

At Irindi's words, Luc felt as if the floor were falling out from underneath him.

The hot angelic glow abruptly went out, leaving the loft in cold blackness. The weight on Luc's shoulders lifted, but he stayed bowed over, knees on the floor. Beside him, Marco's laugh rumbled low.

"I told you not to trust the boy," he said, and then sprang to his feet. "Don't bother looking for him—he was gone when I arrived. Irindi came to me earlier and instructed me to join you."

"Then who is Dimitrie?" Luc rose slowly, his mind racing with tangled thoughts. The sharp edge of panic brought a wash of gooseflesh over his skin.

"He doesn't belong here, that much I know," Marco answered, strolling to the loft door and shoving it open once again. "He lied and took on a territory that wasn't his. He's either a glutton for punishment or"—Marco looked over his shoulder at Luc—"someone else wanted him here."

Marco peered out toward the rectory. "Where is Lady Ingrid?"

Luc went to his cot and sat down. He needed to think. He needed to know why Dimitrie would have come here, or who would have sent him.

"Forget Ingrid for a moment." A demand for Marco to stay away from her rolled to a halt on the tip of Luc's tongue. *Receive him accordingly.*

Hell and damnation.

"We need to find out who Dimitrie is," Luc said.

"And we will," Marco replied. "The very moment he returns. Though I can't promise I'll ask very nicely."

Whatever the reason, Luc suspected it had to do with Ingrid. Perhaps even with Axia—could she have sent Dimitrie here somehow? And all this time Luc had allowed him to be close to Ingrid. He closed his hands into fists and surfaced her scent.

She filled him with alertness. She wasn't asleep. Luc went to the loft door and saw something he hadn't before: the lights were on in the rectory's front sitting room and in the servants' ell. And Ingrid was crossing the churchyard for the carriage house.

Marco saw her coming.

"This will be much better than hibernation," he murmured.

At least Marco couldn't harm her now. Luc wouldn't have to worry like he did before. But what if Marco felt something . . . *more* for her, the same way Luc did?

"You're a Wolf," Luc said, thinking of all the dog gargoyle statues scattered along the abbey roof. "Only Dogs should be guardians here."

Marco held up his hands. "Then there must be a handsome wolf gargoyle hidden somewhere amongst all those ugly dogs."

Ingrid's call traveled from below just then. "Luc?"

Marco moved toward the loft stairs in anticipation.

"Are you here, Luc?"

She appeared at the top of the stairs, her eyes landing on Marco first, then on Luc's half-dressed form. She stood inert, as if both sights were unexpected hazards.

"Lady Ingrid," Marco greeted her, his eyes a touch too intense.

He was scenting her. The angels had to be laughing at Luc just then. *Your human charges are now his.* Irindi had given Marco exactly what he wanted, and there was nothing Luc could do to change it.

"Where were you?" Ingrid said to Luc as she edged carefully around Marco, clutching the top of her cloak around her throat. "Grayson's missing from the rectory and my father wanted the carriage. Dimitrie said he couldn't find you."

Luc took up his shirt and began to pull it on. "Grayson had a run-in with Léon."

Ingrid gasped. "Oh God, is he hurt?"

"Léon just tangled him up in a bit of silk webbing and gave him a warning for you to stay away from the Daicrypta. Grayson's on his way back right now."

She watched him button his shirt. "Wait. You went out."

"Of course I did," Luc replied, tucking his shirt into the waist of his trousers.

"Dimitrie didn't," Ingrid said thoughtfully, almost to herself. "Not until ten minutes ago, at least. He took my father out in the carriage instead."

Luc crossed a glance with Marco. He didn't care for Lord Brickton, but he also didn't want the imposter anywhere near one of his humans.

"I don't understand," Ingrid said. "If you were called to Grayson's side, why wasn't Dimitrie?"

Luc didn't want to tell her that he'd been taken for a fool. Marco, on the other hand, had no reservations. He sauntered away from the top of the stairs, arms crossed.

"Because the boy lied to all of you," Marco said. "He isn't your gargoyle."

Luc's chest felt air-light when she looked to him first, and not Marco. Luc nodded.

"It's the truth. Irindi knew nothing about Dimitrie. He was never assigned to the abbey."

He belonged somewhere else. A gargoyle always had a territory, even shadow gargoyles. The question of where Dimitrie's territory was pricked at Luc like a warning.

"But you do have a new gargoyle," Marco added.

Ingrid held Luc's gaze. Her corn-silk brows furrowed, and a twist of apprehension knotted itself deep in Luc's stomach. *Her* apprehension, not his.

She knew who it was, and she gasped his name.

CHAPTER TWENTY

"**M**arco."

Ingrid had felt the difference the moment she'd entered Luc's loft. Before, Marco had tended to look at her as if she were something to eat. Now, his eyes looked upon her with a fierceness that reminded her of Luc's.

"At your service," he murmured, and she imagined him making a low, mocking bow. A quick glance over her shoulder showed him doing just that.

"But then why has Dimitrie been here?" she asked, a cool glove of worry sliding down her ribs, enclosing her stomach. Luc's chest expanded, as if he felt her worry, too. "Why has he pretended to be our gargoyle?"

"I plan to ask him as soon as he returns." Something in Luc's voice told Ingrid she didn't want to be there when the inquisition occurred.

She drew her cloak tighter. It was freezing outside and in, and yet there were Luc and Marco without coats. Luc, without shoes.

"It won't be for a while yet. My father and Dimitrie will likely be out until dawn searching for Grayson," she said. Luc looked away, turning his ear as if he'd heard something.

"Your brother is back, but he's alone," he announced.

"Excellent. The sooner I scent him, the better," Marco said, striding toward the open loft door.

"What do you mean?" Ingrid asked.

Luc avoided her eyes, joining Marco at the door. "He can't trace any of his human charges until he's scented them."

"I've had the rapturous pleasure of meeting your brother before, Lady Ingrid, but at that time I wasn't guardian of this territory," Marco explained.

Luc's whole body had gone rigid. He hadn't liked Dimitrie telling Ingrid about their scenting abilities, and he probably still felt that the less she knew, the better. He didn't want her to be a part of his world. The realization shouldn't have hurt as much as it did.

"I don't like that my father is with Dimitrie," Ingrid said to Luc. "If we don't know who he is or why he's been here, we can't trust him."

"I know," Luc said, ripping his shirt free from the waist of his trousers again. "I'll find them."

His fingers weren't fast enough to satisfy what must have been an overwhelming need to flee, because two of his buttons popped off as he was shucking his shirt.

Ingrid saw a swath of pale skin along Luc's chest and stomach before she spun around.

"Keep her safe." Luc's whisper hadn't been for her, but it was so quiet in the loft she had heard anyway.

"Do I have a choice?" Marco returned.

Ingrid ticked off the seconds. She would give Luc ten before taking a peek. Less than half of that had passed when she heard the distinct sound of wind filling a pair of massive feather-less wings.

"He's gone," Marco said. "And rather put out, if you ask me."

Of course he was. This was Luc's territory. His home. Having to share it with Dimitrie had been difficult enough for him. Now Luc had to share this place with Marco. For an *eternity*. Ingrid would have wanted to fly away, too.

She turned back around and saw Luc's clothes on the floor, his shirt atop his trousers, looking as if he had simply vanished.

"I'm a Duster," she said softly, glancing up from Luc's clothes. "You want me dead. You want my brother dead."

Marco straightened and pulled a frown. "I never wanted you dead, Lady Ingrid. If I had, would I have helped you escape the Underneath? I was too curious about you to wish for your death."

And now he wouldn't lay a finger on her. She let her shoulders relax. There was nothing to fear anymore; at least, not from him.

"Who is this Duster you call Léon?" Marco asked.

"He has arachnae blood. He had said he was going to the Daicrypta. I thought it was to have his demon blood removed," Ingrid answered, recalling Monsieur Dupuis's offer to do the same for her. But Léon couldn't have had his blood drained. Not if he could still make silk webbing.

"If I had found him cocooning your brother in silk, I would have gladly killed him," Marco said.

"Then I am relieved you *didn't* find him." She turned for the stairs. Marco might not be able to lay a finger on her, but that didn't mean he wasn't dangerous.

"My lady," he said in parting, and she thought how strange it was for him to address her by her proper title all the time.

She held still on the top step. "Why did Irindi choose you?"

"I was slipping into hibernation," he answered. "Maybe the Order understands I'm more useful guarding a territory than turning to stone upon another one."

She gripped the banister and faced him. "But why *you*?"

"Would you rather have Dimitrie?" he countered.

She would rather have only one gargoyle to sense her, to be able to locate her and feel everything she happened to feel. Irindi had been right, though: Luc did need help. The Waverlys weren't easy humans to protect.

"Does it matter what I want?" she asked.

Marco laughed as she took the steps down and exited the carriage house door.

Back in the rectory, she found Gabby, Grayson, and their mother at the dining room table. They sat in complete silence, the steaming cups of tea before them untouched. Ingrid walked in hesitantly and gripped the back of a chair. She didn't want to sit and shook her head at the footman as he approached.

"He is going to take us back to London," their mother said, her hushed voice steady. She lifted her eyes to Grayson, whose rumpled state made sense, considering he'd recently been wrapped in spider webbing. "Not you. You he will leave here, to manage the gallery. *My* gallery."

She didn't say it possessively. It wasn't a bitter statement, but one of extreme sadness and disappointment. Ingrid and her siblings had done this to their mother, Ingrid knew. They had been careless and selfish, and everything she had wanted for so long, had been able to experience, even just briefly, was going to be taken away from her.

"We won't go," Gabby said. "If we all refuse to leave, he can't make us."

"Oh, my dear girl, that is all very idealistic," Lady Brickton said, slowly pushing her chair back and standing. She still wore her dressing gown and a white lace-trimmed sleeping hat. "But your father holds the winning hand here. It is his title we bear, his holdings that support us, his connections we require. If you haven't realized that yet, now is the time to start."

Mama left the room, her steps quick and efficient. She was going to start packing. Ingrid knew it without having to ask.

"How could you leave?" Ingrid asked Grayson.

"You could have at least had the decency not to get caught," Gabby added.

Grayson stood abruptly, knocking back his chair. "As if the two of you haven't left this place in the middle of the night before. I just had the misfortune of being seen by a maid. Funny," he said with a cutting glare at Gabby. "She didn't witness Nolan Quinn climbing up to your window."

Gabby scowled at Grayson, and Ingrid was about to chastise her but bit her tongue. Luc had come to her window before. He'd come into her room and kissed her. And, well . . . he hadn't been wearing much in the way of clothing. She sincerely hoped Nolan's visit had been more decent.

"Well, good. Once you're here all by yourself, you can sack her," Gabby said.

"He will not," Ingrid said, tempering her sister's ire. "She probably thought she was doing her job."

"Snitching on Grayson is her job?" Gabby cried.

The footman by the swinging doors that led down to the kitchens stepped forward.

"If my lord and ladies would permit?" he said, his head bowed.

Grayson rubbed his temple. "Yes?"

The footman straightened. "I wish to vouch for the maid in question, my lord. She did not witness your departure, but was told by another servant that you had left and that you had seemed rather distressed. The other servant bade her to inform Lord Brickton at once, my lord."

Grayson lowered his hand. "Which servant was this?"

Ingrid let go of the chair as understanding hit her. "Dimitrie."

The footman, looking surprised, bowed again. "Why, yes, my lady."

Gabby surged from her seat. "Why would he do that? He's our—"

She stopped to clear her throat. Grayson thanked and dismissed the footman, who seemed entirely too grateful to leave.

"He's our nothing," Ingrid said, voice low. Her brother and sister squinted in confusion.

"Our nothing?" Grayson repeated.

"He lied. He's not our—" Ingrid paused and looked to the kitchen doors. "Protector."

Now wasn't the time to share the big news about who exactly was.

Gabby tossed up her hands, her dressing gown looking like a half-inflated lace balloon. "Then what is he doing here?"

"I don't know," Ingrid answered. "Luc doesn't know, either. But it's clear Dimitrie wanted Papa to know Grayson had left."

Grayson withdrew to the mirrored sideboard. Ingrid watched his reflection. Like her, he seemed to feel not anger but the need to understand. To piece it all together. He met Ingrid's gaze in the mirror.

"If this isn't his territory, what is?" he asked.

Ingrid went for logic. "It has to be close. If he has humans to protect somewhere, he couldn't keep himself far from them for very long."

"Unless he doesn't have permanent human charges," Grayson said.

The rectory doorbell cranked its grating blare. The three of them held still an alarmed second before dashing into the foyer. Without waiting for Gustav, Grayson threw open the door. A bleary-eyed messenger boy stood on the front step. He held out an envelope and yawned.

"What is this?" Grayson asked.

"Some people refer to them as letters," the boy said, his English as proficient as his sarcasm.

Grayson grabbed the note from the boy's gloved hand and slammed the door without tossing him so much as a sou.

"That wasn't very kind," Gabby said, fighting a smile.

Grayson flipped the note over and read the handwriting. He looked at Ingrid and held out the small envelope. "It's addressed to you."

Ingrid took the note but was wary of opening it. Something was wrong, and she somehow knew that when she read this note, things were going to get much worse.

She took the envelope and walked to the credenza beneath the foyer's mirror. Slowly and methodically, she lifted the penknife and slit the envelope open. The note inside was on fine card stock, a marbled gray, with an address stamped at the top and slanted handwriting inked below:

Dimitrie is delivering your father to me presently. He will remain unharmed for now. I told you that you would end up coming to me.

M. Robert Dupuis

The dusky blue hour of four in the morning found them on their way back to Hôtel Bastian. Gabby's eyes burned. She hadn't slept and yet somehow she'd become caught in the center of a nightmare, the kind that spun in frenzied circles; the kind where she couldn't run fast enough or move her body the way she wanted.

Luc had returned to the rectory within minutes of the letter's arrival. He'd followed Dimitrie and Lord Brickton to a grand Montmartre town house and watched from the skies as they approached the door. Lord Brickton's shivery unease had dripped through Luc's chest the whole time. Gabby's father had known something was off, and yet he'd gone inside the town house anyway.

"He's concerned, but not hurt in any way," Luc had told them. He'd waited, circling overhead, devising a way to get inside if

Lord Brickton required him. But when nothing more happened, Luc had turned back for the rectory instead.

"He isn't going to harm Papa," Ingrid said now, all five of them—Gabby, Grayson, Ingrid, Mama, and Luc—riding in the hired hackney.

Their own landau was still in Montmartre, outside the Paris seat for the Daicrypta.

"He's using Papa as leverage," Ingrid said.

"As trade, you mean," Gabby said, still cold despite the ratty rug that covered her legs. "You for him, isn't that how it is? We should have pushed Dupuis off the balcony at that dreadful artist's salon."

"Gabriella," Mama sighed. It was a halfhearted admonishment. Gabby was certain that in truth Mama agreed.

"Marco will bring Constantine. Maybe he can tell us more," Luc said, his posture rigid. Gabby wondered if he planned to leap from the moving hackney should the urge to shift come over him.

"Léon said not to go to Dupuis," Grayson said. "His warning sounded serious, Ingrid. It has to be bad."

"So you would leave Papa there?" Ingrid asked.

"I would try to think of another way, that's all."

"And what if there isn't another way?" Ingrid shot back.

"There is always another way, my dear," their mother said, her gaze fixed to the window and the rising light. "We simply need more heads than we currently have to think of it."

Her optimism was strange to hear. In fact, her insistence on accompanying them to Hôtel Bastian had been so out of the ordinary that no one had dared object. No one argued with her now, either.

When they arrived at Hôtel Bastian, they went straight up to the third floor and pounded on the dungeonlike door. Luc stood with them, and Gabby was certain he would force his way into Alliance headquarters if need be. Thankfully, it wasn't required. Rory opened the door, half asleep and for once not wearing his vest of daggers. Gabby figured it couldn't be very comfortable to sleep in.

The sight of them crowded on the landing was enough for Rory to yank the door open wide and permit them all in. Less than five minutes later, the common rooms were noisy with the mumblings of awakened Alliance, including Nolan and Chelle. Gabby let out a breath of relief when she didn't see Carrick among them.

"Then Dimitrie is the Daicrypta's gargoyle?" Nolan asked.

From what Luc had seen and what Dupuis had written in his note to Ingrid, it made the most sense that the Daicrypta had planted Dimitrie within the abbey's territory. To get close to Ingrid, Gabby suspected.

"But how did the Daicrypta know the Order planned to pair Luc with another Dispossessed?" Nolan asked.

He stood in the center of the open kitchen area. Because of the stove, it was the warmest spot in the apartment and the place where everyone had chosen to congregate. Lady Brickton had been given a chair close to the stove, and Gabby and Ingrid stood behind her.

"That's what we want to know," Gabby said. "We told no one other than you, Vander, and Chelle."

"What about Constantine?" Chelle asked, seated on a zinc-topped counter. "Did Ingrid tell him as well?"

One of the Alliance men Gabby didn't know spoke up. "He was Daicrypta once. Maybe he still is."

"He isn't behind this," Ingrid said. "And no, I didn't tell him. We don't talk about things like that."

Gabby wondered what they did talk about. How to aim lightning? How to put a stopper on it?

"There are many Dispossessed who knew," Luc said, speaking for the first time. Rory and Chelle, along with a few Alliance Gabby didn't know, looked at Luc with marked reproach.

"There you have it, then," the same man who'd doubted Constantine said with a wave of his hand toward Luc.

"You can't place blame on the gargoyles without proof," Grayson said. "There were others who knew."

Ready to argue, the man stood up from the chair in which he'd been reclining. Nolan held out a hand toward each of them.

"Grayson is right. There were others," he said. "I told my father when we were in Rome. He could have told someone else."

Gabby thought again of Carrick and wondered at his absence. Not that she wished to even look upon him, but still.

"Where is your father?" she asked.

Nolan lowered his hands. "He said he would be patrolling late tonight."

To make up for time lost during their lovely dinner, no doubt. Gabby's eyes traveled past Rory and caught on his puckered brow. He was scowling at the floor, his hands on his hips. As if feeling her eyes on him, Rory glanced up. He couldn't hold her gaze very long.

"Rory?" she asked. "What is it?"

Nolan and the rest of the kitchen turned their attention toward him. Rory didn't look as tall or threatening without all that blessed silver strapped to his chest. In fact, he looked a bit like a cornered cat.

"It happened while we were in Rome," Rory began. "Uncle had a visitor. I didna think a thing of it—he's part of the Directorate and deals wi' peace ambassadors from time to time."

Rory held the note Ingrid had brought aloft. "Uncle's visitor was this man. Robert Dupuis."

CHAPTER TWENTY-ONE

The sun was slow to rise. At least, it felt slow. Ingrid took a restless turn around the roof of Hôtel Bastian, running her hand over the curved wrought-iron balustrades. The roof gravel crunched under her feet, the pink dawn fully under way now. A few stories below, her family and members of the Alliance continued to convene. They were tossing around ideas on how to retrieve Lord Brickton, speculating about whether Carrick would have been in league with the Daicrypta, and why, and above all, about how to keep Ingrid away from Dupuis and his bloodletting machines.

She had said she'd needed air and gone to the roof. Really, though, she was trying to devise a way to sneak out of Hôtel Bastian and give Dupuis exactly what he wanted.

How could she sit back and allow something awful to happen to her father when she could stop it? He'd been infuriating since he'd arrived in Paris, but before, in London, when Ingrid had been younger, he'd been different. Better. And right now his life was in her hands.

If she went to Dupuis, the risk of death was there, of course. She wasn't too proud to admit that it scared her. The blood draining could go badly; her organs could quit if they were deprived of the blood needed to sustain them. Yes, she could die. But if she didn't go to Dupuis, her father most certainly would.

The roof door opened as she was leaning against the corner balustrade, gazing down at the street below. Luc had let her go to the roof alone, but she knew he would be keeping watch, surfacing her scent time and again to make sure she was okay. She didn't have to turn around to know it wasn't Luc who'd come to the roof. She could always feel Luc's eyes on her like two fingers pressing against her skin.

"They said you were up here." Vander closed the door behind him.

"I'm going to Dupuis," she said, dispensing with pleasantries.

"I thought you might try to," he said.

Vander's boots crunched over the gravel toward her. He stopped a distance away. Most likely to stay out of her field of dust and avoid sapping her of her lectrux power, the way he had been this whole time.

Ingrid turned away from the ledge, her arms crossed over her middle. It was cold, and she had left her coat in the apartment. "It's my decision to make."

Vander's hair was unruly, from the wind and from his having been drawn from his bed at so early an hour. It tossed like wheat stalks in a summer storm.

"No one has ever had anything as powerful or . . . or *extraordinary* as angel blood before," he said. "You can't just hand it over to a member of the Daicrypta."

"What if I don't?" she asked. "What if, after it's done, I'm able to destroy it somehow?"

It was a grasping theory. Was angel blood even destructible? Did it look like blood or was it something else entirely? No one knew. This would be the first procedure of its kind, and that was why everyone was so scared.

Vander's response was predictable and irritating. "It's too risky."

"He's my *father*," Ingrid said. It was as simple as that. He wasn't perfect. In fact, he'd been acting like a pompous old goat. But he was still her father.

"I don't care about your father."

Ingrid balked at him. "How can you say that?"

"Because it's the truth. It's coarse, but it's the truth. If I have to protect one of you, it will be you." Vander took a few steps closer to her field of dust. Dawn crested the cityscape and shed fresh light on his old coat. "It will always be you, Ingrid."

He was making his choice—who to stand behind, who to sacrifice. It was the right thing for him. Ingrid wouldn't begrudge him his decision. That didn't mean it was right for her, though. It wouldn't be right to stay safely in the back of the line, protected on all fronts. If she allowed it, if she allowed something awful to happen to Papa, how would she live with herself for the rest of her days?

She'd rather have no days left than endure that. And if this was to be her last day . . .

Without stopping to think, without a thought for propriety or prudence, Ingrid rose to the tips of her toes and kissed Vander soundly. She had startled him, and she stumbled backward with him. Vander grabbed her arms and steadied their footing.

"What was that for?" he whispered.

She shrugged. "Just in case."

Ingrid expected another question, a demand to know what she'd meant. He quizzed her silently, thoughtful eyes behind a pair of wire spectacles, slightly askew.

Vander brought his mouth to hers. It wasn't an elegant kiss, or a tentative one like they'd shared in the library. This one was untamed. Ingrid felt it deep in her stomach, reaching low between her hips. Vander settled his hands around her waist and pulled her closer. This time she understood the prickling thrum in her arms and hands. Vander's touch stirred her dust, and whether he wished for it or not, he claimed it for himself. How was it possible that his hands had the power to change her? As they stroked up her back, then dove again for her hips, Ingrid could pay little attention to anything but them.

When the roof door opened she was slow to pull away from him. Vander kept his hands around her waist.

A throat noisily cleared across the roof.

"My lady, Mr. Burke, I do apologize for, ah . . ."

Monsieur Constantine had arrived, and when Ingrid looked, she saw Marco towering behind him. They both came out onto the roof, followed by Nolan and Chelle. When Gabby appeared in the mouth of the doorway next, Ingrid eased out of Vander's hold. Grayson emerged after Gabby, and then finally Luc. He wouldn't look at her.

A sudden stirring of guilt ripped through her so fast and strong it made the roof feel as if it had tilted beneath her feet. Ingrid had never been so disappointed with herself. She shouldn't have done it. She shouldn't have kissed Vander when she had already given her heart to Luc. Even if Luc were to hand it right back to her again and again, it would still belong to him.

She took a step away from Vander. It wasn't fair to him, these things she felt for Luc. And she would always feel them.

"I am quite sorry about this, my lady," Constantine said to her as he and the others spread out over the roof.

Her teacher took a seat on the edge of a raised garden bed filled in with snow and propped his hand on his cane.

"I did wonder if Monsieur Dupuis would stoop to violent means, but this tactic is rather surprising. And the senior Quinn's involvement is distressing. I wonder what his goal is."

Nolan looked as if he'd been gnawing on oiled leather for the last half hour. He had to be humiliated and furious and, like everyone else, utterly confounded.

"We don't know anything for certain," he said in a feeble attempt to defend his father. Carrick still hadn't shown, and his connection to Dupuis, his having known Luc was to receive a second gargoyle, didn't do him any favors.

Ingrid searched for her mother, but the countess hadn't taken the trip to the roof. "Where is Mama?" she asked Grayson and Gabby.

"Resting," Grayson answered. "And just so you're aware, she agrees with our decision to find another way to bring Father back. Although I'm tempted to forget all about him."

"That's a terrible thing to say!" Ingrid looked to Gabby for assistance, but her sister was inspecting a trellis woven through with withered black tomato vines.

"He's a bastard," Grayson said. He sighed and ran a hand through his hair. "I know we have to get him, all right? I'm just tempted not to, that's all."

Luc and Marco stood apart from the crowd. Probably without even realizing it, they had come to stand side by side, looking like sentries with their arms crossed over their broad chests.

"There is no other way," Luc said. "The Daicrypta grounds are well guarded, and the place is sprawling. Marco and I couldn't go in there on our own and expect to come out."

"I believe Luc is correct," Constantine said.

"There has to be." Gabby stood with her feet wide apart, as if getting ready for a sword fight. "My sister is not turning herself over to this madman!"

Ingrid had moved even farther away from Vander's side, but she still felt his intense stare.

"No. She isn't," he said.

Ingrid bristled. She knew it only came from a desire to keep her safe, but she didn't like Vander—or anyone—making a decision for her.

"What if we do nothing?" Chelle put in. "What if we act as if Dupuis's note never arrived?"

Constantine stood up from the raised bed edge, leaning heavily on his cane. "It would be most unwise to underestimate Dupuis, or to take his threats lightly. He *will* harm Lord Brickton should Lady Ingrid refuse this summons."

"So I won't refuse it," Ingrid said, turning away from Vander when he took an angry step toward her.

She'd already made up her mind.

"Ingrid, stop," Grayson said, his fingers loosening the collar of his shirt. "It's only been a few hours. We have time."

"And we're wasting it right now," she retorted. "I'm going to get Papa out of there, and then I'll deal with whatever happens next."

Grayson and Gabby set in on her immediately. Each pitched their voice above the other to be heard, but they were essentially saying the same thing: that she was insane and rash and making a ludicrous decision. She was simply waiting for their throats to give out on them before she attempted to make her argument.

Luc stepped away from Marco's side and silenced them both. "I'll take you."

He was finally looking at her, his gaze steady and cold.

"You . . . you will?" She hadn't expected the offer from anyone, let alone Luc.

"He won't," Vander growled. "You are not going to drop her off at Dupuis's door."

Luc spared Vander a withering glance. "Do you actually believe I would leave her, Seer? I'll stay with her the entire time. If Dupuis or his occult practices threaten her life, I'll be there to end his." Luc returned his steadfast gaze to her. "And to take Ingrid home safely."

Vander started to protest again, but Nolan held up a hand to interrupt. "We haven't discussed Axia yet."

It would have been nice not to ever discuss the fallen angel again. The mimic demon's portrayal of Axia's pale serpent had been enough of a reminder to last Ingrid a very long time.

"Axia won't allow Ingrid to discard the one thing she needs to make her a full-fledged angel again," Nolan explained. "She has to have demons watching Ingrid at all times. There must be one corvite for every ten ravens in Paris. As soon as she hears what's happening, she'll make her play for Ingrid."

Damned corvites. There had been black birds roosting on every roof as far as Ingrid could see from the top of Hôtel Bastian. The corvites could have been listening.

"So we should expect demon obstacles on the way to Montmartre," Marco said with a little too much pep. "My first day as your gargoyle is certainly proving to be entertaining, Lady Ingrid."

Luc didn't bother to turn and look at Marco. "*I* am taking her," he said.

"Two gargoyles are better than one, brother."

Ingrid had had enough bickering. Decisions needed to be made, and she needed to get moving. Now.

"Luc can fly me over," she said, though the last time she'd flown over Paris with Luc she had been terrified.

"No," he said quickly. "Corvites aren't the only demons with wings. I can't fight with you in my arms."

Ingrid avoided the death glares Gabby and Grayson were sending her. Gabby had taken up pacing the roof and Grayson had unbuttoned his collar most indecently. They both must have known there was no point in protesting any longer. The decision was made.

"So what do we do?" Ingrid asked.

Luc looked uncomfortable. Whatever he was thinking, it wasn't making him happy.

"We go to common grounds," he answered. "And we ask the Dispossessed for help."

Hôtel du Maurier was no place for a human girl, especially one most gargoyles would consider diseased with demon blood. Luc had understood the risks when he decided to take Ingrid there— *only* Ingrid. Vander Burke had stormed over that condition, but Luc had ignored him. He'd found it relatively easy and unexpectedly satisfying, too.

He and Ingrid had left for Hôtel du Maurier midmorning, and now he stood on the threshold of Lennier's second-level apartments looking directly into the face of the gargoyle he'd least wanted to see: Vincent, the sour-faced Notre Dame guardian.

"You again," Luc said coolly.

Vincent saw Ingrid and flared his nostrils. "Is this your demon girl? How dare you bring her here?"

Ingrid had stayed on Luc's heels as they'd made their way through the abandoned and dilapidated town house. Now she'd just about adhered herself to his back.

Luc pushed against the door, nudging Vincent out of the way. He kept a hand on Ingrid's wrist and pulled her in behind him.

"I thought you protected Notre Dame," Luc said. "And yet this is the second time I find you playing the role of Lennier's butler."

Vincent's cheeks hollowed as he shifted his narrow jaw, his color rising from beeswax to pale rose.

"Your human is welcome, Luc, but tell us why the two of you have come here together," Lennier said from his usual chair before the fire, basking in the warmth.

"The gargoyle I brought earlier, Dimitrie, told us lies. He wasn't assigned to the abbey. He's part of the Daicrypta, and they now have one of my humans imprisoned," Luc said, his hand a shackle around Ingrid's wrist. He had a feeling she didn't mind the closeness, not with Vincent's hooded eyes watching her.

"Another angel's burn for you, then?" Vincent said with a distinctly pleased sneer.

"He hasn't been harmed yet," Luc ground out.

Why was Vincent even here? Lennier didn't keep friends, and he didn't make allies among the other castes the way some did. Luc watched Vincent stride around the room, his head held high, as if he lived here.

"What do you need, Luc?" Lennier asked, genuinely concerned. That was what set the elder gargoyle apart from all the others, even Luc. He truly did want to help whenever and wherever he could.

"We will not help free your human charge," Vincent said.

"We don't need help freeing him. I'm going to take care of that myself," Ingrid said, her voice tremulous. She was angry. Luc could hear it, feel it. She didn't like Vincent or the way he scared her.

Vincent turned his back on her, a purposeful snub, and walked to a window that overlooked the inner courtyard.

"Luc?" Lennier prompted.

"We expect the fallen angel Axia to intercept us in some way. Either through her hellhounds or the other demons she seems to have control over in the Underneath," he answered. "She won't want Ingrid to reach the Daicrypta."

Lennier rose from his chair, his long, craggy fingers tightly gripping the armrests. "Why not?"

"I'm going to let the Daicrypta drain the angel quotient of my blood," Ingrid answered.

It was good that she still believed this.

Luc was sure Lennier believed her, too; she said it with conviction. Of course, there was no chance in hell that Luc was going to allow Dupuis to drain one drop of Ingrid's blood. He just needed to get her there, free Lord Brickton, and then escape with both his humans.

"You ask for added protection," Lennier summed up.

"We have some from the Alliance," Luc said. "But we could use more."

Vincent spun away from the window. "These are your humans. As such, they are your burden, not ours."

"It is an opportunity to work with the Alliance," Lennier said, his watery blue stare floating toward Vincent.

"The *Alliance*," Vincent scoffed. "They would make us their pets, complete with leash and collar. Abide by their laws? Suffer their punishments? We are not on this earth to serve the Alliance, and yet that is exactly what they want. They want our obedience, our fealty, and they want to take it by force. Well, they will not have mine. I will not lower myself to assist them, either. Them or a half-breed girl."

"That's a relief," Luc said. "It would have been awkward having to tell you that you weren't invited anyway."

Vincent's lips thinned as he struggled to come up with a response. Failing, he crossed his long, musty-smelling cape tightly across his front and, with a curt bow toward Lennier, left the apartment.

Ingrid released a pent-up breath against Luc's shoulder, her nose brushing against him. He let go of her wrist, feeling absurd that he'd been so worried about Vincent's presence. The Notre Dame gargoyle was a rotten crab apple with antihuman sentiments, and just like a rotten crab apple, he could be taken care of with one solid boot stomping.

"I hear rumors that Marco has joined you at the abbey." Lennier's raspy voice somehow made the chilly apartment feel colder.

"He has," Luc answered. Gargoyles gossiped more efficiently than servants, it seemed.

"I will tend to things," Lennier said, and Luc knew that he'd succeeded, at least at this first junction.

The elder gargoyle gestured toward the open doorway leading to the inner rooms. "Rest. We will wait until night has fallen."

CHAPTER TWENTY-TWO

From his seat by the fire, Lennier closed his eyes as if he meant to nap. Ingrid knew it was a dismissal.

"But we can't just wait. Nightfall isn't for hours yet," she said.

Lennier kept his eyes shuttered. After Vincent's show of hatred, Ingrid supposed Lennier's response was rather kind.

She knew having more gargoyles on her side was essential, and that they wouldn't be enthusiastic about flying in daytime skies, but any number of things could happen to her father before nightfall.

Luc silenced Ingrid with a finger to his lips and then waved for her to follow him. He walked through the open doorway, entering a sparely furnished dining room. Did the Dispossessed eat or drink? She'd never seen Luc do either, but then, she didn't see any of the servants eating or drinking.

They walked a short, lightless hallway located off the dining room before Luc found where Lennier wanted them to go.

It was a bedroom, with a four-poster bed and a single glass door to a terrace overlooking the courtyard. The hearth was cold and black, and there wasn't so much as a splinter of wood in sight to build a fire. The chimney couldn't support one anyway, Ingrid figured. If anything, they'd smoke out a nest of squirrels or mice. There were blankets on the bed, at least, though they were sun-faded and an unfashionable chintz.

Ingrid hovered near the door, watching Luc take a turn around the small guest room. "I don't feel like resting," she admitted.

He stopped to peer outside. "There isn't much else you can do until Lennier says it's time to leave."

"And we must do what Lennier says?"

"He's our elder," Luc said, his brows vaulted. "And the elder is king of the Dispossessed. It's how things are done."

Ingrid stepped over a battered hooked rug, charred along the fringe from lying so close to the hearth. Hôtel du Maurier gave off such a sad aura, as if it had been bottled up and sealed off while it waited for a family to return to it. From what she had seen, no family had lived here for many years. Perhaps it had been decades. Lennier was the master of the house, and she was certain he liked it abandoned.

"Who was that other man?" Ingrid asked.

Luc grumbled and came away from the window. "Vincent. A Notre Dame gargoyle. They're all like that." He leaned against one of the bed's lusterless posters and crossed his arms. "Forget him. He's nothing."

Ingrid wasn't as confident about that as Luc seemed to be. Vincent had made her nervous in ways Marco and Yann never had—and they hadn't exactly been nice.

"Is this place dangerous?" she asked. It felt like it should be.

The whole estate seemed set apart from the rest of the world. Luc had led her to it through the Luxembourg Gardens, the entrance arcades tucked into a corner of the park. Ivy and vines camouflaged the arched entrance, and the town house itself, dilapidated as it was, could have easily been overlooked.

She didn't belong here. This was a place where men could freely transform into beastly figures. A place where unfamiliar rules held sway.

"I wouldn't have brought you here if I thought I wouldn't be able to protect you," Luc answered. She didn't fail to notice that he hadn't really answered her question. It *was* dangerous, then.

Ingrid walked around him, toward a small dresser topped with an aged mirror. A spotty silver brush and comb set had been left to tarnish on the dresser. She ran her fingers lightly over the engraved silver.

"If you don't want me in here, I can leave," Luc said. He looked at her in the mirror.

"Don't," she said quickly to his reflection. "Please don't."

They were alone in a bedroom, but considering they were on gargoyle common grounds and Vincent had acted as though he wanted to drain her blood himself, she would forget propriety for a little while.

Luc held her gaze in the mirror. "What I told you the other morning. About my sister and that priest . . . about what I did . . ."

The topic change was so abrupt that Ingrid could only blink.

"I told you I wasn't sorry, and that's not going to change. If you're uncomfortable with that—"

"I'm not."

Luc sharpened his focus on her. "You ran away. You couldn't get out of that carriage fast enough."

She remembered it with a pang of guilt. "I wasn't running from *you*."

Oh, good Lord. Luc had trusted her with a secret he'd kept under lock and key for who knew how long, and she'd dashed away as if her stockings were on fire. Why wouldn't he have thought she was running from him?

"It was a mistake to say anything." He turned away from the mirror.

Ingrid did as well, catching his arm. He was too solid, though, and she couldn't swing him back around. "It wasn't what you did. It's what happened to you because of it."

Luc held still. "What do you mean?"

"The way you died. When you were telling me what happened I saw it all—the gallows, the noose, the black hood. The crowds shouting for your death. It was awful and I hated it. I hated imagining you dead."

He had turned back to her by then, his expression guarded.

"I didn't stay dead for very long. They threw my body in a shallow grave." Luc cocked his head. "At least there were only three feet of earth to claw through instead of six."

"It's not funny," Ingrid said, not understanding how he could speak so casually about death and coming back to life.

"Of course it isn't funny. For a second I thought I'd been buried alive."

"Not that! Your death, Luc. It made me sick just thinking of it. That's why I got out of the carriage so fast. I needed air. I couldn't breathe. I didn't want you to be dead."

He startled her by smiling.

"I am dead, Ingrid," he said softly. "I've been dead for hundreds of years. Why should that bother you?"

She didn't know what to say. Why should it bother her? How could it not?

"You're not dead. You're standing right in front of me, breathing, talking." Ingrid poked him hard in the chest. "Solid, see? You're not some ghostly specter. You're *alive*."

Luc seized the hand that had poked him and held it away from her side.

"I do feel alive sometimes," he whispered. Ingrid pulled her hand back, but he counterpulled and, no surprise, won. She stumbled closer to his chest.

"There is so much that we don't feel as gargoyles. We don't feel hunger or thirst. We don't have to sleep, though some of us do it out of habit. Or boredom. You have no idea how bored I've been before. No dreams, no goals, nothing to do but protect. Nothing driving me but that one act, and most of the time my human charges never even needed me."

Luc drew her hand to his cheek. Breath stuck fast in her throat, Ingrid uncurled her fingers and touched him. He was warm, his skin like velvet. He pressed her hand against him and exhaled, long and hard.

"I never thought I'd have such difficult humans to take care of." Before she could quarrel, he went on, "But I've never felt more alive than I have since meeting you."

He turned his cheek until his lips were against her palm, his breath hot. "You're dangerous, Ingrid. You make me feel things that I shouldn't."

He kissed the heart of her hand.

"Luc." It was the only coherent word revolving through her mind. There was nothing else, just Luc and his lips, and she knew that she wanted this. She wanted him to keep talking and touching her. She wanted Luc to kiss her the way he had before.

He let go of her hand, but she kept it against his cheek, willing the moment to stretch on.

"Is he courting you?" he asked, his voice hoarse, his eyes sooty malachite.

Vander. He was there now, stuck within the spare inch or so left between Ingrid and Luc. Reminding her that she'd kissed him just a few hours before. How could she have been so thoughtless?

"No. But you should know—"

Luc kissed her, stealing away the rest of her confession. Ingrid let it go, tasting again the wild spice of his lips, his warm breath as it mingled with hers. She gave herself over to the touch of his tongue, the rock of his body as he crushed her closer. He wanted to make her a part of him, and she wanted that, too. To dissolve into him, sink deeper, into a place without end. He explored her hips and hitched them flush against his own.

Luc dropped his chin and gave her a gentle push away. He breathed deeply, his jaw tight and eyes closed.

"Are you . . . changing?" She'd known it couldn't last. His curse might allow a kiss, or perhaps even two. But his body would forever revolt against what it wanted: her.

Luc shook his head and opened his eyes. They were surprisingly serene. "Not yet. Knowing that it's coming this time helps."

Ingrid didn't understand how, but it made her happy nevertheless. She lifted her hand to his mouth and traced his full lower lip, the same way she had in the underground arcade. It moved beneath her fingers as he spoke.

"If we try hard enough we can sometimes stave off a shift. Not for very long. A minute. Maybe two." With another gentle push, Luc moved Ingrid backward. Her skirts brushed against the mattress. "It won't be easy. I don't know if I can do it."

Ingrid smoothed the front of his shirt with her palms. She wanted him to try. She wanted it so badly the need for it weighed heavy in her chest. Luc locked his hands around her waist and lifted her to sit upon the mattress. He inclined toward her, but Ingrid leaned back. If they kissed again, his hold on his shift might break. She wanted him to stay as he was for as long as he could.

"Perhaps we should . . . talk," she said.

Luc raised one of his dark brows. "Talk?"

"It might help you to not change so quickly."

Luc put one knee onto the mattress, then the other, until they bracketed her legs.

"What do you want to talk about?" he asked.

Ingrid edged backward, pushing herself toward the headboard. He followed. On hands and knees, Luc crawled over the ugly chintz coverlet.

"I really don't know very much about you," she answered, trying to keep her voice steady. The predatory shine in his eyes was distracting her. "What did you do when you were human? Did you go to school?"

Ingrid's back hit the mound of pillows and she swallowed hard.

"I never went to school. I needed to work my family's farm, a small place outside the old Paris wall. Goats, pigs, chickens. A couple of cows." Luc came down beside her, the headboard creaking against his weight. She tried to picture him tending farm animals. Tried to imagine what his parents or sister might have looked like. People from so long ago. Dead for centuries. And yet, here Luc still was.

"I taught myself to read, but that wasn't until after," he said.

After. If anyone had a clear-cut before and after, it was a gargoyle.

"Do you like to read?" she asked. Luc's eyes followed the motion of her lips.

"Not as much as I like doing this," he answered, and to stop her from speaking again, Luc cupped her chin and ran his thumb along her lips.

Ingrid lay still against the pillows, uncertain. Barely breathing. What did Luc intend? Her mind ran wild with ideas, all of which she wanted. When Luc reached for the folds of her creamy blue skirt, he hovered over the silk, as if afraid to touch her.

He took a long moment to run his eyes down the length of her body, and then his hand settled lightly on her leg. His palm barely ruffled the silk at first, but as he traveled from her thigh to the arc of her hip, he grew bold. He angled her toward him and wrapped his arm around the small of her back, pulling her closer.

Ingrid flattened her palms against Luc's chest, her head tucked into the curve of his neck. His skin was still smooth and white, without a single patch of obsidian. He was tense, though, his breathing ragged. But they were still touching. Lying beside one another.

"It's okay if this is all it can be," she whispered.

He buried his nose and mouth in her hair, his breath hot against the crown of her head. "I want more. You do, too."

Ingrid closed her eyes and pressed a kiss to Luc's neck. His skin was warm and he smelled of clean cedar. "How much more?" she asked.

His laughter gusted against her scalp. He pulled back until his face was over hers. "All of you."

Ingrid laughed, trying hard not to blush. "I meant how much more *here*? Now. Before you change."

"Let's find out," he whispered. Luc lowered his mouth to hers. She breathed him in, wishing they could stay like this for as long as they wanted.

"They won't forgive me for this," Luc whispered, his mouth still brushing against hers.

Ingrid froze stone-cold beneath him. With an awkward slap of her hands against his chest, she shoved Luc away and covered her throbbing lips. Oh, how stupid! How unbelievably *reckless*.

"I'm so sorry," she said through her trembling fingers. "I forgot where we were. Lennier . . ." *The window*. She rolled out from underneath Luc and off the bed, landing behind the four-poster.

They were on gargoyle common grounds. They could have been seen.

Luc followed her off the bed, shaking his head. "I didn't mean them. Lennier left a few minutes ago. There's no one here. I would have felt them." He tapped the back of his neck, just below his skull. He could feel the presence of other gargoyles?

"I meant the Order," he went on. "They know everything I do. Everything I feel."

His body had tensed, the muscles along his jaw rippling with some hidden effort. He must have been trying not to shift.

"What will they do?" Ingrid asked. They were angels. Their punishment couldn't possibly be as bad as the violent death the Dispossessed would order.

Luc shook his head again and clenched his eyes shut as a tremor rippled through him. "I don't know. Irindi warned me—"

His voice broke into a shriek. Luc's eyes flew open, alert and focused. "Your father."

"What do you—" Ingrid stopped as Luc kicked off his boots and tore at his shirt, buttons popping off and spinning to the floor.

He shot up toward the ceiling, the muscles beneath his creamy skin bulging, his shoulders broadening; jet scales quilted his skin, clambering like vines up his neck, along his face, and to the crown of his head, where his ears had sharpened into clipped points.

She understood now. Something was happening to her father.

Ingrid didn't turn away as she usually did. She watched with determined bravery as Luc transformed into a sexless, scaled monster even before his trousers had hit the floor.

Ingrid went for the balcony door and threw it open a bare second before he could smash through it. Luc's wings unfurled and he soared into the sky, a black stamp against the bleak clouds.

And then he was gone.

Oh God. Papa. Ingrid sat on the edge of the bed, the balcony door still open. Waiting until nightfall had been a mistake.

She couldn't stay in this room another second.

The dim hallway seemed to tip side to side as she ran down it, into the spare, depressing dining room that no one ever ate in. The receiving room was empty, but even if Lennier with his crazy, long white hair had been inside, she would have surged right past him.

The peeling wallpaper along the corridor and the faded carpet in the stairwell blurred as she ran. She passed the dead cat in the downstairs corridor without flinching as she had the first time, then bolted through the dingy ballroom, toward the open doors, and into the courtyard.

But there was nowhere to go.

Ingrid came to a stop just in front of a stone fountain with a nine-headed Hydra waterspout. One of the snakelike heads had cracked and slid off and now rested in the dry basin.

She stared at the coarse gray stone serpent, its carved fangs having weathered to blunt ends. Just as Luc's had, her body felt as if it was revolting. One moment, throbbing with desire, the next, squeezed tight with guilt. How could this world be real? How could any of it be possible?

She sank to the ledge of the basin and dropped her head into her hands.

"Your father must have met with difficulty for Luc to have flown off in such haste."

Ingrid jumped up from the stone fountain. Vincent stood within the columned entrance to Hôtel du Maurier. He had his black cloak folded around him, and in this natural light, his complexion appeared even whiter.

"And Lennier," Vincent said, taking languid steps across the courtyard toward her. "He hardly ever leaves his territory. You must be feeling rather abandoned."

She lifted her chin and met his gaze. "Not at all."

Vincent's slow smile made her think of a slinking cat. The balcony door to the guest room was right there, in plain view. What if Vincent had seen her and Luc? But hadn't Luc said he'd have been able to sense another gargoyle's presence? Vincent must have only just returned.

"What do you want?" she asked.

Vincent stopped at the fountain and ignored her question. "Have you met many of my kind?"

She ground a heel into the gravel, prepared to run if need be. As if she could get far. The man could sprout wings, for heaven's sake.

"A few," she answered. Marco and Yann. Dimitrie and Lennier. Gaston, Constantine's gargoyle. And of course, Luc.

"There are hundreds of us in Paris. Thousands the world

over," Vincent said, his attention turning toward one of the several pitted and cracked flowerpots rimming the base of the fountain. In one, a single white Christmas rose, though stunted, had managed to bloom.

Vincent ran his fingers over the fragile petals. "No one ever thinks of a garden in winter. When one chances upon such a thing, the flowers are a welcome sight, though an unnatural one. The Dispossessed are much the same. No one ever thinks of us. No one knows to think of us. And yet, here we are, at humans' beck and call. Here to be plucked, to serve, and when we are no longer useful, discarded."

Vincent lifted his eyes and held her gaze with unsettling frankness. He strangled the thin stem of the rose and pulled.

"Does that sound fair to you, my lady?" He rolled the stem between his fingers. "The Dispossessed you've met have done you a disservice by sympathizing with you so quickly. I assure you, dear human, they are in the minority."

He sniffed the air, thinning out the waxy bridge of his nose. "I can smell your demon blood from here. Like fermented wine. It tempts, but not without the slightest hint of revulsion."

Ingrid put a stopper on her fear. She could *not* be afraid of Vincent, not with Luc gone to help her father. She couldn't give Luc a reason to turn back and help her instead.

"You won't touch me." Her voice surprised her. It was strangely calm and, even more strangely, confident.

Vincent tossed the Christmas rose to the ground. His smirk became a laugh.

"I would be doing Luc a favor in the end," he said.

It happened then. Not a spark in her shoulder. It was something else. Ingrid started to feel . . . she didn't know how to describe it. She started to feel full and heavy, yet incredibly light. Like all of her blood had stopped its natural flow through her veins and started to push down, hard, toward her feet and fingertips. Ingrid swooned, her eyes fluttering shut. The top of her body grew light and airy, the bottom swollen and gravid. And then even the engorged sensation filling her fingertips and toes had gone, and she felt totally and mercifully erased. As if there were nothing left of her at all.

Just like the night in the churchyard when Marco and Yann had cornered Grayson.

Ingrid opened her eyes, and even though it was still day, the space around her shone bright, as if the clouds had all peeled back and the sun had dropped closer to the earth. She blinked at the glaring whiteness. Looking down, she saw she was suspended in the air—and Vincent was on his knees, his chest and head pressed low against the courtyard gravel in a bow.

"Leave here," Ingrid said. Her voice rang out hollow yet canyon-deep.

It wasn't like last time, when she hadn't understood what was happening. This was her angel blood coming to life after so long being dormant. Why now? Why not earlier, when she'd been in grave danger? She felt its power and saw its weight as Vincent, still bent forward in a bow, scuttled backward like a cockroach.

Ingrid gave him a push with her mind and his body responded. Vincent crawled back toward the stone arcades that led into the Luxembourg Gardens.

The glow she cast flickered. Her body started to fill back in. Ingrid strained against it, waiting for Vincent to pass under the arcades and out of sight. It was like fighting against a sunset. As soon as he disappeared into the park, Ingrid let go. She collapsed to the ground, onto her side, and a rush of cold air filled her chest. She shivered, her limbs heavy and tired. If Vincent rushed back into the courtyard right then, she would be finished.

And there it was, the crunch of gravel under a pair of approaching feet. She was too exhausted to feel afraid. *I would be doing Luc a favor in the end.* Perhaps he would be.

The boots that stopped next to her face, which was flat against the frozen ground, were not Vincent's. Ingrid turned her eyes up and saw Yann staring down at her. He made no move to help her stand.

"Are you certain you wish to drain your angel blood?" Yann asked. Lennier must have found him and sent him to common grounds.

Ingrid pushed herself up. The urge to go back to her guest room, crawl into the faded four-poster, and sleep overwhelmed her.

"I have to," she said.

Yann continued to scrutinize her. Ingrid met his stare with a long stare of her own. His eyes were an impossibly flat cement-gray. When he transformed, the feathers of his eagle wings matched their coloring.

"When it's gone, how will you protect yourself against gargoyles like Vincent?" he asked, and with a twitch of his lips added, "The kind that are nothing like Luc. The kind that would rather harm humans than help them."

Ingrid recalled Luc saying the same thing. There were gargoyles that relished harming humans.

"Vincent is one of those gargoyles," she guessed.

"And you've just made him very angry," he replied.

A shriek from above drew their attention to the sky. A pair of blue-scaled wings circled the courtyard. Dimitrie. Gabby had mentioned how beautiful his scales were; how they matched the striking blue of his eyes. He looped through the air above the courtyard once more before hurtling up into a bank of gray clouds and out of sight. A second later, gravel scattered near the fountain. Dimitrie had dropped something.

Yann went for it. He crouched down to pick it up but stopped. Still crouching, he raised a hand and waved her over. Ingrid approached, wondering why he had hesitated. As soon as she cleared his shoulders and saw the object, she understood perfectly. Ingrid let out a short scream and clapped both hands over her mouth.

Lying on the gravel was a dismembered finger, leached of color except at the ragged, bloodied base. A signet ring circled the red fleshy stump. The flat black onyx oval showed a family crest in gold leaf. *Her* family crest. It was her father's signet ring.

Her father's severed finger.

CHAPTER TWENTY-THREE

"**Y**ou shouldn't be here."

Gabby sat straight-backed on the driver's bench of Constantine's brougham and attempted to ignore Nolan's statement. He slapped the reins and grumbled something else under his breath before raising his voice again.

"For the devil's sake, Gabby, you haven't had nearly enough training!"

She fought the urge to hit him over the head. She'd been fighting it all day, actually. Ever since he'd refused to allow her to accompany their caravan from gargoyle common grounds to the Daicrypta mansion.

"If my sister, who can't so much as swing a butter knife effectively, is inside this brougham, then I can most definitely be here as well," she said.

It had taken convincing Chelle, Vander, and Rory that she could be of use before Nolan had held up his hands in surrender. However, he hadn't given up objecting.

"Your sister is part of the bargain. You are not. At least your mother had the good sense to stay at the abbey and wait."

"My mother! You want me to sit at home with my mother! Nolan Quinn, you are the most infuriating man I've ever had the displeasure of meeting."

Ingrid must have been listening. She was just behind the driver's box, enclosed within the slim, lacquered-wood brougham Constantine had lent them for the night. Luc had said he'd take Ingrid to Dupuis, but the more Gabby, Grayson, and the others had stewed over it, the more they had all realized that *not* helping was nothing short of neglect. So they had shown up at gargoyle common grounds at dusk and waited for the black velvet blanket to drop over the skyline.

"Would you stop complimenting me, lass—I thought we were arguing," Nolan said.

Heaven help her, she was likely to commit murder tonight! Gabby shut her mouth and kept her eyes firmly ahead, on Vander and his horse. He led their caravan, with Lennier directly above the brougham and Yann in the sky behind it. Grayson, Chelle, and Rory were all positioned along the route to the address Dupuis had given them, and Marco was pacing the route in its entirety from the sky.

No other gargoyles had accepted Lennier's invitation to help, and Luc had not returned to Hôtel du Maurier by the time they had left. Which had led Gabby to believe her father was still in danger.

"If Dupuis is torturing my father again . . ." Gabby touched the pommel of her sword, hidden within her cape. Two more daggers rested in makeshift sheaths, one in each cloak panel, and a third was safely tucked inside the lip of her boot.

She hadn't been allowed to see the severed finger when she'd arrived at Hôtel du Maurier, but Ingrid had told her about it, saying Gabby shouldn't look. For once, Gabby hadn't argued.

"There's no use worrying yourself. The only way to stop Dupuis now is to . . ."

Nolan's words trailed off and Gabby waited for him to finish consoling her. The carriage light formed a bright aura around his dark profile, with steam curling off the hot glass lantern. Nolan stared straight ahead.

"Is there something the matter?" Gabby asked.

Nolan turned to her then. In the passing light of a streetlamp, Gabby saw his eyes. They looked at her in an empty, uninterested way.

"Nolan?"

Something was wrong with him. He turned back to the road and pulled hard on the right rein. The wheels cut sharply, veering off rue Tronchet and down a narrow branch road. Gabby braced herself to keep from sliding off the bench.

"This isn't the way. Nolan, what are you doing?"

No reply came. He kept his gaze on the road ahead, slapping the reins and building speed, taking the carriage farther from the planned route.

"Nolan, stop!" she shouted. He didn't so much as flinch.

It wasn't him. *Inside* it wasn't him.

She didn't know who or what was at the reins, but it wasn't Nolan Quinn.

Gabby reached inside her cape and grabbed hold of the sword's handle.

It's not Nolan, she told herself as the brougham careened down a second street and started back for the river. If some sort of possession demon had taken control of him, then would blessed silver work to draw it out again? Nolan had been right: she didn't have nearly enough training.

She heard Ingrid pounding from inside the carriage, her muffled voice shouting. Her sister knew something was wrong. Marco would know, too. Gabby looked skyward, but the carriage jerked roughly. She had to do *something*. If Marco scented a demon inside Nolan, he wouldn't be as hesitant to exorcise it as Gabby was. And he certainly wouldn't do it gently.

Gabby pulled the sword from inside her cape and swiftly brought the blade edge down across the tops of Nolan's wrists. It was a tap, really; hardly enough muscle behind it to slice a tender roast. Still, green sparks danced out of the flesh wound, and Nolan's hands dropped the reins. He winged his arm and the point of his elbow jammed Gabby in the ribs, hard. The carriage wheels lurched to the right as they hit a raised sidewalk, sending the whole brougham into a dangerous tilt.

Gabby screamed, knowing what would come next. It had happened before in Vander's phaeton, when the traitorous Alliance member Tomas had kidnapped Gabby and taken her to the Métro construction pit. They were going to crash and roll. Only this time, there wouldn't be a slope of forgiving rock gravel and dirt to catch her.

She heard Ingrid's muffled scream as the brougham, still speeding, teetered onto just two wheels. And then Gabby was out of her seat, falling toward the black pavement. She threw up her hands and hit—but not the ground. A pair of iron-strong arms slammed into her side, hooked around her, and swung her sideways out of her fall. She dug her fingernails into albino scales as the elder gargoyle, Lennier, threw out his white wings and dragged them to a stop.

Gabby clung hard to him and slowly looked up into his face. His scales had the luster of seed pearls, and his eyes—inexplicably human, even set as they were within scaled skin—were far gentler than Luc's.

"Thank you," Gabby whispered. Lennier's lashless lids closed briefly in acceptance.

She rolled out of his grip and, with a shaky landing, watched him spiral up into the sky. She looked back toward the brougham, expecting to see a wreck. Instead, Yann was underneath the nearly sideways carriage, his thick, furry lion's arms raised overhead to keep it from crashing to the street. He pushed until it landed again on all four wheels, then followed Lennier into the sky.

On her next breath, Gabby saw the empty driver's box.

In the center of the street, a sprawled body.

"Nolan!"

He stirred and moaned, his cheek flat against the street. Gabby ran to his side as Vander's horse closed in.

She turned Nolan onto his back. "Are you badly hurt?"

He groaned again. Blood seeped from gashes on his forehead and lip, and his coat was torn at the shoulder.

The brougham door whacked open. Without waiting for assistance, Ingrid jumped out. She stumbled on the landing. "Gabby! Are you all right?"

Vander pulled his mount to a stop and leaped from the saddle. He took one look at Nolan and swore.

"There's demon dust everywhere. What happened?"

The shrill blare of a police whistle echoed down the block. Nolan ground his teeth and maneuvered himself to his side. "I think it was a possession demon."

He saw his wrists then, the two shallow slices. "Nicely done, lass."

"I'm so sorry." Gabby reached for them. "I didn't know what else to try."

The whistle sounded again, and this time voices accompanied it. Gabby pulled her hands back. Their near accident had drawn attention.

A slapping noise, like the ripple of canvas sails, came from above. Luc's massive jet body landed with a fierce *whump* on the street just inches from Ingrid.

"Go, Luc, you'll be seen," Vander said as a lamp quavered into view down the block.

Luc wound his arm around Ingrid's waist and flushed out his wings.

Gabby held out her arm. "Wait, not with—"

Luc shot up, into the sky and out of view, taking her sister with him.

The smell of spring grass and rich black soil drove into him. Luc breathed it in. A litany of images and emotions stole him away from where he was. For a moment Luc forgot the grinding pain of the heavy mercurite chains twined around his body.

Ingrid.

The dank cellar hole where he'd been imprisoned most of the day blurred out of focus. Luc felt her—her yearning for air, the panicked cadence of her heart, the bitter tang of fear rising in her throat, choking her.

Ingrid was afraid. She needed him. And he couldn't move.

The mercurite ate into his flesh. The muscle and skin under the thick chains had long since hardened to stone. With the chains wound around him from his shoulders to his knees, most of Luc's body had crystallized, including his wings. Those had been pinned into place with a curved, mercurite-dipped rod.

The disciples had put Ingrid's father on the roof of the Daicrypta den like bait. Tied to a chair, Lord Brickton had seen Luc and screamed in terror. Luc had thought him a fool, until he'd touched down on the roof, having rushed headlong into a trap.

They had been waiting for him, armed to the teeth with mercurite. Brickton wasn't the fool—Luc was. And now here he sat, a useless pile of stone and flesh, naked, in the dark, and unable to protect. Unable to shift, though the urge hammered against him incessantly.

Gabby's heady scent of water lily and hibiscus fluttered in but then left. What the hell was happening out there?

Honeyed light filtered through the door as it creaked opened. Dimitrie's gangly figure stood within the entrance. Luc held still, already having learned that the more he struggled against the chains, the more they burned anew.

"Let me go," he muttered. "My human needs me. I need to *go*."

Dimitrie stepped inside and shut the door behind him. "I can't."

"Traitor," Luc seethed.

His night vision showed Dimitrie's outline in gray and white. His shoulders hung forward, his head slumped down so Luc saw the crown of his head.

"You know nothing," Dimitrie replied.

"I know you're keeping me from my human," Luc growled. "I know that if anything happens to her I'll shred you like a wet paper bag."

Dimitrie lifted his head. "Would you?"

Luc sat on the dirt-packed floor with his head pressed against the damp cellar wall, his wings hanging limply behind him. Was it just the pain, or had Dimitrie actually sounded hopeful?

Dimitrie dropped into a crouch. His eyes looked like two black beads to Luc.

"You don't know, do you? How lucky you are." Dimitrie's soprano voice cracked.

Luc barked a laugh, which shifted his shoulder, which burned like hell.

"Don't laugh. Your abbey . . . your humans. You don't know what I'd give to have what you do."

Luc ground his teeth as the mercurite chain fixed around his chest tightened. The need to shift, to go to Ingrid, was making his ribs expand.

"So you thought you'd pretend for a little while, is that it?" Luc asked.

"I did what my humans told me to do," he answered. "I've learned it's better to give them what they want. And they want your human girl very badly."

Marco. Luc had to depend on Marco. He wouldn't let anything happen to Ingrid. He *couldn't*.

"You don't know what it's like," Dimitrie went on. "I have many humans here, Luc. Scores of them, but not all are Daicrypta. The Duster chained to a bed in a third-floor guest room? She's my human. The unconscious homeless man the disciples brought in off the street last night to try a serum on? He's my human, too. Possessed humans, unwanted asylum patients, prostitutes—every kind that slips through the cracks without another person knowing or caring. Those are the people Dupuis and his disciples bring here. Those are the people they perform their experiments on.

"Protecting them would mean fighting Dupuis and the disciples. You know I couldn't do that. Everything I am forbids me to touch them. So I have humans who are injured—sometimes even killed. And I have humans who do the killing. You tell me: what am I supposed to do?"

Luc stared at Dimitrie's washed-out face. The poor bastard. The endless scores of angel's burns along his back made sense now. Once, Luc had tried to plan what he might do if Grayson went after Lord Brickton, or vice versa. The two despised one another. Which human would Luc protect? Which would he fight?

"All those times Irindi punished you," Luc said. "Didn't you ask her what you should do?"

Dimitrie snorted and stood up. "I could ask all I wanted. Do you think she ever answered? Do you really think the Order cares?"

No gargoyle would be so asinine as to think the angels cared.

"They won't help me, but you can," Dimitrie said.

"What makes you think I'd help you with anything?" Luc asked, but then thought back to how hopeful Dimitrie had looked when Luc had threatened to kill him.

"If I let you go, you'll do it. You'll end me," Dimitrie said.

"The Dispossessed has its rules. I can't just kill you."

Even though Luc wanted to. Half out of fury and half out of pity.

"You can if I endanger your humans," Dimitrie replied, his gray lips pulling into a taunting sneer. He leaned over, coming closer to Luc. "If I killed one, Lennier would allow you your revenge. Which one will it be?" He tapped his chin. "Oh, wait. I think I know."

Luc braced himself for the pain and swept his bound legs in an arc across the floor. He caught Dimitrie's ankles and sent the shadow gargoyle flat against the dirt.

"If you kill her, I'll make sure you rot here for eternity," Luc said, his throat hoarse, his entire body gripped by the mercurite sting.

Dimitrie pushed himself up, laughing. He grabbed hold of the chains binding Luc's legs. Luc saw the darker shade of gray around his hands and realized Dimitrie was wearing gloves.

"I don't think you will," Dimitrie said. He started to unravel the coiled chains.

Luc's body stayed stiff, a spiral of stone and flesh. If the trace amount of mercurite on Gabby's wounded shoulder had left his hand frozen for nearly an hour, how long would it take for his body to recover from this amount of exposure?

"I'll tell her something from you," Dimitrie said. He tossed the chains aside and reached for the curved rod pinning Luc's wings together. "If you have a message. Anything you want her to know before I kill her."

He drew the rod out with one fast tug. Speed didn't help. It hurt worse than when they'd thrust it in.

"You won't do it," Luc said. He tried to move his arms. They wouldn't budge.

"You won't be going anywhere for a while," Dimitrie guessed. "With you here, and Ingrid about to arrive at my doorstep, who is going to stop me?"

Marco. Dimitrie didn't know about Marco. Luc kept his lips sealed. He tried to test his wings, but the muscles along his back and shoulder blades had calcified.

"That's what I thought," Dimitrie said. He got up and walked to the door. "It's a pity, Luc. I can tell she is your favorite. But I can't exist like this."

Dimitrie closed the door behind him.

CHAPTER TWENTY-FOUR

Ingrid dug her nails into the jet scales along Luc's arms. It was like trying to puncture a hillside of shale. He held her tight against his concrete abdomen as they flew over the rooftops of Paris.

He'd come for her.

She still didn't understand what had happened, but there had been demon dust. Vander had seen it, said it was everywhere. And then Luc had just landed, grabbed her, and flown away again, all before she could take a full breath.

"Luc!"

Wind tunneled down her throat and canceled out her scream. He had taken her from whatever danger lay on the ground, but what about Gabby? Why hadn't he taken her sister as well?

Ingrid squeezed her eyes shut and tried not to flail. A bubble of nausea rode up her throat, and though they were flying straight, she still felt as if they were corkscrewing through the air. She had nearly fainted the first time she'd flown with Luc, but this dizzy spinning sensation was something different. It felt oddly familiar.

She fought the spell as shifting currents of wind tossed her legs side to side. Luc hadn't pinned them up as he had the first time. The air filled his wings and took him higher into the dense cloud cover. The lights below finally disappeared, and then Luc was hurtling through cold black clouds. Ingrid's cloak and dress were sodden, her skin had numbed to ice, and her head throbbed and spun—and then went still.

Just like that, the nausea was gone.

Ingrid knew what it had been.

"Luc! Lower!" she cried out, but again, ate her own words as wind filled her throat. She tucked her head to keep the icy mist from pelting her eyes.

The same fast, debilitating dizzy spell had come over her in the profane cemetery lot. The mimic demon had been latching on to her. Burrowing through her memories.

The *mimic*?

Luc's arms went slack.

Ingrid gargled a scream as her whole body swung down, perpendicular to the ground, far, far below. Her fingers dug for purchase on the shalelike scales. The mist had made them slick, though, and he slipped out from under her hands.

It isn't Luc was the absurd thought floundering through her mind as she fell. It was the mimic. It had finished playing with her. Now it was time for her to die.

Weightlessness felt strange. As if the sky were both pushing her down and sucking her back up at the same time. She couldn't breathe. Couldn't move. Couldn't even scream. The wind blew the pins and combs from her hair as fingers of wind rotated her body in the sky. Her cloak flapped like useless wings at her sides.

She wouldn't see Luc again. She'd be dead and he would still be a gargoyle and how could this be happening? Ingrid rushed to grab hold of his image—she only had a few seconds left to think of it. It wasn't his human form that slid into her mind, though. Not the raven hair and soft warm skin, but his tempered-steel scales, the brawn of his chest, the magnificent spread of jet wings. That was the Luc she wanted to cling to.

The front of Ingrid's body slammed hard against an unforgiving surface, driving the air straight out of her lungs. The strike hadn't hurt half as much as she thought it would, and her body undulated as it might upon a wave. She dragged in a rough gasp and—*she was still breathing*.

Opening her eyes, she saw the Paris skyline scrolling by underneath her and the scaled body of the gargoyle she'd crashed into. Marco! She lay prostrate along the knuckled ridge of his back, his russet wings stroking the air at her sides. They enclosed her in a safe embrace on each upward stroke. She wound her arms around his neck and straddled him, digging in with her knees until her muscles shook. Ingrid buried her face in his coarse scales.

"Thank you, thank you, thank you," she sobbed, and was answered with a shriek that vibrated through his back.

Ingrid had only just evened out her breathing when Marco dove into a sharp slant. The peaked roof of a palatial old mansion rushed at them, along with a brightly lit circular drive. Marco shifted his weight, throwing down his legs and landing on the drive with startling finesse.

Ingrid fell off his back without an ounce of grace. She landed on her rump and stayed there. The stillness of solid ground was glorious.

"Lady Ingrid."

Nolan's father ended her reprieve. He stood within the open front door of a medieval-looking estate. Ingrid remained where she was, her legs too rubbery to attempt standing. He came into the courtyard, his eyes fixed on her. "I feared you would not come," he said, and for a moment he did look afraid. Afraid and relieved at once.

"You," Ingrid said. A spark of electric static fired through her shoulders. Her arms and legs—her whole body—were so wet and cold that the burn of the sudden flare hurt. Just as it had hurt that time on Constantine's grounds when she'd been sprawled in the snow, and again, in the sewers. Ingrid gasped as more sparks lit and fired underneath her skin.

"Where is my father?" she asked, wobbling to her feet.

Carrick raised his palms to her in a gesture of peace. "He is uninjured. The severed finger came from a test corpse. The intended effect seems to have been achieved, however, for here you are."

Ingrid stepped in front of Marco. He blew a shot of steam from his wolfish nose and stayed close behind her.

"You're a traitor to the Alliance," she said.

Carrick blinked twice at the accusation.

"I cannot argue. I went against my vows. Everything I hold sacred." Carrick Quinn, though taller and rounder than Nolan, still had his son's easy swagger. He came toward Ingrid. The gas jets hinged to the façade of the mansion threw half his face into shadows. "And you should be grateful that I have, Lady Ingrid, because the Alliance very much wants *you* dead."

It was inevitable. Grayson had known it that morning when he'd been standing on the roof of Hôtel Bastian, listening to Ingrid insist she sacrifice herself for their bastard of a father. Grayson's temperature had catapulted, his pulse had gone full tilt, and even though he'd fought it off all day, a part of him had known he wouldn't win.

He was going to shift.

Standing along rue de Clichy, in the slim alley between two apartment buildings, waiting for Constantine's brougham to clatter by, Grayson knew his time had run out.

There were two of them this time. He breathed in their

musky odor and his skin shivered like horseflesh throwing off flies. This was it. At least Chelle wasn't there to see it happen.

Grayson ducked farther into the shadowy alley and arched his back. Letting go didn't hurt. It felt good. It was a release, like taking off shoes that pinched, or wet, cold clothing. As his body fell forward, muscle and bone shifting and moving like liquid into their rightful places, Grayson heard what the hellhounds wanted.

Come with us. Mistress says it is time.

Grayson kept his eyes on the sleek, pale fur of his bulging paws, each one easily the size of a Christmas ham. He smelled things he hadn't before: the wet limestone of the buildings shouldering him, the rotting carcass of a roast fowl in a row of metal trash cans, a sickly sweet rose perfume drifting from an open window above.

His mistress wanted him, and he had a sudden urge to acquiesce. Like an undertow, it sucked and pulled, making him want to roll over and submit. It was nearly as strong as the urge to shift, and just as hard to resist. But Grayson *could* resist. If he tried hard enough, he *could.*

No, he thought. Immediately, the apprehension of the other two hellhounds crept inside Grayson. He looked up and saw their cloudy brown shapes and glowing coal eyes. They were nothing but bond servants. Dogs to be commanded. They had no thoughts of their own, no needs or desires or goals except for those of their mistress.

Grayson was different. He saw that now. He had changed form, but if he tried he could keep his human side intact. He was willing to bet Axia hadn't anticipated that.

She wanted Grayson to lead her hounds. She'd given him this curse at birth. She'd made him what he was. From the first breath he'd ever taken to this one right now, Axia had designed him to belong to her.

He breathed in and realized even angels made mistakes.

If Axia wanted Grayson to lead her hounds, he could do just that. Just as Axia wished, he could be their master.

But she would not be his.

You will serve me, Grayson thought, and took a bold plunge toward the two creatures. He didn't have Luc at his side this time. He didn't need him. The hellhounds backed off, letting out thin whines. Their eyes lowered toward the pavement and they crouched in submission.

Grayson craned his furred neck to see out into the wide boulevard. Ingrid would be passing by soon. What better way to help her than with a couple of Axia's pets at his beck and call?

"I'm going in."

Gabby slid back against the eight-foot brick wall enclosing the Daicrypta grounds just before one of the four muscled guards would have seen her peeking through the iron bars of the front gates. The building was a small medieval-looking palace atop the butte of Montmartre, and it seemed appropriately fortified.

"No, you are not," Nolan said. He stood at the curb, rubbing his hand over one of his hastily bandaged wrists. He'd been uncharacteristically quiet the rest of the way to Montmartre. The few times Gabby had tried to capture his attention, he'd looked away from her, his jaw set.

"My sister is inside, and we have no idea where Luc is," Gabby argued, her voice hushed.

Yann had shifted into human form long enough to explain that a demon—not Luc—had snatched Ingrid into the air, and that Marco had gone after it. Ingrid and Marco had arrived safely at the Daicrypta, Yann later reported, and had been led inside. Vander had been chastising himself ever since. The mimic demon had been posing as Luc, and Vander had not known. The mimic's dust had been a shade of light blue, like a gargoyle's.

"I agree with Nolan. You should not go inside. Besides, Marco is with her," Chelle said. She and Rory had joined the caravan as it had wended up the hilly eighteenth arrondissement, but so far, they hadn't met Grayson. Gabby couldn't worry about him just then. She was far too preoccupied worrying about Ingrid.

"Marco is not Luc," Gabby said. It was an obvious statement, and she wasn't sure the others would understand what she meant by it. She wasn't entirely sure *she* did.

Luc had protected all of them at one point or another, but it was Ingrid he preferred. Gabby had known it from the beginning, and she was certain she hadn't been the only one, human or gargoyle, to see it. Within the branches of the leafless trees lining the street were two sets of gleaming eyes. Watching. Waiting for someone to say more about Luc and his human girl.

Gabby kept her lips pressed together.

Vander had his crossbow loaded and ready at his side. The closest streetlamp, hanging from a curlicue of iron ten yards away, gave off clouds of yellow steam. Vander's eyes shone with purpose.

"I'm going in with you," he said.

Nolan clapped a hand to his head. "Of course you are. Storming the castle in true Gawain fashion, are we?"

Rory, who had been quietly observing them as he leaned against the brick wall, now spoke. "Ye're both acting on emotions. Look at it rationally—we've no idea about the innards of the building, how many guards or their positions, where they've been holding yer da, or where Ingrid's been taken. The two of ye would be charging headfirst into disaster."

Every word of that was true, and yet Rory's caution only made Gabby more desperate to go inside. As reckless as it might be, at least she would be doing something. Sensing that the effect of his words had been the exact opposite of what he'd intended, Rory pushed off from the wall and came toward her.

"*Laoch*, I know what's in yer heart." He touched her gently, his hand a loose cuff around her wrist. Gabby stilled. "But making danger for yerself won't help Ingrid or yer da."

He held on to her. His stare demanded something that his touch didn't. He wanted to know she understood.

"Then we need another way," Gabby said.

Polished silver flashed at their side as Nolan withdrew his broadsword. Rory released Gabby's arm abruptly and stepped back as two figures, cloaked in shadow, approached from across the quiet street.

"Who goes there?" Nolan called.

One of the figures held up his hands. In one hand was a cane.

"A friend," Constantine replied in a hushed tone.

Nolan kept his sword steady. "And your companion?"

Vander brought his crossbow up. "A Duster."

Constantine came closer, though the second person held back, reluctant.

"Léon," Vander said.

Chelle, already with her hands at her red sash, took out two of her throwing stars. Rory moved with the same stealth, leaving only Gabby without a weapon in hand. She didn't rush to follow their lead—instinct told her this Duster wasn't a threat.

"Wait!" Léon mirrored Constantine and held his hands in surrender. His tall, lanky build made him seem younger than the rest of them somehow.

"The boy returned to me this evening." Constantine laid a gloved hand on Léon's knobby shoulder. "After hearing what he had to say about this place, I thought it wise to find you immediately. You cannot enter that building."

Ice locked Gabby's chest as solid as a winter harbor.

"Ingrid is already inside," she replied.

And her father, though shouldn't he have been released by now?

Léon put his hands down slowly. "Then you must get her out."

Gabby's thoughts exactly.

Nolan lowered the tip of his sword. "Which would require us to go in. Weren't we just ominously told *not* to do that?"

"Léon has knowledge of the layout of rooms," Constantine told them, ignoring Nolan's sarcasm.

"And I know where they will be taking her," Léon added.

"Time is of the essence, Mr. Quinn," Constantine said.

Gabby turned to Nolan, who seemed to be contemplating an apt reply. Since when did he make all the decisions? This was *her* sister. *Her* family.

"Can we get in without being seen?" she asked Léon, wary of him and yet desperate enough to hope that he meant well. She didn't know him. He had murdered his family. But he had tried to warn Grayson, and he was here now with another warning.

"It's possible," he replied, his haunted eyes drifting up toward the tangled branches of the nearby trees, where Lennier and Yann still hid, waiting. Léon jerked his chin. "Monsieur Constantine told me about them. He said we might need them, and he is right. We can't do this without wings."

CHAPTER TWENTY-FIVE

Ingrid had expected the Daicrypta mansion to be just as inhospitable inside as it appeared on the outside. Judging from the blocky, weathered limestone complete with parapets and towers, she'd envisioned large, drafty halls, arched wooden doors, and torchlight.

She had not imagined what opened up before her now.

Ingrid stepped inside a carpeted guest chamber decorated with creamy silk wallpaper and drapes, fine beveled mirrors, potted palms, a slim writing desk and chair, and small-scale replicas of all six Lady and the Unicorn tapestries. The elegance of the room far surpassed that of her own at the rectory.

"I hope it's suitable," Carrick said as he entered behind her. Everything about the place had been alarmingly tranquil as they had wended their way to the second-level guest room.

Though Dupuis had not joined them, a number of disciples, as Constantine had called them, had come to stand in open doorways as Ingrid had gone past. They had stared at her with unabashed curiosity. They were picturing her blood, most likely. Wondering how it would look trapped in glass vials rather than in her veins.

Marco strode into the room as well, wearing his human skin and a pair of ill-fitting trousers. He'd refused the shirt Carrick had taken from the Daicrypta disciple who had given up his pants. Why don a shirt when he could intimidate them all with his broad, chiseled torso?

"I won't be here long enough to enjoy the room, I'm sure," Ingrid replied, purposefully cool. "Now, for the last time: I want to see my father."

Carrick gestured toward the writing desk's chair. Ingrid remained on her feet, with Marco standing so close to her side that she could feel the heat radiating from his body. His presence gave her a fraction of confidence, but she still longed for Luc. Worry kept closing in on her, dashing her concentration. Where *was* he?

"I assure you, your father is perfectly fine," Carrick said.

He'd said the severed finger had come from a corpse, but what proof did Ingrid have of that?

"I'm *here*," she said, her patience worn thin. "I've done what Dupuis has asked. Now let him go!"

The papered walls and hanging tapestries muffled her shout. Carrick could have been lying. Marco hadn't yet scented her father, so he was unable to tell what was happening to him.

"I will see to it personally," Nolan's father said, putting on a cajoling tone that only made her more irritated.

"You'll forgive me if I don't believe a word you say," she replied as she crossed the room. Earlier she'd been able to command Vincent. She wished she could do the same with Carrick now.

At the window, Ingrid shoved aside the heavy drapes and tried to open the sash. It wouldn't budge.

"Nailed shut, I'm afraid," Carrick explained.

To bar an escape, she guessed.

Marco came to the same conclusion. "The tricky thing about glass, Alliance fool, is that it shatters."

She backed away from the window. "I have two questions. I want answers for both, or else Marco and I will be leaving and you will have an open gap here instead of a window."

Marco looked giddy with anticipation when she turned to face him and Carrick. "Where is Luc? And why does the Alliance want me dead?"

The first question was, of course, the crucial one, although a small, dark corner of her already knew the answer.

Carrick began with her second question. "The decision was made by a handful of the highest-ranking Alliance leaders."

"The Directorate?" Ingrid asked. "Why would they want me dead?"

"Why wouldn't they? Learning of a fallen angel's intentions to reclaim her blood from you and then form a demon-human army was enough to give us all nightmares. We asked you to come to Rome, if you remember. We *could* have kept you safe in confinement there. But you refused, and considering you aren't officially Alliance, we had no right to force you. Spilling your blood, dashing it out of your veins before Axia could take it for herself, was the next most commonsensical answer."

Ingrid couldn't form words. She had trusted the Alliance. They were supposed to help her, not try to *kill* her.

"Was there no one who objected?" she whispered.

"It was a unanimous vote," he replied. "The sacrifice of one girl to ensure the safety of millions was deemed acceptable."

The small hairs on the back of her neck stood on end as Marco stepped up close behind. He towered over her, the crown of Ingrid's head reaching his collarbone.

"*You* were supposed to kill her?" he asked.

With those words, Ingrid heard all the vicious things Marco wanted to do to Carrick. Nolan's father, however, remained aloof.

"Not I. A mimic demon."

Ingrid jerked back, stepping on Marco's bare feet. He braced her shoulders to keep her from falling.

"The Directorate authorized its release from our holding chamber at Hôtel Bastian with orders to target you. I released it myself," Carrick said.

Ingrid rolled her shoulders until Marco let go of her. She didn't mind his touch, but she didn't want Carrick to think she needed Marco to make her feel safe. She still had powers of her own. Sometimes.

"You've captured demons?" she asked.

"Certain breeds," Carrick answered.

Ingrid puzzled over how they'd captured them—and where the demons would be kept. At Hôtel Bastian? She recalled the strange room she had stumbled into, with the freezing, steel-fronted drawers. The pressure gauges and Rory's flash of annoyance that she had gone inside. Was that the holding chamber?

"And you can give these captured demons orders?" she asked.

"Not all of them," a new voice answered. It came from the doorway. Robert Dupuis stood with his hands clasped at his waist.

Ingrid had nearly forgotten what he looked like. He was plain enough to be easily forgettable. A head shorter than Carrick, and leaner. When he closed the door behind him, she saw that his fingers were long and feminine.

"Do you like your room here?" Dupuis asked. Ingrid stood rigid, wary of him. "Do you accept it?"

What an odd question. She hesitated before nodding. "Yes."

Dupuis grinned. "The Daicrypta has spent decades perfecting the practice of demon capture and command. We have seen fit, in some instances, to share what we know with the Alliance."

"I thought the Alliance and Daicrypta weren't on friendly

terms," Ingrid said. Nolan and Vander had drawn their swords when Constantine had mentioned the Daicrypta in the sewers.

"They needn't be friendly in order to be useful to one another," Dupuis answered.

"So the Daicrypta decided to show the Alliance how to capture demons, hold them prisoner, and then give them orders to kill people?" Ingrid asked.

Dupuis bowed his head, a smile playing on his lips. He steepled his fingers together in front of his chest.

"Mademoiselle, do you really think us so vile? My purpose in life is not to hunt and destroy. I leave that to the majority of the Alliance."

Carrick sealed his mouth into a tight grimace.

"It would be ignorant to reject the demon reality. They are among us and will continue to be among us," Dupuis said, coming farther into the room. He turned to admire the tapestry nearest him while he continued to speak. "No amount of blessed silver can close the rift between our world and the Underneath. Accepting demons and learning from them—specifically, how to control them and bend them to our will—is the educated way to deal with them."

Carrick had kept his eyes fixed on a corner of the room as Dupuis had spoken. His fists were clenched, his expression granite. He and Dupuis were definitely not friends.

"I still don't understand. You voted to have me killed. You released the mimic demon. And yet last night Chelle told me that you were desperate to align Grayson and me with the Alliance. Why?"

Carrick sighed. "It's difficult to explain. In short: I changed my mind. But by then, the mimic was already hunting you. I don't want you to die, Lady Ingrid. With the raw electrical power you generate, you could become one of the Alliance's most valuable hunters. Once your angel's blood is destroyed, Axia and her Harvest will no longer threaten our realm, and you will be *useful* to the Alliance, not a hazard. Of course, my decision to save you will cost me my life, and I wanted things under way while I was still here to manage them."

Ingrid wanted to scream in confusion. "But they still want me dead?"

"Right now, yes. Make no mistake, Lady Ingrid. My agreement with Dupuis is not authorized by the Directorate," he said, fists still locked, the skin at his knuckles blanched. "I did vote for your death. I did release the mimic. I thought it was my duty."

He flexed his fingers. "I wasn't always a member of the Directorate. I was a fighter, like my son. I believed in the Alliance and what I thought was its mission: to eradicate demons from the face of the earth."

His body lost its tension bit by bit as he spoke, and as he loosened up, more words flowed.

"When I did ascend to the Directorate, I saw a new side of the Alliance. Intrigue, politics, deception. None of which I liked, but I quickly learned that once you become a part of it, there is no leaving." Carrick paused to meet her eyes. "Mine was the final vote cast. Had I broken from the total accord, my fate would have been sealed just as yours had been."

Ingrid parted her lips, stunned. They would have killed him? She didn't know the Alliance at all.

"You changed your mind, though," she said. Carrick nodded, the motion slowed by some invisible weight.

"I couldn't hold with it. The death of an innocent young girl might be acceptable to the other members of the Directorate, but it isn't to me. I'm a man of honor. Of integrity. In my soul, I'm a fighter, not a politician. The Alliance is supposed to uphold certain morals." He reached up with his hand and made another tight fist. "Using a demon—the very thing we hunt—to slay a human girl is beneath us. It's beneath *me*, and yet I did it." He threw his hand down. "I'm ashamed, Lady Ingrid."

He was. She could feel the burn of his shame with every word.

Still, it had come to him too late, and it was definitely too late for her to forgive him.

"How has luring her here saved her?" Marco asked. "It looks to me as though you've only taken my human from certain death to very likely death."

Dupuis parted his lips to speak, but Carrick cut him off.

"The Alliance has never succeeded in capturing a mimic. The one I released had originally been captured by the Daicrypta."

"They are exceptionally tricky," Dupuis said, that unsettling little smile still on his lips. "When Monsieur Quinn asked for my help, I gave it . . . on one condition."

Ingrid imagined that Dupuis required some sort of payment. Not money, however. By the state of their accommodations, she didn't think they needed it.

"He asked for your angel blood. As soon as he has it, he'll stop the mimic," Carrick explained. "I am here to make sure Dupuis upholds his end of the bargain."

The blood Axia had hidden within Ingrid was the only thing standing between the fallen angel and her planned Harvest of Dusters. Once it was gone from Ingrid's veins, the Directorate would no longer see Ingrid as a threat. It was the angel blood, Axia and her Harvest, that the Directorate feared.

"And what happens to the angel blood afterward?" she asked, recalling Vander's worry about the Daicrypta getting their hands on it. "Couldn't Axia simply send one of her demon pets after it? The blood should be destroyed."

"We will study it first," Dupuis answered, fingers still steepled.

"And then, by our agreement, it *will* be destroyed," Carrick finished. Dupuis bowed in agreement.

Destroying it right away sounded like a much better idea to Ingrid. Perhaps there would still be a way for her to do so.

"What of you?" she then asked Carrick. "The Directorate

will know that you've betrayed them. That you've bargained for my life."

He let out a mirthless laugh. "I am already done for. The mercurite only saves us so many times before it starts to eat away at us from the inside. To be truthful, I'd rather be taken out quickly by a skilled Alliance assassin than waste away in my bed, my insides rotting and my brain turning to mush."

Marco, his arms crossed tightly over his broad chest, replied, "If you'd rather not wait for that assassin, I'd be more than honored to do the job."

Ingrid nudged him with her elbow. "Stop, Marco."

She had no doubt, however, that he would do it, and that he'd do it with relish.

"Come, Lady Ingrid," Dupuis said, crossing to the door and opening it. "The sooner we drain your angel blood, the sooner my disciples and I can recapture the mimic."

Marco came out from behind Ingrid. His torso and arms flickered once with amber scales before returning to human skin.

"I had another question," Ingrid said. "Where is Luc?"

Carrick looked to Dupuis, whose annoying little smile withered. Both men then shifted their attention to Marco.

The gargoyle took in a deep breath, arms still crossed over his broad, naked chest. A low, gurgling growl escaped on his exhale.

"They have him," Marco answered, meeting Ingrid's stare. "I suppose we should do as they say."

Lennier dropped closer to the sloped roof of the Daicrypta building, Gabby clasped to his albino body. He released his hold on her and she fell less than a foot to the slate-topped roof. The pitch was slight. She barely slid an inch before Nolan took hold of her arm and steadied her, Lennier already flying away.

He and Vander had come to the roof first, in case a disciple had been stationed there, as Alliance were on the roof of Hôtel Bastian. Constantine had left, and Nolan had ordered Chelle and Rory to stay below on the street. He'd tried to order Gabby as well, but considering she wasn't officially Alliance, she hadn't been under any obligation to comply.

Yann's feathered wings hovered overhead, beating cold air down around them. He lowered Léon to the roof and then spiraled up and away. The Duster landed sure-footedly, though he still looked sick with nerves.

"What now?" Vander asked as his eyes swept along the dark roof.

Gabby didn't see a roof door or a skylight to drop through. Léon picked his way down the roof toward a knee-high balustrade of carved stone. Gabby followed. Once closer, she noticed a dog-headed gargoyle protruding from the exterior of the stone railing. It reminded her that this was Dimitrie's territory. Would he sense their arrival?

"The room Dupuis assigned to me is just below," Léon said. Gabby tilted forward until she could see the double-hung top-floor window. "The window had been nailed shut, but I was able to pry the nails up before I escaped."

"Through the window?" Gabby asked.

"No," Léon said. "The window was my first plan, but things happened too quickly. I wound up escaping from the draining room."

A cold wind gusted up over the ledge. *The draining room.* That was where they would be taking Ingrid. Or maybe they'd already taken her there.

"Climbing down is too dangerous," Nolan said, still higher up on the roof's slope.

Gabby swung her leg over the parapet.

"Stop, Gabby!" Nolan barked.

She felt something cinch around her waist, and then a lurching tug. She fell forward, her legs still straddling the stone balustrade. Her hands landed on glistening ropes that had latched around her middle. Léon stood with his arms outstretched, silk webbing having streamed from each fingertip.

"Léon, let her go." Nolan extended his broadsword, both hands on the handle. Vander touched his arm.

"No, don't," he said. Nolan glared at him. "Don't you remember how strong that silk is? He can lower us to the window."

Gabby tested the silk webbing with her hands, stretching and pulling it. It was tacky but strong, each length of silk the thickness of her pinky finger. With ten of them wrapped around her, Léon could lower her with ease.

"You will not fall," Léon whispered.

She threw her other leg over the parapet.

"Gabby—" Nolan called, but with a quick breath, she let her backside slip off.

The webbing cinched tighter but held. She dangled midair, feeling a momentary flutter of panic when she began to drop smoothly toward the window. The room was black. When she hissed up to Léon to stop lowering her, she gripped the sill and within seconds had opened the window and climbed inside.

She took her dagger, sliced through the webbing, and waited. A few minutes later, Nolan and Vander joined her inside the room, and then Léon himself climbed down the side of the building, his sticky fingers clinging to the exterior limestone.

"The draining room," Gabby said as soon as he'd ducked inside. "How do we get there?"

Léon wiped his hands on the sides of his trousers, then shook them out. "It's in the basement."

"Excellent. We have five possible floors on which to get caught," Nolan muttered.

"There are guards on every floor at every flight of stairs," Léon added. "But there is a servants' stairwell two doors down from here to the kitchens, and from there, a set of stairs to the basement rooms. The draining room is the one farthest down the corridor."

Gabby knew it was just five floors, but it felt as though he were giving them directions to Africa.

"Léon and I will draw the guards and disciples away," Nolan said to her. "I know I can't keep Vander from Ingrid, and I'm quickly learning you're as stubborn as you are impatient."

He took Gabby roughly by the arm, dragged her toward him, and crushed his lips to hers. She breathed in sharply through her nose, too stunned to kiss him in return before he broke off and stepped back.

"What was that for?" Gabby asked, a little dazed and embarrassed. Vander and Léon had edged away from them, toward the door. "Luck?"

"No," Nolan said with his trademark arrogant grin. "It was because I love you."

He didn't wait for her response. He withdrew his sword and he and Léon charged out of the room, making whooping noises and catcalls to draw the attention of whatever guards lurked at the top of stairs.

Gabby drifted across the room to Vander's side, Nolan's voice still ringing in her ears. She knew she had to have a ridiculous expression on her face because Vander laughed.

"Well, in that case, I'd best keep you alive, Lady Gabriella," he said. Then, together, they fled the room.

CHAPTER TWENTY-SIX

It was worse than Ingrid had imagined.

The style and warmth of the posh upper floors had deceived Ingrid into thinking the room where Dupuis planned to drain her blood would be just as elegant and charming.

It wasn't.

The room, located in the basement, was a medical nightmare. A series of steel-topped tables lined one wall, and strewn about them were all sorts of beakers and tubes and sharp-edged instruments. The walls themselves were just the stone foundation, the low ceilings constructed of plaster and hewn beams. The harsh electric light only made the room feel more cramped, and the corners were draped in shadow.

Three wheeled gurneys, each outfitted with leather restraints, were positioned against the wall directly in front of Ingrid as she walked in, Marco on her heels. Beside each gurney were serpentine tangles of tubing attached to cylindrical copper-and-glass vats.

No wonder Léon had run away from this place.

"The average human body holds approximately five and a half liters of blood," Dupuis explained as he came to stand beside the vats. His long fingers traveled over the twists of clear rubber tubing. "We shall draw out your blood, separate it in this system, and then immediately pump the filtered blood back into your body."

He brought his hands back into a steepled position. "The transfusion will be lengthy, I am afraid."

Ingrid tried to keep her trembling to a minimum. She had to do this. They were holding Luc against his will. Feeling her fear and being unable to come to her must have been excruciating for him.

"How will these machines know to withdraw my angel blood and leave the rest of it?" she asked.

Logic always calmed her. If she could have something to concentrate on, some specific focus, perhaps she could get through this. Because it was clear, now that she had followed them into this nightmare room, that if she didn't give Dupuis her blood, her father and Luc would never leave this place alive.

"We've never drawn angel blood before, but we have drawn demon blood. It has a different cell structure. We've developed a way to magnetize and pull out those different cells," Dupuis said, his cheeks flushed with either excitement or pride. Neither one suited the moment. "This separating system will draw out every cell that differs from your human cells, and will therefore only return those that are human," he continued, lifting up a second tangle of tubing, which ended with a needle.

Ingrid held up her hand as his explanation settled. "Wait—*all* the cells that aren't human?"

Carrick cleared his throat. He was leaning against a steel-topped table, one arm hooked around his stomach, a sheen of sweat on his forehead. She remembered that the mercurite poisoning was eating him from the inside.

"If you drain both her demon and angel blood, how much blood will she be left with?" Marco asked.

"She won't survive," Carrick said, his voice strained. "We agreed on the angel blood, Dupuis. You said you could remove it and leave the rest. The Alliance can still use her if she has her demon gift."

Dupuis transformed his face into a carefully drawn mask of regret. "Yes, well, this is where the risk enters. I cannot guarantee she will survive."

"But you can guarantee that you'll have your angel blood," Ingrid said. "You don't care if I live or die."

"Of course I do not care," he replied, hardly concealing his amusement. "However, it would be better for our reputation should you live. So we shall try our hardest, yes?"

Carrick gritted his teeth as he tried to straighten. "What is this, Dupuis? The girl's angel blood. *That* was the deal."

Dupuis ignored him. He didn't even glance his way as he reached for a white coat on a wall hook. "If you would remove your dress, mademoiselle. Your undergarments will be sufficient."

Ingrid retreated a step. "No. Not until my father and Luc are released, and I want to see them leave."

"Not at *all*," Marco argued. His voice rose to where Ingrid knew it might cross over into a shriek. "I've heard enough. We're leaving, Lady Ingrid. Should anyone attempt to stop us, brace yourself for the sight of blood."

Dupuis began to turn switches and dials on the cylindrical vat, unmoved by Marco's threat. "You sound quite protective, gargoyle. Take a moment to search yourself. What is the tie that binds you to this young woman?"

He flipped a lever and a humming sound shook the vat. The lightbulbs brightened.

"Lady Ingrid has come to me willingly," Dupuis added, and with a glance toward Marco arched one of his brows. "She has accepted her room here. She is on my territory. By Daicrypta edict, she is now my ward, and the human charge of my Dispossessed."

Marco came forward, stepping in front of Ingrid and staring hard at Dupuis. But he didn't speak. Ingrid watched as the sinuous muscles along his ribs and torso stretched. He was breathing in. Scenting her. Marco exhaled and looked over his shoulder at her. "You are no longer my human."

The room went cold around her. His bond to her had been severed. Marco was going to leave.

"Your dress, mademoiselle," Dupuis repeated.

Ingrid kept her eyes locked on Marco's, while in her unfocused side vision Dupuis slipped his arms into the sleeves of his white lab coat.

She couldn't look away. The expression on Marco's face was new; it didn't seem to belong to him. Sadness melted into disappointment, and then changed again, this time into something much more familiar: anger.

He moved fast and mercilessly.

Marco had half shifted before he reached Dupuis and grabbed fistfuls of his white coat. He jerked him off the floor and, with a piercing shriek, threw Dupuis as he might a sack of potatoes straight into Carrick Quinn's hunched frame. The two men landed on the stone floor in a heap of arms and legs, taking with them one of the steel tables and the instruments upon it.

Marco turned back to Ingrid as the scream of metal and breaking glass assaulted her ears. His wolfish snout crumpled back until his face was once again human. Marco surged toward her, his great wings folding into his body as his scales softened to skin.

"Lady Ingrid, come with—"

Marco stopped—and shattered out of his skin once again, transforming so quickly that Ingrid threw her arms up before her face. She heard a shriek, then two more, and when she lowered her arms, Marco was down flat on his back, a long knife handle protruding from his abdomen.

Dimitrie entered the room through the open door. He was in human form, and he held a crossbow, fitted with a dart.

"Marco!" Ingrid yelled as she rushed toward him.

Dimitrie caught her by the arm and pulled her back before she could reach the gargoyle. Marco screeched in pain, rolling onto his side as he grasped the knife and ripped it from his armored stomach.

Dupuis had shaken himself off and stumbled to his feet. "Finish him, Dimitrie."

"No!" Ingrid screamed, clawing at Dimitrie to let her go. Marco had only been trying to protect her, even though he wasn't required to any longer. She had to do something to help him. "I'll do it, I'll give you the blood, just—just stop!"

With one easy shove, Dimitrie knocked her to her knees and sent her skidding to the far side of the room. He raised the crossbow toward Marco, who writhed on the floor, and fired again. A dart buried itself in Marco's back, just under his right wing. His anguished shriek reverberated off the walls.

"I asked you to finish him," Dupuis barked.

"The mercurite will hold him," Dimitrie replied.

"Mercurite?" Ingrid pushed herself up from the cold floor, but she couldn't reach Marco. Dimitrie stood between them.

"Our weapons are dipped in it," Dimitrie answered. "It's the only way humans can protect themselves against the Dispossessed."

"But you're one of them!" Ingrid screamed.

Marco growled on the floor. His body rippled out of true form until he lay naked, facedown. His wings folded and nearly disappeared into clean gashes just beneath his shoulder blades. The one closest to the mercurite dart remained half formed.

"No he isn't. He's a Shadow bastard and a traitor," he spit, his grating voice tremulous.

Dimitrie didn't deny it. He only grimaced. "Be thankful I didn't aim for your heart, Wolf."

Dupuis brushed off his coat and walked away from Marco's prostrate form. The blood-draining machine droned on. "Get her ready, Dimitrie."

Luc crawled out of the basement storeroom, his human body still a grotesque fusion of flesh and stone. He couldn't scent Ingrid. She had been there one second and gone the next, and no matter how hard he tried, her rich, earthy essence wouldn't come.

He dug his fingers into the rotting wooden doorframe and hauled himself up. It had been half an hour since Dimitrie had left with the promise of Ingrid's death on his lips. Luc threw his head back and cracked it against the soft wood. If her scent was gone, that meant she was either in the Underneath with Axia and no longer his human charge, or she was dead.

If Axia had somehow snatched Ingrid back to the Underneath, Luc would simply go after her again. Surely he could find demon poison somewhere in this Daicrypta prison. He would ingest it and cross into the Underneath, and like last time, once he and Ingrid shared the same realm again, he would be able to scent and trace her.

But if she was dead . . . if Dimitrie had taken her from him . . . The boy had been right. Luc wasn't going to let him rot here for eternity.

He felt the telling chime at the base of his skull. Dimitrie wasn't far.

Luc forced himself to move forward. The darted tips of his leathery wings dragged along the floor. He was half naked and half scaled, and he could barely move. Where the mercurite had touched him, his jet scales had been frozen in place, calcified to flinty stone. In the last half hour they had softened to something more like wet cement. Still. How was he supposed to destroy

Dimitrie like this? And if Ingrid wasn't dead, if he had to go into the Underneath . . . how could he rescue her?

The single electric bulb lighting the dug-out corridor hummed and brightened before a wire inside snapped. The light fizzled, dropping the corridor into a tunnel of mixed grays.

He heard a voice.

"Is someone there?"

Brickton. His oiled-leather scent traveled fast up Luc's nose. He was hard-pressed not to gag on it.

"Hello?" Ingrid's father called again. There was a closed door to Luc's right, with a chain draped through the handle and affixed to an iron ring driven into the stone. Luc stared at it a moment, considering. The man wasn't in any danger. Luc sensed fear, but that was only because Ingrid's father was a fool, and ignorant to everything going on around him.

Perhaps it was time to enlighten him.

Luc closed his hand around the chain and swore. Mercurite. Cursing again, he grabbed the iron ring staked into the stone and tore that out instead, then threw the door open. Brickton sat tied to a chair in the center of a small storeroom much like the one Luc had been kept in.

"Tell me who you are," Brickton pleaded. His eyes darted around, blind in the dark. "Dimitrie?"

Luc tested his footing, shuffling forward awkwardly.

"I'm the one who can save you," Luc whispered.

Brickton gasped. "Then by God, man, untie me. Get me out of here!"

He struggled with the ropes that bound his wrists. Blackness seeped down the tops of his hands, Luc saw. Blood. He'd chafed his skin raw trying to escape.

"I can't say I'm inclined to do that yet." Luc tested the slender bones framing his wings. They twitched as they straightened, making a popping sound. Lord Brickton stopped fidgeting.

"What do you want, then?" he asked.

Luc lifted the bridge of one wing and touched Brickton's flaccid cheek with the arrowed tip.

"I want you to leave Paris," Luc answered.

He flexed his long, rigid talons, wet cement turning to tidal clay.

"I will, I will," Brickton said, voice reedy with desperation. "I promise, I'll take my family and—"

"Your family stays," Luc said. "*You* leave. Forever."

Brickton gargled an objection. "They will come with me. I cannot possibly leave them—"

"They stay in Paris, or you stay right here."

This time Ingrid's father swallowed his argument. He closed his eyes and nodded.

Luc sheared through the ropes that bound Brickton's wrists and ankles.

"Go," he snarled. Brickton didn't waste a moment. He sprang from the chair and stumbled forward, arms outstretched to guide him through the darkness.

A muffled crash from somewhere else on the basement level drew Luc's attention from his human's staggered escape. He didn't know how far the man would get, but that wasn't his concern just then. Dimitrie was. Again Luc called up Ingrid's scent. Reflex. Habit. Again, he was left hollow.

A scream followed the crash, and he lurched toward the door, the chime at the base of his skull driving him into motion. Luc pulled at the trigger in his core to coalesce, but he stayed disfigured, half gargoyle, half human, as he trudged through the corridor toward the pandemonium.

CHAPTER TWENTY-SEVEN

Chelle stood just outside the Daicrypta gates. The mansion was barely visible behind the immense brick wall enclosing the grounds, which ran the full length of the block. Scores of trees grew in a straight row behind the wall, acting as a second barrier to curious eyes. Grayson watched her pace the sidewalk for close to a minute. She'd bounce up onto the balls of her feet, turn, walk, bounce up restlessly, then turn and do it all over again.

Grayson hadn't meant to take so long, but he'd been stuck in that side alley for longer than he'd expected. Letting his human form go and changing into his hellhound one had been easy. Natural, even. It was changing back that had proven difficult, especially with two hellhounds at his side. It seemed that his body wanted to stay in harmony with theirs.

Grayson had managed, though, and he'd kept it that way as he'd walked up the hills of Montmartre, the hellhounds following him through a circuitous route of alleys, roofs, and park squares. He held himself in, keeping his muscles tight, imagining his bones as immovable iron. Staying human had taken so much of the last hour's focus that when he crossed the dark street toward Chelle, he still hadn't quite worked out how the two hellhounds concealed in the shadows behind him were going to be useful.

"Where've ye been?"

Rory appeared at Grayson's side with phantom grace.

"I'll tell you if you promise to keep your hands off that silver," Grayson answered.

Chelle hurried toward him. "I started to think something had happened."

She looked and sounded furious, and when she came to a stop just beneath his chin, he knew better than to try to touch her.

"Where are Lennier and Yann?" Grayson asked, searching the sky and the roofs of nearby homes.

"Gone. Why?" Chelle stared up at him, her nose crinkling. "What happened? You smell like . . ."

Like a hellhound. She could smell it on him.

"I've brought two hellhounds with me," Grayson said. "They're under my command."

Chelle pulled back and the *hira-shuriken* came out, two flashes of silver in her skilled hands.

"What have you done?" she whispered.

"Trust me, Chelle. They aren't going to attack," he answered, and letting out all his breath, summoned the hounds forward with a single thought: *Come.*

He didn't need to look to know they were there. Chelle's squint softened and her eyes grew round and alert. Rory came flush against her side, a knife in each hand. At least the gargoyles weren't there. Grayson wouldn't have been able to convince them not to attack.

"We can use them," he said, though it was difficult to speak and hold himself together at the same time.

"Call them off," Rory ordered, his vigilant eyes never wavering from the hellhounds slinking up behind Grayson.

Stay, he thought, and in the next second Rory's brows slanted down in surprise. The hounds had lowered themselves to the paving stones.

"They won't hurt you," Grayson said, hoping he was right. He'd led these beasts here. To Chelle. If anything happened to her . . . if he failed . . .

"How are you doing this?" she asked, eyes flicking from Grayson's face to the hounds behind him.

"I don't know, really, and I don't know how long it will last, but I'm going in."

Chelle shook her head. "Nolan and Vander have already gone after Ingrid, along with your stubborn little sister. Stay here with us—and send *them* away," she said with a glance at the hellhounds.

"I can't," Grayson said. "If my sisters are in there, I'm going in, too."

Chelle gritted her teeth and let out a frustrated grunt. "Do you think I wish to stand out here twiddling my thumbs on the sidewalk, Grayson Waverly? Don't you think I would rather be inside with Vander and Nolan doing something useful?"

A clamor rose suddenly from within the walled estate and the three of them shot to the gates and peered around the ivy-wrapped wall. The front doors to the mansion had been thrown wide, and three men scrambled into the circular drive.

"Father," Grayson murmured, watching as the Earl of Brickton, stripped down to his trousers, waistcoat, and shirtsleeves, swung a Grecian vase wildly at one of the two men chasing him. The vase hit the man's temple and he staggered, clutching his head.

Grayson's father saw the closed front gates and doubled back, bolting away from the circular drive and out of sight.

"Damn." Grayson leaned against the wall. He hadn't forgotten about his father, but he hadn't really cared, either. Hadn't worried about him the way he was worrying about Ingrid.

He turned back to Chelle and Rory and stopped. The hellhounds were gone.

A yelp, then a low growl sounded from behind the wall.

"They jumped it," Rory said, glaring at Grayson. "Was *that* yer command?"

No. Grayson grasped the sides of his head, his insides turning to fire as the urge to shift consumed him. He had to stop them. They were under *his* command.

"I thought—" he started to say, barely able to breathe.

He heard his father scream and his muscles and bones twisted and popped. He threw back his head and a growl ripped from his throat. Before he'd even finished shifting, Grayson had sprung into the air and over the Daicrypta wall.

Ingrid watched with dread as Dimitrie closed the door and threw a heavy bolt into place. He set his crossbow on one of the steel tables, and with carefully controlled motion, turned to her. "My human told you to undress."

She backed away.

"Touch her and I'll slice off your fingers and feed them to you," Marco grumbled, still immobile on the floor.

Dimitrie laughed at the improbable threat as a hand wrapped around Ingrid's ankle. She shrieked and kicked her leg, but Carrick Quinn's fingers clung like briar thorns. He was still on the floor, his face a mask of agony.

"Forgive me for . . . what I've done." He gasped before letting her go. She spun away, and Dimitrie caught her in his gangly arms.

Carrick fought to rise to his knees. A cough ripped from his throat. Blood flew from his mouth and splattered onto the floor.

Ingrid stopped struggling.

"He needs help!" she cried to Dupuis. The Daicrypta doyen was still fiddling with the machinery.

Carrick was a traitor, yes, but he was also Nolan's father.

"The mercurite poisoning is incurable, I am afraid," Dupuis answered, uninterested. "If he is lucky, the internal bleeding will finish him off within the hour. Dimitrie?"

Dimitrie grabbed the collar of Ingrid's blouse and wrenched the fabric apart. A handful of abalone buttons scattered, leaving bare skin and the lace top of her camisole exposed.

While Marco roared another vow to tear off more of Dimitrie's appendages, Ingrid sank her teeth into the gargoyle's forearm. It took Dimitrie by surprise, though she doubted it hurt. He only pushed her away and swore.

"Forget the clothes!" Dupuis snapped his fingers. "Get her on the gurney."

The bulbs overhead brightened again, their shrill hum rising to a scream. Ingrid squinted up at the glowing orbs of shuddering white light. She needed her electricity. Needed it *now*. She stared at the hot white glass and the wires inside strained to brighten. Ingrid gasped as dual currents clawed down her arms and prickled at her fingertips.

"Stop her," Dupuis ordered. The lightbulbs had drawn his attention. They hummed louder, grew brighter. Dupuis's look of alarm told Ingrid exactly what he didn't want her to realize: the power-draining machines weren't pushing the bulbs to their limits. *She* was.

"Dimitrie, now!" Dupuis shouted.

The gargoyle leaped forward and clamped his hands around her shoulders. She seized his arms in return, and where her fingers dug in, flickering braids of electricity tasseled out. She saw them quiver over his shirt; felt them tunnel through his flesh, into his nerve endings. The straining lightbulb above them popped and went black. Dimitrie shook, sick gurgling noises low in his throat. Ingrid screamed when he shot back, out of her grasp, as if blown by a heavy gale. He landed hard on the floor and didn't move.

Ingrid's knees buckled. She landed on one, her hands flat

against the floor. Her palms stung, the muscles in her arms trembled, and yet this time, something was different.

She still felt it. A tickle just beneath her skin. It wasn't much. But it was *there*.

"My sincerest apologies," Dupuis said, so close behind her that she flinched and started to turn.

His arm came toward her face and struck the side of her head. Ingrid went down into a swirling black fog.

CHAPTER TWENTY-EIGHT

Gabby and Vander had made it to the basement level, but not without a pack of disciples on their heels. The three men now trailed them through a maze of narrow corridors. For a bunch of students, they were suspiciously well armed.

"Here," Vander hissed, and Gabby darted to the right, down another corridor.

The bulbs snapped and flickered as Vander and Gabby approached a new ruckus: the draining room. It had to be.

Vander slammed into the door, twisting the handle and throwing all his weight against the solid wood. It rattled but withstood his assault. He backed up and went at the door with the heel of his boot instead, kicking and stomping with crazed ferocity.

A disciple came around the corner and Gabby raised her sword in time to feel his blade bite into hers. His thrust was far more powerful than hers, and it shoved her blade down to the floor. Vander turned, buried his foot in the disciple's gut, and cracked the crossbow against his temple.

"Thank you," Gabby breathed.

"My pleasure," he replied as he kicked the door again. Gabby heard wood splinter and the door flew open.

There were three people on the floor of the draining room. Though Gabby recognized them all—Dimitrie, Carrick Quinn, and a completely unclothed Marco—her eyes went straight for Ingrid, who was unconscious and strapped to a gurney that Dupuis was rolling out of the room through an open door along the far wall.

"Dupuis, stop!" Vander brought his crossbow up and aimed. But Dupuis ducked low behind Ingrid for cover, and then they were gone. The next second, another disciple charged into the draining room, his *katana* slashing through the air toward Vander.

Gabby intersected it with her blade, but the force of this man's swing was also superior to her own. Her blade hit the stone floor and he shoved her back. Gabby tripped over Marco's splayed form. She landed on her rump, her legs and skirts covering *his* backside.

"Oh, for the Lord's sake! Can't your clothing shift with you?" She struggled off him as Vander and the disciple crashed into a table and upset a host of medical tools.

"Last I was aware, it wasn't my clothing that was cursed," Marco growled. "Now, if you please, Lady Gabriella, I've got a mercurite dart in my spine. Take it out and let me kill some Daicrypta scum."

Gabby turned toward the door Dupuis and her sister had disappeared through. It was shut, but that didn't matter. Marco could get to Ingrid faster than any of them.

Gabby gripped the silver fletching feathers. She closed her eyes, and with a grimace, ripped the dart out of Marco's back. His roar of pain drowned out the telltale sound of steel and silver clashing in the corridor. It had to be Nolan and Léon out there.

Carrick moaned from his spot on the floor by yet another

overturned table. Dimitrie had been near Nolan's father a moment ago, but he was gone now. Gabby made a beeline for the closed door across the room, stooping quickly to pick up an abandoned dagger. She recognized the dull pewter sheen of the blade: mercurite-dipped. She slipped it into her cape, making one of her dagger sheaths do double duty. If she found Dimitrie, she wouldn't hesitate to use it.

Marco grasped the collar of the disciple Vander had been battling and threw him against the stone wall. The disciple crumpled to the floor.

Vander cleared his throat. "Yes, well . . . thank you."

Marco reached the door Dupuis had escaped through just as Gabby did. It wasn't a plank of wood like the rest of the doors she'd seen in this godforsaken mansion. It was made of thick, smooth stone and had no handle. She pushed it. Nothing happened. In her side vision, she saw Nolan and Léon barrel into the draining room.

Nolan went straight to his father's miserable form. "What's happened?"

Léon stayed at the entrance, facing the corridor. Silk streamed from his fingertips, and Gabby heard the muffled cries of more disciples.

She found a small gap between the door and the wall with her fingertips. She strained to pull the door out. Nothing. Marco knocked her hands aside and dug his own fingers into the gap. He hauled on the slab of stone, and slowly, it sank into the wall like a pocket door.

"You can't stay here," Nolan said to his father. "I have to get you to Benoit—"

"Listen to me," Carrick interrupted. "The Directorate. Don't trust them. Tell Rory."

Gabby heard Carrick laboring for breath and felt a pang of worry. Her father. She had to find him, too, but Ingrid needed her more. In another few seconds she, Marco, and Vander would be able to squeeze through the gap and go after her. Traitor or not, she knew Nolan wouldn't leave his father's side.

"I can't locate your sister," Marco said, the muscles in his upper body cording as he heaved aside the slab door. "She accepted a room here and is Dimitrie's human now."

Vander slid in front of Gabby and helped push the slab with both hands, though Gabby was certain Marco didn't require the added strength.

"We'll find her," he said, and finally, the gap was wide enough for them to go through.

"Nolan?" Léon called, his voice distracting Gabby before she could step inside the tunnel. There was a muffled silence out in the corridor. "There is something coming."

Ingrid's head jerked to the side. The fast creaking of wheels and the rocking motion of her body nearly lulled her back into the swirly black fog. Until she remembered.

Dupuis.

Ingrid wrenched herself to consciousness. She was on her back, moving through the dark. She turned her face away as a glaring lightbulb flashed overhead. She tried to sit up and realized in a sudden panic that she couldn't. Dupuis had her restrained on a gurney. Leather straps buckled each wrist, thigh, and ankle, as well as the width of her chest. Cinched tight, her legs had gone numb. Her wrists ached.

But it was still there. The barest electrical current swarmed at the tip of each finger.

"I do wish you had not chosen to be so defiant."

Dupuis's voice came from near the crown of her head. He was behind her, pushing the gurney, and he sounded a touch breathless.

"Did you plan to have those silly Alliance friends of yours rush in at the last minute to rescue you?" Dupuis chuckled.

His breath wafted over her face. Paired with the musty, water-on-rock odor of the corridor they were winding through, it made Ingrid fight back a gag.

"Where are you taking me?" She wriggled her fingers. It wasn't enough of an electric current. This was a languid Thames, whereas she needed Victoria Falls.

"Did you know, my lady, that we have spent decades draining the blood of demons? The discovery of demon-blooded humans such as yourself prompted us to develop mechanisms that would make the process far less lethal." Dupuis took the gurney around a sharp bend. The metal frame scraped the wall.

"It is unfortunate that we have now been driven from those mechanisms. They might have spared your life. We do, however, maintain our original machinery."

He was still going to drain her blood.

"Now I will have to take it all and separate it later," he explained with the same sort of sigh a maid might give upon finding a just-cleaned floor dirty again.

"You were never going to destroy it," she said, her voice shaking as the wheels traveled over uneven floor.

They were underneath the estate, in some twisting tunnel. Wherever they were going, Ingrid dreaded their arrival.

"Destroy it? No," he said, amused. "It will be the Daicrypta's most valuable leverage."

They passed underneath another glaring bulb. Ingrid winced and felt the pressure in her hands build.

"Your blood can do the one thing the Alliance wishes it could do," Dupuis went on. "They have their mercurite weapons and their dreams of regulations, but you saw your gargoyle back there—the threat of mercurite did not stop him from trying to help you. Gargoyles will never adhere to Alliance regulations unless they are *forced* to."

Ingrid wriggled her fingers, remembering the courtyard at Hôtel du Maurier and the way she'd forced Vincent to submit. With her blood, the Alliance could control the Dispossessed?

"We have the technology to proliferate blood samples in the laboratory, you see," Dupuis went on excitedly. "One or two liters of blood can become hundreds of liters, possibly thousands. Enough for every Alliance fighter. Can you not imagine what the Directorate would be willing to give for such power?"

Perhaps the Directorate would want it, though Ingrid couldn't imagine those she knew, like Vander, Nolan, or Chelle, giving themselves angelic powers.

Dupuis rolled the gurney under another humming bulb, and Ingrid, instead of wincing, purposefully stared into the white glass as it rushed overhead. New static swelled within her arms.

"But these are details you need not worry yourself over," Dupuis said dismissively.

Because she was going to die. There was no one coming for her now.

Dimitrie was her gargoyle, but he wasn't going to help her. Marco had a mercurite dart in his spine, and if Luc was being held in mercurite as well . . .

The only person who could save her was *her.*

Another bend in the corridor and the metal rim of the gurney nicked the wall again. The friction threw off a spark. They passed another lightbulb and the slender bones in each of her fingers ached with another gradient of pressure.

Electricity begets electricity, Constantine had once said. She could absorb an electric current and let it fuel her own. .

The lightbulb popped and flickered to black as they passed by.

Dupuis continued to push her, his hands gripping the metal of the gurney. Though Ingrid's wrists were bound, her fingers were free. She clamped them around the cold rods at her side and unloosed the pools of electricity that had welled up in each fingertip. All she did was *think* it and the current traveled out, through the metal, singing past her ears. It shivered over her scalp and lifted her hair on end for a split second before it hit Dupuis. He stopped, made a strangled noise, and fell—taking the gurney with him.

Ingrid let go of the metal rods before her fingers could be crushed, but the impact still hurt. Her head snapped to the side, pulling tendons along her neck. The gurney leaned on its side, wheels spinning. Behind her, Dupuis moaned and cursed. The jolt hadn't been strong enough. He'd be up and raging within a minute.

But she had controlled it. She had finally understood the electricity that had always seemed to ebb and flow as it saw fit. Even though she was still trapped, Ingrid felt like letting out a whoop of joy.

Dupuis crawled into view, his arms quivering as he held himself up.

"Metal and lightning," he whispered. "Very clever, mademoiselle. Though you, like your Alliance friends, are shortsighted."

Her eye caught on the next bare lightbulb ahead. Ingrid stared at it, pulling the light toward her, and the energy filled her, brimming in her fingertips.

There was a noise then. Something dragging along the floor. A rattling came next, followed by a low, shaky hiss. Ingrid's focus on the lightbulb was severed as Axia's serpent moved into the spill of light up ahead. Bleached of color, nearly translucent, its scales seemed so much paler than those of the mimic that had stalked her in the shopping arcades. And this one wasn't moving with the same taunting rhythm. It skated toward them fast.

Dupuis stumbled to his feet just as the serpent reared up, flattened out its regal hood, unhinged its jaw, and struck. Ingrid watched in detached horror as Dupuis's head disappeared, crown to neck, in the massive serpent's mouth. Long fangs punched through Dupuis's shoulders, and his arms went slack. The strength in his legs gave next, and when the serpent extracted its fangs, the man crumpled, twitching, to the floor. Ingrid let loose a scream.

"Ingrid!"

Vander's shout sounded like it came from a great distance. Blood roared through her ears, and she hoped she'd imagined it. She didn't want Vander here, with this demon serpent. It wasn't the mimic—Luc had said that it wouldn't harm anyone but Ingrid. This was the real serpent. Axia's pet.

It curled toward her, sliding around Dupuis's convulsing form. Though it was futile, Ingrid struggled against the leather straps until the snake's fangs closed around her bound arm. They stabbed through her sleeve and into flesh. The searing burn of demon poison was instantaneous.

Feeling electricity under her skin was a patch of kitten fur compared to this. The burning intensified and climbed, carving wide, deep paths at a reckless speed. Ingrid gasped for air as it tore through her arm and obliterated any electric current the lightbulbs had given her.

The gurney wobbled as the serpent slid down the length of it, the tapered end of its tail coiling around the metal frame near Ingrid's feet.

"Ingrid!" Vander's voice came again. But it was just an echo. He wasn't close.

The gurney started moving again, in the same direction Dupuis had been taking her. The metal side scratched along the floor, grinding and grating and sending vibrations through Ingrid's body. With Dupuis, she hadn't known where she'd been going, but there were no mysteries now. The demon poison burrowing into her, spreading far and wide, would allow Ingrid entry through a fissure somewhere in Paris, straight into the Underneath. Straight to Axia's hive.

CHAPTER TWENTY-NINE

Luc had followed the sounds of clanging metal, the screams and shouts, and the incessant throbbing at the base of his skull that assured him another Dispossessed was close. And Gabby. He'd followed her scent, a beacon cutting through a sea of gray, spooling waves.

He stepped over a writhing cocoon, one of at least a half dozen scattered throughout the corridor. It was the kind of destruction an arachnae demon would leave in its wake, but it wasn't a giant spider standing in the doorway up ahead. It was a boy. A human boy with viscous silk dangling from each fingertip. It had to be the Duster everyone had been talking about.

The boy held his hands down as Luc struggled toward him. His muscles and bones had gone from tidal clay to beach sand, and his jacket of scales had come out over most of his human skin, but it was still an ugly patchwork. His motions were cleaner, less jerky and pathetic, but barely so.

When he came upon the Duster, the boy scuttled to the side.

"Luc? Good Lord, is that you?" Gabby was across the room, flanked by Vander Burke and Marco. They stood within the slim mouth of another doorway.

Luc couldn't reply in any human way, so he kept heading toward them, his wings still dragging.

Marco stared gravely. "What did they do, bathe you in mercurite?"

He scanned the room. No Ingrid. No Dimitrie. The chime at the base of his skull had been for Marco.

Gabby looked from Luc to Nolan. He knelt beside the elder Quinn, who had blood streaked down his chin. "I'm staying with him," Nolan said.

"But—" Gabby started.

"Go," Nolan replied, then more gently, "We'll be fine here, but Ingrid needs you."

Luc's body reacted on instinct. His wings spread open and the last patches of skin snapped into hard jet. He didn't even feel the pain.

"Ingrid's alive?" Luc asked. Only Marco could understand his gravelly cry.

"For the moment," he replied.

Luc sagged forward. Alive. Ingrid was alive. He felt sick with relief. But why couldn't he trace her? Bring up her scent, or feel her?

"I don't know what they've done to you, Luc, but we have to go. Now," Gabby said, her short sword clenched in her palm, her foot already inside the slim gap.

Vander's patience broke. He pressed himself through the opening. Gabby immediately followed, and Luc started for the gap as well.

Marco blocked the opening. "You couldn't feel her because she isn't our human any longer. She's Dimitrie's, though I doubt the Shadow bastard can do anything to protect her."

"He promised to kill her," Luc said, his shriek resounding off the stone walls.

"Well, he can't do that now, can he?" Marco replied. Luc didn't know what Dimitrie could or couldn't do. The rules were blurry here.

"Get out of my way," Luc growled, starting forward again. He could hear Vander shouting for Ingrid inside the tunnel and envy burned in his chest. That should be him in there, not Vander.

Marco blocked him once more. "Look at yourself. You aren't in any condition to go with Lady Gabriella. I will."

Luc stilled, suddenly seeing things the way Marco must. The way any other gargoyle would. He should have wanted to charge into that passageway to protect his human charge—Gabby.

Protecting her had not crossed Luc's mind once.

Marco cocked his head as he realized it. "Lady Ingrid is not our human any longer. Your responsibility to her is severed. Go after her now and the Order will know, brother."

They knew last time, when Luc had taken demon poison and gone into the Underneath to rescue Ingrid from Axia. He had chosen to put himself in danger for a human who wasn't his own. Irindi had accused Luc of having an affinity for Ingrid and had warned him to curb it.

He'd tried.

Luc didn't know what the Order's punishment would be this time. It didn't matter. "Let me pass," he said.

Marco's hooded eyes barely concealed his annoyance. "Luc, I'm trying to help—"

A scream pricked Marco's sentence. It came from far away, buried by layers of stone, wood, and plaster. Yet even severed from Ingrid, Luc felt it keenly in the pit of his stomach.

He barred his forearm across Marco's brawny chest and shoved him against the stone door. "She may not be mine, but I am still hers."

Luc pushed off from the other gargoyle and bolted into the dark passageway. He conjured a trace on Gabby and followed it, spreading his wings as far as the walls would allow. His feet had barely left the floor when each injured wing collapsed. Luc's bare soles hit the floor and he was forced to run after Gabby and Vander. He went as fast as he could but longed for his wings. Damned mercurite.

Ahead, in a sphere of electric light, Luc saw a body on the floor of the tunnel.

"Don't stop, Luc!" came Vander's shout from farther down the tunnel. "I see crypsis dust! It and Ingrid's dust lead this way!"

Axia's pet has her. Luc ran faster and caught up to Vander and Gabby at a short set of stairs. At the top, a hatch door had been left flung open. The cold air felt good on Luc's scales as he climbed into a grassy courtyard. It made the one at Hôtel du Maurier look like the Paris slums. This was a true lawn, a miniature Luxembourg Garden. Stately trees, their trunks gnarled and scored with age; a tiered fountain surrounded by a sunken garden; an arched footbridge spanning a small, iced-over pond. Five stories of block limestone, corner turrets, and leaded-glass windows towered over them on all sides, casting dim light over pockets of the lawn. Far beyond, an outbuilding had its lights on. A short stretch of open arcades linked this outbuilding to the main estate and appeared to be the only exit.

In the center of the lawn was Axia's pet crypsis, the tip of its near translucent body knotted around a hospital gurney. Ingrid lay tipped over, strapped into place with wide leather buckles. She thrashed beneath them, struggling wildly. *Alive.*

Vander, still a good ten strides ahead of Luc, stopped and leveled his crossbow at the demon snake. The snake's tail lifted the gurney from the grass and shielded itself by wagging it back and forth in front its body like a pendulum.

"Don't, Vander!" Gabby shouted, holding her own daggers indecisively.

Vander cursed under his breath, lowered the crossbow, and charged the serpent instead. He tore across the grass like a madman, a battle cry rending the air. With a flick of her tail, Axia's serpent swung the bobbing gurney, catching Vander in its path, and swept him away. He cartwheeled through the air before landing flat on his back, his weapon lost on impact. Ingrid, hanging upside down, her hair a waterfall of corn silk, screamed Vander's name.

The serpent's tail swished again when its pearly diamond-shaped eyes locked on Luc. It tossed the gurney aside and started to slither toward the gargoyle.

Gabby didn't waste a moment.

She streaked toward the gurney, which had tumbled to a rest, again on its side, next to the fountain. Her desperation overwhelmed Luc, fermenting in the back of his throat until it was all he could sense. The snake changed its course, flicking its tapered tail toward Gabby and coiling her waist in one thick loop. Luc raced toward the serpent, driven by the immediate burn of Gabby's panic.

"Gabby, no!" Ingrid screamed.

Before Luc could reach her, Gabby plunged the dagger she'd been holding through the milky scales squeezing her. The serpent hissed and spit, arching and undulating until it had uncoiled Gabby and bucked her off. Luc forced his wings to open despite the agony of it, and pushed off the grass. He'd barely caught her before his wings crinkled shut yet again, sending them both crashing to the ground.

"Move back," Luc ordered Gabby, who lay stunned behind him, as the serpent targeted him once more.

He considered his pathetic wings and poisoned muscles. They had made him weak. Nearly as weak as a human. He realized then that Vander hadn't charged the snake thinking he could best it. He'd done it because there was nothing else *to* do.

Luc made his decision. He would leave this place with Ingrid, or he wouldn't leave at all.

Ingrid screamed as the serpent glided over the lawn toward Luc.

As always, Luc's wings were two sheets of night, his scaled armor reflecting facets of onyx. But there was something seriously wrong with his true form. As he rushed to meet the serpent's attack, his right leg seemed to buckle with every stride. He should have been flying, not running.

Luc threw his legs forward at the last moment and went into a slide, narrowly avoiding the strike of venomous fangs.

Ingrid caught a flutter of something out of the corner of her eye and, when she looked, saw Vander coming for her. She shook her head fiercely. "No! Help Luc! Your crossbow, Vander, help him!"

He ignored her plea and fell to his knees at her side, attacking the leather straps.

"Forget the buckles. He's hurt, Vander!" she cried, twisting wildly under his hands.

"Stop moving!" he shouted right back.

Her wrists fell forward as he loosed the straps around them; then he started on the ones binding her ankles. Luc dodged another strike, but he was limping and faltering, looking more like a fly with one wing than the massive, powerful gargoyle Ingrid knew him to be.

Her ankles dropped to the grass just as the tip of the serpent's tail swept Luc's feet out from under him. The snake rolled and undulated, its regal head and tapered fangs stabbing toward Luc.

"No!" Ingrid screamed.

A piercing shriek and a blast of air fanned down over their heads. Marco's russet wings cut toward the serpent with hummingbird speed. He sank his talons into the demon and swiped it off the ground. The snake wriggled and bucked, but Marco held it skillfully as Yann dove toward the serpent. The edge of one feathered eagle wing sheared through scale and flesh, and Marco let the serpent fall in a hailstorm of green sparks. *Final* sparks.

Vander released the chest buckle and caught Ingrid as she fell. She'd done far too much falling lately. She eased back so she wasn't sprawled in Vander's lap and pushed her hair out of her eyes.

"Are you hurt?" he asked, and immediately found the fang bites on her arm. The searing burn was still there, but the pain had leveled off. Her angel blood would destroy the poison soon enough and she'd be fine, but Luc . . . There was something wrong with him.

She stood, her legs feeling quivery and her head cotton-stuffed.

"Ingrid!" Gabby bypassed Luc and threw her arms around her sister as if they had been parted for months instead of a single evening.

Ingrid watched Luc with her face half buried in Gabby's hair. His wings dragged like wrinkled elephant ears. The sight of his struggling, wounded body lanced through her. He stopped a good yard away.

He wasn't her gargoyle, not officially. Yet once again he'd come for her. Gabby must have sensed Ingrid's distraction because she let go, stepped aside, and followed Ingrid's gaze.

Ingrid staggered forward. Luc opened his arms to her and she fell into them. His scaled obsidian plates were hot and unforgiving, and it felt like embracing a sun-warmed boulder, but she didn't care. Luc was alive.

"I want to be yours again." She whispered the wish into his chest.

Luc loosened his arms and Ingrid wondered if she'd been

wrong to wish it aloud. She peered up at him. Felt the prickling of Gabby's eyes on her back. Vander's glare. Luc stared down the short slope of his doggish nose. It was a barely pronounced muzzle that left his face more human than monster. He was still hideous, though. Ingrid was too honest to say he wasn't.

Luc ran his rough-knuckled hand down the curve of her cheek, his deadly talons tucked safely into his palm.

"*Ingrid,*" Vander barked. "You and Gabby have to leave. Go through the arcades."

Luc withdrew his hand and everything around her slid back into focus. "But Papa," she said, turning to Vander. "He's still inside."

Luc shot a curl of steam from his nostrils and made a gravelly noise in the bottom of his throat. His form began to degenerate then, much more slowly than usual. His wings crackled and snapped as they pleated into his back.

Gabby whirled away from Luc, and Ingrid did the same, though she pinked in the cheeks thinking about his last shift. How she'd watched without shame.

"Nolan is inside, too. We can't leave him," Gabby said.

Vander picked up his crossbow. "I'm not leaving him."

"Your father isn't in the building," Luc rasped from where he stood, behind Ingrid. Pain laced each word. "He and Grayson are close, but . . . I don't know. Something is wrong. Ingrid, the Seer is right. You and Gabby have to go."

Luc was staying, though she didn't understand why. Gabby took Ingrid's arm and led her toward the arcades. She glanced over her shoulder and saw Luc, returned to true form, and Vander. They were waiting, watching. They wouldn't move until she and Gabby had successfully gone.

Ingrid's feet slipped over the grass, slick with icy night dew, as they approached the stone arches and the thick columns that ran the length of the arcades.

A shadow peeled off from one wide column. Ingrid dragged Gabby to a halt.

"Dimitrie?" Ingrid whispered. Her breath hung as a cloud before her.

The gangly boy came toward them. Gabby jerked her hand from Ingrid's grasp and withdrew a dagger from her cape, but Ingrid held up her arm.

"Stop. He won't hurt us. He can't. He's—" Ingrid paused, knowing the words would be bitter. "He's my gargoyle."

"He isn't mine," Gabby retorted, dagger still poised. "Back off."

Ingrid turned around. Luc and Vander had already started toward them, Vander with his crossbow raised and Luc stretching his wings as far as they could go. From this distance, Ingrid noticed a hole in each wing. Her stomach rolled—and then her pulse fluttered. Because coming up behind Luc and Vander was another Dimitrie.

Just as Ingrid saw it, Luc froze. He turned and saw the other Dimitrie in his human form.

One of them was the mimic.

The Dimitrie closer to Ingrid lunged for her. Gabby planted her foot in Ingrid's side and shoved her down, slicing at Dimitrie's reaching arm with her dagger. He vanished, and Gabby stumbled through the space where he had just been standing.

"It's the mimic, Gabby!" Ingrid shouted as it reappeared a few feet away.

Gabby swiftly sheathed the dagger and withdrew her sword. She swung, but the mimic ducked out of the blade's path, laughing. *Playing.*

Ingrid got to her feet and saw Vander running toward them—and Luc half running, half flying away. He skimmed over the lawn, his wings a swell of ink, toward the real Dimitrie. The smaller gargoyle simply waited, his twiggy arms lifted at his sides, palms turned out in a gesture of supplication. He looked so young, like a boy lifting his face to a summer rain.

Luc smashed into him. His wings blocked out everything but their legs as they plowed into the ground.

"Luc, now!" Vander screamed.

And then Ingrid knew. She knew what Luc was going to do.

A shriek rent the air. The ground shook and Ingrid dropped to her knees, Gabby falling with her as the shriek died away to a pitched whine. It had come from the mimic. Ingrid and Gabby stared at the demon as it lit in a flurry of color. It was no longer Dimitrie, but a jet-scaled Luc, then a near-translucent serpent, then a man again: Jonathan. The mimic faded into Anna's image before becoming someone Ingrid had never seen before. It continued to change, shuffling through image after image—all the disguises it had worn—until the very shape of the mimic began to dissolve. Like a sugar cube in tea, it disappeared a little more with every transformation.

It gave one final flicker and was gone.

Vander helped Ingrid up, then Gabby. Slowly, all three of them turned. Ingrid knew what Luc had done, but she wasn't prepared to see it.

He had his back to them, his wings once again listless. He stood over Dimitrie's still body, prostrate on the grass. Luc held something in his talons. Something round and strange, and Ingrid squinted to see what it was.

She bit back a scream.

CHAPTER THIRTY

Dimitrie's head.

Luc held Dimitrie's *head,* his talons curled into the boy's mop of blond hair. Gabby lowered her sword. She wanted to vomit. The night couldn't possibly get any worse.

It did, however, and promptly.

Gabby heard panting behind her. She held her sword aloft as another figure rushed down the length of the arcades, the slap of feet on the paving stones reverberating off the vaulted ceilings. She nearly dropped her weapon when her father stumbled past a column and slipped on the frosted grass.

"Papa!" Gabby and Ingrid exclaimed.

He looked at them with confusion before waving his hands wildly. "Go! Go! Run!"

Something must have been chasing him.

Gabby and Vander raised their weapons once again. Lord Brickton's eyes landed on her sword.

"Gabriella, what are you—?" He didn't finish his question but tore the handle of her sword out of her palm.

"Papa—give me that!"

Lord Brickton wheeled toward the arcades just as a hellhound streaked through and onto the lawn. Vander fired his crossbow a second too late; the dart missed and the hellhound ripped across the grass, toward Gabby, Ingrid, and their father, who chopped clumsily at the air with the sword.

Ingrid, however, threw her arms forward, palms flat, fingers splayed. Veins of lightning crackled through the air and hit the oncoming demon. The hellhound reared up onto its hind legs, then crashed backward as briars of electrostatic energy shivered over its fur.

The hound wasn't down one second before a second dart from Vander's crossbow speared its chest. Gabby's father cried out as the beast burst into a green cloud and vanished. He staggered back when Ingrid turned to face him.

"What did you just do?" he said, his voice spiraling to a frantic pitch.

Ingrid looked to Gabby, her wide blue eyes pleading for help. How could they explain any of this to him? But just then the doors to each wing of the mansion swung open, and the Daicrypta disciples braved entering the courtyard. They flooded out, surrounding their quarry within moments. Gabby did a harried count and found a neat dozen. They each held odd-looking, crossbow-like contraptions. She didn't know what they were but thought it wise to consider them deadly.

"Papa, give me my sword," Gabby said through clenched teeth.

"Don't be absurd," her father countered. "Where did you get this to begin with?"

Yet another thing she couldn't explain easily. The disciples advanced slowly. Dupuis was dead, but they clearly still wanted Ingrid's blood.

"Vander?" Gabby called. "Please tell me you have a plan."

"I was hoping we could make that a group effort," he replied.

Gabby focused on the approaching disciples closest to her. Even if she had been holding her sword, there was absolutely no way she could take them on all at once. The closest one called out in French, ordering them to lay down their weapons. He had barely finished speaking when a tangle of white silken rope looped around his chest and arms and snapped him off his feet. The other two disciples went down next, each of them wreathed in thick silk.

Léon! The Duster was climbing out of the basement-level hatch with Nolan just behind him, and Carrick leaning heavily on his son's shoulder. Léon cocooned yet another disciple, but not before the strange crossbow contraption went off. It fired not bullets or darts but a glittering, tightly woven net. Léon's silken webbing snarled the net midair before it could come down on top of him, and he slung it aside.

"Behind you, Gabby!" Nolan shouted. She turned to see a second hellhound leap from the arcade roof, land atop a disciple, and with one massive paw, crush his head into the ground.

Luc let out a shriek and surged forward, even though his wings barely lifted him from the ground. He collided with the hellhound and scrabbled with it for a few paltry moments before the beast raked a claw through one of Luc's already damaged wings. He went down, and the hellhound lunged toward Ingrid yet again. A glimmering net reached Ingrid first, clobbering her to the ground. Small spikes along the border of the net pierced the earth and held her flat to the grass.

The hellhound roared to a stop and, with an angry yowl, darted in another direction.

A second net caught Vander in the side and took him down as well. Gabby heard a shrill *ping* as spikes shot out of the net's border ring and bolted into the earth. She crouched, trying to pry up the spikes.

"Gabby!" Vander rolled beneath the strange net and aimed the silver bow straight at her. She screamed and ducked and a dart whirred past her. It struck an oncoming disciple in the shoulder.

As the disciple fell, Gabby saw Marco's wings above the courtyard. His bestial talons snatched a disciple by the collar of his monkish smock. Marco spun him through the air and sent him crashing through one of the latticed windows.

Gabby's father pulled her to her feet and started to drag her to Ingrid's netted figure. Luc had struggled over to her and was prying up one side of the silver net while roaring in pain. Whatever the net was made of, it wasn't gargoyle friendly. Ingrid crawled free and Luc collapsed. Brickton abruptly dug his heel in the ground and came to a halt, Gabby treading on his ankles.

Two red lantern eyes peered out from the dark of the arcades. Another hellhound.

This one hung back, however, watching the chaos unfurl in the courtyard.

"Stay away." Her father's order trembled on his lips.

The hellhound emerged slowly. Hesitantly. Not at all like the others.

"Lord Brickton, lower your sword," Vander commanded.

"I will not!" he shouted.

"Papa, stop!" Ingrid cried. "It's not a hellhound!"

It wasn't. Even Gabby could see that. This one was smaller than the others. It was furred, but it wasn't the same. It was wearing *clothes*.

"What in God's name is it, then?" their father spluttered, the point of the sword still aligned with the beast.

Gabby slapped his wrist and yanked the sword down hard. "It's your son. It's Grayson."

* * *

Grayson knew he should shift. His father stared at him, pure revulsion brimming in his eyes. This was his son. A monster. An
aberration, and he most certainly wanted to kill it.

Grayson couldn't shift, though, not with the remaining hell-
hound on a tear around the courtyard. He couldn't understand.
He'd had the hounds under his sway. He'd brought them to heel.
What had happened?

We serve Mistress first.

The answer trickled into his mind with crystalline lucidity
compared to the muffled, underwater voices of his sisters and
father. Their arguing burbled around him while the hound's
thoughts continued clearly.

You serve her now as well. Bring the one Mistress wants.

Ingrid. They'd come for Ingrid. And Grayson had led them
straight to her. The hounds had played him for a fool. They'd
never been under his control at all.

He caught sight of the beast across the courtyard. It clam-
bered onto the exterior limestone like a thorny vine, defying
gravity as it ran along the stone façade, perpendicular to the
ground. A disciple shot one of the Daicrypta's gleaming nets, but
the hound evaded it and the net shattered a window instead. The
hellhound streaked along the exterior stone, clawing over windows and shutters and balcony railings, red eyes focused on its
prey: Ingrid.

Silver flashes slashed the air over Grayson's shoulders, announcing Chelle's presence. One of her *hira-shuriken* gouged the
limestone, but the other sheared through the hound's flank. The
beast stumbled and Grayson charged toward his twin. Axia's pet
would not succeed—she would not have Ingrid's blood, and she
would *never* be his mistress.

Chelle hadn't hindered the beast. It arced off the wall,
scoring the frozen ground with its claws upon landing. Someone
was shouting, a new voice burbling up in a muffled pocket of

air. And then someone else dove into the path of the oncoming hound.

Nolan's father held no weapon, but he ran toward the demon with crazed determination. Grayson slid into position, blocking Ingrid, and watched in awe as Carrick Quinn ran full tilt into the hellhound's enormous maw.

The beast clamped its jaws around the man's torso and ripped him from the ground. Carrick's war cry went silent as the hellhound darted past Grayson and Ingrid and disappeared through the dark arcades.

CHAPTER THIRTY-ONE

Nolan's scream drowned out Gabby's. She watched his broadsword cleaving the air as he chased after the demon and his father. There was nothing to be done for him. Gabby knew it, and if she did, so did Nolan.

Pangs of shock and sadness drummed her in the stomach. She would have gone after Nolan had it not been for her brother, covered in swaths of greasy yellow fur and crouched on all fours in front of Ingrid.

"Stay away from her!" Lord Brickton screamed, jabbing Gabby's sword toward Grayson. Her brother yelped and growled as he avoided the point of the blade. Why didn't he shift back?

"Papa, stop!" Ingrid and Gabby shouted together, each of them pulling at their father's sleeves.

More screeching came from above, the shadow of wings and long, whiplike tails swerving through the air. Lennier and Yann had returned, and with Marco, Chelle, and Rory, they were driving the disciples back inside the mansion. Vander, however, was still stuck beneath one of their bizarre nets. Luc had freed Ingrid, but the silver must have been laced with mercurite—he could only crawl toward Grayson, who was still at the end of Lord Brickton's sword.

"You're a monster," Brickton moaned, the sword trembling in his grasp. "A murdering monster. This is how you killed her, then, you wicked beast. *This* is what you are."

Gabby stared, not understanding. Grayson hadn't killed anyone. He couldn't have.

Her father raised the sword. He was going to do it. He was going to kill his own son. Grayson hunched down and roared—and Gabby knew that her brother would not be the one to die.

Luc must have known it as well. He stopped crawling, and from where he lay, battered and broken, he lashed out his long, darted tail and clipped Brickton's ankles. Marco compounded the strike, slamming into her father's chest with the force of a bull. Her father went down and Gabby's sword pinwheeled through the air, landing yards away.

"Grayson, shift! Change back!" Gabby cried.

Lennier and Yann circled above like vultures. Grayson wasn't human to them just then. He was a demon. A threat.

Yann dove first.

Gabby heard the spring on Vander's crossbow release. A dart shot through the gaps in the netting and pierced one of Yann's razored wings. He spun wildly off course—and Lennier immediately plunged down, his great white wings tucked back, talons extended.

"Grayson!" Gabby screamed.

Her brother bounded away, but he still didn't shift. Maybe he couldn't, Gabby thought. She reached into her cloak and gripped the handle of a dagger. If she could pierce Lennier's wing, just wound him, as Vander had done to Yann, it would buy Grayson time to shift. Or escape. Gabby didn't care which, so long as her brother was still breathing.

She hurled the dagger as Lennier swooped low. The blade was in midflight when Léon's silken ropes lassoed Lennier's leg and pulled him back. The dagger sailed past Lennier, who took one swipe at the arachnae silk and sheared himself free.

A second dagger was in Gabby's hand and then whirling toward Lennier before she could take another breath. He unfurled his wings, exposing the steel cage of his chest, and the dagger plunged through the albino scales. Lennier dropped, heavy as a stone. His body plowed a deep rut into the earth, and then he lay still. Utterly still.

"Gabby—" Ingrid's hand landed on her shoulder and jerked her back. "What did you do?"

Gabby stopped breathing.

She reached inside her cloak and touched the one remaining dagger. The familiarity of it made her stomach clench. It was one of her own. She'd thrown two daggers. One blessed silver and one—

Oh God.

The mercurite-dipped blade. The one she'd pocketed, intending to use it on Dimitrie.

Yann touched down beside Lennier and crouched over the elder gargoyle's body. His lion's tail slashed back and forth, his white and gray speckled wings flat planes at his sides.

His tail stilled, and Gabby knew for certain which dagger had speared Lennier's chest.

Almost instantly Yann took flight in a reverse flip and came for her.

Rory slid underneath Yann, his daggers weaving through the air. His aim was true, and Yann veered off course long enough for Marco to leave Brickton and hook Gabby around the waist. He rocketed into the air, and as they spiraled up, Gabby craned her neck to look down. Lennier was no longer a gargoyle but a flaccid old man, his long white hair splayed on the ground—and her dagger was embedded in his heart.

Chelle approached Grayson, her arms open and hands facing out.

"It's me," she said, as if he couldn't already recognize her. Couldn't already smell her blood sluicing through her veins.

"Change back, Grayson." Her voice was muffled but firm. Calm. She wasn't afraid.

"Close your eyes," she suggested. His heart rampaged hard in his barrel of a chest. He had to calm down.

He closed his eyes to the sight of Rory prying the steel-like net off Vander; to Ingrid helping Luc to his feet, their gargoyle protector looking half dead; to the gargoyle lying motionless on the ground, now a mound of white hair and pale crepe-paper flesh. Gabby had only been trying to protect him. She never would have killed that gargoyle on purpose.

He had to change back. He had to explain.

His femurs cracked as they shrank. The hulking muscles along his neck and back compressed and his cartilage reshaped. The wicked February-night wind licked his human skin next.

When he opened his eyes, on all fours, the frosted grass dampening his trousers, Grayson felt another pair of eyes boring into the crown of his head.

Grayson got to his feet. A pair of hands shoved him hard in the chest and propelled him back to the ground.

"We trusted ye!" Rory towered over him. "Ye said the hellhounds were under yer command."

"They were." Grayson rebounded to his feet. "At least, I thought they were."

"*You* led them here?"

Nolan crossed through the dark arcades, the tip of his broad-sword slicing into the earth as he dragged it.

Grayson didn't know how to explain what had happened. "I'm sorry—"

"No, you're not. Not yet." Nolan flipped up his sword and drove it toward Grayson. Vander slammed his crossbow into Nolan's silver blade and brought it down.

"Not now," he said, raising his eyes to the Daicrypta windows. "We need to leave. Before they have another fit of bravery."

The skin under Nolan's eyes looked bruised as he stepped back and saw Lennier's lifeless body for the first time. He stilled. "What dagger is that?"

Rory bent to extract it, the blood black on the blade. "Mercurite."

Nolan forgot his fury with Grayson and turned it on Rory. "Do you have any idea what you've done?"

Rory calmly sheathed the bloodied dagger. "I know what I've done tonight, cousin, but I dinna think Gabby does. 'Twas her deed, no' mine."

The last ounce of Nolan's color drained. He took a panicked look around the courtyard and, when he didn't see Gabby anywhere, ran for the arcades once more. He passed Luc and Ingrid, who were already limping in retreat. Vander hurried to shore up Luc's other side.

Grayson felt someone approach from behind. He knew who it was. He'd always been able to feel his father's disappointed glare before meeting it head-on.

"What are you?" his father asked.

Grayson sucked in a breath and saw Ingrid stop up ahead, her eyes bouncing between him and their father. She'd begged to know what happened that night in London. Well, Grayson was done hiding.

"I'm exactly what you thought I was." He turned toward his

father. Brickton appeared unusually old and haggard. Undone. "Did you never wonder how I ripped out her throat?"

Beside him, Chelle let out a gasp. *Good,* he thought. Let her hear it, too. He'd been fooling himself, thinking he could hide from what he truly was. Best to tell them all and get it over and done with.

"*I* did," Grayson went on. "I wondered. I tried to imagine how human teeth could manage such carnage. Obviously, human teeth didn't."

He wanted to see shock spread across his father's face, but Brickton didn't acquiesce. Ever unflappable and hard, he only flared his nostrils.

"You are no longer my son."

A bitter laugh crawled up Grayson's throat and he bowed low. "With pleasure, my lord."

Grayson had spent his life feeling tethered to the man standing just feet away. As the invisible threads finally released him, the gulf of freedom was as invigorating as it was terrifying. It spread out before Grayson, open and empty and full of promise. Bad or good, Grayson didn't know, but it was promise just the same. He wasn't afraid to drift out into that open gulf. He backed toward the arcades.

"Grayson, stop. He doesn't mean it. He can't mean it."

Ingrid's voice was so small and uncertain. Grayson knew she didn't believe a word she was saying. He'd once known everything his twin felt. Everything she thought. She had been inside him, a second person. Lately, though, he'd lost her. As he walked away from her now, ignoring her pleas for him to stop, to come back, he realized it was better this way. Not for him, but for her. For them all. She didn't want him to be a monster, but he was. Chelle wanted to believe that he was more human than demon, but he wasn't. The sooner they realized these things, the sooner they could get on with their lives.

A hand rested gently on his shoulder. It was Léon, his expression drawn. Another murderer. The only person Grayson pitied more than he did himself.

"Come" was all Léon said.

And Grayson went.

CHAPTER THIRTY-TWO

Constantine's brougham rolled down the steep, winding streets of Montmartre, toward the frozen Seine. Vander was at the reins, his mount from earlier fettered to the back and trotting behind. Ingrid sat on the driver's bench with him, the winter wind rustling what remained of the brittle poplar leaves overhead. She didn't care about the cold. She would rather turn to a block of ice than ride in the back with her father. After what he'd said to Grayson, Ingrid didn't know if she would ever be able to forgive him.

Ingrid pressed a little closer to Vander's side and wondered when she would next see her twin. The way he'd left hadn't given her much hope that it would be anytime soon.

"At least Léon is with him," Vander said, as if reading her thoughts.

Ingrid was grateful for that. The Duster had killed his family, but he wasn't evil. He'd made a mistake. An awful mistake, just as Grayson had in London. Her brother was not a monster. He might think so, but she did not. Ingrid would let him be for now. Eventually, she would find him.

"I'll bring him home," she whispered.

Vander lifted the arm she was leaning against and looped her with it. She was full against him now, his fingers still tightly gripping the reins. She had no desire to pull away from the embrace. Vander felt solid and strong, and Ingrid breathed evenly, repelling the feelings of guilt before they came too close. She didn't think she was Luc's human again just yet, or that he could sense her. He was inside the carriage with her father, having shifted back to his human form as much as could be done.

The mercurite had hurt Luc more than Ingrid wanted to think about. He wasn't immortal or infallible, and she'd hated seeing him struggle. She also hated the image that pressed against her eyes whenever she closed them: Luc, standing over Dimitrie's body. The boy's head dangling from his talons.

A shudder worked down her arms. It had nothing to do with the cold. Ingrid tried to pull away, but Vander's arm kept her encircled.

"Vander, it isn't safe," she said.

"For whom?" He glanced down at her, lamplight reflecting off his spectacles. "I don't mind absorbing your dust, Ingrid. I'm not afraid of it. In fact . . ." He shrugged, one corner of his mouth kicking up. "I like being able to feel you this way. No one else can. Just me."

Something intimate passed between them. It felt like a kiss without their lips actually meeting. The soft, pale flesh along the underside of her forearm prickled, invisible needles poking lightly at her fingertips.

It scared her how much she wanted to stay there against him, letting him soak up her dust. How long would it take for him to absorb it all? The idea of being normal, of giving it all away to him, even for just a little while, both tempted and frightened her.

Ingrid pulled away again, and this time he let her sit up.

Disappointment pulled his lips back into a straight line. He focused on the road ahead.

"You owe him nothing," Vander said softly, his jaw tight. He knew to whom her thoughts had traveled. With a wrench of guilt, she wondered if she'd always been so very transparent. "If he's made you any promises, Ingrid, I can assure you they're lies."

Ingrid closed her eyes. She couldn't talk to Vander about Luc right now. She'd just watched her brother walk away from her, and she knew it was selfish, but she wasn't ready to watch as Vander did the same thing.

"No, Vander. It's just . . ." She shook her head. "I don't know if I can go to Hôtel Bastian anymore. What Nolan's father told me, about the Directorate voting to have me killed . . ." Ingrid closed her eyes at the unexpected tug at the bottom of her throat. The sting of tears.

"If the Alliance is my enemy—"

"I am not your enemy, Ingrid." Vander's voice cracked like a pistol shot. "I don't understand why the Directorate would do something like this—if they even did vote to release that mimic on you. Carrick Quinn was half mad with mercurite poisoning, remember. He might have been acting on his own."

He hadn't been. Ingrid knew it, and somewhere underneath his denial, so did Vander. "They are going to discover I'm still alive."

"I'll take down the entire Directorate before I let them hurt you." He slapped the reins and the horses trotted faster. "You are safe with me, Ingrid. I promise you that."

She knew she was. It was the rest of the Alliance that worried her.

He held both reins with one hand and laced his fingers through hers. He lifted her hand to his mouth. He didn't kiss it, but breathed out hot air to warm her. Her lips parted as the warmth reached inside, curled around her stomach, and gave a slow, seductive tug.

Ingrid dragged in a ragged breath and unlaced her fingers from his. She couldn't do this. Not after what had happened between her and Luc at gargoyle common grounds. The way they had kissed and touched, their limbs twined together on the bed in that guest room, had left no room for anyone to edge between them. Neither of them had spoken the actual words, but she and Luc had made a promise to one another.

Ingrid looked away from Vander. "I think I know how to use the electricity now. I need to practice." It was a flimsy excuse. Vander's touch stirred her, but was it *him*? Or was it him disturbing her dust? She didn't know. God, what was she going to do?

Vander, gracious as ever, simply nodded. "That's good. I knew you would. You were amazing back there, you know. The way you took down that hellhound." He let out a laugh as the horses trotted toward the Île de la Cité. The round towers of the old prison were black against the mottled blue of the oncoming dawn.

"Why are you laughing?" she asked.

"It's just I wonder what the Earl of Brickton thought when he saw lightning streak from his daughter's fingertips."

Oh, she was certain she would hear exactly what her father thought of this entire night all too soon. Though, pleasantly enough, she found she didn't dread it. What her father thought didn't matter much just then.

"He'll never let me return to London now," she said, a smile playing upon her lips.

Vander's amusement faded. The carriage took the first small jump onto the cobbled bridge leading onto the city island. He glanced down at her. "Do you want to go home?"

Ingrid squared her shoulders, her velvet cloak suddenly heavier than usual. "I'd rather face off with a dozen more hellhounds or crypsis serpents than return to London." She sighed. "And it's not my home. Not any longer."

Paris was. The abbey and rectory. Hôtel Bastian. Clos du Vie. In Luc's arms, or folded within his great, protective wings. And though it left her feeling conflicted, she knew home was here, beside Vander.

He let his rigid posture go and allowed his leg to relax against hers. He said nothing but urged the horses onward, across the bridge connecting to the Left Bank. The abbey wasn't far. She could see the belfry towers rising above the trees. This was her home, but it wasn't perfect. It was both beautiful and savage, a safe haven with evil knocking at the door.

The problem, Ingrid was coming to realize, was that there were no hard and fast rules when it came to evil. It could change shape. Be one thing one moment and something else the next. It could be demon. Gargoyle. Human. Angel.

Ingrid wondered what evil would look like the next time it came knocking.

CHAPTER THIRTY-THREE

Marco broke the lock on the rear kitchen door with one twist. He pushed the door open and stood aside, his mouth a taut line. He hadn't spoken to Gabby yet. In Luc's carriage-house loft, Gabby had sunk to the cold wooden planks and waited, eyes squeezed shut, while Marco returned to his human form and dressed.

His usual smooth sarcasm, his coy, dangerously playful air, had not returned along with his human skin. She'd seen this man in his birthday suit, she realized, and it had left *her* feeling exposed. Now, as he glared at her, waiting for her to enter the kitchen, she felt not only exposed but afraid.

Marco was her gargoyle. He couldn't harm her. But that certainly didn't stop him from looking like he wanted to.

Gabby stumbled inside, her legs still wobbly from the fast flight high over Paris. Her dress was damp and cold, torn in spots from the fighting at the Daicrypta estate. A low fire was going to cinders in the hearth, and Gabby walked toward it, craving warmth.

Marco slammed the door behind them.

"You'll wake the servants," Gabby said, staring at the glowing embers under the grate.

"I scent your mother, her lady's maid, and your father's valet," Marco replied, coming closer to her than she liked. "The rest have quit the house."

Her father's disappearance must have been the final straw. Gabby held her hands out to the pathetic fire.

"Good for them," she said. If she could flee this madness . . . No. That was a lie. She wouldn't flee. She wouldn't leave Nolan or the Alliance. Her hair hung limply around her face, ripped out from the pins, her hat lost long ago. She lifted her hand to push the strands back. The pads of her fingers brushed the bumpy scars along her cheek.

She'd forgotten all about them.

"I killed him," she said, suddenly not caring at all about her blasted face. She'd killed someone. Her breath came faster. "The dagger, it was the one I took from the draining room floor. The mercurite one. I didn't know. I just . . . I just grabbed it and threw and I didn't mean to." She swung around and there Marco was, less than an arm's length from her. His amber eyes were sooty in the low hearth light.

"You pierced his heart," Marco said, unblinking. "We are not immortal, Lady Gabriella. Whether the dagger had been of silver or mercurite doesn't matter. A knife in the heart means death to human and gargoyle alike."

"But I didn't aim. I just threw. I swear it, I didn't want to kill him!"

"Then you should not have been so careless." Marco spun away from her and stalked to the long farm table in the center of the kitchen. He braced himself against it.

Gabby grasped for something to say. Her throat hurt too much. If she tried to speak, she knew she would only let out a sob. Marco was right. He was so right that it ached. She'd panicked. Forgotten everything Chelle had taught her. And now Lennier was dead.

"Forget your conscience for a moment," Marco said, and she remembered he could pry his way into her feelings the same way Luc could. "As we speak, every single Dispossessed in Paris is learning that their elder is dead. That he's been killed by an Alliance fighter."

"I'm not Alliance—"

"Do you think any of them will care?" Marco pushed off the table, sending it screeching across the tiles. "Yann isn't the only gargoyle who will be out for your head. Hell, if I weren't your guardian, I'd be one of them."

Marco let out a sigh and his grimace softened. He'd likely felt Gabby's flash of alarm.

"It isn't safe for you here," he said, gentler than before. "There is a gargoyle named Vincent who will want to take on the title of elder now that Lennier is gone. He is no friend to the human race, and it would be ignorant to think he wouldn't try to make an example of you to prove his power."

Marco's wolfish sneer appeared even more dangerous in the shadowy kitchen.

"Lennier was the first gargoyle to ever speak with the Alliance. The one who brought peace between us. For hundreds of years he worked to keep that peace. But a new elder means new rules."

Gabby needed to sit. The chairs at the table were too far away, so she simply lowered herself to the warmed slate around the hearth. Nolan had told her about the gargoyle who had ended the wars between the Alliance and Dispossessed. It had been *Lennier.*

The kitchen door flew open and cracked against the plaster wall. Gabby leaped to her feet as Nolan crossed the threshold, his broadsword thrust in Marco's direction.

"Get away from her," he snarled.

Marco groaned. "Human, relax. My tie to her is stronger than my loyalty to Lennier."

Nolan lowered the broadsword, if only a few inches. "Will they come here?"

Gabby realized that Nolan had already pieced together what Marco had just explained. The Dispossessed were now her enemy.

"Why shouldn't they? Sacred ground keeps demons at bay, not gargoyles," Marco answered. "Luc and I can only protect her so much. She needs to leave Paris."

A chill darted up Gabby's spine. "I will not."

Leave Paris and go where? Running from the mess she'd made wasn't an option. It would be cowardly.

Marco twisted toward the swinging doors that led into the dining room. "Lady Brickton is coming. I'll attempt to detain her with the riveting details of our evening's events." He started for the doors. "I think we rather got along when we met this afternoon, don't you?"

Marco didn't require an answer. He knew perfectly well that Gabby's mother had detested him. Of course, she'd hired him on the spot when it had been made clear to her that he was going to be as much a fixture to the abbey as one of the actual gargoyles set along the roof.

Nolan sheathed his sword once Marco had left, his hand clasped around the hilt. Gabby crossed the kitchen toward him. She wanted to pry his fingers from the sword and lace them with her own. Kiss each clenched knuckle until he let go of the tension that gripped him.

"I'm so sorry," she whispered, reaching for his hand.

Nolan stepped aside. "I know you didn't mean to kill Lennier."

He didn't look at her and Gabby pulled her hand back. "No, I mean about your father."

Anguish cut across Nolan's face. He didn't respond, but the muscles along his jaw worked with tension. She thought he might say something about his father. A few of the insubstantial words one was supposed to say in situations like these. Not as if witnessing a father getting killed by a hellhound was a situation one often found oneself in. Still. Nolan only took a deep breath and continued to avoid her eyes.

"Marco is right. You need to leave Paris. And if Grayson knows what's good for him, he'll do the same."

Gabby frowned. "What do you mean? Why would Grayson need to leave Paris?"

When Marco had taken her from the closed-in Daicrypta courtyard, her brother had been in hellhound form. Had she missed something?

Nolan held his spine straight as a rod. "He led those hellhounds to the courtyard, Gabby. He was in league with them."

A snort of laughter escaped before she could tamp it down. Nolan seared her with an icy glare.

"That's absurd," she said. "My brother planted himself in front of Ingrid. He was going to fight that hellhound. He *would* have if—" She stopped. If Carrick hadn't thrown himself in the beast's path.

"Rory said your brother had them under his command. Grayson admitted that it was true."

Gabby refused to believe it. She shook her head, something hot boiling up inside of her. The innate desire to defend her brother. "There must be a piece missing, then. Something we don't know. Grayson wouldn't have put any of us in danger, not on purpose."

Nolan balled his hands into fists. "My father is dead. The hellhound your brother was controlling *ate* him. He will answer to the Directorate in Rome for what he's done."

Gabby bit her lower lip to keep herself quiet. She wanted to argue. Insist that her brother was innocent. But then, her father had just accused Grayson of killing someone as well. He'd called him a murdering monster, a wicked beast. Gabby shut her eyes as if she could block out the memory. It couldn't be true. Nolan and her father were wrong. Her father had always disapproved of Grayson, and Nolan . . . well, he didn't know Grayson the way she and Ingrid did. Besides, he had just seen his father die.

Maybe all he needed was a little time. Space to calm down and see things clearly.

"Isn't there someplace safe in Paris where no avenging gargoyles can find me?" she asked, the forced change of topic rough. It took Nolan a moment to adjust, but if anything, he only appeared more irritated.

"I doubt Lady Brickton will be open to your moving in with me at Hôtel Bastian," he said. Normally he would have delivered a suggestion like that with an arched brow and a sly grin. It would have kindled a blaze inside Gabby. But Nolan's words were flat, his expression emotionless. "And then you wouldn't have any gargoyles bound to you," he went on, all cold logic.

Nolan's glossy black curls swept over his forehead, falling over one eye. He pushed them back and looked at her. She had never seen him so sad before. Gabby wanted to go to him. Slip her arms around his waist, hold him close.

"There is no safe place in Paris. You need to go."

She stared at him, willing him to take it back. Or, barring that, at least look regretful. *I don't want you to leave, lass, but I can't have you in danger here.* Or *I don't know what I'd do if you got hurt again, Gabby.* She could imagine him saying such things.

He licked his lips and shifted his attention to the stacks of bowls and folded napkins on the table.

"I don't have anywhere to go," she said, and then something awful came to mind. "Unless I go back to London."

Her father would likely instruct his valet to begin packing as soon as he returned to the rectory. Whether he'd order them all to leave with him, Gabby wasn't certain. He'd seemed rather frightened of his own children earlier.

"I'll send someone with you for protection," Nolan said. Gabby could only stare at him. How easily he'd accepted the idea of London.

"Can't it be you?" she asked, grasping for a connection to him. He met her eyes, but only for as long as it took for her to see the rejection he was about to deliver. He'd broken her heart before he could even part his lips.

"I need to stay in Paris and deal with what happens here." *Because of you and what you've done.*

"And what about the Directorate? Your father told you not to trust them," Gabby said, desperate to think of a way to convince him to let her stay. To hear him say he *wanted* her to stay.

"I'll speak to Ingrid and Marco and find out what he told them." He still wouldn't look at her.

"I don't want to leave you." Gabby cringed at how needy she sounded. She couldn't feel sorry for it, though, because it was at least honest. Nolan had kissed her earlier. He'd told her that he loved her.

He struggled for a response now. Nolan, who always knew what to say.

He chose action instead of words, breaching the arm's length he'd kept between them. He cupped the nape of Gabby's neck and pressed his lips firmly against her forehead. He pinned her there, his fingers pressing on the back of her neck until she felt a tremor passing through them. Then he let her go and walked away, toward the door he'd burst through a few minutes before.

"Nolan—"

"I'll come for you when I can." And then he was gone, the door clicking softly behind him.

*　*　*

Luc took the last step up into the loft, ready to collapse and lay still for a thousand years. His unmade cot looked more welcoming than a bare, crepe-thin pallet had a right to. Still, he would have fallen into it had it not been for Marco. The Wolf was leaning against the loft door, which was rolled open to the sky purpling toward dawn.

"You weren't exaggerating about those humans of yours," Marco said.

Luc shifted his gaze from the cot, determined not to show how badly the mercurite had affected him. He'd never been subjected to so much of it before. He limped lightly toward the open loft door as if every step weren't killing him.

"Of *ours,* you mean," Luc replied.

"Oh, so now you're willing to share them with me?"

Luc ignored him and watched the rectory. He felt Lord Brickton's presence. Gabriella and Lady Brickton. One of the maids. Brickton's valet.

Luc waited.

A light went on in her room. The sweet scent of spring replaced the dead bite of winter in his nose. He breathed her in and forgot the mercurite tainting his muscles and bones. Ingrid appeared in the window. She drew aside one panel of sheer gauze, and Luc felt her eyes searching the carriage house. Looking for him.

"If you continue to be so obvious, brother, you will surely die."

Ingrid let the panel fall back into place. Luc watched her figure turn and disappear. He didn't care. Let them rip him apart. Let them send him to hell or wherever dead gargoyles went.

Ingrid was alive. He'd killed another gargoyle, but he'd done what he'd needed to do to protect her. No gargoyle would mourn a shadow like Dimitrie or care to punish Luc for destroying him.

Not when there was Lennier's death to avenge. A new elder to be determined.

"Why don't you do it yourself, then?" Luc asked. Marco could. He was bigger. Older.

Marco moved away from the open door. "Kill the only gargoyle I can trust to protect one of my humans with or without being compelled to do so?"

There was more to it than that. There had to be. Marco had destroyed René with relish. Luc still remembered the gleam of disgust in Marco's eyes, the curl of his lip, when he'd discovered that René had consorted with a human girl. The difference, Luc figured, was that Marco had not known René's girl. He knew Ingrid. Though Marco would never admit it, she intrigued him. If he destroyed Luc, he would only alienate her.

"Lady Gabriella is leaving, and I assume it will be with their dear father," Marco said. "Her brother is no longer our concern."

Luc felt the loss of Grayson as well, along with the pervasive sadness lingering in Ingrid's chest because of it. There would be no feelings of regret when Brickton left, he was sure. That would leave Lady Brickton, Ingrid, and a single lady's maid.

"Three humans. Two gargoyles. I like the new ratio, don't you, brother?"

White light poured through the loft. It curled over Luc and threw him face-first onto the floor.

Luc had known it would come, but he still swore under his breath as his knees and forehead bashed into the wooden planks. Irindi's burning presence sent Marco sprawling as well.

"This happens to you a lot, doesn't it?" he muttered.

"Silence," Irindi intoned.

They obeyed. Outside, the wind kicked up. It battered the old roof slates and thrashed the bare-limbed trees.

Luc tried to think whether any of their humans had been injured. The severed finger had not been Lord Brickton's, and he had rubbed his own skin raw on those ropes. Ingrid had been bitten by a crypsis, but at that time she'd belonged to Dimitrie, not Luc or Marco. Gabby, by some miracle, hadn't received so much as a scratch.

The angel of heavenly law wasn't here to punish them with angel's burns.

Then again, her presence never boded well.

"Luc Rousseau, you have erred."

Of course he had.

"You have not heeded my warning regarding the child christened Ingrid Charlemagne Waverly."

It always came back to her.

"Your affinity for her will no longer be tolerated."

Lennier's guest bedroom flashed into his mind with sharp focus. With everything that had happened since then, Luc had forgotten. Ingrid's lips. His hands exploring her body. The two of them sinking onto the mattress. The way he'd fought the shift.

"You will be removed from l'Abbaye Saint-Dismas."

Irindi's hollow voice stabbed him like a mercurite-dipped blade. No. *No.*

"Irindi—"

"Your new territory awaits approval. That is all."

Irindi's departure was usually a relief. This time, however, Luc wanted to gather her light back. Keep her here and convince her she was wrong.

He and Marco breathed heavily as they straightened, their breath rolling out as fog in the cold loft.

This couldn't be the end of everything.

The abbey was his. The rectory and carriage house, the cemetery and grounds. It all belonged to him. *Ingrid* belonged to him, and she wanted it that way. *I want to be yours again,* she'd said.

He'd done this to himself. He'd known the Order wouldn't forgive him a second time, and yet he'd still kissed Ingrid. He had still desired her in a way no Dispossessed should ever desire a human.

"You have too much human left inside you," Marco said, his tone curiously soft.

Luc growled. He was *not* human. No part of him was. What human had talons sharp enough to peel through the skin of a boy's neck? What human was strong enough to shear through tendons and cartilage, vertebrae and a spinal cord, all to rip off a head? What human would be able to stomach such an act?

"I'm no human," Luc said.

If Marco disagreed, he kept it to himself as he crossed to the loft stairs. This place would be his now. Luc didn't know when he'd be severed from the abbey or the humans living on its sacred ground. He didn't know where he'd be sent, or even whether his new territory would be within Paris. But it would happen. He'd have new humans, and their scents, their emotions, would settle right into the knowing place inside him where he'd kept Ingrid and her family.

"I will protect them all, brother," Marco said before descending the loft stairs.

The promise did little to comfort Luc. Ingrid would be lost to him. His home, taken away. And he had no one to blame but himself.

CHAPTER THIRTY-FOUR

Ingrid knew she would find him in the belfry.

It wasn't instinct that brought her into the abbey just before dawn. It wasn't the same sort of knowing that Luc had with his humans that led her up the narrow, winding steps to the bell tower, bathed in watery blue light. She wished to feel Luc the way he no doubt felt her again now that she was back in her room at the rectory. She longed to have that knowledge, to be able to experience everything he did and felt. But no. It was logic, pure and simple, that told her where Luc would be.

Vander had delivered her and her father to the rectory less than an hour earlier. After he had helped her to the ground and opened the carriage door, he'd found Brickton alone. Luc had already fled. Ingrid figured he would want to be alone, in a place where he could avoid Marco and any human who might try to find him.

Her father was not one of those humans.

He had already commenced packing his belongings. His harried instructions to his valet could be heard throughout the rectory, along with his declarations that he would never be returning to Paris, that the gallery was officially finished, and that he no longer had an heir. Ingrid had soothed Mama's panic by explaining that Grayson was in fact alive, just out on his own for now. And when Lady Brickton had outright refused to leave Paris until her son came home, her husband hadn't objected. He didn't care. So long as he was gone on the morning train.

Gabby had also started packing, but in a much more somber and quiet manner. After Lennier's death, Ingrid thought Nolan's and Marco's advice wise. The gargoyle named Vincent had mentioned that there were Dispossessed out there who practically salivated for reasons to attack humans. Ingrid knew her sister loathed the idea of going home, especially now that there would be whispers about her scars. If London could keep her safe, though, it would be worth the humiliation.

Ingrid spotted Luc behind the massive bronze bell. He crouched against the belfry wall, his elbows hooked around his knees. She couldn't see his face yet, but he was definitely in human form. Her pulse raced faster when he was like this. When he was in his scaled, true form, he couldn't speak. She didn't long to touch him. His gargoyle form erected a kind of safe, impenetrable wall between them.

"I spent the last thirty years here," Luc said before Ingrid could come around the curve of the bell and meet his eyes.

She walked beside the railed parapet. The parched wooden boards complained under her weight, reminding her that the bell hung suspended over the tower shaft. It would be a long fall.

"You're safe," he added.

She smiled. "I suppose I trust you."

As Ingrid came around the bell, he leaned his head back against the rough stone and watched her.

"Someone once told me that gargoyles turn to stone when they hibernate." Ingrid didn't want to mention Vander by name.

Luc tucked in his chin. He wore old work clothes instead of formal livery: canvas trousers and a loose white linen shirt rolled to the elbow, never mind the zero-degree-Celsius weather.

"We don't feel it," he said. "When we sleep we don't feel anything. Not until a human comes around, at least."

Ingrid inched closer to him. Her feet crunched over loose rock. When she looked down, she saw broken pieces of stone littering the wooden boards. She crouched and picked up one shaped like a crescent. The inside curve was smooth, the exterior rough and weather-worn. Luc had slept here for thirty years. When Grayson had moved into the abbey a handful of months ago, his stone casing must have shattered.

"Yours?" she asked, holding it out to him.

Luc saw what she cupped in her palm. "It's not really stone. More like a crust our scales build up over time."

He let out a sigh and pushed himself to his feet, wincing when his legs straightened. Ingrid followed, her hand closing around the small piece of him.

"Are your wings going to heal?" she asked. She couldn't stop thinking about the gaping hole in each one.

She also couldn't stop thinking about Dimitrie's head hanging from Luc's talons.

"In a few days," he answered. He faced the Seine and the flying buttresses of Notre Dame. Morning light was always so perfect and clear. Ingrid liked its honesty. After being swamped in darkness for so long, the first hour of sun as it crept over the city revealed the truth like no other time.

She wanted to be as honest as the morning sun.

"In the Daicrypta courtyard, when I told you I wanted to be yours again, I meant it. Not just as your human charge, but as *yours*."

If he had been in obsidian scales right now, this would have been easier. Instead, she had to watch his human face remain impassive, his cut-jade eyes fixed on the frozen Seine. She had to wait for him to speak.

He didn't.

"I know you've said it's impossible. I must sound like I've gone mad." She let out a laugh. "Perhaps I have, but, Luc, I—" She stopped before the words could tumble out. She hadn't even known they were there, waiting on the tip of her tongue. *I love you.*

"I'm being sent away," he whispered. Luc kept his gaze trained on the waking skyline. "Irindi is giving me a new territory."

Ingrid rocked back onto her heels and gripped the open window ledge. She mirrored Luc and turned to stare out at the city. She didn't see it, though. Rising panic blinded her.

"But *this* is your territory," she said.

"Until I'm assigned a new one. The Order can do as they please."

Ingrid closed her eyes, and strangely enough, she could see again. Luc, in Lennier's guest room. Luc, crawling over the bed, toward her. He'd told her the angels would know, that they wouldn't forgive him.

"Because you kissed me," she said. "Because of what we did."

"No. It's my *affinity* for you. At least, that's how Irindi referred to it."

"They're doing this because you care for me?" Why wouldn't caring be considered a good thing? What sort of angels were these?

Luc finally let go of his roof gazing and met her incredulous stare.

"Your offer to be mine?" he said with a gentle arch of one brow. "You're right. It is impossible. It is completely insane. You're a human, Ingrid. I'm not—not anymore—and we could never be . . . *human* . . . together." The way he said *human* stirred her. She knew what he meant, even though the word itself sounded utterly innocent.

"The Order knows everything," he went on. "I can keep secrets from the Dispossessed, but not from the angels. They know that I want to tell you yes, that I want to make you mine. They know . . . they know I've fallen in love with you."

Ingrid lost whatever she'd been planning to say next. She'd had words lined up, ready to go, but they'd all scattered now.

"But . . . but you . . . ," she stammered. "You said you couldn't love. You said you lost the ability when you became Dispossessed."

"I lied." Luc moved back from the ledge. "Did you really believe lust was all I felt for you?"

She had. At first. But she remembered how hard she'd worked to convince herself of it. How exhausting it had been. Ingrid shook her head.

"I'm sorry if I hurt you," he said before striding away to the corner of the belfry. "I wanted to tell you the truth before I left."

Luc braced his foot against the solid bronze bell and kicked. The bell swung, crying out its disturbance with deafening gongs. Pigeons roosting along the roof took flight, swirling away in a panic of gray and white wings.

Ingrid had to wait for the bell to slow its dance back and forth to cross to the corner. She came up behind Luc.

"There has to be something I can do."

"You can promise me that you'll make existence for Marco extremely boring," Luc replied quickly. Marco had already saved her life—like Luc, once or twice when he hadn't been required to. She knew Marco was capable. She could trust him. But she didn't want him.

"I'll come with you."

Every muscle in Luc's back, and throughout his neck and

arms, went rigid. He gave the slightest turn of his head to show he'd heard her.

Ingrid couldn't believe she'd actually said it. She wouldn't take it back, though. She wanted him to say yes too desperately.

"I don't know where I'm being sent yet," he said, voice low and husky. "I'll have new human charges. I'll be bound to them first, not you."

"But if I stay with you, I'll always be your human charge."

Luc looked at her fully now, and not with his earlier earnestness. She heard her proposal for what it was: a request to live with him.

"I can exist in the top of a tower like this." He gestured around them. "I can live in a sewer line beneath my territory, or in an attic, or in a dovecote. I can pose as a servant, like I have here, or hide within the walls of a home. I don't have to eat or drink or sleep or keep warm. You can't do those things, Ingrid. You can't stay with me."

Of course she couldn't. Heat rushed to her cheeks when she thought of how naïve she must seem to him.

She stared at the tips of her boots peeking out below the hem of her skirt. "I know. I'm sorry, I just . . . This is all my doing."

She looked up and noticed that the light had changed. It was already becoming less crisp as the sun shimmered over the horizon.

When she met his eyes again, they had softened. The corner of his mouth pulled into a mischievous grin. "If memory serves, I kissed you first."

He had. Twice. And now Irindi was going to take him away. What if Ingrid never saw him again?

Luc turned and walked toward the belfry stairs.

"You're not leaving yet, are you?" she asked.

Luc paused at the top step. The bell hung between them. It still swayed, though the hammer inside no longer chimed. He shook his head and attempted a smile, but it fell quickly.

He let his eyes rove over her, interrupted every few seconds by the lip of the bell. When Luc continued down the steps and out of sight, Ingrid remained where she was. She didn't know if she could move, not yet. Her legs might not support her. Because she had the awful feeling that Luc had been lying to spare her a good-bye.

Acknowledgments

Before I started to write this book, my husband worked for months to transform a run-down cabin on our property into an official writing haven. Thank you for giving me my own space, Chad, and for understanding how much I needed it. It's the fourth-best gift you've given me. The first three? Our beautiful daughters, Alexandra, Joslin, and Willa (who actually ask permission before entering the writing cabin!).

As always, I have an endless amount of gratitude for my fabulous agent, Ted Malawer, and my insightful and supportive editor, Krista Marino, along with Beverly Horowitz, Barbara Marcus, Jodie Hockensmith, Johanna Kirby, and the entire team at Random House Children's Books. Thank you for the love and dedication you've all shown this series.

I'm also blessed with the best critique partners and friends: Maurissa Guibord, Dawn Metcalf, and Cindy Thomas. I'll let you rip my manuscript to shreds any day, ladies!

A special thank-you to the HB&K Society—Amalie Howard, Cindy Thomas, Danielle Ellison, Kristi Cook, Arianne Mandell, and Kate Kaynak—for welcoming me into their annual retreat and for an incredible amount of friendship and support.

I wrote most of *The Lovely and the Lost* during summer vacation, so a big thank-you to my mother-in-law, Charley, and our wonderful babysitter, Anna, for entertaining the girls while I sequestered myself in the cabin.

Though this book is dedicated to my parents, Michael and Nancy Robie, they deserve one more thank-you here. They deserve much more than that, actually, but if all I have are words, the best ones would be "I love you."

WILL THE WAVERLYS SURVIVE?
Find out in the final book in the
DISPOSSESSED trilogy,

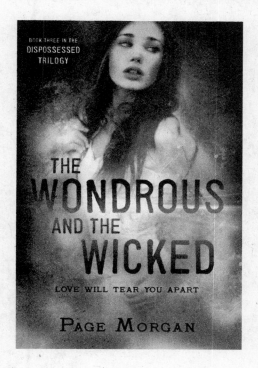

Excerpt copyright © 2015 by Page Morgan. Published by Delacorte Press,
an imprint of Random House Children's Books, a division of
Random House LLC, a Penguin Random House Company, New York.

CHAPTER ONE

PARIS

LATE MARCH 1900

Ingrid should have brought a sword.

She crouched in a most unladylike manner on the narrow quay beneath the Pont de l'Alma, considering ways to pry a manhole cover free. The tarnished brass disk had to weigh at least five stone. She needed to lever the blasted thing up if she wished to descend into the sewers before daylight broke over the city.

Entering miles of dank, serpentine sewage tunnels alone was a risk at any time of the day, but Ingrid needed to slink her way in, and she preferred to do so without being seen. She had to find her brother. Grayson had been gone for nearly a month, and she'd started to have that old bubbling awareness again. The caged restlessness that always beset her when she simply *knew* her twin was in trouble.

The sewers were as good a hiding place as any, and Grayson had most definitely been hiding. For a month he'd been on his own in Paris, avoiding Ingrid and their mother. Had Gabby still been in the city, instead of in London, Ingrid was certain he would have steered clear of their younger sister as well. Anything to avoid facing the reality of their grim situation: that he and Ingrid were Dusters—humans who had been given demon blood at birth. A rogue guardian angel had gifted them this blood, and with it, inhuman abilities. Ingrid could create electricity at her fingertips. As for Grayson . . . his ability was a bit more complicated, and much more dangerous.

Well, she was finished waiting for him to come home. She needed her brother—even if he *was* a hellhound some of the time. Ingrid would find him and drag him back to the abbey by the ear if she had to.

She untied the silk drawstring pouch cinched around her wrist and withdrew the petite hand dagger she kept for emergency use. When Vander Burke had given her the four-inch blade of blessed silver with its polished ebony handle a few weeks prior, he'd intended for her to use the weapon to fend off hungry Underneath demons trespassing in the human realm. Ingrid, however, was perfectly content using it to try to lift this sewer manhole cover.

She scraped the point of the blade along the rim of the cover, searching for a gap. It was nearly impossible to see in the predawn darkness. The point slipped into a crevice and Ingrid pushed against the weight of the brass disk with all her strength.

"You are not going down there."

She paused at the low, surly voice. She'd wondered if Marco might follow her. Butlers didn't usually keep such close tabs on the members of the family they worked for, but Marco was more than just the butler at l'Abbaye Saint-Dismas. And Ingrid was more to him than just his employer's daughter.

The dagger had barely raised the cover an inch, but she continued to hold it propped open.

"Not by myself," she replied, glancing quickly over her shoulder to where he stood. "My gargoyle wouldn't be so negligent as to allow that."

Marco came around to stand before her. The dark gray merino of his butler's livery was a few shades darker than anything else around them. Sunrise was closer than she had thought.

"If you'd help me with this, please?" she asked, pushing on the handle again. With his strength, Marco could easily rip the cover up and toss it aside.

Instead, he set his foot on the cover, forcing it to slam shut and her dagger tip to pop free.

"And as your gargoyle, I am forced, once again, to keep you from getting yourself killed." He crouched down until his eyes met hers.

Marco's dark features were even darker than usual in the coming blue of dawn. Ingrid had once feared the scowling face before her. Even more, she'd feared him when he would take on his true form—a thick, cinnamon-red jacket of reptilian scales, featherless sienna wings, and long, wickedly sharp talons. At one point, not very long ago, Marco had considered killing her. That was before he'd been assigned to the abbey and become her gargoyle protector. Before everything that he was forbade him to harm her.

"I'm not afraid of what I might find in the sewers," Ingrid said, though the tunnels were rife with demons. Her last visit beneath the city had been with two demon hunters, Vander Burke and Nolan Quinn, and she hadn't known the first thing about protecting herself.

Things were different now. Ingrid knew how to use her demon half, powered by the blood of a lectrux demon. She knew how to summon electricity and store it in her fingertips, and more importantly, how to release a current of lightning without completely draining her reserves. If she came across a demon threat in the sewers, she was certain she could subdue it.

Marco leaned forward. "Then why, Lady Ingrid, could I taste your fear in the back of my throat?"

She clenched her teeth and beat back a wave of nausea. Marco himself didn't make her uneasy. It was his vivid connection to her that did. He could sense her so intimately that if he held still and drew up her scent, catalogued within his memory, he could feel the beat of her heart echoing his own. He could feel her every breath, the shift in her pulse, even her emotions. He could find her and be at her side within moments.

These things were all meant to help him keep his human charge from harm. Still, Ingrid didn't want him to have such access. She didn't want him to be her gargoyle.

She wanted Luc.

Ingrid turned her head toward the Seine to avoid Marco's stare.

"I'm worried for Grayson, you know that," she said. "I have to find him."

"Human, your impatience is infuriating," he growled, standing tall. "The only thing you're going to find down there is a quick fissure straight to Axia's hive."

Ingrid let out a sigh and stood up. The crown of her head reached just below the starched points of his white collar. Marco wasn't entirely wrong. She was certain there were plenty of fissures in the sewers that led to the Underneath. She was also certain that Axia, the fallen angel who had created all of the Dusters, had not forgotten about Ingrid and the angel blood still circulating through her veins. Axia wanted that blood back. It was hers, after all.

Axia had also given Ingrid and Grayson her angel blood at birth, unlike her other seedlings, thinking to safeguard it from the toxic Underneath should the Angelic Order ever banish her to that realm. After sixteen years, the angel blood had finally grown strong enough within the twins' bodies for Axia to reclaim. With it, she could return to the human realm for something she called the Harvest. What that was, exactly, was still a mystery to Ingrid. It wouldn't be good, that much she suspected.

Axia had already reclaimed Grayson's angel blood. If she reclaimed Ingrid's portion, she would be able to begin her Harvest.

"I'm not going to hide on sacred ground forever," she said to Marco as she slipped her dagger back into her purse.

"And your brother isn't going to come back to you until he is ready."

Ingrid cinched her purse and curled her hands into fists at her sides. "He's in trouble."

Her brother's hellhound blood had made him do horrible things. He'd killed a girl in London. Ingrid couldn't imagine the guilt Grayson had to be suffering. What if he couldn't live with it? What if he decided *not* to live with it?

"Think me cold and callous if you choose, but *you* are my human charge. *He* hasn't been since he quit the rectory and started residing elsewhere," Marco said. "I warn you: if you attempt to climb down that sewer hole again, I will strip off my clothes, coalesce, and fly you back to the abbey kicking and screaming. Trust me—you don't want that." His deadly serious gaze softened as he flashed his teeth. "Or perhaps you do. I am rather stunning when unclothed."

Even poor light couldn't hide her blush from his night vision. Marco picked up on the pinches of color and laughed.

"My mother should toss you out on your ear," Ingrid said. "You are by far the worst butler I have ever met."

Marco gestured toward the wide stone steps that led to the street. She groaned and reluctantly started walking toward them.

"Lady Brickton adores me," Marco replied, following her. "And I am a marvelous butler."

She supposed he was rather efficient. He had no excuse not to be, not with over four hundred years of various servant duties under his belt at his former territory. That didn't mean Ingrid felt the need to praise him.

"Mama is terrified of you," she said. Her mother knew what Marco was. She also knew that as the Dispossessed assigned to the abbey and rectory, he would not be going anywhere even should she dismiss him.

"Terrified is exactly how I prefer my humans," he countered. "I need to work on finding a way to frighten you into obedience."

"Threatening to remove your clothes was quite enough. I—" Ingrid's retort fell silent on her lips as a man appeared at the top of the quay steps.

Since arriving under the bridge, she had only needed to pause for one vagrant who had shuffled by, wheeling along a wooden cart filled to the brim with his meager belongings. Ingrid had hidden in the shadows until he'd passed, the dark having been a much better veil a half an hour ago.

There was no avoiding this new stranger. The rising light cast him in shades of blues and purples, and Ingrid could tell by the cut of his trousers and heavy greatcoat that he was not some ragtag vagrant. She paused at the bottom of the steps, thinking to stand aside and allow him to descend first. *This isn't London,* she reminded herself. This man wasn't going to recognize her. Though she'd been in Paris for over four months, she wasn't a true part of society here. No one but her mother would care that she was on a quay this early in the morning.

Marco stepped close behind Ingrid, his brawny chest brushing against her shoulders. Though he said nothing, she felt him rigid with menace as the stranger took the first few steps down.

"Relax," she whispered, but at the tail end of her plea came a familiar sharp *twang*.

She knew the sound: the spring release of a crossbow.

Marco caged Ingrid with his arms and with unnatural speed pivoted her away from the stone steps. He moved with such swiftness that he drove the breath from her lungs and her vision blurred. Marco stumbled as something hit him, and with a grunt and a growl, he shoved Ingrid.

"Run," he rasped. "Go!"

His thrust propelled Ingrid forward, but she stumbled to a halt, disobeying her gargoyle yet again. Had that man actually *shot* at them? She turned back toward the steps in time to see

Marco's human body erupt into true form. His butler's uniform ripped apart at the seams as his spine cracked and lengthened, his legs grew and bulked with muscle, and a pair of massive wings unfurled out of his back. He flexed those wings, raising them into great sails, and shredded the last clinging remnants of his jacket. Ingrid stared at the dart embedded in Marco's ribs.

Marco's battle screech echoed off the quay wall as the stranger tossed his spent crossbow aside, drew a sword, and slashed it toward Marco's enormous form. With one swipe of his talons, Marco sent the sword clattering to the ground. He raked his claws toward the man again with unrelenting ferocity. Ingrid swiveled around and squeezed her eyes shut, but she still heard it: the rip of flesh, a short squeal of agony. And then silence. An awful silence, slowly being pushed back by the pounding of her pulse and the burble of the swollen Seine.

Ingrid turned toward the quay steps, certain of what she would see. Marco's wings drooped slightly as he twisted at the waist and wrenched out the embedded dart. The stranger lay on his side next to Marco's long, spiked tail.

"Is he . . . is he dead?" Ingrid whispered. Marco couldn't answer her while in gargoyle form, and he wouldn't be shifting back into human form here, not with his clothes in tatters.

Instead, he threw the bloody dart and the man's discarded sword and crossbow into the river. The current swallowed them. Marco scooped up the limp body with one arm. He then stalked toward Ingrid, fury powering every step. She pulled in a breath and held it as the eight-foot gargoyle, his wolfish face crumpled into a scowl, surged toward her. She knew he wouldn't hurt her, but she'd never been more terrified of him.

Marco broke into a run. His wings snapped open and caught a gust of wind a mere second before he hooked her around the waist with his free arm. Ingrid slammed against his chest, and she clung to him as he lifted off the quay and into the low blue light of dawn.

CHAPTER TWO

The man wasn't dead.

He'd groaned during the flight to Hôtel Bastian, the rising sun nipping at Marco's tail the whole way to rue de Sèvres. Marco had landed on the roof of the town house with such force that the Alliance member standing sentry had actually cried out. He'd recovered quickly and run inside to alert the others, leaving the door open, the invitation explicit: gargoyles were not often permitted inside Hôtel Bastian, but this was obviously an exception.

The injured man hacked a wet cough as Marco shrugged him off his plated and scaled shoulder, dropping him carelessly on a steel table inside Hôtel Bastian's medical room. More blood leaked through his teeth and over his lips.

The gashes across his chest were fatal; of that Ingrid was certain. Marco's talons had ripped a path from the man's right collarbone to his left ribs, and with every heartbeat, blood rushed from the carved trenches, drenching his overcoat and shirt and—

Ingrid stared at the sash, wide as a cummerbund, wound around the man's torso. Even soaked nearly black with blood, she could see what color it had originally been: bright crimson. The color of the Alliance.

Marco had brought them here, to Paris Alliance faction headquarters, for a reason.

Ingrid heard the thud of feet approaching the room and expected Marco to shift back to his human form. But he remained true and turned to face the door. The first person to rush in would meet with the sight of a gargoyle's intimidating height, brawn, and fury.

This wasn't the first time the Alliance had tried to kill her.

Nolan Quinn charged through the door of the medical room. He was occupied with tucking in the rumpled tails of his linen shirt and strode right by Marco without more than a swift glance of acknowledgment. The gargoyle emitted a snort of disappointment through his long, wolfish snout.

The man on the table gurgled on more blood, and Nolan swore under his breath. "What happened?"

"We were on the quay beneath the Pont de l'Alma—" Ingrid began.

"What demon did this?" Nolan barked as he threw open a cabinet door and pulled down a familiar black glass bottle.

"Mercurite won't help. He doesn't have demon poison in him," Ingrid said. Nolan slammed the cabinet door and spun toward her.

Gabby had once told Ingrid how much she adored Nolan's eyes, as bright as a morning glory and as sharp as one of the Alliance's blessed silver blades. Ingrid, however, squirmed beneath them now. He shifted his glare toward the gargoyle standing behind her.

"Marco had no choice. This man tried to kill us."

Nolan lifted his chin and the anger drained from his face. He set down the bottle of mercurite and approached the table.

Nolan inspected the wounds but didn't attempt to staunch the bleeding. Ingrid figured he knew a dead man when he saw one.

"What is your name?" Nolan asked him. "Who sent you?"

Another Alliance member rushed into the medical room, giving Marco his desired reaction. Hans, the new faction leader in Paris, pulled up short and stumbled past the pair of half-open wings. Finally satisfied, Marco crumbled from his true form. His wings pleated and sank into his back, his barrel chest and hulking thighs slimmed, and his slate scales disappeared beneath dark olive skin.

Ingrid turned aside. It was startling how accustomed she'd become to naked men waltzing about. She'd long lost any desire to peek.

"Why does his name matter? He'll be dead in less than a minute," Marco said, joining the conversation now that his vocal cords allowed him to speak instead of screech. "He attempted to kill Lady Ingrid and he is Alliance. What your father told us was true, and this proves it."

The man jerked and arched his back. He hissed a long, reedy death rattle, and then his spine hit the table.

Marco grunted. "He shouldn't have lasted this long. It's not good for my ego."

Hans moved to Nolan's side and frowned, causing two deep creases to bracket the space between his eyebrows.

"Are you certain he tried to kill you, Miss Waverly?" Hans asked.

After Carrick Quinn, Nolan's father, had died in the jaws of a hellhound, Hans had come up from Rome and taken command of the faction. So far, he'd been quiet and unsmiling the few times he and Ingrid had met.

"Does the wound in my back look like a paper cut from when he shot an invitation to tea from his crossbow?" Marco growled.

Ingrid squeezed her eyes shut. Marco's quick temper would not help things. A lot had changed within the last month. Nolan and the others had put up with Luc's presence from time to time, but ever since Ingrid's sister had accidentally killed the Dispossessed elder there had been a complete breakdown between the gargoyles and the Alliance. The tenuous accord Lennier had nurtured between the two groups for centuries had all but shattered.

"Enough," Hans said in his soft yet authoritative voice. He had his eyes on the crimson sash. "Were there any witnesses?"

Ingrid hadn't yet decided whether she liked Hans. She hadn't liked Carrick, and for good reason—the man had released a mimic demon and given it orders to attach itself to her, torment her, and ultimately, kill her. He and the rest of the Directorate had agreed that the sacrifice of one human was acceptable if it meant that Axia could never reclaim her angel blood and set her Harvest in motion. They had no more of a clue about what Axia's exact plans were than Ingrid or anyone else, but they had decided that the safest route would be to spill Ingrid's blood and never find out.

Nolan's father had tried to redeem himself in the end by going against Directorate orders and attempting to save Ingrid's life. Clearly it had worked. Here she stood, still alive. However, Carrick had told her flat out not to trust anyone from the Directorate. Hans wasn't a part of the Directorate, though he did have their ear.

"No," Ingrid answered. She hadn't seen anyone else on the quay, and she hoped no passersby had witnessed Marco's transformation or the brutal killing. If they had, the poor wretches would likely have nightmares for the rest of their lives.

The door to the medical room winged open once more, and the only female Alliance hunter in Paris strode in, her cropped black hair wildly mussed and flattened on one side, presumably from a bed pillow. Chelle stood at least a head shorter than Ingrid, her petite frame drowning in a baggy shirtwaist and wide-legged canvas trousers. As if her eccentric clothing required one last detail to top it off, she was also barefoot.

Chelle approached the body without hesitation. No one needed to tell her what had happened. It was all there for her to piece together: The red sash. The deep slashes delivered by a set of talons.

"Well, has anyone looked yet?" she asked.

Ingrid frowned. "Looked for what?"

When no one answered, Chelle sighed and boldly lifted the man's limp arm. Her frankness and tenacity more than made up for her unintimidating stature.

She pushed the man's coat and shirtsleeve down, revealing a tract of coarse black hair on the top of his forearm. On the pale flesh underneath, something had been inked into his skin. Ingrid craned her neck. It was an arrow, the head aiming toward the man's blue-veined wrist and the fletching curved in half crescents toward the crease of his elbow.

Nolan moved away from the table, muttering a long string of curses. Chelle dropped the man's arm.

"What does it mean?" Ingrid asked.

"Only one sort of Alliance member receives the Straight Arrow," Chelle answered. "An assassin."

Ingrid looked upon the dead man with new horror. Carrick Quinn had spoken of Alliance assassins. He'd said the Directorate would send one to end his life for betraying their orders. Ingrid had feared that they might send one for her as well once they discovered the mimic demon had failed. But after a month had passed with Marco practically adhered to her side and no trace of danger, she'd let herself breathe again. Too soon, apparently.

"Let's not speculate," Hans said, pinning Ingrid with his cool glare. She had relayed Carrick's confession to Hans, but it had gone unaddressed.

Like many Alliance fighters, Nolan's father had been exposed to mercurite, a tincture of mercury and silver used to destroy whatever poison a fighter became infected with after a bite or gash from a demon. But mercurite was a poison of its own. After years of use, it started to eat away at the hunter's internal organs, including his brain.

By the time Carrick had set the mimic demon on Ingrid, he'd been suffering badly. Even Nolan had noticed how different his father had been acting. They all believed he'd been half mad with mercurite poisoning, and of course, the Directorate had denied ever having voted to have Ingrid murdered.

Even she had started to question Carrick's confession. The body on the table, and the tattoo on his arm, removed any lingering doubt.

Marco moved closer to Ingrid, mindful to keep his bared body out of her side vision.

"It's hardly speculation," he said. "The Alliance wants my human dead, and this proves what we've already tried to tell you."

The knotted tangle in the pit of Ingrid's stomach tightened a little more every time Marco called her that. *My human.* As if she belonged to him.

"Or this man could be connected with the Dusters that have been disappearing," Hans murmured. "Miss Waverly is a Duster, after all."

At Ingrid's last session at Clos du Vie, where she practiced gathering and storing electric pulses in her fingertips, Monsieur Constantine had mentioned that a few of his students had not arrived for their scheduled lessons. They had not been seen at their homes, either.

"He isn't connected," Marco said. The finality in his voice brooked no argument.

Chelle tapped the sole of one bare foot against the tile floor and glared at Marco. "Of course he isn't. We already know who is. Or I should say, *what* is."

Ingrid risked a glance over her shoulder. Chelle's hostility toward the Dispossessed wasn't new, but she was accusing them of harming Dusters. Oddly enough, Marco didn't make a sarcastic retort. He cut his eyes away from her, toward the body on the table.

Nolan had taken up the unpleasant task of searching through the dead assassin's coat and trouser pockets, most likely for any identifying information. "Marco is right. Assassins aren't trained to hide the bodies of their targets, and none of the missing Dusters have been found," he said. "Though a seasoned assassin would have known better than to approach his target *and* her gargoyle."

Finding nothing, Nolan reached for a length of linen toweling. His hands were smeared with blood from his search.

"The ink on his arm does look fresh," Chelle noted. "He could have been newly initiated."

"I said we should not speculate," Hans barked. "Now go wake the others. I want to know who this man is. Perhaps someone will recognize him."

Chelle swallowed her retort and left the room.

Hans kept his gaze on the dead assassin. "I'll contact the Directorate. Until I receive word, perhaps, Miss Waverly, you should remain in your home."

He didn't wait for Ingrid's response. He stole out of the room and left her gawping. Stay in her home?

"He doesn't know the Waverly women very well, does he?" Nolan said, raking a hand through his tousled black curls. Then his amused grin faded. "Have you heard from your sister?"

Ingrid shook her head, startled he'd mentioned Gabby. He hadn't, not once, in the last month.

He rubbed his mouth, his palm scraping over the shadow of a beard. "I need to send a telegram to the London faction," he said, his eyes glazed. Concern pulled his dark brows into a slant.

"You don't think . . . *Gabby* isn't in danger, is she?" Panic flooded Ingrid's body and suffused her with heat. "Do you think an assassin might go after her?"

Why did Gabby have to be so far away? Bloody London! Her

sister had been banished from Paris for her own safety against any retaliating gargoyles, but what could keep her safe from an assassin? And what about Grayson? The restless urge to find him, the notion that he was in trouble, made sense now. What if—

A hand clamped her shoulder. Marco. He'd felt her cold rush of fear. "Stop. She isn't the one with angel blood, and I would bet my wings that is what this is about."

Nolan paused at the door. "I didn't mean to alarm you, Ingrid. I just have to make sure she's all right." Without another word of comfort to spare her, he disappeared into the corridor.

Ingrid stood beside the table, alone in the medical room except for the naked gargoyle at her back. Hans had advised them not to speculate, but it was indisputable to her what had happened that morning: an Alliance assassin had attempted to kill her on orders from the Directorate. They still wanted her dead. And here she was, standing in the lion's den.

But she was safe. With Marco, she had a shield, someone who could read her primal instincts perhaps even faster and more effectively than she could. She had known the sound of a crossbow releasing its arrow, but she hadn't been able to move or think quickly enough. Marco had, and without hesitation he'd taken the shot meant for her.

"You saved my life," Ingrid whispered, still staring at the assassin's body, at the deep gashes to his chest that had stolen *his* life. She didn't feel as if she could say thank you to Marco. She wasn't thankful that someone lay dead in front of her.

"It's nothing," Marco replied in that bored tone of his. She was most certain it *was* something to the gargoyle, though. When had he last killed a human?

Ingrid moved off to the side, toward a window, unable to stare at the body any longer.

Yes, she was safe with Marco, and perhaps she and Marco bantered more easily than she and Luc ever had, but there was still something missing between them. A warmth, a tenderness.

The ever-present want—*need*—that had been between her and Luc. They had tried not to notice it for a while, and then, when that hadn't worked, they'd tried to overcome it. To actually touch and kiss and love one another. Because Ingrid did love him. And he loved her. He'd confessed it to her the morning the angels had taken him away to some other territory.

"Where is Luc?" Ingrid asked as she parted the black velvet drapes and looked out.

An older gentleman stood smoking a cigarette on a terrace directly across the street. The balcony doors opened, and his wife handed him a scarf and a hat. Just regular people doing regular things. Normal. Something Ingrid would never be again.

"I know you know where he is," she went on.

She reached into her skirt pocket and rubbed her thumb along the curved fragment of stone she kept with her at all times. It was the irregular-shaped piece of Luc's shattered stone shell that she'd picked up in the belfry, the place where his stone-crusted body had hibernated for over thirty years. The fragment was the only piece of him she had left, and she often found herself rubbing its smooth underside as if it were a talisman.

"Marco, can't you understand? I need to know."

He spoke through gritted teeth. "Why? He couldn't have saved you this morning. He isn't your protector any longer. I am."

Ingrid closed her eyes, knowing she'd hurt him. He pretended not to have feelings, but she didn't believe it for a second.

"You'd best get used to me, Lady Ingrid, unless you feel like joining your sister in London. Trust me, I wouldn't attempt to stop you."

"I didn't mean it that way." She sighed, letting go of the stone fragment. "I know how much you do for me—"

"What I am *forced* to do, may I remind you, Lady Ingrid."

By the angels, yes, she knew. Marco was compelled to protect her. And perhaps that was her answer. Perhaps the moment Luc had been removed from the abbey and rectory he'd stopped caring. Had he confused protection with love? It wasn't a new thought for Ingrid. Every day that passed without a word from Luc drove that fear a little deeper into her heart.

"I know it's dangerous . . . what I feel," she said after a stretch of silence. She spoke to the pane of glass, her fingers balled into the velvet drape.

"I know he can't . . . perhaps doesn't . . . feel it, too, but I'm not asking to see him. I just want to know where. I promise, I'll stay away, but—" Ingrid stopped herself. *But I love him.*

Marco was her gargoyle, but he was still a Dispossessed, and the Dispossessed had strict rules among their own kind. General relationships with humans were frowned upon. Romantic relationships were forbidden, and punishable by death. Gargoyles were not immortal. This was simply their second life, one that stretched on and on for an eternity, or until they were killed—something that was usually difficult to accomplish, with their steely scales and stony muscles. However, a horde of gargoyles could easily rip another gargoyle apart.

Marco said nothing, and after another stretch of silence, Ingrid turned around. The medical room was empty. Marco had left noiselessly, though she didn't know if it had been before her bumbling half confession or after. Or during. All she knew was that she was alone in a room with a dead body.

Strangely, she didn't feel any lonelier than usual.

About the Author

Page Morgan has been fascinated with *les grotesques* ever since she came across an old black-and-white photograph of a Notre Dame gargoyle keeping watch over the city of Paris. The gargoyle mythologies she went on to research fed her imagination, and she became inspired to piece together her own story and mythology for these remarkably complex stone figures. Page lives in New Hampshire with her husband and their three children. To learn more about her and her books go to pagemorganbooks.com.

Look for the other books in the Dispossessed trilogy, *The Beautiful and the Cursed* and *The Wondrous and the Wicked,* available from Delacorte Press.